STALKING MIDAS

Debbie Burke

Tawny Lindholm Thriller Book 2

Advance Praise for *Stalking Midas*

"Debbie Burke touches all the right bases in her new novel, *Stalking Midas*, set in Northwestern Montana during a biting winter you can feel in every scene. The novel is a study in human frailty, redeemed by the open heart and immense courage of her wounded hero protagonist, Tawny Lindholm. Nothing is spared in this story – murder, torture, racism, sexism, ageism, misogyny, off-the-rails maternity and paternity, heinous fraud, and the darkest seeds of human cruelty – all of it woven tightly within a plot that builds and then roars with finality. It's rare to find narrative terrain this emotionally resonant, making *Stalking Midas* a special treat for thriller readers, indeed." – **Larry Brooks**, bestselling author of *Story Engineering, Darkness Bound, Serpent's Dance*

"*Stalking Midas* is strong on characterization and witty banter with a chilling villain in a ripped-from-the-headlines compelling plot. A real page turner." – **Jordan Dane**, critically acclaimed bestselling author of the **Sweet Justice Series**

CONTENTS

ACKNOWLEDGMENTS

Many friends and colleagues offered invaluable assistance with this story. Sincere thanks to critiquers and beta readers: Betty, Val, Barbara, Holly, Marie, Ann, Karen C., Debbie E., Dawn, Sue, Leslie, Sarah, Phyllis, and Lin. You are the best!

My special thanks and gratitude to Tom Kuffel, Rabbi Allen Secher, Jordan Dane, and Larry Brooks.

Most of all, to Tom, who makes it possible for me to follow my dream.

CHAPTER 1 - WHITEOUT

Cassandra Maza targeted cranky old folks, ones so ornery that only ankle-biting Chihuahuas or feral cats could tolerate them. Their bitter isolation from family and friends made her work easier. Case in point: her eighty-two-year-old neighbor, Lydia, in whose bedroom Cassandra now sat.

A January blizzard rattled the windows of Lydia's condominium at Golden Eagle Golf Resort. The elderly woman slumped in her recliner, feet propped up, eyes half-closed. An empty tea cup dangled from a finger. She'd finished the brew Cassandra had prepared for her and it was working nicely, giving blessed relief from Lydia's incessant complaining about her arthritis.

Cassandra rubbed lotion into Lydia's bare foot, toes warped and twisted. "Doesn't this feel nice, dear?"

"Muggins," Lydia whispered. Her Shih Tzu's name. The rag-mop dog yapped from inside the coat closet where Cassandra had secured him.

"I'll take very good care of Muggins, darling," she murmured as she lifted Lydia's robe to expose gaunt thighs and cotton underwear. She slipped a syringe from her pocket and removed the plastic cap with her teeth, then slid the needle into the deep crease in the groin where a puncture would never show. Her aim was good.

Lydia jerked but Cassandra held firm until the potassium

emptied in the femoral vein. She used her elbow to compress the flesh for thirty seconds to prevent bleeding.

The fragile teacup crashed to the floor.

By the time Lydia's heart stopped, Cassandra had recapped the syringe, returned it to her pocket, and was rummaging in the dresser drawer.

The dog's barking rose to a high-pitched staccato.

Cassandra plucked a ruby and diamond choker from a jewelry box and admired the light dancing in the facets. Had Lydia's late husband once cherished her? More likely, the foul-tempered old woman caught him cheating and had extorted the necklace as penance.

She tucked it in her cleavage, then closed the drawer and released the frantic dog from the closet. Muggins raced to Lydia and catapulted into her lap. No response.

At the front door, Cassandra paused to don her coat. "Don't worry, Lydia darling. Muggins will soon be playing with doggie friends."

Crouching against the blast of windswept snow, she hurried to her own condo at the opposite end of the four-unit building. The whiteout masked her movement if anyone happened to be looking out a window. By the time she reached home, the blizzard had already filled in her footprints, wiping away any trace of her final visit with Lydia.

~~~

If a lawyer saves you from prison and gives you a job, you'll do anything he asks. At least that's how Tawny Lindholm felt. Otherwise, she wouldn't be driving at a crawl in the middle of a Montana blizzard in January.

Two hundred cookie-cutter condominiums lined the maze of looping lanes in Golden Eagle Golf Resort, ten miles outside

Glacier National Park. She needed to find the unit where her boss Tillman Rosenbaum's father lived. The father he refused to talk to.

A good six inches of fresh snow already layered the street, more heaped on the curbs. Tawny parked her Jeep Wrangler in front of what she hoped was the right building and crunched through white banks, shuffle-scuffing on the buried walkway. Icy bullets stung her cheeks and nose.

She pounded on the door with her gloved hand. Waited. Her teeth chattered.

At last, the door swung open. Moshe Baruch Rosenbaum filled the entrance, a startling preview of what her boss would look like in thirty years. Long lanky limbs, tight iron-gray curls, and a jutting lower jaw that dared the world to take a swing at him. He could have been Tillman's older identical twin, except this man was black. That explained her boss's bronze skin tone, which, until now, she'd assumed came from a tanning booth.

"What?" Moshe Rosenbaum snarled.

Tawny smiled with as much warmth as she could manage in a wind chill of twenty below zero. "Mr. Rosenbaum, my name is Tawny Lindholm. I wonder if I could have a few minutes of your time."

"You're too old to be selling Girl Scout cookies." The door started to close.

"I'm not selling anything, sir. I work for your son and he asked me to—"

"I have no son!" His baritone roar sounded like God in a cave.

Even though she'd anticipated the rebuff, Rosenbaum's fury unnerved her. She forced her smile wider, despite chattering teeth. "Sir, I need to talk to you. It's important."

The elderly man glared down at her.

Tawny often felt the same rage from Tillman and had

learned to stand up to him. Would that work with his father? She met his angry, dark eyes with a steady gaze and took a chance. "Mr. Rosenbaum, you know as well as I do that your son is a big pain in the ass. If I don't do what he says, he'll fire me and, sir, I really need this job."

Moshe Rosenbaum's stormy expression didn't change, but after a few seconds, he turned on his heel, leaving the door open to allow blowing snowflakes—and her—to enter. In the welcome warmth of the vestibule, she forced the door closed against the blustering wind.

The ammonia stink of a neglected litter box immediately assaulted her nose. She glanced around for the cat as she stepped out of snow-caked boots and shrugged off her hooded parka. A low, menacing growl drew her attention. A Siamese, as big as a bobcat, sprawled on the back of a massive leather sectional, its tail swishing. Blue eyes narrowed with a threat.

A second cat rubbed hard against her legs and purred like an idling jet. Tawny stooped to stroke its calico head.

In the great room, staghorn chandeliers hung from the cathedral ceiling that was constructed of peeled log beams. Two-story-tall windows faced the golf course, invisible at the moment because of the whiteout. Cats three and four flanked a river-rock fireplace that was the size of the entrance to a gold mine.

A wide curving stairway led to the upper level. Cats five, six, and seven lolled on the steps, grooming themselves or clawing the carpeting. No wonder the place reeked. A litter box would need to be the size of a pool table to accommodate all the felines.

Tawny breathed through her mouth. No relief.

Tumbleweeds of cat hair floated across the slate floor with every step she took. Pizza boxes, tall stacks of books and newspapers, and rumpled clothes littered the great room. If

Moshe Rosenbaum aspired to hoarding, he'd made a solid start.

Tawny mentally reviewed the information Tillman had related when he'd called early that morning from his office in Billings. Moshe Baruch Rosenbaum was seventy-five, divorced four times, a semi-retired financier. Private pilot until suspension of his medical permit after a heart attack three years before. Golfed six days a week in season. His net worth should be a healthy seven figures.

Yet his condo was in foreclosure and Tillman wanted to know why. He suspected fraud.

She'd argued, "Your dad's not going to open up to a complete stranger."

"He'll open up to *you*," Tillman retorted. "You're pretty, not threatening, someone he's likely to trust."

Yeah, trust was her specialty. Because she'd trusted the wrong man, Tillman had to rescue her from criminal prosecution. Now she was stuck working for a lawyer she didn't like but felt indebted to.

And here she stood in the senior Rosenbaum's home without a clue how to tackle her assignment.

She needed a conversational opener. *Well, Mr. Rosenbaum, your son thinks you're being scammed. How's the rest of your day going?*

Tawny longed to join the man in front of the glowing fireplace but hesitated. Instead, she picked up the calico for warmth. She wondered if her shivers felt like purring to the cat. "Sir?"

He snapped, "Call me Moe."

"Moe." She shifted the cat to her other arm and offered her hand.

"Bah!" He ignored her gesture and moved to the kitchen, long legs scissoring just like his son's, and picked up a mug with a teabag label hanging over the rim. "Why's a nice girl like you working for a prick like him?"

Plenty of family animosity to go around. "He helped me out of a bad situation."

In sock feet, Tawny crossed cushy carpet that once might have been the color of ivory, now a mottled gray-brown. In the kitchen, wadded fast food sacks and take-out containers cluttered the granite counters. She noticed a commercial six-burner range partly buried under golf shoes, sneakers, and sandals. She'd always wanted a stove like that but could never afford it, while Moe treated his like a shoe rack.

A kettle steamed on the only exposed burner. She set the calico down and asked, "Do you mind if I have some tea?"

He jerked his head toward the stove. "Help yourself."

Grit and crumbs on the cold slate floor poked through her socks. She tentatively opened cupboards, looking for a mug. Jumbles of papers stuffed the shelves but no dishes or tea. "Uh, where do you keep cups?"

He frowned. "Dishwasher."

Duh, of course. She opened it to find glasses and mugs full of slimy water, mingled among apparently clean. Despite her chill, disgust made her give up the quest.

Moe wandered back to the fireplace, slopping tea on the carpet. A raggedy green golf cardigan hung on wide bony shoulders. He wore leather house shoes like her grandpa used to wear, broken down from years of sliding into them, the backs permanently flattened under his heels. He paused to stroke the growling Siamese. The cat continued to watch Tawny with suspicion.

Tawny wondered if Moe was simply a slob. Or was he losing control? She remembered Grandpa, no longer able to cope as once-familiar surroundings slipped away, leaving him to drown in the bottomless well of dementia.

She moved to the tall windows. Snow still blew sideways

across the fairways but seemed to be winding down. "Great location for a golfer. How long have you lived here?"

He scowled at the fire, not looking at her. "Get to the point." No wasted small talk, just like his son.

"Tillman saw a legal notice about your home, sir. He's concerned."

"I'm deeply touched." Sarcasm must be genetic. "What kind of trouble were you in?"

His unexpected question jerked Tawny back. She gulped. "I killed a man in self-defense."

At last, Moe turned to her, a slight lift of one bushy eyebrow. "Well, aren't you the hotshot?"

She perched on the arm of the sectional, noticing rips in the leather, no doubt caused by cats. "It's not something I'm proud of. But your son helped me and I owe him. Besides, he pays better than any other job I could get. I'm fifty, never went to college, and I've been out of the work force for eight years. I'm grateful for the job and want to do my best."

He pulled on his long chin. "So he's taking advantage of your undying gratitude. Over and above the outrageous fees he undoubtedly charged you."

She poked stuffing back into the torn leather. "He took my case pro bono."

Moe's eyes were so dark they almost appeared black. They narrowed as he scanned her figure up and down, his insinuation clear.

She'd filled out a little since the modeling career of her youth, but still fitted into her daughter's skinny jeans. She tugged on her auburn french braid and held her gaze steady. "No, sir, I am *not* working it off in trade."

An unexpected grin lit the old man's face. "You're all right. Straight shooter. No beating around the bush." He moved away from the fire and folded onto the couch, knees high. The

Siamese stalked along the back, hopped down, and curled on his lap. "So what about my affairs are you supposed to meddle in?"

Tawny swallowed. She'd started out with honesty-is-the-best-policy and it had worked so far. At least he hadn't thrown her out yet. "Your condo is in foreclosure."

He flipped a long-fingered, veined hand. "Nonsense."

"There's a notice in the newspaper. I have a copy in my car." Which she'd purposely left outside in case she needed to make a hasty retreat. "I'll get it if you'd like to read it."

"And send you out into the storm?" He slid the cat to the side, rose, and strode toward a closed door off the great room. "Look it up online. Come on."

Tawny followed him to a dim room, where wood shutters blocked the windows. Through the murk, she made out a built-in desk with a computer.

Somehow Moe found the *on* switch and the monitor lit up, casting a bluish glow through the cluttered office. He stubbed his slipper on a stack of file folders, sending them cascading across the floor. When he pulled the chair out, the casters ran up on the disturbed pile, making the chair slant sideways. He didn't notice and sat down, even though he was tilting to the right.

The walls appeared to be closing in until Tawny's eyes adjusted. Then she realized they weren't walls, but instead floor-to-ceiling rows of bankers boxes, perched precariously, overlapping in a jigsaw like an OSHA inspector's nightmare. An earthquake, or even a semi-truck passing by, could spell disaster.

Claustrophobia made shivers creep up her neck. "Moe, I can't see a thing. I'm turning on a light." She felt along the door frame and flipped a switch. A single bulb lit up, the last working one in the ceiling fixture.

The cat box stink coupled with the creepy dark office overwhelmed her. Backing into the living room, she said, "I need to go to my car."

Moe ignored her, bent over the computer.

In the entry, she slipped into her boots and coat and went out, quickly closing the door to keep the friendly calico cat from following her.

After the gagging stench, the blizzard felt refreshing, cleansing. She climbed into the Jeep and longed to drive twenty-five miles straight home to Kalispell. Let Tillman take care of his own father instead of foisting the job off on her.

But the elderly man clearly needed help. And if Tawny knew anything, it was how to take care of the aging and ill— her grandparents and parents, then eight years dealing with her husband Dwight's cancer. Besides, Tillman paid twenty-five dollars an hour, three times what she could hope to earn as a home aide without certification or license.

She took a deep breath and started the Jeep to fetch cleaning supplies.

~~~

Forty minutes later, Tawny returned to Moe's condo, the reports from Tillman tucked under her arm. She toted a large sack of kitty litter, light bulbs, and bleach, all packed into a new plastic litter box. Having left the front door unlocked, she knocked but entered without waiting for Moe to answer. "Hello?"

The calico cat placed gentle paws on her leg. Tawny rubbed under its chin. "You're sure a lot friendlier than your owner." She felt the vibrations as the cat's throat stretched long, eager for attention.

The door to the office stood ajar, the inside even murkier

than before. She peeked in. Either Moe had turned off the lonely light or the last bulb had burned out. The monitor provided the only illumination. "Hi, I'm back."

He didn't acknowledge her or seem to notice her presence. Instead, he stayed focused on the computer, sitting in the chair still crookedly canted up on files he'd knocked over earlier.

The Siamese bodyguard had taken a sentry position on a shelf above Moe's head, tail switching. A low growl rumbled when it spotted Tawny in the doorway.

In the utility room, she held her breath while she dumped the lumpy contents of the litter box into a garbage bag. She knotted it tight and set it outside the back door. In the laundry sink, she filled the plastic tray with bleach and water. She poured litter into the new box. A marmalade cat immediately hopped in and took advantage of the clean restroom.

Within an hour, she'd filled more garbage bags with trash, replaced light bulbs, and swept up the largest fur balls.

"What the hell are you doing?"

Moe's baritone snarl made her jump. She faced him with what she hoped was a reassuring smile. "Just tidying up a little. Hope you don't mind."

He snarled, "Who asked you to?"

Tawny pressed her lips together. "Your cats did. Have you cleaned their litter box in the past six months?"

Again, the angry, "Bah!" and a glare that could roast flesh.

She added, "Some light bulbs were burned out. I replaced them."

He pulled himself straight, six-five at least, and skewered her with his squint. "Don't you think I'm tall enough to reach them? If I wanted them replaced, I'd have done it. You're pretty damn presumptuous, aren't you?"

She lifted her chin. "Yes, sir, I am."

"What are you, an auditor or a maid?"

"If I see something that needs doing, I do it."

He studied her, one eye narrowed. "You're snooping in my finances."

Tawny went to the cluttered dining table, where she opened the folder of reports. "Would you like to see what Tillman emailed me?" She pushed the papers toward the glowering old man. The Siamese leapt onto the table, squaring off with Tawny. It hissed, teeth ready to sink into her arm. She backed out of range.

Moe's hands swept sideways, like an umpire signaling *safe*. "It's all online. But it's wrong."

At last, an opening. "What's wrong about it?"

The Siamese paced the table, then sat. Maybe it had decided not to attack her. For now.

Moe answered, "Says the mortgage is six months in arrears."

"You've been making payments all along?"

"Yeah, yeah."

His too-quick response made Tawny wonder. "Then we need to fix their mistake, right? Do you have anything to prove you made payments? Like canceled checks or your bank statement?"

"All online. I shut the computer down." The set to his jaw left no doubt he'd shut the subject down along with his computer.

Tawny was already on shaky ground. He could throw her out and Tillman would be pissed. The situation required a little finesse. "Moe, I'm hungry. Would you like to go out for lunch?" She offered a conspiratorial wink. "On my expense account."

An unexpected twinkle brightened his eyes. "My son pays?"

She smiled. "Yep."

A full-blown grin spread across his narrow face. "In that case, we're going to the golf course restaurant. I'll change." He loped up the steps two at a time, scattering stairway cats.

Tawny picked up her furry calico shadow. "Nailed it, kitty."

~~~

A half hour later, Moe reappeared, shaved and snappy, wearing a beautifully tailored sport coat over a polo shirt the color of lime sherbet. An Irish tweed driving cap sat on his head at a jaunty angle, and a force field of cologne surrounded him. When he held her coat for her, Tawny caught a glimpse of the dash that had attracted four women enough to marry him.

A door off the kitchen connected to the double garage, where a black Lincoln Navigator and a golf cart were parked. Tawny noticed a bumper sticker on the golf cart: *Don't drink and drive. You might hit a bump and spill your drink.*

Outside on the street, the blizzard had blown out most of its fury but thick snowflakes still fell. Several new inches of white covered her Jeep.

Tawny asked, "I counted seven cats, right?"

"There's two more upstairs," Moe replied. "They like climbing up on the open beams." His harsh tone softened a bit. "You like my cats?"

She smiled. "All except your Siamese. He'd like to claw my eyeballs out and eat them."

Moe nodded. "Protective. Loyal. Devoted. Unlike my children." He turned the wheel too quickly. The big SUV slid around a corner in a wild fishtail. "If I'd known what a pain children are, I'd have gotten a vasectomy at age twelve and spent my life with cats."

Tawny bit her lip at his driving and wondered how deep she dared to dig into his family details. "How many kids do you have? Tillman? And...?"

"A daughter, Shoshanna, his younger sister."

"And Tillman gave you three grandchildren. How about Shoshanna?"

Moe hawked deep in his throat, powered the window open, and spat. "He didn't *give* me bupkis. I've never even seen those grandchildren."

Whoops. Not a good path to go down. "I'm sorry."

"Why? It's not your fault my son's an asshole and my daughter's a pathetic mess who can barely feed herself."

"I just meant I'm sorry for the situation. It's sad." Tawny's children, Neal and Emma, meant everything to her, despite her daughter's often-annoying behavior. She couldn't imagine speaking about them with the disdain and anger Moe obviously felt toward his. Based on Tillman's phone conversation early that morning, the bitterness went both ways.

She changed course. "What's the Siamese's name?"

A long silence stretched. Moe seemed to have zoned out, his jaw slack. She watched him from the corner of her eye, wondering where his mind had gone.

After a couple of minutes he finally spoke again: "Rambo." He glanced sideways at her. "Appropriate, don't you think? He was feral, roaming the golf course. I was playing golf one day and he jumped on the back of another guy in the foursome, attacking like hell, trying to get the protein bar the man was eating. Scared the shit out of him. He had to have IV antibiotic infusions for weeks because of infection."

Tawny shuddered. "Rambo seems to have mellowed a little now."

"I threw my jacket over him, bundled him up, and took him to the vet. He was half-starved and meaner than piss. Vet gave him his shots, dug some BBs out of his hide, and—God forgive me—neutered him. But it did settle him down. Once he realized I'd feed him no matter how ferocious he acted, he decided I was his savior and I belong to him."

"Are all your cats rescues?"

He nodded. "They have brutal backgrounds but they're survivors. Now they don't have to worry. I provide for them."

Even if you're lax in cleaning the litter box, Tawny thought. Still, she warmed to Moe's compassion, although he tried to hide it, as if kindness was a quality to be ashamed of. She wondered again about dementia, with his herd of cats, the mountains of clutter in his home, and his sudden loss of focus in the middle of their conversation.

He wheeled into the golf course parking lot, where a pickup with a plow was clearing big banks of snow from the entrance. They parked and scuffed on the slick sidewalk to the door. When Moe pulled the handle, it was locked.

"Well, fuck me very much!" he said. "Do you know what I pay in dues to this dump?"

Tawny pointed to a sign: *Restaurant open 4 p.m. Thursday through Sunday.* "Winter hours."

"Goddamn!" Moe thumped the glass hard and kicked at the base. "I spend thousands here and now they can't be bothered to take more money off my hands."

Tillman's bad temper appeared genetic. "Let's go into town," she suggested. "How about Chinese? It's only about ten minutes away and I know they're open." Her daughter worked at the Lucky Dragon Restaurant and Casino, owned by the family of Emma's boyfriend, Jim Tang.

As soon as Tawny made the suggestion, she thought better of it. She didn't want to take this rude grouch any place where people knew her. She might never be able to return.

Moe's face contorted. He pounded again on the glass then cupped his hands to peer inside. Another kick. The glass rattled dangerously.

She gripped his arm. "Moe, come on. This isn't doing any good. We'll find another restaurant." She forced a grin through gritted teeth. "Remember, it's Tillman's treat."

He banged one last time then spun on his heel toward the Navigator.

The snow plow driver had stopped to watch the elderly man's antics and dipped his head at Tawny. She made a *what-can-you-do* face and got back in the SUV. Moe revved the engine too high. Before she could fasten her seatbelt, he jammed it into reverse and raced backward.

The Navigator jolted to a stop with a loud crash.

Her head whiplashed. "Crap!" She grabbed the armrest, too late to brace herself against the impact.

He shifted into drive. The big car lurched forward, climbed a snowbank, and drove through a white-shrouded juniper hedge, branches whipping the side windows.

She looked out the back window. He'd rammed a landscape boulder. The Lincoln must have body damage. "You just hit a rock as big as a buffalo."

"So what?" he snapped. He ignored the path cleared by the plow and instead bounded over snow-covered shrubs, knocking down a carved wooden sign for Golden Eagle Golf Resort.

Tawny realized he knew perfectly well that he was vandalizing the property. What a jerk, throwing a tantrum because of a closed restaurant. "Moe, calm down or let me out of the car. You're not going to kill me with your crazy driving."

He stomped the brakes, making the SUV skid sideways. Tawny sucked in a breath as they slid toward a ditch. The car stopped, inches from tipping over the edge.

They glared at each other.

She recognized the snap in his dark eyes, so like his son's. "If you want to wreck your rig, fine, but you're not doing it with me. Take me back to my car. If you can't drive like a sane person, I'm calling nine-one-one." She drew her cell from her coat pocket as if it were a gun.

He continued to glower at her.

She reached for the door handle. A mile-long trudge back to her Jeep through deep snow in bitter cold didn't appeal, but if she had to, she'd do it.

"Wait," he said. "You can't walk in this weather. You'll die." His voice had lost the raw anger and instead sounded apologetic, maybe.

"I could die if I ride with a maniac." The words slipped out before she could stop herself.

For an instant, she wondered if he'd dump her at the side of the road but instead he accelerated cautiously. When he bypassed the lane to his condo, Tawny started to protest but he waved his hand and gave her a sheepish wink. "Thought you wanted Chinese."

Again, she noticed a mischievous flicker that must have charmed his four wives, at least temporarily. "Only if you're finished with your tantrum," she answered.

CHAPTER 2 – HAZARDOUS CONDITIONS AHEAD

Because of the blizzard, the Lucky Dragon was nearly empty except for two customers waiting for takeout.

"You're sure my son isn't shtupping you?" Moe shoveled in sweet and sour with chopsticks.

Tawny compressed her lips. "Quite sure."

"Then he's as big an idiot as I thought."

"The choice might not be up to *him*." Despite Tillman's many faults, thankfully, he had never put the make on her.

Moe splayed his hands, wiggling the chopsticks. "Of course. And that answer proves you're way too smart to get mixed up with a putz like him."

She speared a mushroom from the platter of chicken with snow peas. In the adjoining casino, cheery jingles played from the gaming machines. Only three customers perched on high stools, tapping the screens. She was glad no one sat close enough to overhear their conversation.

Through a mouthful of fried rice, Moe asked, "You killed a man and he got you off?"

Tawny pulled on her braid. "That's not my favorite topic of conversation."

He shrugged and concentrated on his food.

"How come you two don't get along?" Tawny wouldn't normally ask such a personal question of someone she barely knew but the crabby old man's intrusiveness had made her bold.

He raised his chin high, looking down his nose at her, the way Tillman often did. "Ah, I see. You don't want to talk about your dirty laundry, but it's OK to ask about mine."

"*Touche.*" She waved a hand. "None of my business."

"You work for him and you have to ask?" His head bobbed. "His mother poisoned the children against me when they were young."

She recalled details her boss had related. "You didn't get divorced till Tillman was an adult."

"Divorced, right. But legally separated for years before that. The children didn't think much of my extra-curricular female companionship. Guess I can't blame them but their mother didn't want a divorce."

"You've been married other times?"

"Once before, twice after. Had a daughter the first go-round. No more since Tillman and Shoshanna, thank God."

Tillman hadn't mentioned another sibling. "Where's your oldest?"

He dropped his chopsticks on the platter of broccoli beef, gulped tea, and thudded the empty cup onto the Formica table. "Dead."

Tawny's heart jerked. "I'm sorry."

He glowered. "What is wrong with you? Why apologize for things you have no control over?" The edge of anger returned to his voice, reminding her of his tantrum at the golf club.

"Moe, I *am* sorry. That's the most terrible loss anyone can endure. If something happened to my children, I couldn't go on."

Silence hung for several minutes. Tawny rearranged her food, watching him, his expression dismal and stormy. She wondered if he might upend the table and start throwing plates. She leaned both elbows on the surface just in case.

Finally, without making eye contact, he said, "She committed suicide."

Even worse. She wanted to squeeze his arm or offer comfort but instead sipped tea.

Her stillness seemed to encourage him because he went on in a low voice. "Her mother claimed it was an accidental drug overdose. Tried to convince everyone that Levona was always mixing up her prescriptions and it happened again but this time fatally." Heavy brows bunched. "Truth is, we'd put Levona through rehab twice before age fourteen. Brilliant musician, played the cello, a real prodigy. Tender-hearted too. She was always collecting injured stray cats, begging me to take them to the vet. I spent damn near as much on vet bills as on her rehab." A sad smile flickered. "But I always knew she'd never live to adulthood. Drugs owned her. They made her impulsive, reckless, self-destructive. Terrible waste…"

A strange light came into Moe's eyes. Did he long for his own death in hopes of being reunited with his lost child? Or as atonement for failing as a father?

"In a way," he went on, "she's the reason I started rescuing cats."

He couldn't save his daughter but he could save what she loved. Tawny murmured, "To honor her memory."

"Yeah, I guess." Abruptly, he shook his shoulders, jerking himself back to the present. Dark eyes bored into hers. She felt the same discomfort when Tillman stared at her like that. "What else do you do for my ungrateful son besides meddle in my business?"

She twirled lo mein noodles, relieved to shift away from painful topics. "Whatever he says. Mostly, I interview new clients, collect background information, ask questions, get people talking."

He folded long arms across his chest and regarded her. "Well, you're damn good at it. I haven't spoken my daughter's name in years."

In spite of regret for opening old wounds, a little thrill of pride at Moe's compliment touched Tawny. She didn't understand why but people did seem to trust her, revealing their dark traumas and secret shame.

"Moshe! Darling!" A woman's voice rang across the

restaurant. She zeroed in on their table, purple cape billowing, like an osprey sailing down to pluck a fish from the lake.

Mid-fifties, Tawny figured, with bouncing platinum curls framing a round face and eyes so blue they had to be tinted contacts. Smiling chipmunk cheeks hinted at overdone collagen. Her spike-heeled boots would be treacherous on ice.

Moe jumped to his feet. The woman enveloped him with her cape and pulled his head down so she could kiss him full on the mouth. When they broke apart, Tawny noticed a lipstick smear. So did the woman. She snatched a napkin off the table, licked it, and wiped the stain like a mother cleaning up a child, except there was nothing maternal in her gesture. Nor in the intimate whispers that passed between them.

Tawny fiddled with a bottle of soy sauce, feeling as if she'd stumbled into their bedroom.

The woman finally greeted Tawny with a wide smile, teeth bleached as blue-white as the snow falling outside. "And who is this, Moshe darling?"

Moe straightened his jacket. "Cassandra, this, uh, young lady works for my son."

Tawny caught his hesitation—he didn't remember her name. She offered her hand to the woman. "I'm Tawny Lindholm."

The woman grasped it. Glitter sparkled in her long, polished, turquoise nails. "Tawny! How lovely to meet you!"

Moe dragged a chair from an adjoining table and seated Cassandra beside him. She immediately clasped his arm in a wordless warning, staking out her territory.

Jealous and possessive, Tawny thought.

Cassandra gazed up at Moe. "Darling, do you remember that adorable little Persian?"

"The one with the bad foot?"

"Yes. The vet took care of it and now she's on her way to

her happy new home." She turned to Tawny. "I run a sanctuary for pets whose owners had to go into assisted living or passed away."

Maybe Tawny's initial annoyance with the smoochy woman had been unfair. "That's really nice. I hate to see animals abandoned."

"Do you have pets?" Cassandra asked.

Tawny shook her head. "Not anymore. We had Labs and Golden Retrievers for years."

Cassandra's smile widened. "You know, we have a lovely senior Golden who'd love to be adopted. Her owner died. Maybe..."

Uh-oh. An arm-twister. With Tawny's soft heart, she had to say no or she'd quickly end up with as many strays as Moe and his condo full of cats. Besides, after Dwight, she couldn't bear the death of another loved one. "Not right now."

Disappointment flashed in the woman's eyes but she recovered by helping herself to a spring roll from Moe's plate. "Too bad. Beautiful, sweet, devoted dog." White teeth bit into the roll. She coyly offered the rest to Moe. He grinned, wrapped his lips around it, then his tongue licked her fingers clean.

Again, Tawny flushed at witnessing a sensuous, intimate moment. If only she could leave. But she was stuck, dependent on Moe to drive her.

He used chopsticks to place a morsel of chicken on Cassandra's pink pointed tongue then faced Tawny. "Cassandra runs a foundation that's really quite extraordinary," he said. "She's building a large-scale luxury animal sanctuary where people can endow their pets' future care. Owners are assured they'll be cared for in perpetuity."

Tawny smiled politely. "Like a trust fund for animals?"

Cassandra lit up. "Exactly! I've seen so many tragedies where the owner passes away. The uncaring heirs just dump

Mommy or Daddy's fur babies at the pound. The pet is the one who stood by the owner until the very end, devoted and loving, while the kids only show up to claim their inheritance."

Moe grumbled and hawked into his napkin. "That'll be my worthless spawn."

Tawny watched the old man, wondering how accurate his assessment was. Tillman could be a real son of a bitch, but he *had* sent her to check up on his father's wellbeing. She felt compelled to defend her boss. "Moe," she said, "did you know Tillman has only lost three cases in seventeen years? That's a pretty good record for a lawyer."

Dark eyes flared. "What the hell do you know?" He shoved away from the table, upending his chair. It clattered against an adjacent table, tipping over a vase of silk orchids that smashed to the floor.

Oh crap, Tawny thought, another tantrum. Shouldn't have brought him here. And should've kept my mouth shut.

The kitchen door swung open and Mama Rose Tang burst through, hot-footing it across the restaurant. The tiny, wizened woman stared up at Moe. "What wrong? You no like your food? My brother make something else for you. OK, mister? Right?"

Tawny jumped up to step between Moe and Mama Rose. "Mrs. Tang, everything's delicious. Just a little accident. Please, bring me the bill and add on for the damage."

Cassandra pulled on Moe's arm until he bent low enough for her to talk quietly in his ear. She rubbed between his shoulder blades, steering him toward the exit, a constant stream of chatter all the way out.

Mama Rose pushed open the kitchen door and hollered, "Wilbur, come here. Clean up mess."

Tawny handed over her credit card, which Mama Rose ran through the terminal. While they waited for approval, a chunky, middle-aged man with Down's Syndrome pushed through the swinging door, carrying a broom and long-handled dustpan. Buzz-cut brown hair accented the irregular shape of his head. Tawny recognized Wilbur, known for riding his old cruiser bike throughout the sprawling county, working odd jobs and delivering newspapers. He picked up the larger pieces of the vase and dropped them in the dustpan. Then he painstakingly swept up every splinter of glass from under tables and chairs.

"My Jim, your Emma," Mama Rose said to Tawny, "lot of time together."

Tawny smiled, glad for the distraction from Moe's tantrum. "Jim's a great guy. You should be proud."

Mama squinted up at her. "I surprise they back together. Bad breakup."

Tawny gulped. Mama Rose would never forget how Emma had broken Jim's heart after high school, ten years earlier, by chasing after a North Dakota oil worker.

Tawny signed the credit card slip, adding an extra-large tip, and bundled up in her coat and gloves. She stepped outside, deciding Cassandra had earned her wings. The woman not only rescued the restaurant from further damage, but saved Tawny from being mortified in front of the woman who might someday be her in-law if Emma and Jim stayed together.

A squeal of tires made her jump backwards.

Moe's Navigator swerved past her and jetted onto the highway, smack in front of an oncoming pickup. The truck jammed on its brakes. On the slushy road, it skidded sideways, hopped the curb, and crashed into a whiskey barrel planter in the Lucky Dragon parking lot.

The Navigator kept going without even a touch to the brakes.

Tawny cringed. The second accident Moe had caused in an hour. Dammit. The man was a menace. His license should be revoked.

She trudged to the pickup. The driver had gotten out to inspect the new dent in his mud-spattered passenger door. The whiskey barrel's wood slats were splintered, the metal bands sprung.

The man straightened as she approached. Cowboy hat, gray ponytail, cigarette in the corner of his mouth. "Sumbitch pulled out right in front of me."

If Tawny ratted on Moe, he'd never talk to her. And Tillman might fire her. But she couldn't let an innocent party be hurt.

"I saw what happened. I know the driver's son." Tawny pulled the cell from her coat pocket. "If you give me your number, I'll make sure he takes care of the damage."

He rubbed the dent with a leather-gloved hand. "Naw, it's an old truck. This'll keep the other dings company." He shrugged with more grace than Moe's bad behavior deserved.

The pickup drove away and Tawny sighed. Now she needed to find a ride back to her Jeep. Tillman had better spring for a taxi.

A snow-covered yellow Porsche Cayenne SUV pulled beside her and stopped. The tinted window lowered, revealing Cassandra. "You OK?"

"Yeah. Thanks for getting him out of the restaurant before he did any more damage."

Her round cheeks glowed red with the cold. "Just have to know how to handle him when he gets upset."

Tawny's teeth chattered. "Could you give me a lift back to Moe's place? My car's there."

Cassandra popped the door lock. "Sure."

Tawny settled into the seat, turning the vents so heat blew directly on her.

Cassandra adjusted the blower to high. "Cold as a witch's tit."

Tawny nodded. "How long have you known Moe?"

Fingers fluttered in turquoise leather gloves studded with rhinestones. "About three years. Most of the time, he's a sweetheart. But now and then, watch out."

"Does he seem to be getting more...?"

"Erratic? Irascible? Mule-headed?" Her laugher tinkled like wind chimes.

"His son is concerned about him. That's why I'm here."

Wipers noisily skidded across layers of ice on the windshield. "Moshe is fine. He's just got a short fuse. Let me tell you something, honey. The older you get, the less you care what other people think. The hell with inhibitions. You do what you always wanted to do but were too well brought up to get away with. He doesn't have a boss who's going to fire him. His wives already divorced him. What does he have to lose?"

Tawny pondered her assessment. Cassandra knew Moe a lot better than she did. "Yes, but he could cause an accident that might kill someone."

"So could anyone, on these slippery roads in this lousy weather."

"I suppose." Still, Tawny felt relieved the pickup driver had let her off the hook as a witness. As annoying as this assignment was shaping up to be, she didn't want to fail Tillman.

"Where do you live?" Cassandra's question interrupted Tawny's thoughts.

"Kalispell. How about you?"

"I keep a condo at Golden Eagle, two blocks from Moshe. But I travel a lot for the foundation." Cassandra turned on the road toward Columbia Mountain and the resort. "The need keeps growing, the project keeps expanding. We Boomers are aging but we're smart and savvy. We want to plan ahead for our pets. Lots of Boomers mean lots of animals will need future care. Most older people would love to have pets—they're so good for our souls—but they're concerned if something happened, who would take care of them? My foundation gives them great peace of mind."

"Where's the sanctuary?" Tawny asked.

"The foundation has optioned acreage in various locations. I can show you mockups of the facilities, if you're interested."

"Sure, I'd like that. Sometime." Tawny wanted to keep the woman's goodwill since she needed Moe's cooperation and Cassandra seemed to have mastered that skill. "How expensive is it?"

Cassandra's chipmunk cheeks swelled with a smile. "I have all that planned out with sliding scales of affordability to fit every budget." She looked sideways at Tawny. "Even though you don't have pets now, you might have one in the future. At your age, you can buy into an annuity very inexpensively, ensuring your costs won't rise with time and inflation."

Uh-oh. The arm-twisting had edged up another notch. "Vet bills are so high, I can't afford a pet, let alone provide for its future."

"I'll give you my card, just in case you find yourself with another Golden." A sly dig for Tawny's earlier refusal.

They turned onto Moe's lane. Snow had completely covered Tawny's Jeep, now a squared-off white lump in the road. "That's my car. Thanks for the lift."

Cassandra braked gently but the Porsche still slid before stopping in front of Moe's driveway. The garage door gaped open, showing the Navigator had arrived in one piece, except for a fresh dent in the rear hatch from striking the boulder.

"Are you going in?" Cassandra asked.

Tawny considered. She didn't want to leave on a bad note because Tillman would no doubt send her back to finish the job. Yet, it had been a rugged day and she still faced driving home on treacherous roads. "Do you think I should? I mean, does he usually get over his spells? Or should I come back another time?"

Cassandra chuckled as she pulled a business card from the visor. "You mean, does he fester and stew? Yes. He may forget what you did that made him mad but he'll remember he's mad at you."

Tawny swallowed. "Then I probably ought to try to make peace."

"Good luck." Was that sympathy or irony in her tone? Cassandra offered her card between sparkly gloved fingers.

Tawny took the card and slipped it in her pocket. "Nice to meet you. Hope your venture is a success. I really can't face having a pet right now but I do admire what you're doing."

The woman beamed. "We animal lovers have to stick together. Poor darlings are at the mercy of those who don't cherish them. I do what I can."

Tawny climbed out of the car and shuffled to Moe's condo. The Porsche took off as she knocked on the door. A long minute passed. Cold seeped through her coat and gloves. She rapped harder with the side of her fist.

The door flew open. Moe glowered. "What?"

Tawny tilted her head sideways, like her yellow Lab used to do to gain favor. "Could I come in, just for a few minutes?"

"That's what you said the last time." He glanced at his Rolex. "That was four hours ago." He stalked away but didn't slam the door in her face.

She took that as a *yes*, entered, and slipped off her boots. The calico immediately trotted over, tail high, and rubbed against her leg despite the snow coating her jeans. Tawny picked her up and nuzzled her. "At least *you're* glad to see me," she murmured in the cat's soft ear.

Moe had retreated to the sectional in front of the fireplace.

Rambo paced behind his owner's shoulders, watching her.

Her old Lab, Ruger, again came to mind. He'd been sweet to everybody, except one of Emma's boyfriends whom Tawny and Dwight had disliked. Every time the boy came to their house, Ruger growled. Tawny and Dwight figured the dog had picked up on their disapproval.

Did cats have similar telepathy with their owners? Would Rambo hold a grudge like Moe?

She set the calico down and sidled past the Siamese to stand before the elderly man. "I didn't mean to upset you. It was disrespectful. But I do know Tillman is concerned about you."

Moe stared into the flames, avoiding her. "He's just afraid I'll leave my money to my cats instead of him."

"Whatever you do with your money is your business," she said. "But all that aside, there's still the foreclosure problem. Can we try to straighten that out?"

He turned his head, pondering, but didn't say no, a hopeful sign.

She moved to the dining table where she'd left the file, put on reading glasses, and shuffled through the papers. She heard the leather creak as he rose from the couch and approached. "Do you write a check for your mortgage payment or is it automatically deducted from your bank account?"

"Automatic deduction."

A step in the right direction. "Does your statement show the deductions?"

"It's all online."

She felt him peering over her shoulder and kept her questions neutral. "Does the bank mail you a paper statement?"

"All online."

"Can we look on your computer to make sure the bank is properly deducting the payments?"

Silence. Uh-oh.

She turned from the papers to look up at him.

A fresh storm gathered inside those dark eyes. "Tillman sent you to find out how much money's in my bank account." His tone sounded low and menacing. "You're supposed to find out what the little prick thinks he's going to inherit from me."

Tawny bit her lip. "I don't think that's the case. Would you just let me look at the deductions for mortgage payments to make sure everything's properly credited?"

An accusation shot out: "You're a forensic accountant."

She couldn't contain her hoot of amusement. "Moe, you're talking to someone who almost dropped out of high school. The only reason I know a little about accounting is because I kept books for my husband's business. Anything beyond that..." She held up her hands in a helpless gesture.

Moe squinted down at her, mouth twisted with bitterness.

Better try another tack. "Tillman drives a hundred and twenty-thousand dollar Mercedes SUV. His practice is doing very well. I've been to his house in Billings. It's a million-dollar estate on the Rimrocks with a view that goes forever—"

"I know," Moe snapped. He folded long arms and stalked to the couch again. "It used to be *my* house. Lost it in the divorce from his mother. He inherited it from her." He flopped down.

Oops. Tillman neglected to mention that. "I really don't think he's after your money. He doesn't need it."

"Everyone needs more money. Or they think they do."

Tawny wanted to throw up her hands. She'd tried but couldn't figure how to dig into the man's finances when he refused to cooperate. If he was being scammed, as Tillman suspected, she didn't know what else to do. "I've taken up enough of your time. I'll leave these records here, if you want to follow up."

From her bag, she retrieved one of the heavy embossed

business cards Tillman had ordered when he hired her: *Tawny Lindholm, Investigative Assistant, Law Offices of Rosenbaum, Withers, and Zepruder, PC.* Her boss's unexpected gesture had surprised her. She'd never had her own cards before, let alone expensive ones. She circled her cell number and placed the card on top of the file.

Moe still sulked on the couch. Rambo crouched beside him, always ready to spring.

She approached but kept out of the Siamese's leaping range. "Thank you for your time, sir. I'm glad to have met you."

He grunted.

At the entry, she bundled up and put on her boots. One last backward look showed Moe ruffling Rambo's fur.

~~~

Cassandra slammed the connecting door between the garage and her great room. Her son Colin glanced sideways from where he reclined on her new dove-gray Chateau Beauvais sofa, a laptop resting on his chest, head propped on a red suede accent pillow. "What's with you?" he asked.

She stalked across the room, the floorplan a mirror image of Moshe's condo, except high-end furniture and original artwork decorated the spotless, orderly home in stark contrast to his shabby trash heap. She yanked open the stained-glass door of the antique liquor cabinet and poured herself a brandy.

Colin lost interest and returned his attention to the laptop.

How could he even read like that, with his neck kinked? Once, she'd been as limber as her tall, athletic, muscular son. Now arthritis stiffened her joints and slowed her movements. She downed the burning brandy and poured another. "We've got a problem."

"What?" Colin continued to stare at his screen.

"Moshe's smartass son sent someone to check on him."

"And that's a problem because...?"

"The son's that high-powered lawyer from Billings who's always in the news. If he's suspicious—"

"Everything's covered."

"Not well enough if forensic accountants start digging."

"Then we move on."

For such a brilliant boy, Colin could be infuriatingly simple. Cassandra's gaze rested on his even features, full lips pouting at being interrupted. He was so handsome.

She slipped behind him, seized a rope of his blond dreadlocks, and yanked.

"Ow!" Colin yelped. "Why'd you do that?" He burrowed into the cushions, hurt in his blue eyes.

From the time Colin had spoken his first words as a toddler, she'd groomed him how to achieve his desires by pleasing people. She'd introduced him like a beautiful exotic pet into circles of wealth where people paid well to be entertained.

Preening, decadent socialites craved the cloying compliments that she and her son showered over them. Therein lay the art: she didn't need to *take* their money—they *gave* it to her willingly, in exchange for the currency of flattery.

Colin had excelled beyond her hopes, becoming a full, meaningful partner in her business by age seven. But he'd never quite grasped how to detach from the human element, how to view targets as objects, not people. She often had to reinforce that lesson, although she didn't like punishing him, but he needed to toughen up.

Cassandra reached out again. He flinched, trapped against the back of the sofa. But this time her touch was playful, flipping the dreads. "What are you doing, darling boy?" She nodded at the laptop.

"Checking Moe's accounts. There's a deferred dividend scheduled to be deposited at the end of next week." Still cowed, Colin avoided looking at her, his gaze fixed on the screen.

"How much?"

"Ninety thousand."

"Nice," she purred. "But I think that's his last sizeable asset. The well is running dry." She stroked his hair. "You're so brilliant, darling." *Follow punishment with reassurance.*

She poured another brandy and watched him tap keys and flick the screen. As much as she needed Colin's wizardry, she also resented it. Technology changed too fast and her mind wasn't as nimble as it once had been. When he tried to explain his hacks, she couldn't follow any longer. Another reminder of aging pinched her.

Age. Her worst enemy. With every passing day, she herself became more like her targets, losing attractiveness and capability, desperate and fearful about the future. Some nights she awoke in cold panic, envisioning herself hopelessly crippled by arthritis, her once-flawless skin crumpled into sagging masses of wrinkles.

Her latest driver's license said forty-six, an underestimation of ten years. With each new identity, she'd shaved off a year or two. She dreaded the day some flunky clerk would squint closely at her, study the falsified documents too carefully, and ask questions.

That woman—Tawny—couldn't be that much younger than Cassandra, yet she still moved with the long-legged, lithe grace of a model. The streaks in her braided coppery hair looked more like sun highlights than gray. A few laugh lines creased the creamy skin around her wide-set brown eyes, but her neck was still firm and unwrinkled.

Cassandra pondered her own ever-increasing investments in lipo, tucks, dermabrasion, and painful collagen injections.

Every morning, she spent two hours applying makeup to give the illusion she wore none.

Damn that woman's casual, effortless beauty.

But more important, Cassandra had to deal with her intrusion. "We need to distract her."

"Who?" Colin's slender finger stroked the touch screen.

"The woman Moshe's son sent."

Colin sat up on one elbow and lifted his broad shoulder in a sexy shrug. "A woman? Not a problem, Mom. You know I can handle her."

Cassandra smiled at her gorgeous son, unzipped her high-heeled boots, and sank on the sofa beside him. "Google Tawny Lindholm, darling."

CHAPTER 3 - STALKED

Tillman called Tawny that evening. He never wasted time with chit-chat, no *hi, how are you?* "So?"

She stretched out on the threadbare velour couch in her living room and pulled her grandma's crocheted green and brown afghan over her legs. "Your dad looks just like you, except darker."

"His mother, my grandmother, was an Ethiopian Jew, making me a quarter black," he snapped. "There've been Jews in Ethiopia since the time of Solomon. But enough Kunta Kinte crap. What'd you find?"

She sighed, dreading his reaction to her failure. "Well, the best thing I can say about today is I made a hundred bucks for cleaning his house."

"Meaning?"

"Tillman, I didn't get anywhere. He's a cranky old man who's too dangerous to still have a driver's license. He's pissed off he's never met your children. He thinks you're after his money. He's got nine cats and his condo looks like a hoarder's training exercise." She tugged on the tail of her braid. "Oh, and he's got a girlfriend named Cassandra who drives a yellow Porsche Cayenne. Hang on a sec." From her jeans pocket, she pulled out the card and read, "Cassandra Maza. Runs a charitable foundation called *This Side of the Rainbow Bridge*, for pets whose owners have died."

Long silence on his end. Must be mad I didn't get results, she thought.

"I really worked, Tillman. But every time I got him relaxed and talking, something would set him off and he'd throw a tantrum. Do you know if he's seen a doctor lately? I'm wondering if he doesn't have dementia, the way he flies into a rage."

Still no response. He wasn't just mad, more like furious. She'd never known him to keep quiet this long.

One last try to redeem herself. "And he's still mourning your half-sister's death."

Long seconds ticked by.

He's going to fire me.

Finally he spoke, deep voice sounding strangled. "What half-sister?"

Tawny almost dropped the phone. Didn't he know? "Levona. Died of a drug overdose when she was a teenager."

"Jesus Christ!"

Finally, the explosion she'd been expecting but still dreaded. "Look, I know you're disappointed but I really did try—"

"I don't believe you!"

Now he'd crossed the line—her line. She might fail but she didn't lie. Hurt by his accusation, she retorted, "I've *always* told you the truth, even when it made me look bad."

"No, no, no! That's not what I mean. I don't believe you dragged all that information out of him. Three different private investigators spent weeks surveilling him, charged me thousands, and not one of them could get him to even open his door. You deliver the mother lode. A lousy hundred bucks to you is the best money I ever spent."

Huh? Not only wasn't he angry, he sounded ecstatic.

"But," she stammered, "I didn't find out about his finances. He says his mortgage payments are auto-deductions but he wouldn't show me proof they've been paid."

"What is wrong with you? You broke into Fort Knox and dragged out stuff I've never known my whole life. Like this half-sister." His deep voice turned pensive. "Haven't thought of this in years. When I was about four, the old man brought some girl to the house. I didn't know who she was but she was older than me, maybe twelve or thirteen. He made a big fuss over her because she played the cello." A pause. "That explains why I never saw her again."

Tawny slumped back on a throw pillow. Despite the sadness of his fractured family, relief softened the knots in her neck. Tillman wasn't going to fire her. She still had a job. Thank goodness.

But, that meant he would expect her to continue investigating.

"Keep it up!" The booming tone returned, like a coach giving a pep talk.

"Doing what?"

"Whatever you're doing that's working so damn well."

~~~

The morning after the blizzard, Tawny's cell rang with a number she didn't recognize.

A deep rumbling voice said, "Go skiing with me."

Sounded like Tillman but not quite. "Moe?"

"The golf course is right out my back door. No lift tickets, no waiting in line."

Tawny looked through the wavy window glass of her ninety-year-old Craftsman bungalow. In the front yard, limbs of the Austrian pine bowed to the ground under the weight of fresh snow. Dazzling sun, brilliant blue sky. The day begged her to be outside in the snapping air. More important, she'd been trying to think of an excuse to convince Moe to allow her to continue the investigation. "OK."

"Do you have skis?"

"Cross country."

"Perfect. That's what we're doing. See you in an hour."

Whatever reason Moe had for inviting her, she wasn't

going to argue. At eleven a.m., she pulled into his driveway. He stood ready in the opening of the garage door, bundled in layers. Green polar fleece showed above the zipper of a tan parka. The tail of a plaid shirt hung below. A hunter-orange knit cap covered his steel-gray curls and ears.

He fidgeted like an impatient child, scuffing his skis back and forth, jabbing holes in the snow with his poles. "Ten new inches. Perfect. Figured you looked like a skier. Downhill, too?"

Tawny stepped into bindings. "Not anymore. Torn meniscus." She pulled her poles and waist pack from the back of the Jeep and shut the hatch.

Moe nodded. "Me, too. Got my knees replaced a few years back and now they're so strong, you could park a truck on my shoulders." He lifted each leg to flex his artificial parts. "It's a bitch going through the airport, though. TSA practically strip-searches me. Wouldn't be so bad if a cute young lady did it but it's always some ugly dude with a big belly and garlic breath."

Tawny had to laugh as she fastened the pack around her waist. A water bottle, first aid supplies, a Swiss Army knife, and bear spray weighed her down but were necessities she always carried in the back country, winter or summer.

"I'm glad for the company," Moe said. "Cassandra won't ski or golf with me anymore. Says the sun's hard on her skin."

Tawny raised her face to the bright blue sky and inhaled deeply. "It's a sin to stay inside on a day like this."

"Come on!" Moe pushed through the side yard between condominium buildings and out onto the rolling golf course, blazing a trail in sparkling virgin snow. He moved like a skater. Long legs scissored in perfect rhythm with the swing of his poles. Pretty impressive for a seventy-five-year-old man with artificial knees.

Tawny hustled to catch up to him as he glided down broad white fairways, over hillocks, and across bridges that spanned a meandering creek. They skied deeper into the course, leaving the clubhouse and condos far behind, not seeing another soul.

Tawny squinted despite wearing sunglasses. Memories surfaced, skiing with Dwight and the kids when they were little—invigorated, excited, cheeks red, exhaling frosted puffs. How she cherished those too-rare days, never to be repeated.

But the wave of longing dissipated as physical exertion warmed her core. Clear, crisp air freshened her mind. Her hips would ache tomorrow but, today, it was worth it.

After a half hour, Moe finally slowed to a leisurely pace where they could talk as they moved into a forested area flanking a fairway. Centuries before, a glacier had pushed boulders into a jumbled wall along the trail. Deadfall trees crisscrossed the rocks.

"So," he said through huffs of steamy breath, "where's your husband?"

A year and a half had passed but Tawny still felt a pinch in her heart whenever someone asked about Dwight. "He died."

Gliding along, Moe glanced sideways at her. "You kill him?"

She skidded to a stop. "No!"

He stopped, too, and peered down his nose at her. "It's a reasonable question. You told me you'd killed a man."

Through clenched teeth, she said, "Not my husband."

"OK, OK." He raised his hands, poles dangling from straps on his wrists. "My son's gotten several battered women off. Thought you might have been one of those."

She squeezed hard on the foam handles of her poles. "I wasn't." Damn this infuriating man and his equally infuriating son.

And damn the tainted past she now had to live with. The previous spring, still reeling with grief from Dwight's death, she'd foolishly fallen into the arms of a man who turned out to be a monster—a monster she had to kill to save herself.

Unperturbed, Moe pulled a water bottle from his belt holster, popped the cap, and drank. "Here I am out in the boonies all alone with a woman who killed a guy. How do I know you're not going to get the itch again?"

Tawny's neck flushed hot. "I've taken enough crap off of you." She turned around to head back to the condo and her Jeep.

"Hey, hey, I'm just kidding." Moe extended his bottle in a gesture that might have been an apology.

She glared at him. "I don't think much of your sense of humor."

"Few people appreciate it." He leaned on his poles and grinned at her. "Come on, please stay." He raised his chin toward the blue sky. "It's a beautiful day and I'd like to share it with a beautiful woman."

His lopsided grin made him look like a bratty little boy who knew he deserved a spanking but also knew he could talk his way out of it.

Deep breaths, Tawny told herself. Don't let him get to you. It's your job.

She pushed off, skiing ahead of Moe for the first time, breaking new trail in pristine snow on another fairway. She focused on the shushing rhythm of the skis, tamping anger into the background. Sweat trickled under layers of clothing. After several minutes, she paused to strip off her windbreaker and tied the sleeves around her waist. Wisps of hair had pulled loose from her braid and blew across her face. She readjusted the waist pack and glanced over her shoulder.

Moe had lagged behind, maybe tired from the strenuous pace he'd set earlier. She caught a glimpse of his orange cap through the skeleton limbs of a larch tree that had dropped its needles for winter.

Ahead, she spotted a line of divots in the snow. Must be

animal tracks. She skied closer to study them, caught a foul smell, and gasped.

Fresh mountain lion tracks. And scat still steaming.

She whipped around and yelled, "Moe!"

The orange cap hadn't moved from where she'd last pinpointed it. The tracks led into the nearly solid wall of conifers a hundred yards ahead of him. By now, the animal could have backtracked to where the elderly man rested.

"Moe!" she screamed again. "Lion! Get out in the open!"

The orange speck still didn't stir. Could he hear her?

She pulled the canister of bear spray from her pack, looped the trigger onto a gloved finger, and clutched her poles tight. As fast as she could, she retraced the trail she'd just cut, skimming toward the line of spruce and pines. Every few seconds, she shouted his name.

No answer.

She slid between trees and stopped fifty feet from where Moe stood.

Frozen, staring up.

A mountain lion crouched atop a massive boulder, looming over Moe. The tip of its tail swished snow. Golden eyes looked from Moe to Tawny, then back to Moe.

Only fifteen feet separated the cat and the man. Moe's face was gray and slack. Bony shoulders stooped. His poles quivered in trembling hands.

Tawny dropped one pole and thumbed off the safety latch of the bear spray canister. In a low, urgent voice, she said, "Moe, wave your poles over your head. Make yourself look big."

He didn't move. His eyes sunk deep in their sockets, lids almost closed. Praying?

Muscles twitched under the lion's sleek fur. Its golden gaze locked on Tawny.

Not close enough to spray. She lashed the air with her pole

and moved toward it. "Go away, get out of here!"

Suddenly Moe came to life. He spun around and tried to run but his feet tangled in the skis. He fell backwards into a deep drift, legs hopelessly twisted in opposite directions.

The lion sprang down from the boulder and bounded toward the helpless man.

Tawny lurched forward, pushing one-handed with the pole. Frantically she squeezed the trigger hard. An orange pepper cloud billowed in the direction of the lion and Moe.

The cat halted, drew back on its haunches, and sneezed. It slunk under a tree.

Tawny skied toward Moe, into the fog of burning spray, holding her breath. Sunglasses partially protected her eyes but only partially. She positioned herself between the cat and the helpless man flailing on the ground. Still on his back, Moe's gloved hands pawed the air, trying to fan away the spray.

She yelled at the cat, "Get out of here! Go!" Hot pepper seared her throat and lungs. She choked. Her weeping eyes felt full of molten sand.

Foam covered the animal's muzzle. Ears lay flat against its skull. But instead of retreating, it sprang forward, landing only five feet from her.

She jabbed at it with the sharp pointed end of her pole. It bared its teeth and yowled, an eerie primal scream that sent a ripple of terror up her back. Curved shiny claws swiped at the pole. She pulled the trigger again. This time, the bear spray scored a direct hit to the animal's face.

The lion jinked sideways, whirling in frantic circles. It shook its head, flinging thick ropey strings of saliva. Sneezing, it rubbed its face through snow.

At last, it turned tail and streaked toward the fairway.

Tawny backed out of the lingering pepper cloud and leaned heavily on her pole, heart hammering. Tears gushed from her stinging eyes. She sucked clean air down her scorched throat. Behind her, Moe sputtered and choked. "Are you OK?" she croaked.

His snorts, coughs, and curses reassured her.

She checked where the lion had gone. In the distance, it leapt over a narrow stream, zig-zagged across the fairway, and vanished into another line of trees a football field away.

She pulled off her gloves and sunglasses. Squatting, she gathered a lump of clean snow to hold against her hot face and eyes.

By the time the snow melted, her eyes still burned but tears no longer blinded her. The spray had dissipated, oily orange residue sinking to the white ground.

She unclipped bindings and stepped out of her skis to trudge over to Moe.

He struggled like an upended daddy long legs spider, limbs bent at odd angles, skis and poles lashing the air. His frantic movements had only caused him to burrow deeper into the drift. Through his crisscrossed skis, his dark skin looked ashy, like a water stain on mahogany. He coughed, hawked, and spat every few seconds. Tears flooded his bright red eyes.

"Hold still," Tawny said. "I'll get you free." She grasped one wet, wiggling leg and unclipped the binding, then repeated with the other. Shoving the skis out of the way, she reached down and gripped his soggy gloved hand in her cold bare one. "OK, on the count of three. One, two, three."

The effort to pull him to his feet almost toppled her but he managed to stand. He swayed while tears poured down the furrows of his cheeks.

She pulled out her water bottle. "Lean your head back." He obeyed and she flushed his eyes. He blinked madly and sniffled. By the time both their water bottles were empty, he looked a little better.

"Can you walk?" she asked.

He lifted one foot, then the other, flexing knees and ankles. They seemed stable.

"Are you up to skiing back?"

He rested a heavy hand on her shoulder. Deadpan, he said, "Are you offering to carry me?"

In the aftermath of panic and adrenaline, relief bubbled up in her chest. She dissolved in helpless giggles. Moe joined in with deep bass chuckles.

They'd survived a mountain lion attack. No blood, no broken bones.

She reached up to hug his neck. He hugged back hard, nearly crushing her ribs.

~~~

An hour and a half later at the condo, Tawny and Moe had changed out of wet gear and sat on the sectional in front of the fire. She cuddled into warm sweats, glad for the emergency clothes and socks she always kept in the Jeep. A deputy was on his way to take a report about the mountain lion encounter. While they waited, Moe had dusted off a bottle of Courvoisier and poured some for each of them.

The Siamese tucked himself against Moe's leg. Sugar curled in Tawny's lap, purrs vibrating against her fingertips as she scratched under her chin. The rest of the cats watched from perches on the staircase and bookshelves.

Moe swirled the snifter and inhaled. "According to Chinese custom," he said, "since you saved my life, now you're responsible for me."

The brandy burned down Tawny's throat and glowed warm in her chest. "If that's true, we're going back out there to give the lion another chance."

He flicked long fingers in yet another gesture that reminded her of Tillman. "He'd take one bite and spit out this stringy old black Jew."

She grinned at him. "You're probably right." She sipped and smoothed away the hair that had pulled loose from her braid during the altercation. "You don't want to hear this, but you and Tillman are so alike, I swear, I have to rub my eyes to know whether I'm talking to the father or the son."

He scowled. "We're damn clones. Why else do you think we don't get along?"

"Too much competition?"

He shrugged. "Let the Ivy League psychiatrists figure that out. We hate each other and that's the way it is."

"Don't you ever want to see your grandchildren?"

He clunked the snifter down on the coffee table. "You saved my life but that doesn't give you free shots at me."

Tawny tucked her legs under her, trying to thaw her still-cold feet. "Moe, for some reason I can't explain, I care about you two, even though you both make it damn hard most of the time. It would be nice to see your family healed."

"Rambo," he addressed the Siamese, "she thinks she's Oprah."

"Never mind." Tawny still had a job to do. "Have you checked any more into your mortgage payments?"

He looked sideways at her, brows pinched, mouth tight.

Dead end. Again.

A bell chimed. Moe unfolded long limbs and answered the door.

The deputy entered the great room. He looked familiar, late forties, shaved head shaped like a bullet, short, but muscle-bound.

Nodding, he said, "Mrs. Lindholm, how're you doin'?"

He recognized her but she couldn't place him.

The deputy took a notebook from his vest pocket and started with questions. Exactly where had they encountered the mountain lion? How large? Level of aggression shown? Male or female?

Moe and Tawny exchanged glances at the last question, both raising eyebrows. Moe spoke up, "Didn't have time to check out the equipment."

One side of the deputy's mouth lifted. "Any sign of cubs?"

"Not that I saw," Tawny answered. "Just a single line of tracks across the fairway, heading for the forest."

"Tell me about the actual incident."

Moe jumped up quickly and set the stage of his living room into the scene of the attack. With lanky arms, he measured the distance from the lion to him, shrinking it from what Tawny remembered. He described the stalking, mimicking the cat's slink. With a swashbuckling leap full of flourishes, he demonstrated how Tawny had placed herself between Moe and the animal. His version transformed her from a scared woman armed with a ski pole into a valiant sword fighter. During his melodramatic explanation, a few seconds of panic morphed into an epic gladiator battle.

Tawny huddled deep into the couch, embarrassed to be described as a heroic wonder woman. Yet Moe's flair almost made her believe his version. He reminded her of Tillman's charisma in the courtroom. Whenever her boss spoke, everyone's eyes were riveted on him.

The deputy turned to her, respect in his expression. "Mrs. Lindholm, is that how you remember it?"

She shook her head, cheeks hot. "Moe's exaggerating. I was on skis. I could hardly *leap* in front of the lion. Besides, by that time, he was lying on the ground. I'm not sure how much he could see."

Moe's retort echoed off the high ceiling: "I was right there.

I saw everything! She saved my life! If she hadn't come flying through the trees, I'd be bloody pulp in the rough off the number thirteen green."

The deputy suppressed a smile and closed his notebook. "Everybody came home safe, that's what counts. I'll give this information to Fish and Wildlife. They'll check out if there have been other sightings in the area, maybe set a trap."

Moe walked the deputy to the door. The men talked in low tones Tawny couldn't make out, except for a few words from Moe: "...gonna call Channel Nine."

Oh hell, not that. After suffering media attention following her arrest, she never wanted her name publicly mentioned again until her obituary.

She took a gulp from the snifter and almost choked. Her head buzzed, already dizzy from alcohol on an empty stomach. If she left now, she might still catch the deputy outside and ask him how to keep the press from finding out.

She pushed the cat from her lap and hurried to the entry where her coat hung on a peg and boots sat in a puddle on the slate floor. Moe closed the door and turned, surprise lifting his brows at finding her beside him.

"Moe, I need to get home. It's getting dark—"

"No way!" He grasped her upper arms. "I'm taking you out for prime rib and champagne. That's the least I can do for the brave heroine who saved my life."

Her stomach growled, reminding her she hadn't eaten since breakfast. She hoped Moe didn't hear the rumble. "Thank you but I really can't." She hustled into her coat while slipping on her boots, then looked up.

Disappointment painted his gaunt brown face. "But I wanted to..."

She didn't mean to hurt his feelings but she couldn't endure a swarm of reporters. "Another time, I promise. I'll order the biggest prime rib you can afford." She kissed his cheek and left.

Outside, the deputy's truck still idled at the curb. She approached the passenger side. He was typing on the console computer, noticed her, and lowered the window. "Mrs. Lindholm, something else?"

"Mr. Rosenbaum is, well, pretty over the top. He made it sound bigger than it was."

The deputy smiled. "He's lucky you're cool-headed in a crisis."

Recognition finally hit her. This deputy had been among the endless parade of law enforcement officers who'd questioned her while her attorney—Tillman—fended them off.

She gripped the window opening. "Is it possible to leave my name out of the report? I'd like to skip any publicity."

"After your previous experience, I understand." His erect posture softened. "My report won't bring much attention, but I expect right about now Mr. Rosenbaum is on the phone to the TV stations."

Tawny pressed her hands to her temples. "Dear God, I hope not."

He nodded but his expression hardened. "Mrs. Lindholm, before you think about driving, the alcohol on your breath is pretty strong. If you get arrested for DUI, you really won't like *that* publicity."

Damn. How did a beautiful ski day turn so screwy?

"My suggestion," the deputy said, "is to go back inside and maybe you can distract Mr. Rosenbaum from calling reporters. Order in a pizza. Hang around till the alcohol wears off."

She sagged against the truck for a few seconds, knowing he was right. "OK."

He added, "Mrs. Lindholm, I never thought you should've been charged. Killing that terrorist saved a lot of lives. You *are* a brave woman."

She pushed off from the truck and straightened. She didn't feel brave, she felt like crap. "Thanks."

He wrote on the back of a sheriff's department business card, then handed it to her through the window. "Here's my cell number. I live in West Glacier so this whole area is my beat, Bad Rock Canyon, on up the North Fork. If there's anything I can ever help you with..." His even, brown-eyed stare held hers for several long seconds.

Tawny put the card in her coat pocket, wondering if the offer was professional, or personal. "OK. Thanks."

She turned away from the truck, feeling the deputy's gaze on her as she dragged her feet back to Moe's door and knocked.

The elderly man's face lit when he opened it. "You changed your mind."

She moved inside and shrugged out of her coat. "The deputy gently dropped a hint about DUI. Your brandy packs a wallop."

"Great! Let's go get prime rib."

Not great. Moe drove badly enough when sober. She shuddered at the thought of him behind the wheel after a few belts of 120 proof. "I'm bushed. Let's do it another time. Can we just stay here and order pizza?"

"If that's what you want." He grabbed his cell. "What kind do you like?"

Her stomach rumbled again. "Anything."

While they waited for the delivery, she prowled the kitchen, seeking a snack. Except for cases of canned cat food, the human choices were curdled, moldy, or shriveled. Moe apparently hadn't visited a grocery store in months. She found an open can of mixed nuts, old and stale, but probably not toxic.

As she munched, she noticed a wad of stock statements

wedged in a half-open drawer among a jumble of hand tools and margarine cups full of loose screws and nails. She glanced in the living room, where Moe knelt on the carpet, entertaining three cats with a stuffed mouse he yanked on a long string.

Should she? She hated snooping but Moe had refused to cooperate. If he was the victim of a scam, she didn't know how else to find out. With her cell camera, she snapped a photo of the first page then rechecked the living room.

Moe was still playing with the cats, dangling the stuffed mouse above their heads. They danced on hind legs and batted the toy. A surprising, sweet gentleness replaced the customary scowl on his face. For all his gruffness, he did love his pets.

She recorded page after page. When nervousness and guilt grew unbearable, she stuffed the papers back amid screwdrivers and wrenches, almost slicing her hand on the exposed blade of an Exacto knife. With all the junk in the drawer, he'd probably never notice.

She hoped.

In the living room, she offered the can of nuts to Moe, who flicked his hand *no*.

"If someone doesn't eat cat food," she said, "they could starve in this house."

He set aside the toy, finished his drink, and poured another, then tilted the bottle toward her.

She shook her head. "Not if I want to drive home."

He flopped on the sectional, crossed long legs, ankle to knee, and stared at her. "So, you're the woman who pitched that terrorist off Hungry Horse Dam."

His words dropped like a bomb. The deputy must have told him.

She went to the tall windows overlooking the snowy golf course and wished she could crash through the glass and escape.

"You're a hero," Moe added. "You ought to be proud."

"Did you ever kill anyone?"

"No."

She hugged herself. "It's not something that makes you proud."

"Granted. But you don't need to be ashamed either." He moved across the room to stand beside her. "My son's a grade A certified asshole but I have to concede he did one good thing in his life. He kept you out of jail on a chicken-shit homicide charge that should never have been brought. Thanks to him, you're roaming around free and you made yourself quite useful today, saving my scrawny ass." Normally hostile eyes sparkled.

His words made her smile.

Moe put an arm around her shoulder and leaned a bristly cheek on her tousled hair, prickling her scalp. His sweater smelled musty, like it had been at the bottom of a drawer for a long time, and his ribs jutted sharply against her side. Still, his warm gesture comforted her. Her palm moved to rest on his back, rubbing the knobby vertebrae.

His reassuring hug reminded her of her grandfather and how much she missed him. Even as Grandpa had descended deeper into dementia, there had still been occasional tender moments, like this one.

Moments to treasure.

Behind them, the front door creaked then swung open. A woman's voice rang out, "Darling Moshe, look what I have!"

Tawny and Moe broke apart and faced Cassandra. She paused in the doorway, holding a pizza box. She was bundled in a silver fox jacket with matching hat and high-heeled boots. Her bright pink lips hung slightly open, frozen in a not-quite-formed smile.

Uh-oh. The hug was totally innocent but they must've looked pretty sheepish in the eyes of an insecure, territorial girlfriend with a house key.

"I didn't know you had company, Moshe." Cassandra's voice oozed sweetness.

The hell she didn't. Tawny's Jeep was parked in his driveway.

"What kind of pizza are we having?" Cassandra minced from the entry to the dining table and set the box down. "I met the boy outside, paid him, and thought I'd surprise you."

Moe maintained a calm, neutral expression, unfazed. With four ex-wives, Tawny figured he probably had lots of experience getting caught.

"I'm glad you're here." He sauntered across the great room, opened the pizza box, and inhaled the aroma. "I have quite a story to share with you. It's been an exciting day."

"I can see that." Again, the forced sweetness. "Mushrooms, olives, and peppers. Lovely."

Tawny wished she'd brought a comb. She hadn't anticipated a tangle with a mountain lion that left her hair looking as if she'd just climbed out of bed. She also wished she could drain the blood that flushed her face.

What the hell? She'd done nothing wrong. Let Moe and Cassandra fight it out between them.

Moe pulled out the first slice, strings of mozzarella stretching long. He offered it to Cassandra. Smile glued on, she shook her head and zeroed in on the bottle of Courvoisier on the coffee table. She sloshed some into Moe's empty snifter and drank it down. He winked at Tawny and took a hearty bite.

The fragrance of yeast and melted cheese made Tawny's mouth water. She moved to the far side of the table, keeping it as a barrier between herself and Cassandra, and took a slice. She wolfed it down faster than a teenager after football practice, and helped herself to second piece.

Meanwhile Cassandra finished another brandy. "What *have*

you two been up to today?" Sounded like a dare.

Mouth full, cool as Paul Newman, Moe said, "A mountain lion attacked me."

Cassandra's blue eyes widened. "You're kidding."

He slowly tore off another slice, crossed to Cassandra, and again offered it to her.

She waved her hands *no* and glared at him. "What are you talking about?"

Moe bit into the pizza and chewed like a cow with its cud, savoring, dragging the moment out.

Tawny watched him toy with the fuming woman. She looked ready to stamp her feet.

"We're all right," he said. "No one got hurt. In case you were concerned." A zing of sarcasm, then more lazy chewing. "The deputy will pass the report onto Fish and Wildlife, if they want to set a trap."

"What the hell happened?" Cassandra shouted.

Moe's gaze rolled over to Tawny. "Do you want to tell her?"

Tawny dreaded getting in the middle of their fight but Moe seemed ready to prolong the suspense all evening. "We were skiing on the golf course. A mountain lion went after Moe. I used bear spray and it ran off."

Cassandra stared at her, disbelief again narrowing her eyes.

The brackets around Moe's mouth deepened. "You are one pitiful storyteller, Tawny."

"I sure am. Why don't you fill in the details? I need to go." She grabbed a last slice for the road and hurried to the door. "Thanks for dinner."

In her Jeep, Tawny started the engine. She hoped three slices of pizza had absorbed enough alcohol to keep her from being pulled over. As much as she wanted out of the uncomfortable situation, part of her longed to hear Moe's explanation to his girlfriend.

~~~

Cassandra glowered at Moshe. He sat on the ripped sectional with his feet propped up on the cluttered coffee table, slowly chewing. He was having too much fun baiting her and she couldn't allow that to go on. It was unacceptable. He had to be slapped back into place.

And that damn woman. She was too pretty, exactly the type Moshe would find irresistible. Of course, *irresistible* was a relative term and Cassandra was a realist. Anyone with two X chromosomes would be irresistible to the lecherous old man. She'd managed to keep him in line. Until now. She needed to reassert control.

Cassandra sidled toward the sectional, raised her arms above her head and fluffed her hair over her face. She thrust her breasts out. "I have something much tastier for you than pizza," she cooed.

A smile spread across the old lech's face.

CHAPTER 4 - ALPENGLOW

An hour later, Tawny sat at the desk in her son's bedroom, now her office, and smiled at the old family photo that wallpapered her laptop screen. Dwight, still brawny before cancer ravaged him, arm slung over Neal's broad shoulder. Tawny and Emma, both with french braids, her daughter's hair a lighter red than Tawny's auburn, the same wide-set eyes except Tawny's were brown and Emma's hazel.

Tawny touched Dwight's cheek on the screen. "I miss you, baby."

With a sigh, she got to work, uploading the photos she'd snapped with her cell. Squinting through her readers, she scanned Moe's stock statements and watched the balance of his portfolio drop from more than two million to under $15,000. The market still hadn't recovered from the 2008 crash four years earlier but even the Great Recession couldn't cause such extreme losses.

Under closer study, she noticed frequent withdrawals from his account, $150,000 here, $180,000 there. She ran a total on the calculator and found he'd taken out $1,970,000 during the past three years. Falling stock prices caused the rest of the loss.

With two fingers, she typed an email to Tillman, hoping auto-correct would fix her errors. Dyslexia made her struggle with reading and writing. Her boss constantly complained about her bad spelling.

She attached the photos, sent the report off, and erased them from her cell. If only her guilt about sneaking could be as easily erased.

The back door banged and voices filtered down the hall to her office. Emma and a man. Tawny shut down the laptop.

Tawny's kitchen hadn't been updated since the seventies before she and Dwight bought the house. Jim Tang lounged at the worn Formica breakfast bar opposite the harvest gold side-by-side refrigerator. Emma hung on him, running her fingers through his shoulder-length black hair.

Tawny greeted him: "Hey, Jim, how's it going?"

He rose from the barstool, which increased his height a whole inch to five-six. Tawny bent down to kiss his chubby cheek and he hugged her. At five-ten, both Tawny and Emma towered over him but his gregarious personality filled any room he entered. "Ma said you were at the restaurant the other day."

Tawny shuddered. "I brought a guest who started misbehaving. Please tell her and your uncle I promise I won't bring him back."

Jim made a face and waved his hands. "Are you kidding? He's no problem compared to rowdy drunks in the casino. Besides, we know him. Rich guy from Golden Eagle, comes in regular, brings his lady for dinner. They like to play the machines, too. He gets kind of demanding, but you gotta expect that in this business. As long as he makes the cash register ring, Uncle Lee doesn't mind at all."

Tawny wondered if gambling was the reason for Moe's financial problems. "He's there a lot?"

Jim shrugged. "Once, twice a month, I guess."

That didn't sound like a problem gambler but maybe Moe spread his business around to different casinos. She'd have to check into that possibility.

Emma grabbed two beers from the refrigerator. "Mom, is it OK if Jim stays over?"

"Sure," Tawny said. Emma's protective daddy might not have approved but Tawny had always been more practical and realistic than Dwight when it came to their daughter. More than anything, she hoped the romance was catching fire again.

"Ma's old fashioned," Jim said with a grin. "She doesn't

want a girl spending the night at the house with me 'cause she thinks that sets a bad example for my little brother. Like he isn't looking at porn on the computer every time she turns her back."

Tawny chuckled and remembered her son Neal's raging hormones during his teen years. At least a computer didn't get kids pregnant or infect them with an STD.

Emma tugged on Jim's hair. "I'm going to take a shower."

Jim's eyes twinkled. "Want me to wash your back?"

"My shower's too dinky. Hang out with Mom." She breezed toward the bathroom off the hall, disappearing with a cute twitch of her slim hip.

Tawny found a bag of tortilla chips in the cupboard. "Want something to eat? I'll make guacamole."

"Yeah, that'd be great."

Tawny cut into an avocado.

Jim pulled on his beer. "You'd be the coolest mother-in-law."

Her heart quickened as she mashed the pulp in a bowl with salt, sour cream, and lemon juice. "What a nice compliment. Are you hinting?"

"If I have my way." Jim's cheeks puffed out.

"Well, I think you'd be the coolest son-in-law," she said. "But I'm not sure your mom would be too happy."

Jim munched on a chip. "Old-fashioned again. I tell her, 'Ma, there's like four Chinese girls in town. Not much choice.' She still thinks I should go to Taiwan and pick one out to bring home, like going shopping for a washer and dryer or a flat screen TV." He rolled his eyes.

Tawny set the bowl of guacamole between them. "She's a lady who believes in traditions." A different concern bobbed in her mind. "Have you asked Emma?"

He shook his head. "I kinda wanted to talk to you first. Do

you think she'll say yes?"

His trust in her touched Tawny but also forced her to tell him the truth. "Jimmy, I don't know if she's ready for marriage. She says she doesn't want to settle down. Flits from one job to the next, one state to the next, one guy to the next." She squeezed his shoulder. "I just don't know if she's ready for a commitment. I'm kind of surprised she's stayed around home as long as she has this time."

Jim's head sank a little. Tawny feared her flighty daughter might pass up the best chance she'd ever have for a lasting relationship, because excitement beyond the next hill proved irresistible.

"When her dad died," Jim said in a quiet voice, "and then you almost got killed, it shook her up a lot. You guys were like rock solid. She thought you'd both always be there for her." With a chip, he traced a pattern in the guacamole. "I guess I hope she'll see me as her rock."

This boy is too good for my flaky daughter, Tawny thought. She rubbed Jim's shoulder. "Maybe you will be. I sure hope so, 'cause you'd be an awesome son-in-law."

Their eyes met and Tawny wondered if she was watching hope die.

"Mo-om!" Emma's voice whined from the hall. "My hair dryer blew the bathroom fuse again."

Tawny sighed. The wiring in her old house badly needed to be replaced. "You know where the panel is," she called. "Go down in the basement and reset it."

Emma bounced through the living room into the kitchen. Her robe flapped open, revealing her nakedness. "Ooh, guac! Cool, Mom."

A grin spread across Jim's face.

Tawny was used to her free-spirited daughter running around the house nude, but this stunt felt like a deliberate slap to her. She pulled Emma's robe closed, tied the sash, and patted her cheek a tad harder than necessary to make the point.

Emma received the message but tossed her wet hair. "If *you* weren't here, I wouldn't bother with the robe." She grabbed the bowl and bag of chips. To Jim, she said, "C'mon, let's go watch TV."

"Don't forget to reset the circuit breaker," Tawny said.

"Yeah, sure."

Meaning Tawny would later have to reset it herself.

Jim followed Emma downstairs to the basement den, dragged by an invisible leash around his heart.

Tawny sighed. Nothing like a beautiful naked redhead to rekindle a young man's hope.

~~~

Tawny intended to take a little time off to give Moe a chance to resolve the spat with his girlfriend. But the next day, he called and invited her to dinner with him and Cassandra at the Alpenglow Yacht Club. Apparently the couple had made peace.

Tawny spent the morning damp-mopping hardwood floors, and scrubbing the master bathroom. When she plugged in the vacuum, the outlet sparked and plunged the hall into dimness—blown circuit breaker again. Dwight always meant to rewire their old house, but was too sick. She clipped downstairs to the basement and reset the breaker on the electrical panel. It instantly popped off again.

Damn. An electrician had given her a bid but she needed several more months to save enough to pay for the work. Either that or jump through hoops to apply for a bank loan. Meanwhile she hoped the wires didn't short out and burn down the house.

While she cleaned, Tawny tried to brainstorm a new

approach to convince Moe to reveal more about his finances. She'd hoped for direction from Tillman after he reviewed the stock statements but his only reaction came in a terse text: *Keep digging.*

Yeah, but which hole?

At five-thirty, Emma flitted through the kitchen door. "Hi, Mom, help me braid my hair before I go to work?" Her long red locks hung loose and tangled.

"Sure, if you help me braid mine," Tawny answered. "Moe's taking me out to dinner tonight at the Alpenglow."

Emma plopped on the barstool at the breakfast bar and swished her hair over her shoulder. "Cool. That's, like, the classiest, priciest restaurant this side of Missoula."

As Tawny combed out her daughter's fine hair, the homey task reminded her of happier years, getting the children ready for school, packing lunches for her and Dwight to take to the shop, the little everyday family chores she cherished.

"I miss Daddy," Emma murmured.

"So do I, honey." As annoying as some of Emma's habits could be, Tawny felt grateful her daughter had moved home. The house was no longer so achingly empty from Dwight's death. "What made you think of him?"

Emma shrugged. "I always think about him."

Tawny finished the braid and hugged her daughter from behind. "I'm glad you're here."

Emma jumped up abruptly. "Oh, crap, I'm late. I was supposed to be at the Lucky Dragon at four." She darted away like a hummingbird, grabbed her coat in the mud room, and vanished out the back door.

Would her daughter ever develop a work ethic? And now Tawny had to braid her own hair.

She showered, put on makeup, and dressed in what passed for formal in Montana, a black beaded sweater, black velvet leggings, and her good suede boots. She hoped the country club parking lot had been plowed because she hated wearing heels on ice.

At seven p.m., when she pulled under the covered portico, she found she didn't need to worry. A valet opened her Jeep door. "Do I win the prize?" she asked the young man.

"Ma'am?"

"For having the oldest car in the parking lot."

He squelched a smirk and offered his arm to escort her to the vestibule.

She'd only been to the yacht club on Flathead Lake once before, years ago at a wedding reception. But she remembered the polished granite, the original Charlie Russell oils on the walls, and the heavy Frederic Remington bronze sculptures in the lobby. Antique Winchester rifles hung criss-crossed above the carved mahogany arch that led to the dining room. She spotted Moe and Cassandra at a table beside a sandstone fireplace.

Their chairs were cozily pushed together and they drank champagne from Waterford crystal flutes. Cassandra caressed the shoulder of Moe's navy sport coat. He was freshly shaved and looked dashing in a sky-blue shirt and burgundy tie.

Cassandra appeared ready for a night on the town in Vegas. A ruby and diamond choker sparkled around her neck. The tops of her breasts swelled over a tight red sequined cocktail dress with spaghetti straps. Her platinum hair was piled high and had been lacquered enough to deflect hailstones.

Tawny scanned the other women in the formal room to make sure she hadn't underdressed too badly. No, she was OK. It was Cassandra who was over-the-top.

As the maître d' led Tawny to the table, she noticed something else looked different about Moe's girlfriend.

Previously her eyes had been bright blue but tonight they were a glowing golden topaz. Amazing the change that colored contacts could make in someone's appearance.

Moe rose with a courtly bow, kissed Tawny's cheek then held her chair. The server poured champagne from a standing ice bucket.

With a dignified air, Moe lifted his glass to Tawny. His resonant baritone reverberated through the muted dining room. "To my courageous rescuer."

When other diners turned to look at her, Tawny wished she could hide under the table. She clinked her flute against Moe's, took a sip, and quickly changed the subject. "Cassandra, what a beautiful necklace." A gift from Moe? Maybe one of the large withdrawals from his stock account?

The woman touched her throat. "Thank you. It was a bequest from my dear neighbor who just passed on from a heart attack. She wanted me to know how grateful she was for taking care of her darling Muggins."

"Muggins?" Tawny asked.

"Her little Shih Tzu. He's happy and frolicking at my temporary sanctuary until the permanent facility is built. My greatest passion is animals."

Moe let out a grunt.

Cassandra fluttered heavily-mascaraed lashes at him. "Don't be sulky, darling. I meant my greatest passion after *you*." She turned back to Tawny. "Animals are simply angels with fur instead of wings. A four-legged angel brought us together, didn't she, darling?" She leaned into Moe.

He nodded, finished his champagne, and poured more. "People are assholes."

Tawny tensed, hoping his remark didn't foreshadow another rage. "What makes you say that?"

Cassandra sniffed. "He means the ones who are forever

dropping off pets on the golf course. I suppose they think everyone who lives there is wealthy and will take them in. Or at least they tell themselves that to justify deserting a helpless animal."

"That's awful," Tawny said.

"Sure as hell is," Moe spat, eyes narrow.

Cassandra rubbed his arm, perhaps to head off an outburst. "I was out for a walk one day and found a dear old Standard Poodle whose hips had collapsed. She was lying under a tree, whimpering. Her owner must have dumped her, rather than pay a vet. She was too heavy for me to carry but I couldn't stand to leave her alone, suffering like that. I didn't know what to do."

Tears trickled from her glistening golden eyes. Moe reached for her hand and laced his fingers through hers.

She dabbed at her nose with a tissue. "Who comes along but darling Moshe? He carried her all the way back to his house. Then he helped me take her to the clinic and paid for her care." More tears caught in her thick eyelashes. "Unfortunately, it was too late. The vet had to put her down. But at least she didn't die alone and in pain. We were with her, weren't we, darling?" Cassandra smiled up at Moe. "How could I not fall in love with a man like that?"

Tawny watched Moe's gaze cast downward, as if Cassandra's story embarrassed him. He gulped more champagne. How could a man with such compassion for animals hate his own son?

The server brought their salads and another bottle of champagne. Moe's fourth glass since Tawny had arrived. How many before that?

The elderly man had fallen uncharacteristically quiet, brooding over his Caesar salad. Tawny noticed apparent confusion about the silverware laid out on the damask tablecloth. He picked up one fork, set it down, picked up a butter knife, tested the blade with his thumb then fingered a soup spoon. Finally, he pushed the salad plate away untouched.

Tawny recognized signs similar to her grandfather's dementia, the inability to identify ordinary objects or remember their purpose. She wondered what her best friend Virgie, a physician, would think about Moe and his erratic behavior. Could Tawny convince him to see a doctor? She resolved to give it a try. Maybe *that* was more important than tracking his financial problems.

A tall, muscular young man approached their table. Startling blue eyes peered out from behind long blond dreadlocks. He wore a silver vest and dress pants but no jacket. A skinny rosebud-pink tie hung loose at the collar of a lavender shirt with french cuffs. Elegant but funky. He came up behind Cassandra and wrapped his weight-lifter arms around her.

"My adorable bad boy!" She beamed at him.

His blue gaze pinned Tawny. "Hel-*low*. I'm Colin, Cassandra's son." He extended a hand across the table to her.

Tawny reached out to shake but he instead lifted her hand to his lips, never taking his eyes off hers. Since he looked younger than her son, the blatant sexuality in his stare felt creepy. Between his lips, his warm tongue stroked her skin. She swallowed a gag and tried to pull free without being obvious. He held on, his leer broadening, as if he knew she wouldn't make a scene in front of his mother and Moe.

Cassandra said, "Colin darling, this is Tawny Lindholm. She's Moshe's—" She cocked her head to the side. "What *are* you, dear? A girl Friday?"

Tawny forced a polite smile and tugged her hand free. She wiped it on her napkin under the table.

Colin's knowing gaze crawled over her. "Tawny Lindholm, I am awestruck to meet you."

"Are you going to join us for dinner, darling?" Cassandra asked.

Dear Lord, I hope not, Tawny thought. The idea of sitting beside him made her shudder.

Colin massaged Cassandra's bare shoulders. "I can't, Mom. I just dropped by to bring your medicine." He pulled a prescription bottle from his pocket and folded her hand around it, as if presenting her with a diamond. "You forgot again, you bad girl."

Cassandra pooched her lips in an air kiss. "You take such good care of me." Mother and son smiled, sharing a secret joke.

Tawny wondered about the strange undercurrent between them. She checked for Moe's reaction but he was staring into the fire, lost in a distant world.

"I have to run," Colin said, dragging his hand from Cassandra's grip. He focused intense blue eyes on Tawny again. "Next time," he said, as if making a promise. Then he glided from the dining room.

Thank goodness he was gone.

Cassandra took out a pill and started to reach for her empty flute. "Darling, I'm dry. Order us another." She reached for Moe's half-full glass, holding it in both hands as she drank.

Moe gestured at the server, while Cassandra resumed stories about dogs and cats she'd rescued. Tawny nodded and asked a few questions but mostly listened to the woman's drawn-out tales of incredible animals. Moe drank steadily and stared into space.

When the prime rib arrived, he dug in and ate heartily, his earlier confusion about utensils apparently resolved. For dessert, Cassandra ordered something flambé which the server prepared with elaborate flourishes at the table. Moe ignored his portion and drank more champagne. His gaze kept returning to the massive logs licked by the fire.

After dessert, Tawny leaned across the table and squeezed his veiny hand. "Thank you, Moe. This was the best meal I've ever eaten."

Dullness blunted his normally snapping eyes but he nodded.

After Moe handed over his credit card, ten minutes dragged by. Finally the server returned, looking nervous, as he bent and spoke quietly in Moe's ear.

"Declined?" Moe shouted. "The hell you say!"

Both Tawny and Cassandra jumped at the outburst. The heads of other diners swiveled to stare.

The server murmured, "Sir, please, I'm sure it's just a misunderstanding. Would you like to speak with the manager?"

"This is bullshit!" Moe's face contorted.

Cassandra rubbed his shoulder. "Darling Moshe, your blood pressure. Please."

The manager hustled over, a regal woman with upswept dark hair. "Sir, we'll work out whatever problem you're having but I must ask you to lower your voice."

"You're the ones causing the problem," Moe bellowed. "Something's wrong with your system."

"Sir, maybe a different card will work."

Clenched fists pounded the table, making glasses jump. "That's the only goddamned card I have with me. Go figure out how to make it work!"

The manager drew herself tall. "Sir, please step outside with me."

He jumped up, grabbed his Waterford flute, and flung it into the fireplace. It shattered like an explosion of multi-colored fireworks. Broken shards tinkled on the sandstone hearth.

Cassandra leapt to her feet and gripped Moe's shoulders, kneading with both hands, but her soothing didn't work this time. Veins throbbed in his forehead and neck. His eyes bulged.

"Come, darling," she pleaded. "Let's go." She grabbed Moe's arm, pulled it over her shoulder, and pressed his palm squarely on one full breast. She led him to the arched doorway. The manager followed.

Embarrassment heated Tawny's face as diners stared at her and muttered to each other. Bussers scurried with brooms and dust pans to sweep up the glass.

Through tight lips, the server asked Tawny, "Ma'am, can I get you anything else?"

She grimaced. "A tranquilizer gun might be nice."

He swallowed a laugh.

"I'll pay the bill and leave you in peace." She glanced inside the leather folder and gulped at the total, $517. I hope *my* card isn't declined too, she thought.

The server returned in under a minute, handing over the folder.

"Did it go through?"

"No problem, ma'am."

"Good." She added a thirty percent tip to apologize for Moe's bad behavior, signed, and grabbed her purse. She wished she'd worn a hooded coat to mask her face as the stares of annoyed customers followed her all the way to the lobby. *Tillman, you better not say one word when I turn in my expense account.*

Cassandra and the manager huddled together, while Moe stalked back and forth, fists hammering his thighs. Cassandra dug in her purse, evidently searching for her credit card.

Tawny approached them. "I paid. Let's go."

Outside, under the portico, they waited for the valet to fetch their cars. Moe's mouth screwed into a bitter pinch. "Idiots!"

"Now, darling," Cassandra cooed. "Two beautiful women

are fighting to pay for your dinner. Most men would find that extremely titillating." She stroked his gaunt face, tickling under his chin with long red fingernails.

His expression softened then he grinned.

"There, that's better. That's my handsome fella." She raised her lips for a kiss and he obliged.

The valet delivered the Navigator first. Moe tipped him, climbed in the car, and jetted away, leaving Cassandra standing there. Tawny gawked open-mouthed at her, as the valet sprinted for the next car.

"You two didn't come together?" Tawny asked.

The woman peered in a gold mirror and applied lipstick. "Lord, no! I'm not crazy enough to drive with him. He's a maniac."

"Very smart. But what about all the other poor people on the road?" Tawny slouched back on one hip. "Whew, what a night."

"I guess I should thank *you* for dinner." Cassandra pressed her lips together, rubbing them sideways. "Not exactly the reward you expected for saving Moshe from the mountain lion, is it?"

"I don't care about a reward but I'm really concerned about him. I thought he was going to stroke out. There's something wrong."

Cassandra slid one hand into a red leather glove, pulling down one finger at a time. Her movements were deliberate, languorous, even sexual. "He's high-strung is all. You're just not used to his ways."

"Well, I guess I should thank you for calming him down. Again."

"You're very welcome, dear."

The valet delivered the Porsche Cayenne. Cassandra slid into the seat, blowing the valet a kiss instead of a tip. The SUV roared off.

Tawny exhaled a frosty cloud, feeling sorry for the valet. Thumbing through her wallet, she only found a twenty. When the man arrived with her Jeep, she handed him the bill and his face lit up.

Oh well, what's another twenty on top of almost seven hundred bucks?

CHAPTER 5 – LOST

Tawny's cell trilled shortly after three a.m. She struggled awake from exhausting nightmares. Moe's number. Crap.

"Moe, what's the matter?"

"You need to come and get me." His voice sounded frantic but slurred.

"Where are you?"

"My car broke down. I thought I could get it home but it died."

She propped herself on one elbow and turned on the bedside lamp. "Are you OK?"

"Damned if I know. Just come and get me."

"Where are you?"

"I—I'm not sure."

Oh no. "Are you near your house?"

"I must have got turned around, leaving Cassandra's place. I think I'm on a highway."

Cassandra and Moe lived two blocks from each other. How could he get lost between her house and his? "What highway?"

Frustration tightened his tone. "I don't know!"

"Moe, you need to hang up and call nine-one-one. They can track you from your phone."

"No! I can't. I want you to come get me."

His pleading scared her. Like a lost child. A bad-tempered, seventy-five-year-old lost child. How to help him? How to find him? "OK, Moe, let's figure this out. Look around you. What do you see?"

"It's dark. Trees. No cars."

That described ninety-nine percent of the state of Montana at three a.m. "Do you see anything that looks like a road sign?"

"There's a horse corral and a barn."

That narrowed it down—not more than five thousand corrals and barns in Flathead County. "Do your headlights still work?"

"Yeah. But the engine's seized."

"Turn on your headlights and see if there are any signs around, like a street sign, a billboard, a mailbox with an address on it."

Quiet on his end. Oh, Lord, she'd never find him. He'd freeze to death, lost, alone, scared. One more minute and she'd call the sheriff.

"Yeah!" Elation lifted his voice. "There's a mailbox, lettering's rubbed off but what's left looks like—I dunno— might be *H, G, Y, forty.*"

Progress, maybe. Highway 40 was about five miles long, a connector between Columbia Falls and Whitefish, over a half hour from her home if she sped. "All right, Moe, does your heater work?"

"No. Dead like the engine."

"Are you warm?"

"Pretty goddamn cold."

"Do you have any blankets or an extra coat?"

"Maybe in the back."

"Stay in the car. Don't go wandering around. I'll be there as fast as I can. Turn on your flashers. I'm going to call the sheriff, too."

"No!" he screamed.

What the hell? "You could freeze to death. They need to look for you, in case I can't find you."

"Just you. Nobody else." A pause. "I don't want anybody to know. It's humiliating. Please. Come and get me."

His plaintive begging twisted her heart. "I'll make one pass, Moe. If I don't find you, I'm calling nine-one-one, no matter what."

She threw on clothes, grabbed extra blankets, and thought about making hot coffee but didn't want to take the time. In the mud room, while she donned her warmest parka, she noticed the porch thermometer read three degrees. Any residual heat in his car wouldn't last long. Every Montana winter, people froze to death stranded in broken-down vehicles. She couldn't bear the thought that Moe might become a grim statistic. She *had* to find him.

The Jeep's heater roared on high while Tawny sped through quiet avenues, down the hill past Woodland Park onto the commercial strip through Evergreen. Heading north on Highway 2, she pushed her speed to seventy-five, past scattered industrial buildings, open fields, and the airport, all the while scanning for deer. In a record twenty minutes, she reached the junction with Highway 40 and veered left at the flashing yellow signal.

The route stretched like a black ribbon through the broad empty expanse of snow, only a few businesses and homes along it, all dark except for an occasional glowing yard lamp. She hoped Moe's battery held out with the flashers going.

She tapped his number and breathed easier when he answered. "OK, Moe, I'm on Highway Forty now. Do you see anything else that's a landmark?"

"Ish blacker than the inside of a cow." His voice sounded even mushier than before. She hoped it was bad cell reception but feared hypothermia had overtaken him.

"I know." She punched on the speaker and set the phone on the seat beside her. "Are you still warm?"

He didn't answer. On the right shoulder of the road, four white crosses marked where fatal accidents had happened.

"Moe?"

"My teeth are ch-chattering."

Damn. "Stay awake, don't go to sleep. Talk to me."

"What d'ya wanna to talk about?"

"Tell me about your work. What did you do for a living?"

"Finance. Investments. Start-ups. I provided seed money for Microsoft."

"Really? Did you get rich on that?"

"Did OK. Gates did better."

"Yeah, he's not hurting. What other companies?"

"High tech mostly. Some boom, shome bushted." His words slurred worse.

"Moe, I'm coming from the east. Do you see my lights yet?" Tawny checked the odometer. She'd gone two miles. Only about three more miles until the road ended at the 93 junction.

"Whissh way's east?"

"Keep your eyes open. You should be seeing my lights pretty soon now. Are your eyes open?"

"Jusht a quick nap."

"Moe, dammit, if you close your eyes, I'm calling nine-one-one."

"Aw right. I'm awake."

In the black desolation, even a lit match should show for miles. Why couldn't she see his flashers yet?

Three does appeared in her high beams. She tapped the brakes to avoid a skid and leaned on the horn. They scattered, loping into the forest. A quarter mile farther, a bloody deer carcass lay on the shoulder.

Five more white crosses. This road was Slaughter Alley.

"Moe, did you hear a horn just now?"

"Huh?"

"Are your eyes still open?"

Too long a hesitation.

"I'm hanging up and calling nine-one-one."

"Way-way-wait. I'm awake."

72

Far from the highway, she caught a glimpse of distant flashing lights reflecting on snow. "Moe, did you pull off the road?"

"Out of the way."

Whatever that meant. But now she felt sure the blinkers were his. "I think I see you, Moe. Turn on your headlights."

Seconds passed. Finally, twin beams shot into the night, perpendicular to the highway. Relief flooded her body. "I got you, Moe."

A half mile farther, she spotted a driveway, tire tracks tamped in snow. When she made the turn, her headlights swept over an empty corral and a sagging, dilapidated barn. She skidded on the slippery lane, spewing icy gravel. The Navigator sat behind the barn, completely hidden from the highway. If not for the headlights, she would never have seen his rig.

Tawny grabbed blankets and hurried to the driver's door. It opened a second before she reached it and Moe's long legs extended. The dome light illuminated his drawn face, teeth chattering hard, and eyelids drooping. She bundled his tall, shivering body in blankets and marched him to her Jeep. He struggled to scrunch his long limbs into the passenger seat but at least plenty of heat blew on him now. His chin sank to his chest.

She put the Jeep in gear and spun the tires. "OK, I'll get you to the hospital. You're going to be fine."

Moe's head jerked up. "No hospital!"

"You're in hypothermia. You need treatment."

"No!" He snuggled deeper in the blanket folds. "I'm getting warmer already. I'm fine."

No point arguing. Let him drift off then take the turn to North Valley Hospital, only a short distance away.

But he didn't sleep. The heat perked him up. Within five

minutes, his speech had cleared, foggy sluggishness fell away, and his posture straightened. "This has the worst legroom of any car I've ever been in. Damn glove compartment is banging my knees."

When Tawny pulled under the emergency room portico, Moe glared at her. "What the hell did you bring me here for? I told you, no hospital. Take me home."

His irritable complaints reassured Tawny. "If you're sure you're all right…"

"Of course I am," he snapped. "I want to go home."

As she headed back to the highway, she asked, "What happened, Moe? You left Cassandra's, then what?"

His hands gestured, animated. "The architect who laid out the roads in the resort was on crack. People get lost all the time in that complex. Weird forks, double-backs, dead-ends." His words shot out in machine-gun bursts. "Hardly a week goes by without someone knocking on my door, asking for directions how to get out. The signage is lousy. They need to drop bread crumbs."

He was struggling hard to find a plausible excuse for getting lost in his own neighborhood. Any excuse but the truth.

"We're at least ten miles from your condo. How did you get on the highway? Did you have any idea where you were?"

"Of course!" he insisted. "I knew exactly where I was. I just got a little off track in the dark. All this damn snow. Covers up my usual landmarks."

Tawny remembered that Moe used to be a private pilot. Surely if he could navigate in the air, he should know his way around by car.

"What direction are we going now?"

His head whipped toward her. "Think you're pretty sneaky. Testing me, like those damn—" His mouth snapped shut so hard that Tawny heard his teeth clack.

What had he started to say? Why did he stop himself? She wracked her brain for a way to ask that wouldn't set him off like a cherry bomb.

"Besides," he said, "it's your fault."

She faced him. "*My* fault?"

A grin tugged at the side of his mouth. "If I didn't have to buy you champagne, I wouldn't have got plastered."

Tawny bit her lip. No sense bringing to his attention that *she'd* paid the bill.

At four-thirty a.m., she pulled into his driveway. "Are you sure you feel OK? I can stay if you want."

He uncurled from the blanket cocoon. "Yeah, that's a terrific idea. Cassandra shows up with morning coffee and finds you spent the night. Or at least what's left of it. Peachy keen."

If Moe's sarcasm survived hypothermia, the rest of him probably would also.

Chapter 6 – Wounded in Action

"Mom, where'd you go in the middle of the night?" Emma asked.

Tawny stumbled into the kitchen at eight-thirty the next morning, groggy in her bathrobe. "Coffee, please."

Emma poured a mug, added milk, and set it before Tawny, who slumped at the breakfast bar. "You look like crap, Mom."

"Tillman's father. He's driving me nuts."

"Why doesn't Tillman take care of his own dad instead of making you do it?"

"Good question." The coffee tasted strong and she willed caffeine to bring her back to life. "Where's Jim?"

"Left a little while ago to pick up supplies for the restaurant before lunch."

Tawny blinked sleep from her eyes and studied her daughter. "How are things between you guys?"

Emma hunched over her smartphone, tapping. "Awesome."

"He's a good guy. Hard to find."

Emma grimaced and swiped the screen, not looking up. "A hard man is good to find."

Tawny chuckled. "Your grandma used to say that." She gulped coffee. "Moe's car broke down. Thank goodness, he's without wheels for the time being. The roads are a whole lot safer when he's not on them."

Emma's thumbs busily tapped the virtual keyboard, oblivious.

"What are you doing today?" Tawny hoped her daughter's answer included a mention of her job. Emma took advantage of Jim's family, showing up for work only if she didn't have a better alternative.

Emma continued to text. Finally she asked, "Were you talking to me?"

Tawny looked down her nose. "No, the other three people sitting here." Moe's sarcasm was rubbing off.

"You sure have been crabby since you started this assignment. Go back to bed, Mom." Emma rose and set her cereal bowl in the sink. "Gotta fly." She kissed Tawny, grabbed her coat, and scooted out the back door.

A shower and two more cups of coffee helped but Tawny's head still pounded from lack of sleep when she arrived at Moe's condo. After several minutes of ringing and knocking in the cold, she tried the knob and found it unlocked. "Moe? It's me."

Sugar greeted her with a *mrreow* and leg rub in the entry. Rambo was nowhere to be seen. Thankfully.

She continued to call Moe's name as she hung her coat on the wooden peg and toed off her boots. In sock feet, she padded to the closed door of his office and knocked. No answer. She cracked it open. "Moe?"

"What the hell?" His deep voice thundered in the murky office. He jumped up from the desk chair and planted himself in front of the computer, arms spread wide, blocking the screen. "I can't stand people sneaking up on me!"

Rambo sprang out of the dark to land at Tawny's feet, clawing at her jeans. His growl echoed Moe's.

Tawny dodged the Siamese's attack, patience frayed. She'd spent half the night rescuing the lost man and now he was yelling at her. Rude, ungrateful jerk, just like his son. "I've been calling you for five minutes."

"Shut the door. I'll be out soon."

"No rush," she snapped. *Better yet, stay there so I don't have to deal with you.*

She tried to nudge Rambo back into the office with her foot

but his claws wrapped around her ankle. Fangs sank into her toes. "Oow!" She kicked to shake him loose but he held on with a death grip. "Moe, call off your cat!"

The lanky man crossed the room in two long strides and bent to grab the Siamese by the scruff of the neck. Being pulled made Rambo sink his teeth deeper. His claws dug harder into her ankle. Needles of pain seared up her leg.

Finally Moe yanked him free, along with long bloody shreds of Tawny's skin.

Her throat constricted. She backed into the great room, leaned against the wall, and grasped her leg with both hands, fighting back tears. Blood seeped through her torn sock.

Moe cradled Rambo, holding him firmly as the cat hissed at Tawny. "You better clean those scratches up. There's alcohol in the bathroom." Then he retreated into the office and closed the door.

Gee, thanks for your concern, Moe. Biting her lip, Tawny limped to the bathroom. There, she pulled open cupboards and drawers, searching for alcohol. At last, under the sink, behind a shoebox stuffed with papers, she located a bottle.

She sat on the commode lid and peeled off her sock. Using tissue, she swabbed the long bleeding wounds and punctures, gritting her teeth against the sharp sting. From her bag in the living room, she retrieved her stash of emergency Band-aids then returned to the bathroom. After dousing her foot and ankle with more alcohol, she applied Band-aids and put her ragged sock back on.

When she started to replace the shoebox, she noticed it was full of folded receipts for postal money orders. She dug deeper through more stubs, made out in thousand-dollar denominations, dates scattered over the past three years. She added the amounts in her head, almost $50,000.

What the hell?

This might be evidence of the scam Tillman suspected.

Tawny smoothed the crumpled papers as flat as possible and carefully laid them in rows on the vanity counter. She snapped photos with her cell, then stowed the receipts in the shoebox, and replaced it under the sink.

The door to Moe's office remained closed. Given the opportunity, she opened kitchen drawers overflowing with papers. She shuffled quickly through the disarray, searching for anything else related to money. Much of the debris was obvious trash—political mailers from past elections, solicitations for free hearing tests, expired restaurant coupons. But finally she ran across an investment prospectus and stock reports. She checked around the corner. No sign of Moe.

She snapped more photos but the booklets were thick. It would take an hour to record all the pages. She considered hiding them in her bag, except Moe might notice their absence. Instead, she shoved them to the back of a drawer, and scattered trash to cover them. Maybe she could retrieve them later.

The throbbing from the scratches and bites grew worse. She took a break to sit on the sectional. Sugar hopped up beside her to be petted. The calico rolled sideways and slipped her paw into the gap between cushions, as if digging for a lost toy. Something crackled.

"What'd you find, kitty?" Tawny ran her hand down the gap and felt paper. She pulled out a crumpled wad—more money order receipts. One by one, she lifted the cushions. The entire twenty-foot-long curved sectional was full of receipts, tucked in crevices and in rips in the leather.

Each was for a thousand dollars, purchased at different post offices throughout the county.

Tawny retreated to the bathroom, spread the new collection on the counter, and snapped photos. Added to the ones in the shoebox, the grand total exceeded $400,000 in three years.

Holy crap.

Who was Moe paying? And why?

The doorbell rang.

She peeked out of the bathroom. His office door remained shut. She gathered all the receipts and stuffed them into the now-overflowing shoebox under the sink.

The bell rang again.

Tawny called, "Moe, someone's at the door. I'll get it."

It was the same deputy who'd taken the lion report two days before, only this time not in uniform. He wore jeans and a leather jacket. A black knit cap covered his bald head. One gloved hand held a large manila envelope. "Morning, Mrs. Lindholm."

"Come in." She closed the door and faced the man. His business card was still in her coat pocket but she'd never looked at it. "I'm sorry but I don't remember your name."

"Oscar Beaudoin." He held her gaze as he'd done before. "Friends call me Obie."

"Friends call me Tawny. Anything new on the mountain lion, Obie?"

He shifted one foot to the other. "Actually, it's my day off, ma'am. Is Mr. Rosenbaum here?"

Ma'am? Maybe she'd misread his earlier interest.

"I'll get him." She limped to the office and rapped on the door. "The deputy's here to see you."

A low terse grunt from inside. "Be there in a minute."

A minute stretched to two, then three. All the cats, even friendly Sugar, had disappeared.

"Do you want to sit down, Obie?" Tawny moved to the couch, longing to take weight off her painful foot.

"I really can't, ma'am. I just need to deliver this." He

gestured with the envelope.

"If you're in a hurry, I can give it to him."

Obie pursed his lips. "I need to hand it to him personally."

Uh-oh. Tawny knew the local cops sometimes worked as process servers. "Is that what I think it is?"

His mouth twitched. "You know Mr. Rosenbaum pretty well?"

"Not really. I work for his son who's an attorney in Billings. He sent me to check up on Mr. Rosenbaum."

Obie rattled the envelope against his thigh and stared out at the snowy golf course.

The throbbing in Tawny's foot worsened. She remembered Moe's story of Rambo's attack on his golfing buddy, how the man wound up with a bad infection. She should get to urgent care soon.

Finally, Moe emerged from the office. "What is it?" he snarled at the deputy.

Obie, well-muscled, but at least eight inches shorter than Moe, stared up at the man. "Are you Mr. Moshe Baruch Rosenbaum?"

Moe's eyes narrowed. "You know I am."

Obie handed him the envelope. "Sir, you've been served." And left.

Moe ripped the envelope open, muttering, "What the hell?" He studied the enclosed papers for a few seconds then threw them on the floor. He stalked back to his office and slammed the door.

Tawny grabbed her glasses and limped over to gather the scattered papers.

Notice of sheriff's sale. The final step in foreclosure proceedings.

She scanned the document. After several minutes of struggling with incomprehensible legal jargon, she understood the gist. His mortgage was more than $261,000 in arrears for six months plus a balloon payment. Sale of Moe's condo was scheduled for April at the county courthouse unless the past due amounts were brought current, including late penalties and filing fees. With a sigh, she set the papers on the dining table. The calico crept out from her hiding place underneath.

Tawny picked her up. "Sugar, your daddy's in big trouble."

CHAPTER 7 – HIT AND RUN

At urgent care, Tawny's best friend, Dr. Virgie Belmonte, entered the treatment room, wearing a white smock. She flipped aside her dark maroon hair, cut diagonally across her face, and hugged Tawny, who sat on an exam table. "What's happening, sweetheart?"

"Glad you were on today," Tawny said. Her friend mostly worked at the Veterans Clinic but put in extra shifts at urgent care.

Virgie washed her hands and examined Tawny's bare foot, now hot-red, swollen, and throbbing. "Who tried to kill you?"

"Vicious Siamese cat."

"When did this happen?"

"Couple hours ago. I wiped it with alcohol, but it hurts like hell."

"Cat had its shots?"

"I don't know."

Virgie washed Tawny's foot then swabbed it with smelly brown liquid. "Looks nasty. Good thing you came in. I'm going to shoot you full of antibiotics and give you an oral prescription to follow up. And we need to find out if the cat's been vaccinated for rabies."

Tawny's gut contracted. "Does that mean shots in the stomach?"

Virgie placed gauze pads over the wounds. "Not anymore. But it's still no fun." She wrapped Tawny's ankle and foot in a figure eight pattern. "How'd you meet this cat from hell?"

"It belongs to Tillman Rosenbaum's father. He's got nine cats in a condo at Golden Eagle Resort with the filthiest litter box you ever smelled."

Virgie's eyebrows arched. "Nine?"

Tawny flinched at the pressure from wrapping.

"Sorry, sweetie." Virgie readjusted her hold. "What's up with Tillman's father?"

"I'm supposed to check on him."

"Why you? Why doesn't he go himself?"

Tawny gritted her teeth against the pain. "They won't talk to each other. Tillman's four-hundred-fifty miles away in Billings and I'm here. He's paying me so..." She shrugged.

Virgie tipped her head to the side. "Filthy litter box, you said? No wonder your foot's a mess. Digging around in all that fecal material, gets under their claws, and anything they scratch instantly turns septic."

Nausea welled in Tawny's throat. "I could have lived without your gory description."

The doctor smirked and continued wrapping. "What are you supposed to be doing, besides serving as a scratching post for the guy's nine cats?"

"Tillman thinks his dad's being scammed. I've never seen two men so alike. The hatred between them is thicker than concrete. I'm assigned to check into his finances but I think his problem may be more than money."

"Like how?"

"He flies into rages over little stuff. One minute he's Prince Charming, the next, Godzilla. We practically got bounced out of Alpenglow Yacht Club when he started yelling curses and threw a Waterford goblet in the fireplace." She shook her head at the memory. "Then at three o'clock this morning, he calls me to come get him because he got lost driving around out in the country."

Virgie finished the dressing. "Might be dementia."

"That's what I was thinking." Thank goodness the wise doctor shared her suspicion.

"Have you talked to Tillman about it?"

Tawny shook her head. "Not yet. But I will."

Virgie drummed her nails on the treatment table. "It's a tough situation. I see it all the time at the VA. It's a lot more complicated than memory problems. These poor old folks start acting weird and their spouses go nuts. The personality can change and, unfortunately, most of the time, not for the better. They sense they're losing control but can't admit it. And talk about driving. Oh. My. God. Several patients threatened to kill me because I had to turn them in and their licenses got lifted."

Tawny nodded. "I've seen this man cause accidents. Even his girlfriend won't ride with him because he's so dangerous." She tried to put her boot on but grunted in pain. It was too tight because of swelling and the bulky bandage.

Virgie dug in a supply cupboard and pulled out a paper slipper. "Try this. When you get home, ice the foot. Come right back if you get feverish or see red lines running up your leg." She watched Tawny test her weight. "Can you drive?"

"Maybe. If not, I'll call Emma."

Virgie hugged her. "Remember, sweetie, this is *Tillman's* father, not yours."

~~~

Fortified with 800 mg of ibuprofen, Tawny sat on her couch, foot propped up on a pillow and draped with a bag of frozen peas. She sent the photos of the money order receipts to Tillman, along with a text: *Pls call ASAP. Imprtnt.*

Emma and Jim arrived home from the Lucky Dragon with a carton of fragrant won ton soup that Tawny had requested. While Jim went in the kitchen for a bowl, Emma knelt beside the couch, wearing a stricken expression. "Mommy, what is this guy doing to you? First, you have to fight off a mountain lion, then he drags you out of bed in the middle of the night, and now you might need rabies shots."

Her hazel eyes glistened and Tawny recognized underlying fear. She pulled her daughter's face to her breast and stroked her fine silky hair. "I'm OK. Virgie says cat bites and scratches usually get infected and she's watching me. But I might need your help."

Emma's head lifted. "I'll do anything."

Jim delivered a bowl of soup to Emma, who picked up the spoon as if to feed Tawny.

"Thank you, honey, but I can feed myself." The bowl warmed her hands as she inhaled the rich aroma. Her queasy stomach was already rebelling against antibiotics and anti-inflammatories. She tasted the savory broth. "Mmmm, this is delicious. Just what I needed."

Emma sat back on her heels, hand squeezed tight on Tawny's thigh, needing physical reassurance. As a little girl, she'd been a clinger. Still was, under stress.

Jim rested one chunky hip on the back of the couch. "What can we do, Tawny?"

"I'm going to try to talk Tillman into paying Emma to drive me and help out at Moe's. If you can spare her from the restaurant, Jim."

"Sure," he answered, too quickly. Then added, "Business is pretty slow right now."

Tawny noticed a flash of relief cross his round face. She'd suspected his family hired Emma out of friendship, not because they needed the help. Mama Rose would probably be glad to reduce the payroll.

"I don't mind driving," Emma said, "but what do I have to do at his place? You said it stinks and he's got a terrible temper."

"Clean house so it doesn't stink. If I can talk him into letting me go through his records, you can help me with that."

Emma threw her head back and stared at the ceiling.

"Sounds boring."

So much for *I'll do anything.* "I haven't been bored for one minute since I met the man."

Jim's cell rang. He left to talk in the kitchen while Tawny ate the soothing soup.

Emma leaned close. "That's probably Mama Rose calling. The swamper who works at the Lucky Dragon is in the hospital."

"That's too bad. Is he going to be OK?"

Emma lifted one shoulder. "You know the guy with Down's Syndrome, Wilbur. Rides that old cruiser bike everywhere."

"I just saw him the other day. He cleaned up the vase Moe busted." Tawny recalled how carefully Wilbur had swept up every shard of broken glass. He took pride in doing his job right.

Emma went on: "When the casino closed last night, he was supposed to wait for Jim's uncle to give him a ride but he took off on his bike instead."

Tawny frowned. "Way too cold to be out on a bike."

"Yeah, but Wilbur doesn't think about stuff like that. Guess he wanted to get home so he left. A car hit him and took off."

Jim returned to the living room, chubby face pinched, eyes shiny with tears. "That was Ma." His voice choked. "Wilbur just died."

~~~

Tillman called back at ten-thirty that night, rousing Tawny from a restless half-sleep.

He started in immediately, all business. "I got the photos. More than four hundred grand in three years. What the hell's he doing?"

"I don't know yet," Tawny answered. "I've been looking for

the usual black holes where money disappears—drugs, gambling, and women. So far, I'm not finding anything too far out of the ordinary. He drinks a lot, takes good care of his cats, and seems generous with his girlfriend but not over the top. He hits the casinos but no big losses I could find. And he's sure not putting a dime into his condo." She took a breath, nervous about mentioning her theory. "But more important, I think he may have dementia."

"Wha-at?" Tillman didn't bother to hide the skepticism in his tone.

Tawny related the sudden tantrums, the erratic driving, the secretiveness, and finally the plaintive late night call when he was lost.

"He's always had a rotten temper," Tillman countered.

Yeah, and passed it down to the next generation, she thought. "It's not just the temper. He blames other people for things he's done. He seems to feel like everyone's out to get him."

"Aa-ay, that's not new either. He always said he got shot by double-barrels of discrimination, being black *and* Jewish. At home, whenever things went wrong, he blamed my mom or Shoshanna." After a second, he added, "Or me."

The way he said it made Tawny think he meant *mostly me.* Despite his dismissive tone, she sensed a hint of hurt. "Tillman, he got lost in two blocks between his girlfriend's house and his. He wound up way the hell out in the country in a broken-down car. He might have frozen to death."

"Leaving the world a better place."

She thumped her fist on her pillow. How could anyone be so aggravating? "Do you want me to keep working on this or not?"

"Did I say anything about stopping?"

"All right, then, but I need some help. My foot hurts and it's too swollen to drive."

"What's wrong with your foot?"

"You'll be getting the bill from urgent care. Your father's cat attacked me."

"You're kidding."

"I wish." She took a deep breath. "Anyway, I'd like you to hire my daughter Emma to drive me and help sorting through records if he'll let me. Everything I've sent you, I had to sneak when he wasn't looking. But I don't like doing that."

"Yeah, I forgot, you're Miss Pollyanna Goody-Two-Shoes."

Tawny gritted her teeth. *Don't let him get to you.* "But now that the sheriff's served him the foreclosure sale notice, I'm going to try to help him with that. Then maybe he'll let me deeper into the other stuff."

"Makes sense."

She couldn't believe it. Finally, agreement instead of snide jibes. "I don't know if it will work, but it's a crack in the dam."

"What else?"

She swallowed. "I need reimbursement pretty quick on some expenses. Last night, I had to charge almost seven hundred dollars on my credit card for your dad."

"What the hell?"

"The restaurant declined his card. He was making a scene. I figured paying the tab was cheaper than bailing him out of jail."

"Goddamn him."

She waited and imagined Tillman pacing, fist clenched, pounding his thigh with each step, just like Moe had.

"All right," he said, "your daughter's on the payroll. Fifteen bucks an hour."

Astonished, Tawny fumbled the phone, which fell between pillows. She longed to shout *Hooray!* She'd half expected him to turn her down flat. At best, she'd hoped for minimum wage. Emma would be thrilled. She retrieved the cell and forced her voice to stay neutral. "All right."

"Fax the charge slip to the bookkeeper. She'll reimburse you tomorrow."

"OK." She wanted to say more but did she dare? "Tillman, I don't think he can help it. At least, not sometimes. I watched my grandpa do a lot of the same things."

Quiet. Then, "What happened to your grandpa?"

"We had to put him in a locked care unit, after he almost killed my grandma."

CHAPTER 8 – GET RICH QUICK

The next morning, Emma drove to Moe's condo while Tawny rode in the passenger seat, her injured foot shrouded in a size twelve slipper that had belonged to Dwight. With a lovely young redhead cleaning his house, Moe's mood switched quickly from dour to beaming. He locked the Siamese upstairs, to Tawny's relief.

While Emma scrubbed the litter boxes, Tawny asked about Rambo's shots. Moe called the vet's office and handed the phone to Tawny. The receptionist reassured her all vaccinations were current, including rabies. She added quietly, "Mr. Rosenbaum loves his cats and takes good care of them. But every time Rambo comes in, he has to be sedated before the doctor can even take his temperature."

No surprise there.

After disconnecting from the vet's office, Tawny reached for the foreclosure papers, still on the dining table where she'd left them the day before. When she picked them up, Moe's glare warned her to back off.

How else to get to the bottom of his money problems?

A new approach had occurred to her in the middle of another restless night. "Moe, you've got a lot of experience with finance. I could use some advice."

He tipped back on the dining chair and regarded her down his nose. "About what?"

Might as well start with the truth. "My husband's medical bills ate up all our savings. I'm starting to get back on my feet now but I'm not sure what to invest in. Do you have any recommendations?"

His bristly chin jutted and he gazed at the ceiling, thinking. "What are you looking for? Something that will give you a big return fast?"

Her shoulders tightened with anticipation. "Yeah, that's what I need. Big and fast."

He rocked back and forth, tugging on his earlobe, studying her. "Are you willing to take a few risks?"

The truth was *hell no*. Instead she asked, "How much risk?"

"How much money are you talking about?"

"Almost five grand." Money she was saving to rewire her house.

A gleam came into his dark eyes. "How would you like to make that into fifty grand?"

Fifty?

For an instant, a thrill coursed through her. Fifty thousand would not only fix the electrical problems but also remodel her outdated kitchen and pay for a new roof. She wouldn't have to beg the bank for a loan. All her worries could be wiped clean.

Then, with a clang of warning bells, the practical side of her brain took over. Way too good to be true. Sounded like a scam. But she played along. "I could sure use the money."

Moe jumped up from his chair. "Come on." He strode to the office.

Tawny dreaded following him into the dark, claustrophobic cave but the lead held too much promise to ignore.

He unloaded boxes from a second chair she'd never noticed before, buried under the junk. Kicking stacks of paper aside, nudging cartons with his foot, he cleared a tiny space for her to sit. He powered up the computer. Long thin fingers scampered like spiders over the keys.

Tawny's vision fell into the awkward mid-range limbo where her glasses weren't strong enough to read the screen. She removed them and tried leaning back. Blurry. Put them on again and leaned forward. No better.

Moe glanced sideways at her.

"Damn glasses," she said. "Can't see with 'em, can't see without 'em."

"Me too. Had my cataracts operated on and got new lenses. Hardly use glasses anymore."

She shrugged. "In that case, I better hope to develop cataracts."

He stretched long arms over his head, fingers laced. "It's a great time to get old. Five minutes of surgery and I've got my fifteen-year-old eyes again. Take a little blue pill and I've got my fifteen-year-old pecker again."

Tawny had to laugh.

Moe leaned into the computer. "OK, look at these returns."

Tawny squinted at columns of numbers on a spreadsheet.

His bony index finger pointed. "See, for an initial investment of five grand, within eighteen months, it's compounded into forty-eight thousand. How's that for a fast, substantial return?"

"Pretty impressive." Too good to be true. Now she needed to be careful with her questions. "Did *you* invest in that?"

He shifted in his chair. "That and a lot of other funds."

Tawny sensed he didn't want to be pinned down. More secretiveness? Or was he involved in something shady?

Could the investment be a pyramid scheme? She wondered if the only way he could recoup *his* money was to drag in other investors.

She remembered the scam that had entrapped her grandparents. She still felt helpless shame that she hadn't recognized the signs earlier, as Grandpa's dementia turned him secretive and suspicious. When he eventually lost the farm, the fraud came to light but by then it was too late. He'd retreated deep into resentment. She never understood why he didn't blame the con man who'd stolen from him but instead lashed out at his family.

At her.

Tawny had tried to help her grandpa just as Tillman was now trying to help Moe. They both were getting attacked for their trouble. The unexpected link of kinship with Tillman surprised her.

She dragged her concentration back to Moe. She needed more evidence. "That sounds really good, Moe. Could you print the information for me?"

"Yeah, later." He opened more screens. "Here, look at this one. It's tax-free and you double your money in six months."

"Tax-free? Like bonds?"

He snorted. "Hell, no. Bonds are for cowards. Offshore is where smart money goes. Bypass the IRS and rake in the dough." He must have read doubt in her expression because he quickly added, "All legal. If the government leaves a loophole as big as Ptarmigan Tunnel, you'd be an idiot not to drive right on through. Three years ago, I put Cassandra in this investment. Going gangbusters. Of course, she had a substantial basis to begin with."

Tawny had been wondering if Cassandra was the black hole where Moe's money had disappeared. She grabbed the opening. "Is she pretty well off?"

"Yeah, if I had *her* money, I'd throw mine away."

Tawny wanted to say *you already have* but bit her lip. Instead she asked, "Where did Cassandra's money come from?"

Moe clicked open more screens. "Heiress to a pharmaceutical company her grandparents started in Europe. Born into money and continues to roll in the dough."

"Nice gig if you can get it."

Moe shot her a look. "Takes money to make money. I've parlayed her trust fund into a nice pile of cash for her foundation."

That might eliminate Cassandra as the black hole. But how

could his girlfriend be making money when he was so broke?

Keep him talking. "How does someone get started with those tax-free deals?"

"I can do it for you."

She'd be damned if she'd turn a nickel of her hard-earned money over to this man. "I'm not ready to invest yet. Just doing homework ahead of time. Would you print that out also?"

"Killing trees. Everything you need's online."

Tawny chewed on her lip, reluctant to share her secret. Heat crept up her neck. "I, uh, don't read very well. It's easier if it's printed. Then I can take my time or ask for help."

"Why didn't you say so?" He clicked keys and pages spewed out of a printer. He handed them over then frowned when he noticed her face. "What are you all red for?"

Tawny felt the flush deepen as he studied her. "I'm dyslexic. Fourth graders read better than I do."

"Bah. Nothing to be ashamed of. Einstein, da Vinci, Muhammad Ali, Magic Johnson, all dyslexic."

She smiled at his effort to console her. "I fall a little short of their league."

Moe grinned. "You're no slouch."

Tawny thought she read genuine affection for her in his eyes. When she'd watched him playing with his cats, the same surprising warmth had transformed his normal scowl. The cranky old guy had a sweet side, no matter how much he tried to mask it.

He shut down the computer. "Enough of this. I'm hungry." He jumped up and strode to the living room. Tawny hobbled after, carrying the printouts, glad to escape the closed-in office.

And maybe, just maybe, she finally held a solid lead in her hands.

Emma had scrubbed the kitchen to sparkling. But there was still nothing to eat in the house except cat food.

Moe prowled through a drawer, searching for take-out menus while scattering junk mail on the freshly-mopped floor. Behind his back, Emma rolled her eyes at Tawny who suppressed a smirk. How many times had Emma similarly messed up something Tawny had just straightened?

She sat at the dining room table, pushing unopened mail aside to rest an elbow. A bright orange flyer caught her eye.

Golden Eagle H/O/A invites you to a FREE lunch and seminar on ELDER FRAUD. Don't get scammed, get educated!

"Moe, did you see this?" She handed him the flyer.

He glanced at it, then returned to tossing papers in search of more take-out menus.

"It's today," she prompted. "Starts in twenty minutes. Sounds interesting."

"Place'll be full of grouchy old neighbors."

Then you'll fit right in, she thought, but said, "I'd like to hear about that." *And I might pick up pointers on what to watch for while investigating you.*

"Go if you want." He flicked his hand in dismissal.

"It's a *free* lunch."

He paused and peered down at her. "Free?"

She pointed at the flyer. "That's what it says."

He closed the drawer he'd been pillaging. "All right, if you really want to."

Tawny winked at Emma.

CHAPTER 9 – THERE IS NO FREE LUNCH

When the three of them squeezed into the Jeep, Tawny had second thoughts. Emma needed to drive, since Tawny didn't trust Moe. Moe was too tall to fit in the back. Leaving her, with a gimpy foot, to clamber into the rear seat. While she tried to massage away the pain, Moe called Cassandra on his cell to meet them at the restaurant.

Even an heiress with a Porsche, expensive jewelry, and furs liked a free lunch.

Ten minutes later, they entered the crowded room. Perhaps a hundred people chatted over drinks or grazed through a buffet line. All looked prosperous, well-dressed, and white, making Moe conspicuous as the only black face in the room, as well as the tallest person.

A barrel-chested bald man stormed across the room toward Moe. "You've got balls, showing up here, Rosenbaum."

Maybe this hadn't been such a good idea. Tawny braced herself and pulled Emma close in case they needed to duck or flee.

"Sour grapes from sore losers," Moe snapped, looming over the shorter man.

"What goes around comes around. You'll get your day of reckoning." The man stalked away, throwing daggers over his shoulder. At the far end of the restaurant, he nudged his wife and muttered to her. She turned to stare at Moe with cold blue eyes.

"What's that about?" Tawny asked.

Moe blew out a sharp breath and flipped his hand as if at a fly. "Business disagreement." He scanned the group. "There's Cassandra." He parted the crowd in his arrow path to her.

Tawny and Emma followed in his wake.

Cassandra's gold silk blouse shimmered in the light of

chandeliers, matching her golden contact lenses. Her hands danced as she told a story to the group surrounding her. Tawny caught a few words about a rescued weimaraner that had swallowed her one-carat diamond earring. Her laughter rippled like water over rocks.

Colin stood near her but a step back from the group. He wore a black dress shirt, open at the neck, with a silver tie hanging loose. Gold hoop earrings glinted through his blond dreadlocks.

Emma pulled on Tawny's arm. "Mom, what a hunk," she breathed. "Who is he?"

Tawny shuddered and gave her daughter's hand a cautionary squeeze. "Cassandra's son. Don't even think about it."

Moe approached Cassandra, towering over the plump-cheeked little woman. Her face brightened and she stretched up for a kiss and whispers.

Tawny noticed the people around Cassandra quickly drifted away, shooting frowns at Moe. They obviously liked her but couldn't stomach him. Was it his race, his general obnoxiousness, or something else?

In defiance of Tawny's warning, Emma pushed forward and faced Colin, eye to eye. "Hi, I'm Emma."

In a lazy drawl, he answered, "You certainly are, Emma." His gaze roamed beneath her clothes. Electricity leaped between the two youngest people in the room.

Tawny wanted to yank her daughter back by the collar, like a disobedient puppy, but it was too late.

Cassandra joined in. "Tawny, you remember my son, Colin." She studied Emma. "Do I detect a family resemblance?"

Jaw clenched, Tawny said, "This is my daughter."

But Emma and Colin had already retreated to their own planet, performing the age-old primal dance of female and male. The sensual curve of Emma's mouth left no doubt where this was headed. Oh, hell, Tawny thought, poor Jim cast aside for another creep in Emma's collection of bad boys.

They settled at a table for eight, leaving three available seats that, despite the crowd, no one rushed to claim. A couple started to take the vacant chairs, then noticed Moe and quickly moved to a different table. Tawny again wondered why he had so many enemies among his neighbors.

Moe and Cassandra leaned together, trading frequent smooches. Emma chattered and Colin moved in close, appearing fascinated by whatever she said.

That left Tawny the odd one out. Her foot throbbed and irritation raked the inside of her stomach, already upset from the antibiotic. Eager for distraction, she scanned the room. Most people were dressed in skier chic apparel or colorful Nordic sweaters, probably made by the resident knitting club. Tawny caught more people eying Moe.

According to the program, the speaker was an attorney from the state agency on consumer protection. Fortyish, with spiked dark hair, in a frumpy green business suit, she showed an engaging smile as she chatted with attendees.

After lunch, the homeowner's association president stood at a podium. "With the recession, fraudsters are crawling out of the woodwork to take advantage of people strapped by the economic downturn. Our generation makes an attractive target for fraud. We have savings, we own our homes, and we're ripe for the taking. I've invited attorney Renata Schliefman to inform us how to protect ourselves."

Tawny leaned forward to listen. Elder fraud hit close to her heart. She'd watched her grandparents end up broke and humiliated after a lifetime of hard work. Now, Moe faced losing his condo. As she looked around, she wondered how many people in the room might have already been scammed.

Schliefman took the podium. "We all know the stereotype victim—the lonely widow whose husband always managed the money. Her kids don't give her enough attention, so she's grateful for phone calls from some charming con man who sweet-talks her out of her Social Security check." The attorney folded her arms and scanned the audience. "Well, I got news for you. Cons aren't going to waste their time. They're going for real bucks. They're targeting you." She pointed a sharp finger into the audience. "And you. And you. And you, in the back in the brown jacket. Every single one of you."

She paused to let her message sink in, gaze traveling from person to person. "You are educated professionals, doctors, lawyers, accountants, stockbrokers, teachers. If you think you're too prudent, too savvy and well-informed to be scammed, well, I have two words for you: Bernie Madoff."

A rumble filtered through the audience. Heads nodded.

Tawny glanced at Moe. Bent forward, he appeared as preoccupied with his smartphone as her daughter often was. The fraud victim profile fitted him like a second skin. She wished he'd pay attention. But it might already be too late.

"Scammers work a tried and proven script," Schliefman went on. "In affinity schemes, they target people of their same ethnicity, nationality, or religion. Madoff befriended people from his synagogue. Here, you might meet the con artist at your church, Sons of Norway, or Ancient Order of Hibernians." She gestured out the view windows. "Or because of a common interest, like golf."

A movement to one side caught Tawny's attention—Emma and Colin, hand in hand, sneaking out of the restaurant. Tawny imagined their conversation: *This is so bor-ring. Let's get out of here.* Damn them.

Schliefman's arms opened wide, embracing the audience. "They gain your confidence and make you comfortable around them. They mention friends who got in on the ground floor of a hot new opportunity." She placed her index finger to her lips, miming for secrecy. In a stage whisper, she said, "The dividends are *fabulous*. But you can't tell *anyone*."

Tawny noticed a number of people shifting in their chairs. Spouses muttered in each other's ears. The attorney was striking a chord.

Schliefman asked, "Do you know who Carlo Ponzi is?"

A man in the rear called out, "Inventor of the Ponzi scheme."

"Close," the attorney answered. "He didn't invent it, but in the nineteen-twenties, he became so successful at the swindle, it still bears his name. He promised people they could double their money in ninety days by selling discounted postal reply coupons. Early investors did receive one-hundred percent profits, not from postal coupons, but rather from money put in by the investors who came behind them. Word spread, and others rushed to get in on this great opportunity, which is how he raised money." She paused dramatically. "Until he ran out of investors. Then it collapsed."

A woman spoke up, "Just like Social Security." Uneasy laughter rippled in the room.

Schliefman worked to keep a straight face. "I'm afraid that discussion goes beyond the scope of today's program. My point is, Mr. Ponzi made millions. Mr. Madoff made billions. The scheme is alive and well in the twenty-first century. Its allure is what we call *phantom riches*. It appeals to our emotions. Who hasn't dreamed of getting rich quick? When someone presents us an opportunity that sounds too good to be true, our logic can fly out the window. Emotion takes over. Ponzi and Madoff and their ilk tap into our dreams and fantasies. They understand how our hopes get the best of us, no matter how smart, well-educated, and sophisticated we are."

Tawny recalled the momentary rush she'd felt when Moe claimed he could turn her five thousand dollars into fifty. When such excitement filled people, no wonder they grasped at dreams. And wound up as victims.

Moe's shoe banged against her chair repeatedly. She glanced at him, his legs crossed at the knees, the upper one bouncing in nervous rhythm, but he remained engaged with his phone, oblivious. She scooted her chair out of his kicking range.

He looked up when she moved, lifted one shoulder, and went back to his phone.

Cassandra caressed the sleeve of the silver fox jacket hanging on her chair, as disinterested in the lecture as Moe.

Schliefman continued, "Victims are reluctant to report when they've been conned because they're ashamed. If you willingly handed over thousands of dollars to someone you later learn is a crook—who wouldn't be embarrassed? In addition, older victims fear loss of independence and autonomy. You worry that if you can't handle your finances, someone might take away control of your money. That's frightening. No wonder people keep the crime a secret. That's why it's easy for scammers to stay in business."

Moe's cell jangled. In a loud voice, he answered, "Yeah?"

People twisted in their seats to stare.

He said, "OK, give me the figures...No, that can't be right...Send it to me anyway."

Tawny wanted to pull him outside but, before she could act, a man hollered across the room. "Hang up, Rosenbaum! Nobody wants to listen to your yammering."

Moe dropped his phone, jumped out of his chair, and searched for the voice. He zeroed in on the same angry bald man who'd confronted him earlier. "Stay the hell out of my business, Quentin!"

The bald man hopped up. "You're the one making it

everyone's business. Take it outside, asshole!"

Moe's dark eyes sparked like a lit fuse. He lurched forward, zig-zagging between tables toward Quentin.

Gasps hissed through the room.

Tawny started to rise to catch Moe but her bulky bandaged foot stubbed against a table leg. Agony shot up her leg. She fell back in her chair, trying not to cry out.

Across the room, Moe had reached the bald man, looming over him. Quentin crouched in a boxer's stance, hands guarding his face, ready to mix it up. Veins bulged on Moe's neck. His jaw jutted, taunting his opponent to take a swing. "Let's talk about who's an asshole!"

"You are, for showing up where nobody wants you!"

Cassandra scurried behind Moe and pulled his arm. "Darling, please." He shook her loose.

The bald man's wife tried to tug him away but he kept lunging forward. "Thief!"

"Lousy cocksucker!" Moe's fist cocked, ready to launch a punch.

Several men pressed between the two would-be fighters, using their bodies as barriers.

After tense long seconds of jostling, Cassandra finally convinced Moe to leave with her. Heads swiveled to watch the troublemaker exit the restaurant. Conversations erupted as people stared in amazement.

Thank you again, Cassandra. Tawny allowed her jaw to unclench.

While the HOA president calmed the crowd, Tawny limped out, carrying Moe's discarded phone and Cassandra's fox coat. In the lobby, she paused to take several deep breaths to slow the hammer of her heart.

She spotted the couple on a sofa in front of the fireplace. Moe's back was to her, while Cassandra sat sideways, massaging his shoulder and talking into his ear. She caught sight of Tawny and motioned *stay away.*

Tawny nodded then held up the coat and phone. Cassandra pointed at a nearby chair, where Tawny set them down, then retreated to the restaurant. Better her than me, she thought.

Schliefman had resumed her talk. Tawny took a seat in the rear near a display table of posters and handouts about elder fraud. When she picked up the attorney's business card, she realized her hand was trembling. She stuffed the card and several pamphlets in her bag.

What a mess. She desperately wanted to leave but Emma hadn't reappeared. A few people turned to stare at her. She averted her eyes and tried to listen to the speaker but her foot pulsed with pain.

Tawny didn't know if dementia or psychological problems caused Moe's erratic behavior. The situation was spinning out of control. She'd worked hard to complete her assignment but so far had failed spectacularly. She needed help.

Even though she figured Tillman was probably in trial, she texted him: *Yr dad almst strted a brwl help!!!*

The audience remained fidgety and restless after Moe's blow-up. Schliefman seemed to sense their discomfort and finished her talk within minutes to tepid applause. Several people, including the bald man, Quentin, and his wife, approached the attorney. Soon a group of about twenty ringed her, locked in low, earnest conversation.

Back in the lobby, Moe and Cassandra had disappeared, evidently in her Porsche. Tawny peered through the windows to the parking lot, searching for her Jeep.

Gone.

Stranded.

She texted Emma *Whr R U?* Fifteen minutes dragged by without a reply, as the audience straggled out.

She returned to the now-almost-empty dining room to find the attorney gathering up pamphlets from the display table. Tawny approached. "Ms. Schliefman, thank you for a very interesting talk."

The woman faced Tawny with a wry smile. "More exciting than the usual groups I address."

Tawny grimaced then said, "I wonder if I could talk with you about someone I think is being scammed."

The attorney cocked her head. "What makes you think so?"

"He should be quite well off but his condo is being foreclosed on. He's secretive about his money but he let slip about a deal he claims can turn five thousand into fifty thousand in eighteen months."

Schliefman whistled. "Too good to be true."

"That's what I thought."

"Is this gentleman a relative?"

"No, he's my boss's father. My boss wants me to dig into his finances but the only way I can find anything is if he tells me. And he isn't talking."

Schliefman crossed her arms. "You're in a tough spot. If an adult of sound mind chooses to blow his money, that's his right. But if you believe there's mental incapacity going on, the son might pursue a conservatorship." She leaned closer and lowered her voice. "By any chance, is the person in question the African-American gentleman who was talking on his cell?"

Tawny shuddered but admired the attorney's perceptiveness. "I'm afraid so."

She nodded. "Thought I noticed you sitting together."

"It was my idea to come to this talk. I hoped it might prompt him to open up about his problems."

Schliefman pursed her lips. "Kind of backfired, didn't it? But that's not your fault. You were smart to try to open dialogue. What's your name?"

Tawny dug in her bag for a card. "Tawny Lindholm."

Schliefman glanced at the card. "Rosenbaum, Withers, and Zepruder. *Well.*" Admiration edged her tone.

"You know Tillman Rosenbaum?"

"Of course. He's your boss?"

Tawny nodded.

"*Well,*" she said again. "If you work for him, you must be good."

Tawny held up her hand. "I'm not a lawyer, just a go-fer."

"He doesn't hire second-rate, no matter what the position."

"Afraid I haven't been very successful with this assignment."

"You're facing quite a challenge, all right. Call me if I can help."

"I will. Thank you."

Out in the lobby, still no Emma.

She texted her daughter again: *Whr R U??? Need my car!*

Five minutes passed before the reply came: *Hangin w/ Colin. B thr in 20.*

Just great.

~~~

A half hour later, Emma wheeled around the resort's circular driveway.

Tawny climbed in the Jeep and slammed the door. "That was damned inconsiderate."

"Whoa, Mom, chill." Emma's face was as innocent as a ten-year-old's and about as mature.

Tawny struggled to keep her voice even. "You are getting paid very well to assist me. That doesn't mean taking my car and running off without asking."

"Take it easy. I thought you'd catch a ride with Cassandra."

"No. You *didn't* think. That's the problem." Tawny hugged herself, disappointment curdling her insides. "Emma, this is the most money you've ever made at a job. You need to meet adult responsibilities. A man could lose his home. I could lose my job. Thoughtless actions have serious consequences. You were selfish and immature."

Emma's smirk said *quit exaggerating.* "Oh, Mom, Mr. Rosenbaum isn't going to fire you because you're a few minutes late. It's no big deal."

If she let out the scream building inside, Tawny feared she might not be able to stop. Her jaw locked tight, holding it in.

She seethed as they drove to Moe's condo. In the driveway, Tawny snapped, "Wait here." At the front door, she knocked and waited. Knocked harder. No answer. Moe must still be with Cassandra. She tried the handle. Locked.

In the car again, Tawny stared straight ahead, too disappointed to look at her daughter. "Drive home."

When Emma didn't move, Tawny turned to find her hunched, shoulders rounded, tears rolling down her cheeks. "I can't stand it when you give me the silent treatment. I'm sorry, Mom. I didn't mean to let you down."

Tawny took several deep breaths. She suspected Emma was playing her, because she'd always been a pushover when it came to her children's tears. Anger started to ebb. "I know you didn't mean to. But you can't just do things on a whim without thinking. You're twenty-seven years old."

Emma sniffled.

Tawny handed over a tissue from her bag.

"It isn't fair." Emma wiped her nose.

"Suck it up. And, by the way, the two hours you took off with Colin are not going on your time card."

Emma looked sideways, like a dog that wet on the carpet. "I wouldn't do that."

Maybe not but Tawny would still double-check before she turned in Emma's hours to Tillman's bookkeeper. "OK then. Let's go home."

The ibuprofen had long since worn off, and the bandage squeezed like a tourniquet on Tawny's swollen foot. Despite a hopeful start with a possible answer to Moe's financial troubles, the day had sure turned into a screaming fiasco.

On the highway, Tawny said, "Tell me about Colin." *Oh, please let him be better than my first impression.*

Emma's face brightened. "He's cool, Mom. Really fun and funny. He made me laugh so hard, I almost wet my pants."

"How sweet."

Emma glanced over. "You know what I mean. He's got this crazy sense of humor. He travels around for his mom's foundation, meets all kinds of weird rich people. He was telling me about this wacky old lady who had bunk beds custom built for her cats but the cats kept fighting over who got to be on top. So she has the carpenter tear down the bunks and build individual platform beds instead. Cost over thirty grand. For cat beds."

"Sounds like someone with more money than brains."

"Yeah, but Colin's trying to convince her to donate to the foundation so he has to play along." Emma slipped into a mock deep voice, "Yes, Mrs. Fudgerucket, that's a brilliant idea, Mrs. Fudgerucket, I'm sure your cats will love it, Mrs. Fudgerucket."

Tawny shifted, trying to find a position to lessen the throbbing in her foot. "Kissing butt sounds like a miserable job."

"Nah, he says it's fun. Gets invited to all these parties at mansions in Beverly Hills, Houston, West Palm Beach."

"Cassandra's foundation must be pretty big. Where's this pet sanctuary she's building?"

"Somewhere over east of the mountains, I think. He

showed me the architect drawings on his tablet. It's awesome, like Club Med. *I* want to live there. Cassandra sure loves animals."

"Yeah, she does." *And she's the only one who can tame the wild animal that Moe turns into.*

Her cell rang. Tillman's clipped, sharp tone. "Court's in recess. What's the problem?"

Tawny related the dust-up at the lunch. "Your dad almost punched a guy out. If people hadn't gotten between them, I don't know what would have happened."

"What makes you think that's any different from shit he's pulled his whole life?"

"You consider this normal?"

"Not normal but it's his usual *modus operandi*. What else?"

Irritation grated that he brushed off her concern. "He told me a little about deals he's involved in that supposedly pay returns that sound too big to be legit. He mentioned offshore and tax loopholes. I'll send you printouts."

"Gotta go." The connection ended. Like most conversations with Tillman, Tawny was left cut off and unsatisfied.

She felt Emma's stare and turned toward her daughter. "What?"

"You didn't tell me Mr. Rosenbaum tried to start a fight. Jeez. If I'd known a boring lunch was going to turn into a riot, I'd have stuck around."

Tawny glared at Emma.

"Just kidding. But now I see why you got so mad that I was gone. Mr. Rosenbaum seems sorta crotchety but who knew he'd go all bat-shit like that?"

Tawny stretched her knotted neck. "This isn't the first time. He flies into rages and throws things. I think there's something wrong with him. I'm afraid he's going to hurt someone."

"Then why do you keep going to his house? He might hurt *you*."

Emma had a point. Tawny wanted to believe the bond she'd forged with Moe would prevent him from lashing out at her.

But with dementia, restraints broke, inhibitions collapsed. Her sweet grandfather had choked his beloved wife to unconsciousness one night in bed. He couldn't explain why and even denied he'd done it. He kept repeating, "Must have been a prowler who broke in," while Tawny's grandmother wept, rubbing her bruised neck.

When Tawny and Dwight finally had to take Grandpa to the locked unit at a senior facility, he'd asked over and over, "Why are you doing this to me?" Her heart still clenched at the memory twenty-five years after his death.

"Mom?"

"Hmm?"

"You're a million miles away. Did you hear me?"

"You were worried Moe might attack me."

"Mo-om. That was five minutes ago. You're not listening. I told you I'm going out with Colin tonight."

Tawny shook memories away as new concern gnawed at her. "What are you guys going to do?"

"Just hang. Find someplace with music and beer, maybe dance, whatever."

She hated the idea that her daughter was attracted to Colin and might hurt Jim but feared nothing would stop Emma from following her wild heart. She was an adult, no longer under Tawny's control.

"What, Mom?" Emma demanded.

Tawny jerked. "I didn't say anything."

"Yeah, but you were thinking it really loud."

"I hope you have a good time."

"Mo-om, come on, don't BS me."

Tawny chewed on her lip, took a breath, and faced Emma. "I'm concerned about Jim."

"Like, what?"

"How's he going to feel if you're dating someone else?"

"We're not married."

"You don't have to be married to hurt someone."

"Jeez, Mom, you make it sound like we were betrothed as babies."

Tawny squeezed her daughter's shoulder. "I'm concerned. Jim really cares for you, maybe more than you care for him. You might not be able to avoid hurting him. I hope you'll think about his feelings before you do something that may not be worth the price."

"God, you're so serious. Lighten up. We're just going to hang."

Tawny extended her hands, palms up. "It's your life and your choices." *No matter how much they stink.*

CHAPTER 10 – BIRDS GOTTA MAKE A LIVING TOO

The next morning, Moe greeted Tawny at his front door, wearing a leather flight jacket and chinos. She'd been surprised at his early call but quickly learned his motive.

"I need a new car," he said. "Let's go to the dealership."

A shudder rippled through her when she stepped inside the entry and hung up her coat. The longer he couldn't drive, the safer the roads would be.

She pulled off boots and changed into soft moccasins that barely accommodated her swollen foot. The redness had improved but frequent jabs reminded her of the Siamese's attack. She still needed Emma to drive but her daughter hadn't come home last night after her date with Colin. Dammit.

Tawny checked the great room, wondering where Rambo lurked. "What about your Lincoln?" she asked. "Don't you want to get it repaired?"

Moe strode to the kitchen. "The hell with it. I was getting sick of parking that aircraft carrier. Think I'd like something smaller and sporty this time." He raised a mug. "Want tea?"

Tawny shook her head. "You can't just desert your car."

"Why not? Didn't look like anyone lives there. Who'll care?"

"Moe, somebody owns that property and they're going to want it gone." Another idea occurred to her. "Besides, don't you want the trade-in value if you buy a new car?"

He pondered, pulling his long chin. "Guess you're right." He stood at the counter, thumbing his phone, and placed a call. "Yeah, I need a wrecker to tow my Navigator." He listened then thrust the cell at Tawny. "Tell him where it is."

She accepted the phone, trying to remember if she'd seen a mile marker that dark night. "It's in a driveway on the north side of Highway Forty. A mile or two east of the Ninety-three junction."

Annoyance colored the tow driver's voice. "You don't have an address or GPS coordinates?"

"No. It's next to an old abandoned barn. A corral faces the road."

"Gee, thanks, I know right where that is."

Tawny understood the man's sarcasm since she'd had the same reaction to Moe's sketchy description. "We'll meet you there. I'll park on the shoulder. Look for a green Jeep Wrangler with a tan top."

"Half hour," he said and disconnected.

~~~

In the daylight, barren, snow-covered fields stretched along Highway 40 for miles, interspersed with clumps of forest, reminding Tawny how desolate the area was. And how easily Moe might have frozen to death.

They passed the deer carcass she'd seen that night. Two bald eagles now picked at the remains. The sight brought back a memory of Dwight. Whenever they'd spotted scavengers on roadkill, she'd moaned in sympathy for the dead creature. Her practical husband always answered, "Babe, the birds gotta make a living too."

Moments later, Tawny led the wrecker down the driveway to the Navigator, parked forlornly behind the ramshackle barn. On the passenger side, the headlight was broken, the fender crumpled, and part of the grille smashed in, damage she hadn't seen in the darkness when she found Moe.

"Told you," Moe said, "car's still here and nobody cares. Could have left it for six months."

She gestured at the fresh dents. "What'd you run into, Moe?"

"Nothing." His brows furrowed, mystified.

"A deer?"

A vigorous headshake *no*. "Kids must have vandalized it."

Right. Tawny tugged on her braid, a small reassurance that reminded her of Dwight and how he used to tease her. Lately, the habit had become more frequent due to Moe and her annoying daughter.

The burly tow driver, wearing coveralls and a Carhartt jacket, knelt on the snow-packed ground to check under the Lincoln. A moment later, he straightened and brushed gloved hands across his prominent belly. "Radiator's got a big ole hole. Looks like something punched through it. Coolant's all run out."

Tawny suspected Moe never noticed and kept driving until the engine overheated and seized. The body damage was minor compared to what a new engine would cost.

Clouds shrouded the top of the ski mountain to the north. A chill wind blew down into the valley. Tawny's teeth chattered in spite of her polar fleece coat. More tire tracks mashed the snow near the Navigator.

"Where do you want it taken?" the driver asked.

Moe flipped his hand. "The Ford shop, I guess, since there's no Lincoln dealer in town."

"You got tow insurance?"

Moe shook his head. "Waste of money."

The driver squinted up at him. "How do you want to pay? You gonna follow me?"

"Yeah, yeah." Moe's impatient tone said he didn't want to be bothered with petty details, no matter how important they might be to the other person.

Once the Lincoln had been hooked up, the wrecker pulled onto the highway. Tawny and Moe followed in her Jeep.

She'd been waiting for an opportunity to ask Moe about

the money orders. Now she needed to choose her words carefully.

"Hey, I forgot to mention," she began, trying to sound casual, offhand. "When I was sitting on your couch, I noticed some money order receipts had slipped between the cushions. Are they important?" She watched him from the corner of her eye.

He shot a sideways look at her then faced the road. "Donations."

"For what?"

"Charity."

"Oh, really? I've always written checks for donations. Makes it easy to keep track of deductions for the IRS. Why do you use money orders?"

"Are you seeking tax advice?"

"No."

"Good. Neither am I." Shut down.

Damn, she had to go at it another way. "My husband and I always used to donate to local charities like the Spay Neuter Task Force. With all your cats, you probably support animal causes too?"

"Yeah."

"Like Cassandra's pet sanctuary?"

He turned in his seat and faced her square on, chin jutting out farther than normal. "I donate to the Curiosity Killed the Cat Foundation. It's a support group for women who ask too many questions."

She held up her hand. "OK, OK. Backing off. I was just making conversation."

He shifted, knees banging the glove compartment. "This is one damn cramped rig. My next car's got to have enough space to stretch out."

Because Moe clearly didn't want to talk about the money

orders, Tawny figured they were probably the key to his troubles. But she couldn't break through his brick wall of secrecy. She knew from dealing with her stubborn grandfather that pushing harder would only raise his resistance. Time to give up for now.

Moe pulled down the passenger visor and pawed through the CD holder. "Got any Sammy Davis Jr.?"

"No, but there's Ray Charles and Otis Redding."

He flipped the visor back up, apparently disappointed in Tawny's music selection. "Sammy was my man."

"Did you know him?"

"Not in person. I wrote him a fan letter when I was a kid, all pissed off and ready to fight the whole world. Told him I was the only other black Jew in America. Figured that made us related somehow. What d'ya know when you're a dumb punk of fourteen?" He snorted and flipped his hand sideways. "Anyway, he wrote back a nice letter, not his secretary, him personally. Told me about his car accident, losing the eye. I wrote him a couple more times, he answered, sent me a photograph. Not those cheesy publicity shots they sent to fans back then but one he'd actually taken himself. He was a pretty accomplished photographer, along with his other talents."

"That was nice of him."

"When he got all that shit for marrying that Swedish actress, I wrote him again, said fuck 'em all, do what you want."

"Was he kind of your role model?" Tawny asked.

Moe shrugged. "Nah. He wasn't even born Jewish, he converted. We were just a couple of outsiders, going our own way, the hell with the rest. Too bad, though, he didn't have *me* handle his finances later on. He wouldn't have wound up in deep shit with the IRS."

Tawny pulled her braid as a reminder to keep her mouth shut. Otherwise, she might have blurted out that Moe's situation wasn't exactly a glowing recommendation for his ability to manage money.

She followed the wrecker as it towed the damaged Lincoln into the service area of the dealership. As soon as Tawny parked, Moe jumped out and strode around the building to the new car showroom. She stayed to watch the driver unload the Lincoln.

When he finished, he approached Tawny's window. "You paying or him?"

"Him. He went to look at new cars." She followed the driver to the showroom, uneasy that Moe's card would be declined again. And again, she might get stuck with the bill, at least temporarily. Her credit card wasn't used to so much activity.

The bright showroom sparkled in comparison to the dull, overcast day. New vehicles gleamed under the lights. A salesman and Moe were deep in conversation beside a low-slung, sinister-looking black sedan with dark headlamps. Looked like an unmarked police cruiser.

She hung back while Moe gave a credit card to the tow driver. He swiped it through a hand-held reader once, twice, three times, then grunted.

Moe had already returned to his conversation with the salesman when the driver said, "Hey, buddy, it's declined."

Tawny flinched. Not again.

Moe whirled, eyes snapping. "Can't you see I'm busy? Get the hell out!"

The driver puffed up quickly, beer belly nearly bumping Moe. "Hey, asshole, pay me."

Moe shoved the man backwards. The driver plowed forward and grabbed the front of Moe's jacket. Moe's hands shot up, gripping the driver's wrists.

The salesman yelled, "Hey!"

Tawny hurried to them. "I'll pay!"

The two combatants glowered at each other, both unwilling to release their holds.

The salesman's eyes were full moons. Other salesmen clustered at a safe distance, muttering to each other.

Tawny pulled Moe's leather sleeve. "Let him go." She hoped he didn't backhand her in a blind rage. Her arm tensed in case she had to block a punch. To the driver, she loudly repeated, "I'll pay!"

The man's gaze slid sideways toward her. He released Moe's jacket, with a slight backward shove, enough to put distance between them but not enough to provoke a violent response. "I don't want a fight. I just want to get paid."

Tawny stepped in front of Moe and stared up at him. "I'll take care of it. OK?"

His chin jutted as teeth ground together with an audible creak.

Distract him. Diffuse the rage. But how? She caught sight of the black car he'd been checking out. "That's a sharp-looking rig, Moe." She nodded toward it. "Have you sat in it yet?"

The rage flickered.

"Why don't you try it out? See if it's roomy enough for your long legs."

The salesman gave a strangled squeak. Tawny caught an expression of panic that crossed his face. He didn't want a madman with declined credit sitting in a new fifty-thousand-dollar car, no matter how big his commission.

Tough.

Moe moved sideways, shooting a parting glare at his opponent, then opened the car door, and slid into the seat.

Whew. Tawny took the tow driver's arm and walked him outside, pulling her wallet from her bag. He swiped the card then handed her the reader to sign with her fingertip.

"Who is that a-hole?" the driver asked, peering at Moe

through the showroom windows.

Tawny shook her head. "My boss's dad."

The driver blew out his cheeks and pulled the printed receipt from the device. "Lady, I don't know what your boss is paying you but you deserve a raise."

"You don't know how right you are." She tucked the receipt into her purse. "Hey, could you tell from the damage what he hit?"

Big shoulders shrugged. "Probably a deer. Looked like blood on the undercarriage."

CHAPTER 11 – WHEN IN DOUBT, SHUT UP

Tawny rejoiced when she woke the next morning, the first day in a long week that she wasn't at Moe's beck and call. Her foot felt better. Finally, she had a chance to go to the Zumba class she'd been missing since Tillman had assigned this miserable task to her.

Emma's bedroom door was closed. Tawny almost pounded on it to scold Emma for deserting her job as driver. But that would only lead to an argument that might make her miss Zumba. She'd handle her irresponsible daughter later.

In the garage, Emma's rust-bucket Hyundai sat with a rag stuffed in the gas tank filler. Tawny made a mental note to bug Emma *again* to buy a replacement cap, as she climbed into her Jeep.

Despite the socked-in, dreary day, Tawny reveled in dancing as her stiff muscles loosened. Endorphins flowed into her bloodstream, muting the jabs of pain in her foot. Built-up tension gradually released. For a brief hour, she almost forgot her frustrating boss, his frustrating father, and her own frustrating daughter.

She left the gym, sweaty and satisfied, and was heading home for a shower when her cell trilled. Caller ID said *Private*. She answered.

"Mrs. Lindholm?" The voice sounded familiar.

"Yes?"

"This is Deputy Oscar Beaudoin with the Flathead County Sheriff's Office."

Half a beat later, the name clicked. "Obie, right?"

"Yes, ma'am. I wonder if you could come to the sheriff's office. We're investigating a motor vehicle accident and your name came up as a possible witness."

Uh-oh. She flashed back to the Lucky Dragon parking lot

120

where Moe had run the pickup truck off the road. Maybe the driver had changed his mind and decided to make a complaint.

"Ma'am, would it be convenient for you to come now?"

"Uh, sure. I'm about fifteen minutes away."

As she pulled into the parking lot of the Justice Center, she realized she had never given her name to the man with the damaged truck. Did Obie mean *another* accident?

In the lobby, she spoke to the receptionist behind the bulletproof window of the sheriff's office. Moments later, a uniformed Obie buzzed her inside. She followed him past the admin desks, several offices, and around the corner into an interview room. He closed the door to the stuffy little cubicle and they sat across from each other at a table.

"Thank you for coming in, Mrs. Lindholm," he began.

"Friends call me Tawny," she reminded him.

"Mrs. Lindholm," he repeated, "do you know Moshe Baruch Rosenbaum?"

He already knew she did. In her previous interrogations, Tillman had always advised the shortest answers possible. "Yes."

"How do you know him?"

"He's my boss's father."

"Is your relationship with him business or personal?"

"I guess you'd call it business. His son is worried and asked me to check up on his dad."

"How long have you known him?"

Tawny ran the days backwards in her mind. The time felt like forever amid the ruckus Moe had caused. "About a week."

"Did you see him last Tuesday night?"

She had to think. "Yes, we went to dinner at the Alpenglow Yacht Club on Flathead Lake."

"What time were you there?"

"From seven to about eight-thirty or quarter of nine."

"Did you drive together?"

"No, I brought my own car and he had his."

"What kind of car was he driving?

"A black Lincoln Navigator."

"Is this the car?" A photo of the Lincoln with its smashed front appeared on the table as if from thin air.

She swallowed. "Yes."

"Was the car damaged when you saw it at eight-thirty or quarter to nine?"

"No."

"So to the best of your knowledge, this damage occurred later."

"Yes." Tawny shifted in the metal folding chair. She'd learned from experience that interrogation room furniture was intentionally uncomfortable. "What's this about?"

"A motor vehicle accident." Obie's even gaze gave nothing away. No trace of the friendly concern he'd shown earlier when he gave her his cell number. Or maybe she'd only imagined it. "Was anyone else with you at dinner?"

"His date, Cassandra Maza, but she came in her own car, also."

"Before you left the restaurant, had Mr. Rosenbaum been drinking?"

Oh hell, how should she answer this loaded question? Moe had polished off most of three bottles of champagne by himself. But unless Obie pinned her down, she didn't want to volunteer that information. "We had champagne with dinner."

"Was he visibly impaired when you left?"

Tawny chewed on her lip, reluctant to lie. "He was upset."

"Why?"

"His credit card had been declined. He became angry and argued with the manager. I wound up paying to keep him from becoming..." The word *violent* came to mind but she couldn't say that. "To keep from upsetting him more."

"You paid the bill then you left, correct?"

"Yes."

"Did you see him again that night?"

"Not that evening, but early the next morning."

"What time?"

Tawny wondered if she should check her phone log but decided no. The deputy might confiscate her cell. He was being too methodical for a mere car accident. She answered from memory. "He called me a little after three a.m."

"What did he say?"

"His car was broken down and he wanted me to come get him."

"Did he say what happened to the car?"

"The engine quit."

"Did he tell you what he ran into?"

Tawny heard a distinct edge in his question. "He only said his engine quit."

"Where did he say he was?"

Again Tawny wondered how much, if anything, she should relate. The carefulness of Obie's questions concerned her. "He was, well, confused. Not sure where he was."

"Did you find him?"

"Yes."

"Where?"

"On Highway Forty."

"Can you remember a mile marker?"

"About a mile and a half east of the Highway Ninety-three junction."

"If he didn't know where he was, how did you find him?"

She related the difficult deductions she'd gone through.

Obie's eyes narrowed during her description and he nodded slightly. When she finished, he said, "We could have used you on some search and rescue missions."

His compliment didn't relax her. She repositioned herself on the hard chair.

He went on: "What time did you find him?"

"I didn't check the clock but probably about quarter to four."

"What was Mr. Rosenbaum's condition when you found him?"

"Early stages of hypothermia. Slurred speech, shivering, teeth chattering."

"Did you detect alcohol on his breath?"

She shook her head. "I was only concerned about warming him up. I didn't notice."

"So there wasn't any noticeable smell?"

The champagne at dinner should have worn off by the early hours of the morning. Unless he'd drunk more when he went to Cassandra's house. Again, Tillman's cautions came back to her. Without a blood test, Moe's alcohol level couldn't be proven in court. As much as she hated drunk drivers, she feared saying something that could contribute to the arrest of her boss's father. "I didn't notice," she repeated.

"What condition was Mr. Rosenbaum's car in?"

"No idea. I was only concerned about *his* condition and getting him home."

"So you did not observe any damage at that time?"

"Too dark. All I know is what he told me, that it had broken down."

"When was the next time you saw his vehicle?"

"Yesterday."

"Tell me how you came to see it yesterday."

"Mr. Rosenbaum called me because he needed transportation. He arranged to have a wrecker meet us there."

"Was the Navigator in the same place as when you last saw

it?"

"Yes."

"Did it appear to have moved?"

"In the daylight, I could see more tire tracks, but I don't think it had moved."

"Mr. Rosenbaum had the vehicle towed to the Ford dealership?"

She nodded. "We followed the tow truck in my car."

"Did the driver say anything about the condition of the vehicle?"

A memory jolted her as sharp as a blow across the face.

Blood.

At the time the driver mentioned it, she'd assumed Moe must have hit a deer or other animal. But the sheriff's department didn't investigate deer collisions with such painstaking attention to detail.

A wave of nausea swept over her. Moe must have hit a person.

And she might have driven him away from the scene of the accident.

Obie noticed her jolt. "What, Mrs. Lindholm?"

Her lip quivered. "Did he hurt someone?"

He leaned on the back legs of his chair, folded his arms, and stared hard at her. "Don't *you* know?"

She shook her head so hard, she felt dizzy. "All I know is what I've told you."

Obie continued to stare at her, waiting. But she had nothing else to tell him. Fear needled her. What had Moe done?

"Please, tell me," she finally said. "Did he hurt someone?"

The deputy rose. "Wait here, please." He left the room, closing the door firmly.

Tawny started to pull the cell from her pocket to call Tillman then thought better of it. An interrogation room would be monitored and she didn't want to say anything that might be used against her. Or Moe. Tillman always counseled, "When in doubt, shut up."

She put on her readers and reached for the photo Obie had left behind on the desk. It was a digital picture color-printed on regular copy paper, which made the quality muzzy. The blood the tow driver had mentioned didn't show in the photo.

Given the deputy's caginess, Tawny felt sure someone had been badly hurt, or killed. Was Moe so drunk he didn't realize what he'd done? Did he just take off and leave the victim lying injured or dead in the road? What kind of person did that? Someone desperate to avoid the consequences of a terrible act? Someone without a conscience?

Or someone with dementia?

Moe had driven his Navigator behind the barn, out of sight from the road. Was he trying to hide the damaged vehicle? He'd wanted to desert it there until she convinced him to get it towed. Did he intend to leave it concealed, hoping he wouldn't be connected to the accident?

She again reviewed what Moe had said that night. He did appear to be in denial about his behavior but she'd attributed that to his embarrassment about getting lost. But she also remembered his inclination to blame others for problems he'd caused. Was this another sign of dementia? Or was he simply a man without the capacity to care about other people?

Dammit, Tillman, she thought, why aren't *you* here now, instead of me? He's *your* father.

Another detail niggled at the edge of her memory. Wilbur, the swamper at the Lucky Dragon, had died in a hit-and-run. Could Moe have...? *Please, God, no.*

Twenty tortured minutes dragged by before Obie opened the door and sat again.

"Well?" Tawny asked.

His demeanor seemed slightly less stiff but his expression still gave nothing away. "Your account of that night and early morning matches what Mr. Rosenbaum told us. We still need to follow up with other witnesses but for now you're free to go. Please stay available for further questions."

The hunger to know chewed on her. "Can you tell me what happened?"

Obie's mouth turned down at one corner. "Mr. Rosenbaum is under arrest. A thirty-seven-year-old man named Wilbur Makepeace was riding a bicycle that night and was struck by Mr. Rosenbaum's black Lincoln Navigator."

Horrified confirmation flashed in Tawny's mind. "Wilbur from the Lucky Dragon in Columbia Falls?"

Obie nodded. "He left work at two-thirty a.m. and started riding home. Sometime after that, a vehicle struck him and kept driving."

"Oh, Lord." Tawny's throat tightened and a sob fought up from her lungs. She dropped her head in her hands, staring at the photo still lying before her.

Poor Wilbur, the simple soul, known for riding his bike everywhere. Despite his disability, he'd earned the respect of the Tang family for hard work and dependability. Tawny recalled the anguish in Jim's voice when he talked about his friend's death.

"Mr. Makepeace was conscious," Obie went on. "Both arms were broken, also his collarbone, and several ribs. He had a severe head injury. But he managed to walk through a pasture to the nearest house. The residents called nine-one-one at four-thirty and he was transported to the hospital. He went into seizures and died later that day." Obie's jaw worked, the thick muscles of his neck swelling.

"Dear God." Tawny blinked hard. While she had been busy warming up Moe, Wilbur was stumbling around somewhere nearby. Maybe he'd seen her headlights going to the barn and tried to call out to her.

But she hadn't heard. She'd driven away, leaving the badly broken man alone in the freezing night.

Obie folded his hands on the table. Tawny noticed his fingernails were bitten down to the quick, one cuticle bleeding. "Wilbur competed in the Special Olympics. Everyone here at the Sheriff's Office knew him. I was on a team with him for the last three years." His broad shoulders slumped and his voice went husky. "He had awesome endurance and guts. He never, ever gave up. And now he's dead."

She tried to swallow a lump but couldn't.

Obie's posture straightened. "You likely won't be charged because you didn't know you were helping a suspect leave the scene of the crime." His hard stare pierced her already-guilty conscience. "But that's what you did."

She stammered, "I-I never saw him. If I'd known he was out there, I would've helped him." Her tears splashed on the photo. Ink ran in blurry circles.

A rap on the door. Another deputy poked his head in. "Mr. Rosenbaum wants Mrs. Lindholm to take custody of his belongings. I've checked them—they're OK to release."

Obie lifted his chin then addressed Tawny, "Would you come with me?"

She wiped her eyes and followed him down the hallway, deeper into the building.

Around the last corner, Moe stood hand-cuffed in front of a table beside a jailer in a black uniform. His head hung, wide bony shoulders slumped, and he looked a hundred instead of seventy-five. The normal snap of his flashing eyes was gone, now flat and opaque. His keys, wallet, and cell lay on the table. When he spotted her, a plea crossed his expression.

"Moe?" she said. "Are you OK?"

A flicker of anger. "Yeah, I'm peachy keen."

His sarcasm reassured her a little. "Do you want me to call Cassandra?"

"Hell, no! You better *not* call her." But the threat sounded hollow. Then the pleading expression returned. "Feed my cats. Make sure they're OK."

"I will." The old man might not know what he was doing at times but he always worried about his cats.

The jailer indicated Moe's belongings on a table. "Mr. Rosenbaum wants you to take these. Please sign this receipt."

Tawny scrawled her signature with a trembling hand then gathered the items into her bag.

The jailer grasped Moe's arm and escorted him down the hall, pausing before a solid metal door that led to the jail. Moe turned to look back at her. In a cracked, desperate voice, he implored, "Call my son!"

~~~

The voice on the phone sent a worm of concern burrowing into Cassandra.

"Ms. Maza, this is Deputy Beaudoin from the Flathead County Sheriff's Office."

She tucked her legs under her on the sofa and took a sip of Zinfandel before responding. "And what can I do for the Sheriff's Office, Deputy? I donate to your fallen officer pledge drive every year but isn't this a little early?"

"Ms. Maza, did you have dinner with Moe Rosenbaum on Tuesday evening?"

She covered her apprehension with charm. "Why, yes, we had a lovely time at the Alpenglow down on the lake. Have you been there, Deputy? The best prime rib in Montana."

The deputy would not be distracted. He kept up the

questions for ten more minutes. Finally Cassandra hung up, confident she'd satisfied him. For now. She ran upstairs to Colin's bedroom and barged in.

He moaned and pulled the tangled blanket over his head. "What?"

"You should have made sure!" Her voice shrilled to the rafters. "Why did you leave before the job was finished?"

"It doesn't make any difference. He'll still be blamed whether he's alive or dead."

Cassandra yanked the blanket from the bed, leaving Colin exposed and naked.

"Hey!" he protested. Blue eyes widened in fear. He raised his arm to protect his face.

She waited several seconds until he lowered it, believing he was safe, before she launched her surprise backhand. It connected with a satisfying meaty slap to his cheek. He held the pillow up to shield himself, cowering.

"Grow a backbone," she hissed and stormed out.

Downstairs, she poured more wine and pondered the situation. The plan should have gone off without a hitch. Between the pill in Moshe's glass of champagne at dinner and the spiked nightcaps at her home, he should have been passed out cold. All Colin had to do was park the Navigator out of sight, slide Moshe into the driver's seat, and wait for winter to finish the job. She'd followed in her Porsche and picked up Colin who assured her that the old man was near death.

Instead, on Wednesday morning, Moshe had called her. He was confused about the night before and let slip that Tawny had brought him home. That he was alive was shocking enough. But more infuriating—he'd called that woman for help instead of Cassandra. *She* should have been his first and only thought.

Ever since Tawny had showed up, Moshe had been

careening farther out of control and that was unacceptable. He should have been bound to Cassandra, dependent on her to the exclusion of anyone else.

She needed to create another opportunity to rid herself of Moshe. And now Tawny Lindholm as well.

CHAPTER 12 – KEYS TO THE KINGDOM

Tillman Rosenbaum arrived in Kalispell on the midnight flight. Through the thick glass wall at the airport, Tawny watched the towering man in a charcoal three-piece suit gallop past other deplaning passengers. At the revolving door out of the security area, he pushed in front of a mother wrestling with a baby in a stroller. The woman glared at him but Tillman took no notice. Carrying a roller bag and leather briefcase, he bee-lined for Tawny.

Long face screwed into a frown, he said, "What the hell?"

His greeting didn't surprise her but still seemed rude when she'd driven out in the middle of the night to pick him up. "Nice to see you too," she answered.

He rolled his eyes and headed for the exit. "I can't believe there's no direct flight between Billings and Kalispell. Had to go through Seattle. Ridiculous."

Trying to keep up with his long strides, Tawny winced with every step toward her Jeep, parked at the curb. Tillman shot a quick but wordless glance at her limp. She opened the rear hatch and he tossed his bags inside.

At the stoplight on Highway 2, she asked, "Which hotel?"

Tillman fiddled with his phone, apparently checking messages that had arrived during his flight. "Your house. I want to talk."

She almost said, well, *I* want to sleep, but stopped herself. The man's father was in jail, charged with a serious crime. She'd cut him some slack. For now.

Tillman had two speeds, full auto and dead stop. Within minutes, his head lolled back and he started snoring, mouth open, while Tawny struggled to stay awake.

At her house, he instantly came to life again. In the kitchen, she retrieved the bottle of scotch she kept on hand for his visits, poured some over ice, and gave it to him. He gulped down the best part of the glass and held it out for a refill.

He plopped on the couch in the living room, elbows propped on his tall knees. She faced him from Dwight's frayed corduroy recliner.

"OK," he said, "give it to me."

Tawny fought drowsiness as she described Moe's tantrum at the yacht club restaurant, followed by his middle-of-the-night plea to rescue him. Then the retrieval of the damaged vehicle, the tow driver's reference to blood, and her interview by the deputy.

"Did you mention drinking?" Tillman asked.

"The deputy asked. I dodged saying how much but you ought to know—Moe polished off most of three bottles of champagne by himself then tried to blame me for being drunk."

"Huh?"

"He claimed if I hadn't saved him from the mountain lion, he wouldn't have needed to buy me champagne to celebrate."

Tillman frowned. "That makes no sense."

"I know. But to someone with dementia, it's perfectly logical. Tillman, he needs to see a doctor. I really think he's got a problem."

"And you're the medical expert because?"

His snideness irritated her but she answered, "Because my grandpa had dementia and I see the same symptoms in your dad. The rages. Blaming other people for things he does. The secretiveness. Most of all, the confusion. How did he get lost in two blocks between his girlfriend's place and his and wind up ten miles out of the way? He had absolutely no clue where he was."

Tillman's jaw jutted, grim, unconvinced. "Probably snockered but you didn't hear me say that."

She pulled on her braid. "I don't think so. It had been hours since the champagne. And once he got warmed up, his speech didn't slur anymore." Another memory returned. "I asked him what direction we were going. He accused me of being sneaky, trying to test him, but broke off before he finished the sentence. I suspect someone—maybe a doctor—has checked him out and Moe didn't like what they told him."

"You ask him?"

She shook her head. "I've been treading lightly. He's so volatile. I think he still trusts me. I'm trying to keep that trust. He released his wallet, phone, and keys to me at the jail."

"Let me see them."

She went to the kitchen, retrieved Moe's belongings from her bag, and picked up the bottle of scotch on the way back to the living room. She offered it to Tillman but he shook his head. Instead, he dug through his father's wallet, spreading the contents across the coffee table.

Less than a hundred dollars in cash. Driver's license. Shopper reward cards. Coupons. The declined credit card. And a slip of paper with handwriting in pen.

Tillman held up the paper. "What do you think this is?"

Tawny put on her glasses and sat beside him on the couch.

The paper had been folded many times, with ragged edges and tears repaired by tape. Letters and numerals had been printed in a small, precise hand.

"Computer passwords?" she said.

"Account numbers?" Tillman suggested. "Banks or stocks?"

"Could be."

Tillman picked up the key ring and jangled it like a bell. "OK, here are the keys to the kingdom. Tomorrow, go to his place and toss it completely. Turn on the computer and see if you find anything with these codes. Look for financial statements like the ones you sent me before. Grab anything that remotely looks like it deals with money."

Tawny sat back and stared at him. "That's intruding on his privacy."

He grimaced. "Screw his privacy. The asshole's in jail. This is the opportunity we've been waiting for. You can turn the place inside out without him stopping you."

"He's *your* father. Why don't you do it yourself?"

He huffed a scotch-scented exhalation. "Because I'll be at the jail, finding out what the hell is going on."

Tawny folded her arms. "I don't like doing your dirty work. It's one thing to get him to open up and confide in me but it's something else to rummage through his life like a burglar."

Now Tillman reached for the bottle again, filled the glass, and gulped it in two swallows. He glared down his nose. "Tawny, you're such a Girl Scout." Not a compliment.

All trace of sleepiness disappeared as her anger welled. "How would you like it if someone pillaged through your business without your permission?"

"Already happened. Ask my ex-wife's lawyer." His tone was matter-of-fact as he rattled ice cubes and sloshed more scotch into the glass. "Look, if what you think is correct, that he has dementia, it's important to establish that to have a chance at getting him off on the criminal charges. You know what I do for my clients. You expect me to do less for my own father?"

Tawny jumped up, eager to put distance between them. "I've already got enough on my conscience because I didn't help that poor injured man."

Tillman unfolded slowly, deliberately, to loom over her. "If you insist on being a goddamn Goody Two Shoes, I'll hire someone else."

"Go ahead!" She stalked down the hall to her bedroom.

Behind the closed door, she pounded her pillow with both fists, then caught a glimpse of Dwight's photo on the dresser. He'd always calmed her down, put problems in perspective.

Why wasn't he with her now, gently tugging her braid to tease her out of her funk?

She grabbed his pillow and hugged it to her chest. "Dwight, what should I do?" Her thumb rubbed the worn gold wedding band she still wore.

He'd say, *Hell, babe, you put up with* me *for thirty-two years. You can weather this.*

The bedside lamp flickered, reminding her of the electrical work the house needed. She couldn't afford to be fired. What was she thinking, defying her boss like that?

She went into her bathroom and stared at her reflection. Fifty years old and trapped in a job that paid well but required her to do things that bothered her. She already felt guilty about the surreptitious cell photos she'd sent to Tillman. Then leaving an injured man alone in the desolate night, even though she didn't know he was there. Now the further intrusion Tillman had ordered.

If Moe was responsible for poor Wilbur's death, could she live with herself if she helped Tillman get him off?

Why hadn't Moe been more forthcoming? She remembered the fear and loss of control Renata Schliefman had described at the fraud talk. Moe still believed he was capable of taking care of his affairs and understandably resented someone else butting in.

But now Moe had lost control in a big way, with his very freedom at stake. Tillman held his father's fate in his hands. If Moe went to prison, undoubtedly Tillman would have to take charge. So maybe he was merely jumping the gun on the inevitable stewardship of the elderly man's finances.

Tillman was standing by his father, even if he was being a jerk about it. She understood that loyalty and had to admire him for it, although grudgingly.

Maybe she *was* being a Goody Two Shoes.

Fatigue crept back, calling her to bed. She splashed water on her face, since she still needed to drive her boss to a hotel for the night. When she emerged from her bedroom, she heard a god-awful noise coming from the living room. What the hell?

Tillman's long legs hung over the end of the couch. One lanky arm fell to the floor, the other thrown above his head, hand nesting in his black curls. Tie loose, collar unbuttoned. His suit coat and vest had been flung across the recliner. He snored like a chainsaw.

She stood there, watching his chest rise and fall, his normally taut, angry expression relaxed in sleep. He no longer seemed like a badass lawyer, but a rather cute little boy exhausted after a hard day's play.

A little boy whose father was in jail.

Aw hell.

She took the afghan from the back of the couch and tucked it over him.

~~~

A soft knock on Tawny's bedroom door woke her. The clock said six-thirty. Still dark outside and would be for another two hours.

The door cracked. "Mom?"

She rose on one elbow and turned on the lamp. "Hi, honey."

Emma, clad in a tank top and lounge pants, moved to Dwight's side of the bed, flopped down, and curled next to Tawny. "What's Tillman doing here? I thought someone was driving a Harley through the house."

Tawny yawned. "Moe's been arrested."

"What for?"

Tawny reached over and stroked silken hair from her daughter's face. "It's bad. The cops think his car hit Wilbur."

Emma drew back. "Our Wilbur? Really?" Her face screwed up, poised to cry.

Tawny pulled Emma into a one-armed hug. Her daughter melted against her and Tawny felt tears dampening her shoulder.

"That's awful, Mom. Poor Wilbur never hurt anyone. He was just a sweet dumb guy everyone liked." She raised her face. "You mean Moe ran over him and then just left him there on the road, hurt? What kind of a creep does something like that?"

Tawny had asked herself the same question through most of the restless night. "Moe's been charged but nothing's proved yet."

Emma pulled away, suddenly stiff and tense. "You sound like that jerk Tillman. When did *you* turn into a lawyer?"

"Nobody knows for sure what happened."

"Yeah, well, the cops wouldn't arrest him if they weren't sure he did it."

Tawny's jaw muscles tightened. "*I* was arrested, remember? Being arrested doesn't make you guilty."

Emma gave her the side eye. "That was different."

The evidence in Moe's situation did sound pretty damning but Tawny said, "Let's wait for the facts before making judgments."

"What kind of facts make it OK to run down a guy on a bike and leave him to die?"

Tawny empathized with Emma's righteous indignation. "I don't know."

Emma rose from the bed. "How long is Tillman going to stay here?"

"He's not. He's going to a hotel."

"Good, 'cause I don't like him or his crazy father. If he's around, I'm going somewhere else."

Tawny pinched her forehead. "I just may join you."

Emma left, closing the bedroom door.

As weary as Tawny felt, she couldn't go back to sleep. Memories of conversations with Moe whirred in her mind, along with Tillman's order to search Moe's condo.

She felt sorry for the old man. During his good moments, his teasing banter reminded her of Grandpa, whom she still missed terribly. And Grandpa couldn't help his dementia.

Maybe it was the weight of responsibility for saving Moe's life twice, first from the mountain lion, then hypothermia. Maybe his assertion of the silly-sounding Chinese custom burdened her conscience.

But had she saved his life only to give him the chance to kill an innocent man?

Did she share guilt because she hadn't stopped him from driving when she knew he was dangerous?

She had no legal authority. She wasn't related to him. There had been no practical way to prevent him from getting behind the wheel. She'd tried to warn Tillman but he'd blown off her concern—until it was too late and a man was dead.

Why wouldn't these guilty feelings go away?

At seven, she heard the shower running in the bathroom down the hall. A baritone voice belted out Springsteen's "Born to Run." She wrapped up in her blue fleece robe and left her bedroom. Emma's door was closed and Tawny didn't expect to see her again until after Tillman left, especially since he'd now taken over the second bathroom.

In the living room, Tillman's roller bag lay open on the coffee table with folded shirts, jockey shorts, and socks strewn across Dwight's recliner. Her boss had certainly made himself at home.

Tawny started coffee in the kitchen and again studied the mysterious codes on the creased paper from Moe's wallet. Since he kept it with him, it must be important.

Tillman strode into the living room, his damp black curls barely clearing the arched doorway from the hall. He wore a fresh starched shirt, Windsor knot in his tie, suit pants. He put a shaving kit away in his bag then bent to peer at her in the pass-through opening between the dining area and kitchen. A trace of eucalyptus scent came with him. "Morning!"

Tawny poured two mugs of coffee and handed him one. "You're certainly cheerful."

"Slept great. Your sofa is very comfortable."

Don't get too used to it, she thought. "Which hotel do you want to stay at? Or do you want to rent a car first?"

"Drop me at the jail. I'll get a car delivered there. Then you head to the old man's place and start digging." His dark gaze drilled into her. "That is, if you can bring yourself to do your job."

She scowled at him. "When you put it like that, you make it damn hard not to tell you to stuff it."

He looked smug, jaw jutting forward. "Tell me whatever you want. But you'll do it anyway because you won't renege on a commitment."

"Since when did I commit to following your unreasonable, immoral orders?"

He grinned, rising from his hunched-over position, and moved to fill the kitchen doorway. "*That's* not the commitment I mean. You're committed to my old man. I heard it in your voice every time you talked about him. For some inexplicable reason, you care about that miserable old bastard. And when you care about someone, you'll do anything to help them. I know you, Tawny."

She turned away and stared out the kitchen window into the still-dark morning, the yard lamp shining on the snow. Damn him for being right. Loyalty and compassion were supposed to be good qualities but right now they felt more like curses. "How is it helping to snoop in his life?"

"Because *I'm* sure he's being scammed. Because *you're* sure he's got dementia. And the only way to help him is without his consent. He's like a sick child who doesn't want a shot but you have to force him because otherwise he won't get better." He opened the refrigerator. "Got any grapefruit juice?"

"No. I'll speak to the catering department about the poor juice selection." What an irritating, demanding man. Still staring out the window, she heard him rustling with a plastic bag of bread at the opposite counter, then the clack of the toaster. "Don't do that—"

Too late. The lights went out, plunging them into blackness.

"What the hell happened?" Tillman asked.

His tall form overwhelmed her little kitchen. She couldn't avoid bumping into him as she fumbled for one of the many emergency flashlights she'd planted throughout the house for when circuit breakers blew.

"Can't use the toaster at the same time the coffee maker's on." She reached around him to the counter, found the flashlight, and lit up the room. "It's an old house and the wiring's shot."

"That's a helluva a way to live. Fire hazard too. Why don't you get it fixed?"

"I plan to, when I have time." *And money.*

The flashlight beam crossed his face and she saw realization dawn in his eyes. He'd read her last thought even though she hadn't spoken out loud. "Tawny, do you need an advance? Just say so."

She ducked his penetrating stare. Emotions tangled inside her—annoyance, humiliation, stubborn pride, but also surprise. She'd just teetered on the edge of being fired yet now her boss was offering to lend her money? "Thanks, but I'm fine."

He was blocking her way and they did an awkward little dance as she tried to move around him.

She gestured at the door to the basement. "I need to go downstairs and reset the circuit breaker."

He said nothing but stepped aside. She left him in the dark kitchen and shone the beam down the steps, hurrying to escape her confusion because his unexpected generosity had touched her.

CHAPTER 13 – CARLO PONZI IS ALIVE AND WELL

An hour and a half later, eight cats greeted Tawny when she unlocked Moe's door. Rambo the Siamese hunched on the back of the sectional and growled but kept his distance. She squatted to pet Sugar and two others that rubbed against her dark brown leggings, leaving mats of fur. "Hi, guys. Want some breakfast?" All except Rambo trailed her into the kitchen. She washed their bowls, then opened can after can of chopped liver, turkey and giblets, seafood medley, and other smelly combinations that the cats found irresistible.

When she set the dishes on the kitchen floor, Rambo streaked in and ate from the middle bowl in the line. The rest of the cats formed a semi-circle, watching him, not daring to approach. After he finished, he sauntered away to groom himself and they rushed the food.

While they ate, Tawny cleaned the two litter boxes, shaking her head at the irony of twenty-five dollars an hour for such a task. Immediately after she poured fresh litter in, a tiger-striped staircase cat hopped in with a *mrreow* that Tawny imagined was offering thanks.

She wandered into the great room. Weak winter sun peeked over the eastern mountains. Feeble rays glimmered through the tall windows overlooking the golf course. Three yearling whitetails minced across the snow. A fluttering cloud of Bohemian waxwings descended to feed on the orange berries of a mountain ash tree. Moe's home was in a breathtaking, peaceful location.

And he sat in jail.

Sadness swelled inside her. Even if Tillman managed to get his father out, he could still lose his home to foreclosure.

And another man had died a brutal, lonely death.

Tawny tried to shake off her melancholy. She pulled the paper with the cryptic codes from her bag, along with new light bulbs she'd brought. Feet dragging, she entered Moe's gloomy office and replaced several burned-out bulbs. Finally she could see just what a trashy mess it was. Maybe she'd have been better off in the dark.

The computer was on but asleep. She scanned through directories without a clear idea of what she was looking for. She opened files randomly, hoping to stumble on financial information.

Moe's accusation that she was a forensic accountant flickered in her memory and she scoffed at the thought. Bookkeeping and simple tax accounting for Dwight's truck repair business made up the limited range of her skills. This exercise was blind fumbling. If she happened to click on a significant file, it would be pure luck.

A spreadsheet popped up, dates going back through the past decade. She couldn't tell if it recorded Moe's investments or his blood pressure. None of the numbers matched the coded scrap of paper.

Another file called *offshore* made her wonder again about tax dodges but she couldn't decipher unfamiliar jargon.

After two hours, she logged into her Gmail account, attached the files she hoped might be relevant, and sent them to Tillman. Let him puzzle out their meaning. This search was way over her head. Her eyes no longer focused, even with her readers on.

Back in the kitchen, she rummaged in the drawer where she'd hidden the financial reports a couple of days before. Not there now. She checked more drawers and cupboards. But the stack was gone.

Had Moe removed them? Did he realize she'd been searching? She'd never been any good at sneaking. He must have noticed. Damn.

Uncertain what to do next, she cleaned up trash, filling four jumbo plastic garbage bags with expired coupons, ads for stores long out of business, and solicitations for carpet cleaning. Clearing the clutter made the place appear much larger and more orderly. Moe would undoubtedly be furious when he got home.

If he got home.

Next she lugged cartons from the office to the living room where there was more room and better light. She stacked boxes in neat rows, knowing her next task would be combing through the dusty records. But she couldn't face that before lunch.

At eleven-thirty, she put on her coat, locked the front door, and headed for her Jeep parked in the driveway.

A red-cheeked couple walked in the street with two Cairn terriers in matching sweaters and booties. A stocking cap covered the man's head and his wife wore a knitted band over her ears. Tawny nodded and smiled, then recognized them from the scam-warning lunch.

Quentin. The man who'd confronted Moe.

The couple paused, exchanged glances, then the woman said, "Where's Moe?"

"Uh, he's not here right now," Tawny answered.

The man studied her. "You were with him at the clubhouse the other day."

She nodded. "Interesting talk."

The couple traded another unspoken message between them. "That's one way to put it," Quentin answered.

"Do you live nearby?" Tawny asked.

The wife said, "Two doors down." Another message passed between them. "We've been seeing your car here a lot."

Keep it vague. "Yes, I've been doing some work."

Quentin said, "Better get paid in advance. Otherwise, Rosenbaum will leave you out in the cold."

She grabbed the opening. "You don't seem to be on the best terms with him."

The man's eyes narrowed. "That's an understatement. Son of a bitch cheated us out of a quarter million bucks. Too bad you didn't let that mountain lion get him."

Even though the lion report never made the news, word still spread fast in the small community.

The dogs wagged their tails and pulled forward on their leashes toward Tawny. Dogs always liked her, which didn't hurt her credibility with their owners. She squatted to pet them. They planted front paws on her thighs as she rubbed their ears. "Cute puppies. Cairn terriers?"

The woman beamed and nodded. Clearly, these were her babies.

Black noses snuffled her leggings, hot on the scent of Moe's cats. Tawny asked, "Do you mind telling me what it was that Moe did?"

Quentin snorted. "Not just us. Half the neighborhood. Him and his blowhard bragging about being King Midas. Arrogant jerk named his company Midas because he claimed everything he touches turns to gold. The truth is, everything he touches turns to shit."

The wife nudged him. "Quentin, your mouth."

The man whipped his head sideways. "No point mincing words, Antoinette. He's a thief."

Tawny straightened, feet gone numb, and remembered a computer file named *Midas* from her search. "What happened?"

"Goes back about three years," Quentin said. "He was president of the homeowners association then. Telling everybody what a hotshot financier he was, how he invested in these funds hardly anyone knew about but yielded fantastic returns. After the crash in oh-eight, our retirement accounts took a big hit. We were looking for something to recoup those losses. Several of us took Moe up on his deal. Not big amounts at first, ten, twenty grand. And the early returns were as good as he promised. Pretty soon, more neighbors wanted to get in on it. And we put in bigger amounts. Great dividends." He frowned at the cloud-shrouded mountains in the distance.

Antoinette's blue eyes grew misty. "We promised our twin granddaughters we'd help them pay for medical school. They're honor students, brilliant girls. We invested their entire education fund with Moe."

Quentin went on: "The dividends stopped. When we tried to get our original investments back, he had a thousand excuses, all of which boiled down to, our money was gone."

Antoinette's lower lip trembled. "And that meant we couldn't keep our promise to our granddaughters."

Oh, Moe, what have you done? Sounded suspiciously like the sort of scam Renata Schiefmann had warned against. "I noticed people at the meeting kept their distance from him."

Quentin snorted. "He's lucky somebody didn't take a nine iron to that big swelled head of his. Not only did he lose all our money, we caught him dipping into the homeowner's association treasury. We bounced him out on his ass as president. He's steered pretty clear of neighbors since then. We were all surprised he showed up at that meeting, especially since the subject was scams. He's already a damn expert in them."

My great idea to go, Tawny remembered. "Did you report him?"

Antoinette shook her head. "Some people wanted to turn him into the police. But he's been our neighbor for twenty years, he was Quentin's golf partner, our close friend. You don't want to believe a friend would treat you so badly." She held up a mittened hand in a helpless gesture. "Maybe we should have."

Tawny didn't know what to say. If Moe was mishandling his own money, that was one problem. Mishandling other people's money sounded criminal. What would Tillman think of his father's hijinks?

"How much did people lose?" she asked.

Antoinette said, "More than any of us can afford to. We need to sell our home. Several of our friends already had to move."

Tawny recalled seeing foreclosure and short sale signs scattered through the resort.

Quentin added, "We talked to an attorney but he said going to court might cost more than we lost. And there was no guarantee we'd win either. Or that we could collect if we did."

Tawny wanted to console them with the news that Moe's house was in foreclosure, too. But she kept her mouth shut.

Their little dogs had lost interest in sniffing. Now impatient, they pulled on their leashes. "We better go," Antoinette said.

Tawny stooped to give the dogs a goodbye pet. "Thank you for talking with me. I'm sorry you've had this problem."

"Not as sorry as we are," Quentin said. "We never thought we'd be pushing eighty and worried about keeping a roof over our heads."

Tawny stood at her Jeep, watching the couple continue down the street, the terriers' bootied paws scrabbling on the ice. No wonder Quentin had confronted Moe at the lunch. By persuading him to go, Tawny had unwittingly tossed gasoline on a fire she didn't know was smoldering beneath the surface of the golf community.

Where had the money gone? So far, she hadn't found evidence of lavish purchases or gambling losses. Hundreds of thousands in money orders left no trail. Had he stashed it in foreign accounts?

But if he still had money, why didn't he pay his mortgage or credit card?

She wondered if the con man had himself been conned.

A chill wind goaded her into her car. She drove to the Lucky Dragon, craving a hot bowl of won ton soup. While she waited, she noticed Mama Rose had replaced the vase Moe had broken. Plastic this time. The memory of Wilbur sweeping up the shattered glass gave her a twinge.

Moe and Wilbur must have crossed paths again late that dark night on the highway. Another wave of guilt swept over her for not helping the injured man but she didn't know he was wandering in the dark.

For all Moe's scratchy edges, Tawny did feel affection for him, as Tillman had pointed out that morning to her embarrassment.

Now she wondered if Moe was a con man and a heartless killer who'd left his victim alone to die in pain. Or was *he* the victim of his own dementia? The more she pondered, the more confusion swamped her.

Tillman had never explained his estrangement from his father. Did he have good reasons for hatred, perhaps related to what she'd uncovered?

Maybe her judgments had been too soft on Moe and too harsh on Tillman.

The kitchen door swung open and Jim's mother came out, carrying a steaming bowl which she placed in front of Tawny. Portions were always generous but today there appeared to be extra shrimp and slices of barbecued pork.

"Thank you, Mama Rose. This smells delicious."

The sparrow-like woman bobbed her head and sat across from Tawny. "Good for cold day. Sell lots of soup in winter. Warm up the soul."

"It sure does." Tawny dipped a porcelain spoon into the broth. "Mmm. Wonderful."

"Where Emma? Jim say she work with you. New job."

"She's helping me out with a project." Except Emma had been a no-show after her first day. Tawny wondered if her daughter had even talked to Jim since her recent fascination with Cassandra's son. A knot formed in her stomach. Emma had let her down but that disappointment didn't bother Tawny as much as the possibility that Jim's heart might be broken again.

Mama Rose leaned forward. "She come back to work here anytime, OK? Now we short-hand because Wilbur gone."

"I'm so sorry for your loss." If Mama Rose knew Tawny was working for the man under arrest for killing Wilbur, she wondered if she'd still be welcome in the restaurant.

Mama Rose picked up the salt and pepper shakers and wiped them carefully with a damp rag. "Wilbur good boy. Take lot of time to train him but once he learn, he never forget. Keep restroom clean. Mop up after drunks. Wash dishes." She polished the bottle of soy sauce and squared up the condiments in a perfect triangle on the table.

"He seemed like a hard worker," Tawny said. "A lot of businesses wouldn't hire a person who's slow."

She nodded vigorously. "Wilbur have other jobs before. People not pay him fair because he don't complain. That wrong. My brother and me, pay fair. Wilbur worth it, very steady, always show up on time."

Tawny silently added *unlike Emma*. Fortunately Mama Rose was too polite to say that.

The woman brushed brimming eyes with the back of her hand. "Sometimes, though, Wilbur not think. Why he go out on bicycle on bad cold night? Not good. My brother say, 'Wait for me, Wilbur, I give you ride home.' But first he have to count receipts, set up for next day, turn on alarm. By the time he done, Wilbur gone, bicycle gone." Her voice shuddered. "So bad."

"Where did he live?"

"He stay in trailer on Whitefish Stage Road. Way dark out there. Too dangerous ride bicycle in winter but Wilbur got no driver's license. He should have wait for my brother. But Wilbur not have patience." She sniffled as she rearranged silk flowers in the vase.

"Did he have lights on his bike?" Tawny asked.

Mama Rose shrugged. "He wear vest that glow in dark. He think that is bullet-proof vest, keep him safe. Poor Wilbur."

Tawny's cell rang. Tillman. To Mama Rose, she said, "Excuse me, this is my boss."

The little woman nodded and moved away, straightening chairs, bussing tables.

"Hi, Tillman."

"Where are you?"

"At the Lucky Dragon in Columbia Falls. Where Wilbur worked."

"What'd you find out?"

"I can't talk here. Tell you when I see you. How's your dad?"

"Still in custody. Damn judge refused to OR him. Arraignment's tomorrow."

That must have been a blow to Tillman's ego. He prided himself on always getting his clients released on their own recognizance, no matter the charge. She dropped her voice low: "I learned a little about the finance stuff. I think Moe might have been swindling investors but then someone turned the tables and swindled him. As soon as I finish lunch, I'm going back to his house and dig more."

"Meet you there."

Good, she thought as she disconnected. Let Tillman sift through Moe's computer. About time he took over his father's problems that he'd shoved onto her.

The front door swung open and Cassandra swept in, elegant as ever in a fur-trimmed leather coat. For someone obsessed with pet rescue, she didn't mind wearing animal skins. Today her eyes were back to the startling blue again. In the nearly-empty restaurant, she immediately spotted Tawny and hurried to her table.

"Where's Moshe?"

Tawny lifted one finger and took an extra-long time chewing a slice of pork to think of a non-committal response. "You haven't talked to him?"

Cassandra's chipmunk cheeks flushed rosy. "I've left messages. I went to his house. While I was driving by just now, I saw your car here. I'm getting frantic."

Tawny twirled the tail of her braid. Tell the truth. "Actually, I haven't spoken to him today."

Cassandra sat down across from Tawny. "This isn't like him. We talk every day, even if we don't see each other."

Under the woman's penetrating blue stare, Tawny lowered her gaze to her soup, knowing she couldn't hide the truth for long if Cassandra kept pushing. Tawny was lousy at deception. "Actually, his son is in town. They might be together."

Cassandra snorted. "His son? Moshe hates him. I can't imagine them getting together unless someone locked them in the same room."

Tawny swallowed. Cassandra didn't know how close to accurate she was.

Maybe Moe's girlfriend knew more details about the estrangement. "Do you know why they don't get along?"

Cassandra pulled off gloves and fluffed her platinum hair. "Because the son's a spoiled, ungrateful brat. Moshe paid for the best private schools, summers abroad, Oxford education, Stanford Law School. Does he say thank you? Does he treat his father with respect? Hell, no!"

"Have you ever met his son?"

"Just seen him grandstanding on TV." Cassandra abruptly stopped and stared hard at Tawny, her blue eyes showing a click of connection. "Now I know why you looked familiar. I saw you on TV. Moshe's son was your lawyer. He got you off. Murder charge, right?"

Tawny nodded as a spasm clenched her gut. Every time she hoped the notoriety might die down, someone else remembered.

Thankfully her phone rang. Tillman again. "Excuse me, I need to take this call."

Distress clouded Cassandra's face. "If you see Moshe, please tell him how worried I am." She left the restaurant.

With a sigh of relief, Tawny answered. "Hi, Tillman."

"You still at lunch?"

"Yes. Moe's girlfriend just stopped by, looking for him. Moe didn't want her to know where he was."

Tillman huffed. "That ain't going to last much longer. It'll hit the news tonight."

"Why'd you call?"

"General Tso chicken, broccoli beef, egg rolls, steamed rice. Bring it to the old man's place."

Tawny bit her lip. "Didn't your mother ever teach you the word *please*?"

The call disconnected but she thought he'd probably heard.

Cassandra had a valid point about his attitude.

~~~

Tillman already waited beside a rental Escalade SUV in Moe's driveway when Tawny arrived. Swinging his briefcase, he approached as she got out of her Jeep. "Where's my food?"

She fisted hands on her hips. "My children had better manners at age three than you do. Were you raised by wolves?"

He rolled his eyes. "Puh-leeze." Sounded like chocolate syrup poured over ground glass.

She grabbed the paper bag on the passenger seat and handed it to him. He thrust his briefcase at her, then unrolled the top of the sack and reached in, opening waxed cartons.

"If you can wait five seconds," she said, "I'll unlock the door and you can sit at a table to eat."

Another annoyed look. The man had elevated impatience to an art.

Inside Moe's condo, the cats scattered except for Rambo the Siamese. He took one look at Tillman and raced toward him.

"Watch out!" Tawny yelled, holding the briefcase like a shield. "That's the one that attacked me."

But to her astonishment, the Siamese not only didn't attack, he rubbed against the lawyer's legs while Tillman strode to the dining table. She followed, keeping a safe distance.

He stared down at her. "This is the killer attack cat that cost me a three-hundred dollar medical deductible?"

Tawny wagged her head. "I can't believe it. He's never been friendly before, except to your dad." Then it dawned on her. "Rambo must recognize you because you're so much like Moe."

"Well, that's insulting." He pulled cartons from the bag, then a pair of chopsticks and wolfed down a couple of bites of General Tso chicken. "Not bad. You say this restaurant is where the dead guy worked?"

The savory aromas tempted Tawny. The soup had tasted good but didn't last. She set his briefcase on the table. When he opened the container of egg rolls, she plucked one out then settled beside him. Rambo hopped on a chair on Tillman's other side, front paws on the edge of the table, sniffing the food.

Tawny nibbled the crunchy egg roll. "His employer started to cry when she talked about him. He was like a mascot for the sheriff's department. Even the deputy who questioned me choked up."

"Yeah, the old man couldn't have picked a victim more apt to tug at the jury's heartstrings. Going to be damn tough to cut any deals."

"He did it then, for sure?"

Tillman looked down his nose. "You know better than to say something that stupid when you're working for me."

Tawny held up her hands. "Never mind." She couldn't get used to the slippery legal definitions of guilt and innocence that were the lawyer's stock-in-trade.

Tillman picked out a morsel of beef and handed it to the Siamese, then shoveled in a mouthful of broccoli. "But, yeah, he did it. Evidence is solid. Blood on the undercarriage is the victim's. Glass from the headlight matches the shards found in the victim. Apparently he hit the guy and the bike went flying, left paint scratches, which also match up perfectly. Looks like the car dragged him about fifty feet. Moe must have swerved into a fence, scraped the guy off the undercarriage. They found strips of his clothing caught on barbed wire. A metal fence post punched through the radiator. He got the car back on the road then kept driving as the coolant ran out. Left a nice trail of antifreeze for the cops to follow. The engine finally quit and he limped into that driveway where you found him."

During Tillman's cold, clinical recitation, Tawny's stomach flip-flopped. The eggroll changed to tasteless grit in her mouth. She went to the kitchen and dropped the uneaten portion down the garbage disposal, then leaned her arms on the cold granite countertop. Anguish tightened her throat. She couldn't imagine the shock, fear, and excruciating pain Wilbur must have suffered.

Tillman glanced up from his food. "Squeamish?"

She shook her head. His expression showed he didn't believe her. Hell, she didn't believe herself. "The deputy said he walked through a pasture to the nearest house. Tillman, it was three degrees that night. And to think I was worried about hypothermia with Moe." She thumped the counter with her fist. "I should have let him freeze to death."

"Didn't I already say that?"

His sharp retort brought her to her senses. "I didn't mean it."

"Yeah?" he sneered. "Well, I did."

"Why do you hate your father so much?"

"None of your business." Not angry, not resentful, just a statement of fact.

"You're right. It isn't." She heaved a sigh. "I feel bad because I care about both of you and now I'm wondering if I was stupid to care about Moe."

"You can't help yourself. You've got a soft heart and you want to think the best of people. That gets you in trouble every time."

Annoyed that Tillman had nailed her so accurately, she moved past the table to the great room, and stared out the high windows at the snowy golf course. Yes, she trusted too easily. Yet she couldn't be like the cynical lawyer, stuffing eggrolls in his mouth while he callously described a man's agony.

"OK, where's his computer?" Still chewing, Tillman stood, glancing around the condo.

She realized he'd never before been in the home where his father had lived for twenty years. That struck her as sad as she led him to the office.

Tillman sat in front of the monitor and tapped keys with long fingers. Thank goodness he took the lead and didn't expect her to fumble around. She felt nervous enough on an unfamiliar computer, without a short-fused boss staring over her shoulder.

"This morning," she said, "I talked with some neighbors. They claim Moe cheated a number of people in the community with what sounded like a Ponzi scheme. If that's true, he conned *them*, but then maybe another scammer conned *him*. That could be why he doesn't have any money to pay his mortgage or credit card bills."

Tillman didn't bother to look up from typing. "That's quite a leap of logic."

In other words, he thought she was full of crap. Oh well.

She squinted at the screen. "The neighbors said his company was named Midas." She pointed to a directory. "There."

Tillman clicked. A new window opened but required a password.

Tawny found the paper from Moe's wallet and handed it to him. "Maybe it's on here."

He tapped various sequences that didn't work. He thrust the paper back at Tawny. "Read these off to me."

She gulped, adjusted her glasses, and studied the printing. Damn him. Between his impatience and her dyslexia, her jaw ached as she ground her teeth. She focused on the first line, struggling to concentrate.

Tillman snapped his fingers. "Come on, I don't plan to spend the rest of my life here."

Hot with embarrassment, she slowly recited a short sequence of letters.

"That's not what I saw," he snarled. "You transposed the

order." But when he typed the last letter, the window opened. "What the hell?" His eyes widened. "He wrote the password backwards. You're brilliant!"

She wanted to cry. Dyslexia, so long her shame, had for once turned into an accidental success.

Tillman plowed forward, scrolling through page after page of figures, names, and dates, scanning faster than she could blink. "Get my briefcase."

Glad to escape, she hurried out of the office. Rambo now stood on the dining table, head deep in the broccoli beef carton. When she approached, he hissed and spat. She raised her hands. "Easy now. I don't want your food, just the briefcase." She sidled closer, muscles tensing to jump back if he lunged. Slowly she reached for the leather portfolio. A growl rumbled deep in his chest but he allowed her to pick it up.

When she returned to the office, Tillman was still intently studying the screen. "There's a new package of thumb drives in my briefcase. Get me one."

She fumbled through several pockets until she found them, and set one beside his scampering hands. After several minutes of watching the incomprehensible, she left to resume her own search of paper records.

Rambo sat on the back of the couch, licking his paw and dragging it across his face. He paid no attention when she cleared away the remnants of lunch. She dropped all the cartons in the trash, since she didn't know which ones he'd eaten from, then wiped off the table.

Sugar and several other cats emerged from hiding and settled in napping perches.

Tawny retrieved the shoebox full of money order receipts from the bathroom and set it on the table, starting a pile for Tillman to review. Next, she tackled the cartons she'd carried from the office earlier. A jumbled nightmare of records dated back more than twenty years. Based on what the neighbors had said, she decided to focus only on material three years old or less. She stacked older files out of the way. Scattered in several boxes, she found tax returns, which she placed on Tillman's pile.

One carton contained old mementoes, a high school graduation photo of Tillman in 1985, his curls in an Afro the size of a beach ball, but the same piercing nearly-black eyes. Yellow news clippings told the story of his impressive academic accomplishments, his admission to the Montana bar, cases he'd won. Over the years, his hair got shorter and his face got longer, the jutting chin more prominent.

A 1995 wedding photo from the Billings newspaper showed his stunning young bride Rochelle with billowing dark hair, wearing a gown with lace covering one shoulder, the other bare. The bride's parents were named but only Tillman's mother was mentioned, not Moe.

Formal birth announcements of Tillman's three children were paper-clipped together but not a single photo of them, maybe because he'd never sent any.

For all Moe's professed hatred, he'd carefully followed his son's life from a distance.

In the same box, she found a 1996 obituary for Tillman's mother, dead at fifty-four, no mention of her marriage to Moe. Between her young age and no cause of death given, Tawny wondered if it had been suicide.

A sad, broken family.

When she checked on Tillman two hours later, he still sat in front of the monitor, Rambo sprawled across his lap.

"You two seem to have hit it off," she said.

Tillman didn't interrupt his work. "Find anything?"

"I set aside the money order receipts and tax returns but not much else. A couple of days ago, I found a prospectus and financial reports but didn't have a chance to look at them. Now they're gone."

He looked up. "What happened to them?"

She shrugged. "Moe might have realized I was snooping and hid them. I've dug around pretty thoroughly and I can't find them."

"What about upstairs?"

Tawny realized she'd never been on the second floor. "Do you want me to look there?"

He concentrated on the monitor. "Of course."

Again, the guilty twinge pinched her. She had known the feeling of having her bedroom searched and violated.

"Well?" Tillman glared at her. "Anytime this week will be fine."

Her temper sparked but he called the shots and it was *his* father in trouble. She spun and left the office, gritting her teeth. *He pays more than any other job I could get.* Although poverty was starting to look better all the time. If only electrical work didn't cost so much.

She paused to pet four cats staggered on ascending stairs, paws stretching through the bannister. "You guys going to let me ransack your dad's bedroom?"

No one protested, so she limped up to the second floor landing where she found a closed door. It opened into a bedroom as murky and dark as Moe's office. She flicked on a switch and the room glowed fiery from an antler chandelier like the ones downstairs, only this one had red light bulbs. A king-size bed with rumpled red satin sheets sat on an elevated platform. Fur-lined wrist and ankle restraints were strapped to the four brass bed posts. A red velvet swing hung from a heavy log ceiling beam. Red brocade drapes covered the windows, blocking all daylight.

Somehow three black cats had gotten into the closed room

and now reclined on the rafters, green eyes watching her.

Tawny had never been in a brothel but she imagined this bedroom approximated one. She wanted to back out and shut the door. Snooping in Moe's bedroom veered into creepy voyeurism. She didn't ever want to know what he did in private.

Unlike the downstairs, this room was almost pristine—tidy, dusted, and orderly. Cassandra's influence?

In the walk-in closet, Tawny found clothes and shoes but nothing that appeared to be money-related. In the bathroom, candles rimmed a Jacuzzi tub. The overpowering scent of musk and vanilla made her queasy. A quick look through cupboards and drawers didn't reveal any financial records.

She started to leave but Tillman's tall, lanky form filled the doorway.

Damn. She'd hoped to close off the room before he saw it. Moe might be a little kinky but that was *his* business, not his son's.

Tillman's gaze swept quickly around. "Well, he's still a horny old lech."

Tawny tried to ease him backwards onto the landing but he brushed past her.

"There's nothing here," she protested, knowing he wouldn't be deterred.

He opened several dresser drawers and pulled out a red pushup bra, which he mockingly held up to his chest, striking a pose. "Bet he looks adorable in this." He reached into the drawer again and whipped out a vibrator, holding it like a microphone under his mouth. His baritone voice belted out, "Oh-oh-oh, I'm on fire."

Not half as on fire as Tawny's face felt. "Knock it off, Tillman. This stuff isn't what we're looking for. It's intruding on his privacy." *And it's embarrassing as hell in front of my boss.*

The lawyer's long face grimaced. "Aw, get the broomstick out of your butt, Tawny." He tossed the bra and vibrator back in the drawers and strode into the bathroom. There, he yanked open the medicine cabinet. Prescription bottles tumbled into the sink with a plastic clatter. He picked up one after another, reading labels. Next he pawed in the vanity drawers, pulling out massage gels, personal lubricants, and more sex toys, strewing them across the counter.

Didn't this man have any sense of shame? She wasn't sure whether she was more outraged or mortified by her boss's behavior. Either way, she'd had enough.

"I'm leaving." She ran down the stairs, scattering the cats, and grabbed her bag and fleece coat, then remembered her promise to Moe to feed the cats. She hurried through the chore and raced out to her Jeep.

She couldn't prevent Tillman from being an asshole, but she didn't have to watch.

CHAPTER 14 – KING MIDAS

Tawny's doorbell rang at six that evening. The towering lawyer stood on her covered porch holding a cardboard carton topped with a bouquet of red roses in protective wrapping. He thrust the roses at her then angled past her into the living room.

"What's this?" Despite her irritation with him, the blooms smelled wonderful, a promise of spring in the dark gloom of winter.

He set the box on the coffee table then peered down at her. "You're amazing."

The intensity of his dark gaze made her back toward the kitchen. She laid the bouquet on the counter and retrieved her grandmother's crystal vase from a high shelf. "Oh, really? Last I heard, I was a Goody-Two-Shoes Girl Scout with a broomstick up my ass."

"Midas Investments, LLC." Tillman pulled off his suit coat, threw it over Dwight's recliner, and knuckled his tie loose. "Got any more scotch?"

Damn him. He brought roses to apologize and now he planned to settle in for a drink or six. But he'd piqued her curiosity. "Cupboard over the fridge." She filled the vase with water and arranged the velvety blooms, inhaling their sweetness. "What about Midas Investments, LLC?"

Tillman easily reached above the refrigerator for the bottle and poured himself a drink. He grabbed a fistful of ice cubes from the freezer and dropped them in the glass. "Those money order receipts you found. The old man's been sucking funds out of investment accounts—both his own and from the trust accounts of clients—and buying money orders."

"Why money orders?"

"Difficult to follow. Good method to make money

disappear."

"Then how can you figure out where it went?"

"Receipts can be traced but it takes time and more forensic digging. But, like you thought, it looks as if he scammed investors, then turned around and got scammed himself. You cracked it."

Strange satisfaction overcame Tawny's annoyance and welled in her chest. She'd figured out what the brilliant lawyer now appeared to confirm.

In the living room, Tillman pulled plastic prescription bottles one by one from the box. "I need a medical expert to check these medicines. Side effects. Drug interactions. Maybe something chemical is causing him to act squirrely."

After setting the vase on the dining table, Tawny curled sideways on the couch, hugging her knees. "I described his behavior to my friend, Dr. Belmonte. She sees a lot of older men at the VA clinic. She thinks he may have dementia."

"She ever testified in court?"

Tawny drew back. "I don't know."

He flopped down on the opposite end of the couch, long legs splayed, and sipped scotch. "I may tap her as a medical expert."

Good luck with that, Tawny thought. Virgie alternated between telling Tawny how cute he was and hating his guts, mostly the latter.

Tillman slumped and let his head loll back, gazing at the ceiling. "The bad news is: we don't have any blood tests for that night but the good news is: neither does the county attorney. If the old man was impaired because of prescribed medication..."

"Does he remember anything about hitting Wilbur?"

Tillman rolled his head sideways to face her. "He hasn't said three words to me. Everything I learned came from the deputies' reports."

She thought she caught a brief glimmer of hurt in his dark eyes. "How can you defend him if he won't talk to you?"

"That's the problem." Back up at the ceiling. "But he trusts *you*. You're the only one he'll talk to. I've got to get him out on bail so you can pump him."

Great. Her responsibility for Moe kept growing heavier. She took a tentative step on dangerous ground. "Maybe he's picking up on your hatred. Pretty hard to confide in someone who can't stand you."

He closed his eyes for a long moment and exhaled loudly. "So did you always want to be Dr. Phil when you grew up?"

No point debating him. Change tactics. "He's kept a lot of mementoes about you. Like your graduation photo."

Tillman ran fingers through his tight black curls. "Yeah, that one's priceless. Back then, I was damn proud of my Jew-fro. My kids laughed their asses off when they saw the picture. Judah shaved his head and swears he'll never let his hair grow more than a quarter of an inch."

Tawny smiled. His son, Judah, was a shy, sensitive, pudgy tween with thick glasses, as unlike his father and grandfather as imaginable. No wonder she'd instantly liked the boy when she met him. "How's Judah doing?"

Tillman shrugged one shoulder. "Who knows at that age? Damn kid's smart enough but he's only getting Bs in school."

She sighed. "If Bs aren't good enough, I'm glad you weren't *my* dad. I was lucky to get Ds."

He shot her another sideways look. "He won't talk to me either. Nobody in my family talks, except to yell at each other."

"Yeah, I noticed that." Her only visit to the lawyer's estate in Billings had been an uneasy walk through a minefield of fresh divorce wounds and resentful shared custody of their three children. Tillman lived in one wing of the sprawling home, while his ex, Rochelle, lived in the other, the kids stuck in between. It was the weirdest arrangement Tawny had ever seen. The family situation no doubt accounted for at least some of his surliness.

He slugged down his drink and went to the kitchen, returning with a half-full glass. "Bottle's empty." He sat on the couch.

Thank goodness, she thought. She didn't want him passing out and spending the night again.

He finished the scotch and set the glass on the coffee table. "Let's see that foot I've invested so much money in."

Tawny had to puzzle out his sudden twist. "You mean, where the Siamese attacked me?"

He nodded.

She peeled her sock off. Scratches and bite punctures still hurt and showed vivid red on her pale skin but antibiotics had reduced the swelling.

"Jesus," he muttered. He carefully took her bare foot in his hands and lowered it to his lap. Long fingers felt cool from holding the icy glass but the gentleness of his touch surprised her. He turned her ankle back and forth, studying the green, purple, and magenta bruises surrounding the wounds and scabs. "Ugly. The Siamese did all that?"

"Yeah, same cat that was hanging on you today like a two-dollar hooker."

When he faced her again, his normally angry eyes softened. "You're something. You tangled with a mountain lion and came out without a nick. But this..."

The moment hung suspended, her naked foot cradled in his hands, his guard down, finally appreciating the difficult challenge he'd foisted on her. She wondered what he'd started to say before his voice trailed off.

His thumb slid the length of the deepest, most feverish scratch with a soothing, comforting touch. The fearsome, aggressive, take-no-prisoners attorney disappeared briefly to reveal a human being she'd never seen before.

A strange, intimate sensuality hovered between them for several more seconds. Part of her wanted him to keep cradling her foot but the rational part made her pull from his grasp. She slipped the sock back on, afraid to meet his unsettling gaze any longer.

Then the feeling vanished when he jumped up and strode to the kitchen. "You got anything else to drink around here?"

She watched him through the archway as he opened the cupboard over the refrigerator and pulled out Dwight's favorite, Black Velvet. He read the label, wrinkled his nose in disgust but splashed some in his empty glass anyway. Even though her husband wasn't alive to drink it, the intrusion still rankled Tawny.

Tillman's crisp, business-like tone returned. "Arraignment's at nine tomorrow. Media will be there. I'll handle them. You keep an eye on the old man. Don't let him open his big mouth."

Tawny gasped. "How am I supposed to do that? Moe can't be controlled."

Tillman yanked a prescription bottle from his pants pocket. "As soon as we get him out from under the bailiff's eyes, you'll give him one of these." He rattled the pills like dice in a craps game. "Keep him mellow yellow."

She drew in a breath. "You want me to drug him?"

Anger flared in his eyes. "He won't take it from me. You're the only one he trusts. It's for his own good. Otherwise, I can't get bail set and he'll rot in jail. You want *that* on your head?"

Tawny hugged her knees again, wishing she'd never opened her door to him. No wonder his office staff referred to him as *Atillman the Hun*. "Damn you."

He stalked to her, glaring down. "You're damning the

wrong guy. The old man started all this nonsense. You and I are just trying to unripple the lake he tossed the boulder into."

She pressed her cheek against her knees, facing away from him. Tillman was infuriatingly right, as he so often was. Then why did his instruction to her feel so wrong?

She heard him gulp down Dwight's bourbon then bang the glass on the coffee table. "I'll pick you up at eight-thirty tomorrow." Harsh footfalls on the hardwood floor, then her front door opened and shut.

Maybe he'd get a DUI on the way to his hotel and she'd be spared from carrying out another of his distasteful orders.

CHAPTER 15 – DÉJÀ VU ALL OVER AGAIN

Tawny waited with the same attorney at the same defense table in the same courtroom where she herself had been arraigned nine months before. A bottle of water chilled her already-cold, twitchy fingers. She sat in the far left chair, Tillman in the far right, while the middle chair was empty, waiting for Moe.

The lawyer wore an impeccably-tailored navy suit and sky-blue tie. He focused on his tablet, flicking and tapping the screen.

Tawny turned to scan the wooden church-pew benches in the gallery. She recognized reporters from local TV stations and newspapers, along with a handful of curious onlookers. Were any of them Wilbur's relatives?

The door from the lobby swung open and Tawny's teeth clenched. Jim, Mama Rose, and her brother Lee entered. Wilbur's work family. They seated themselves on the opposite side of the courtroom in the first row behind the county attorney's table. She'd been dreading the moment when they would learn she was helping the man who'd killed their employee. And, now, here it was.

Hot blood climbed her neck and burned her cheeks. She forced a small smile to them. Jim nodded but Rose and Lee only stared back at her, eyes flat and blank.

Tawny hoped Emma had warned Jim beforehand but her daughter had been scarce the past couple of days, either not coming home at all, or slipping in after Tawny went to sleep. She didn't answer texts, a *leave-me-alone* signal.

A door between the judge's bench and the jury box opened. A bailiff led tall, stoop-shouldered Moe, wearing an orange jail jumpsuit, into the courtroom. When they reached the defense table, the bailiff removed the handcuffs and turned away.

Without a word, Tillman directed Moe to the vacant chair between himself and Tawny then went back to working on his tablet.

Moe's narrow, unshaven face was gaunt, eyes sunken. He didn't respond when Tawny squeezed his hand, as cold as her own. She held on anyway, overwhelmed with a sense of déjà vu from her own court appearance. She'd been in his seat, faced what he now faced. She leaned into his ear. "We're going to help you, OK?"

His breath smelled sickly, worse than merely the lack of a toothbrush for a few days. A crust of dried drool caked the corner of his mouth. "Are my cats all right?"

She peered into his bleary eyes. The whites were tinged yellow and road-mapped with blood vessels. "They're good. Eating like little piggies."

As Tillman had previously instructed, Tawny pressed a pill into Moe's hand. "Take this," she whispered in his ear. She added a silent prayer, *Please.*

He blinked at the pill and said loudly, "What is it?"

"Shhh." She checked to see if the bailiff had noticed but thankfully he was talking with the clerk. She set the bottle of water before Moe and muttered, "Your medicine." She hated to lie but, as Tillman had said, it was for his own good. "It'll make you feel better."

She wanted to reassure him that they'd rescue him but she couldn't bring herself to offer up that whopper. If he was as guilty as it appeared, he should pay the penalty, yet memories of her own arraignment overwhelmed her with empathy for him.

The judge entered, a woman from out of town, filling in during the sick leave of the regular judge. She was fortyish, with sharp serious eyes that missed nothing, deep grooves around her mouth, and red reading glasses sliding down her nose.

"Good morning, everyone," she said. Then her gaze rested on Tillman. "Mr. Rosenbaum, I didn't expect to run into you clear across the state."

He rose and gave a courtly bow. As always, his startling height and courtroom presence amazed Tawny. "Good morning, Your Honor. Montana is a small town, isn't it? A fortuitous accident that once again allows me the pleasure of appearing before you."

Moe chose that instant to make an obvious show of popping the pill in his mouth. He slugged down a swig from the water bottle.

The brackets around the judge's mouth deepened. She stared hard at Tillman. "Mr. Rosenbaum, I sincerely hope you did not just allow your client to ingest an illicit substance, in my courtroom, in front of my face."

"Of course not, Your Honor. My client—"

The judge cut him off with a *stop* gesture. "Counsel, my chambers, now."

Tillman shot a lightning bolt glare over his shoulder at Tawny, as he and the county attorney trailed the judge out of the courtroom.

Crap. The only thing worse than drugging Moe was getting caught. She should have refused. Now he'd fire her, for sure.

"What the hell's going on?" Moe grumbled in her ear.

"I don't know," she answered.

"He's supposed to get me out of here."

Tawny said nothing as a knot formed in her sour stomach. It tightened as moments of waiting stretched long. Would she and Tillman wind up in jail beside Moe?

After five tense minutes, the judge and attorneys finally returned. Tillman didn't look at Tawny as he took his seat. Which was worse—his previous ferocious glare or this refusal now to make eye contact?

"Let's proceed," the judge said.

The charges against Moshe Baruch Rosenbaum were vehicular homicide, leaving the scene of an accident, failure to report a bodily injury accident, and failure to render aid.

"How do you plead?" the judge asked.

"Not guilty," Tillman answered immediately. "Further, Your Honor, I move the charge of vehicular homicide be dropped for lack of evidence—no blood alcohol test, no Breathalyzer."

"Nice try, Mr. Rosenbaum," the judge said, "but I find there is sufficient evidence to warrant the charge. Due to the serious nature, I am temporarily suspending the defendant's driver's license. Now as to bail?"

The county attorney said, "Because of the victim's death, we are requesting bail of a hundred thousand dollars."

Tillman spoke up, "Your Honor, my client has no prior criminal record, has lived in Flathead County for more than twenty years and owns property here, so there is no risk of flight. Further, he is elderly and in poor health, therefore no danger to the community. And lastly, Your Honor, since he is my father, I take full responsibility for his appearance in your court. I ask you to release him on his own recognizance."

The judge's gaze flicked among the players, coming to rest on Moe. "I understand, Mr. Rosenbaum, but the charge *is* very serious. Bail is set at fifty thousand."

During the exchange, Tawny noticed Moe gradually sank in his chair, eyelids drooping. She pinched his hand to wake him. He turned to her with a dopey smile. *What the hell did I give him?*

For the next ten minutes, Tillman hammered out scheduling details with the county attorney, judge, and clerk for upcoming hearing dates.

Moe's head lolled several times. Under the table, Tawny sunk her fingernails into his palm. His head jerked upright. She had to keep him conscious.

The judge frowned. "Mr. Rosenbaum, is your client all right?"

Tillman leapt to his feet. "Your Honor, this experience has been extremely stressful on him. Once he gets home and has a good night's sleep, he'll be much better."

She stared over the top of her red glasses. "I certainly hope so."

~~~

Moe snored in the back of the rental Escalade despite the radio blaring Springsteen's "Murder Incorporated" at skull-splitting volume. Tillman steered through the traffic circle around the old courthouse building.

Tawny punched down the radio volume. "Am I fired?"

He snorted. "I'm an asshole but I wouldn't hold you responsible for doing what I told you to do."

The knot in her stomach eased. She felt as if she'd run a red light and narrowly missed being T-boned. "Are you in trouble with the judge?"

"Hell, no," he scoffed. He reached in his pocket for a prescription bottle and offered it to her.

She put on her glasses and read the label, *Lisinopril 40 mg.* "That's blood pressure medicine."

"Right. Which my beloved father desperately needs for his heart condition and that he was deprived of taking while in jail. As his devoted, concerned son, I felt compelled to ensure he took his prescribed medication at the earliest possible opportunity." A sardonic smirk pulled at his mouth. "Because *if* the poor sickly man were to have another heart attack while in custody, Flathead County would be responsible for his medical bills. Our esteemed judge would not want to risk that liability."

Her boss was slick. Tawny turned to check Moe, mouth hanging open, dead to the world. "Now I suppose you're going to tell me drowsiness is a side effect of Lisinopril."

"Absolutely."

"I never noticed that side effect before."

"Funny, isn't it?"

She faced him. "What did you really give him?"

He braked for a red light then turned onto a side street. "The less you know, the less likely you are to get in trouble. I'm trying to protect you."

She pondered for a moment. "Yeah, right. Also, if I don't know, I can't testify against you."

For an instant, she thought she'd offended him. Then a broad grin. "You're learning. Getting smarter just by hanging around me."

She made a face at him. "I'm turning as cynical and disillusioned as you are."

"Tawny, you'll *never* touch me in cynicism."

"I hope not."

He rounded another corner and pulled up in front of her house. "Get your car and follow us."

She opened the door and shook her head. "I need some time off."

"How am I supposed to handle him if you're not around? He only trusts you."

"You keep saying that but I've been with him for days now. Surely you can take care of him for a couple of hours." She got out. "He's *your* father."

"Don't remind me."

She shut the car door, climbed the porch steps, and picked up the morning paper. The Escalade still idled at the curb. She suspected Tillman wasn't chivalrously waiting to make sure she got inside but rather hoping that she'd change her mind. With a wave, she went in the house and locked the door behind her. She dropped the newspaper on the coffee table, slipped off her boots, and collapsed on the couch, feet up.

The nerve-wracking court appearance, the abrasive personalities of father and son, and the blaring radio had made her head throb. She closed her eyes but knew sleep wouldn't come, no matter how weary she felt.

After the hearing, she'd looked for Jim and his family but they'd ducked out. She worried about their anger and hoped it didn't spill over onto Emma and Jim. She'd hate for that wedge to drive the couple apart. Mama Rose was already suspicious of Emma, unfortunately with justification. Tawny didn't want to give Mama any excuse to pressure Jim into ending the relationship.

Emma's footsteps sounded in the hall. "Mom?"

"Hi, honey."

Emma's hair was gathered into a messy, bird's nest bun, and she wore a long nightshirt. One tattooed fist rubbed sleep from her eyes. "What's happening?"

Tawny sat up and patted the couch beside her. "Just finished Moe's arraignment. Tillman got him out on bail."

Emma flopped next to her, leaning against Tawny's shoulder, and yawned. "So that old creep is bopping around free, and poor Wilbur's dead."

"Moe's hardly free. The trial is still hanging over his head."

Emma rolled her eyes. "How can you stand to work for that jerk when he's trying to get a killer off?"

"That's the way the system works. Everyone, guilty or not, is entitled to a fair trial. But you're right. I'm not happy about it. You've got to understand, Moe is Tillman's father. He's standing by him." She hugged her daughter. "Just like I'd stand by you, no matter what."

The side eye told Tawny how corny she sounded.

"Jim and his family were in the courtroom," Tawny added. "Did you tell them about me helping Moe?"

Emma stretched her neck. "Haven't talked to Jim for a while."

Damn. Tawny hoped the overnights had been with him. Apparently not. "You guys were pretty tight. Did something happen?"

Emma shrugged. "Nah, just been hanging with Colin." When Tawny tensed, Emma must have felt it because she pulled away. "We already had that talk, Mom. I'm not Jim's property."

"I didn't say anything."

"You don't need to. You're *so* obvious." Emma rose and flounced to the kitchen. "Did you drink all the coffee?"

"Feel free to make more."

Emma huffed at the inconvenience but ran water in the carafe.

Tawny put on readers, picked up the newspaper and flipped through, spotting an obituary for Wilbur Makepeace. "Wilbur's funeral is today at noon. Doesn't sound like he had any relatives."

"He didn't," Emma said. "Jim's mom and uncle are paying for everything."

"Do you want to go with me?"

Emma bent to grimace in the pass-through window. "After Daddy's funeral, I swore I'd never go to another one." She rattled silverware in the drawer. "Are you going? I mean, really, Mom, isn't that too gross, with you trying to get Wilbur's killer off?"

Tawny pondered. "Seems disrespectful not to go. Do you think Jim's family would resent me being there?"

"How should I know? Remember, I don't do funerals." She carried a bowl of cereal to the dining table and sat. "Hey, can you loan me a hundred?"

Tawny's jaw tightened. Time for the showdown. "What happened to your job?"

Emma's hand flicked the air. "I thought you laid me off when you started driving again."

"You hardly got laid off, Emma." She moved from the couch to stand over her daughter. "You didn't show up."

"I've been busy." She concentrated on her cereal.

"So have I. I needed your help. But you weren't there." Tawny gritted her teeth, wondering how she'd failed so miserably to instill a work ethic in her daughter. One more try. "Mama Rose wants you back at the restaurant."

"Yeah, maybe."

That did it. "Emma, I've been really patient but I can't keep supporting you. You live here rent free, you let me down big time, and now you expect me to lend you money. Not going to happen, little girl."

Emma's eyes flashed. "So you want me out? Fine." She jumped up, sloshing milk from the bowl onto the floor. "I won't clutter up your precious space any longer."

Tawny took her arm. "This is your home. But you need to take some responsibility."

Emma yanked away. "Forget it. I'm gone." She stomped down the hall to her room and slammed the door.

Tawny raised her eyes to the ceiling. Dear God, her daughter seemed to have stepped into a time machine that regressed her back to age thirteen.

Why did strangers find Tawny so easy to talk to, but not her own child?

~~~

Despite temperatures in the low twenties, Tawny craved fresh air and exercise, especially after the blow-up with Emma. She limp-walked the eight blocks from home to the landmark brick funeral home on Main.

A number of sheriff and police vehicles parked on surrounding streets. In a handicapped zone, a group of people with special needs debarked from a van and walked together toward the entrance, reminding her of Wilbur's participation in Special Olympics.

When she entered the hushed lobby, the chapel was already full. Through the open door, she saw a blue-enamel open casket. Wilbur was dressed in a bright blue suit, pale blue shirt, and royal blue tie. Blue must been his favorite color.

Jim, Mama Rose, and Uncle Lee sat in the front row. Employees she recognized from the restaurant and casino filled the next two rows. Uniformed deputies were interspersed with teammates from Special Olympics, wearing medals and ribbons. Obie caught her eye and gave a slight nod.

Tawny signed the guestbook then stood at the rear since all seats were full, except beside Jim's family, where she didn't dare intrude. The accident had been on TV and the front page of the newspapers. She wondered if Wilbur knew how many friends wanted to bid him farewell.

The phone vibrated in her pocket. She stepped out to the lobby and found a text from Tillman: *I need you. Hurry*. Seconds later, a follow-up message: *Please!*

He really had to be desperate to add *please* to his commands.

She ducked into a restroom and called him. "What is it? I'm at Wilbur's funeral."

"At the condo, Moe woke up and went nuts. Chased me outside with a butcher knife. I'm in my car in the driveway.

You've got to get up here and talk to him."

A knife? Damn. "Tillman, you don't need me, you need a SWAT team."

"He keeps yelling for you."

"You want me to go in there when he's got a knife?"

"Hell, no! Talk to him through the door or window."

Tawny gripped the phone so tightly her hand cramped. She thought of her grandfather's unwitting violence that he not only didn't remember but denied. Moe needed to be in a facility where he couldn't hurt himself or anyone else. Why couldn't Tillman understand that?

A strange sound came through the phone. If infuriating, abrasive Tillman weren't on the other end, she would have thought it might be a sob. "Tawny, please."

Pain clutched her chest. She stared at the restroom mirror, surprised to see how close to tears she looked. Deep breaths. "I'm on my way."

~~~

Forty-five minutes later, Tawny sat in Tillman's Escalade in Moe's driveway, not believing how badly the lawyer's spiffy appearance had deteriorated from a couple of hours ago. Tie pulled loose and crooked, collar unbuttoned. Red rimmed his dark eyes. Strain lines ran deep in his cheeks, and the deep furrow between his brows looked painful. She grasped his cold hand and he squeezed back hard enough to make her flinch.

"I've faced down some bad-asses," he said, "but, Christ, my own father. I want to kill him."

The feeling seemed to be mutual. "What's the problem between you?"

"It isn't me. It's what he did to my mother."

"What?"

"She adored him, absolutely worshipped him. When she found out about his philandering, it killed her."

"Betrayal really hurts."

"No, *literally*. One day at school, I came down with the flu. Must have been about twelve, thirteen. Called my mom to pick me up. No answer. Called the old man. Told me to take a bus home, he was too fucking busy. Found out later, he was too busy fucking...with a honey. I get home and my mom's on the bathroom floor, overdose of pills. I called nine-one-one, gave her CPR. She pulled through but she was never the same.

"For over a decade, he continued to screw around and she kept trying to kill herself. In and out of psych hospitals. She finally succeeded with a razor blade in the bathtub."

The harsh coffee-tinged exhalation of his sigh brushed Tawny's face. A lump solidified in her throat. "I'm sorry." She rubbed his hand between both of hers, trying to warm his icy fingers.

What must his childhood have been like, wondering every time he came home if he'd find his mother dead?

Tawny remembered more details Moe had dropped. "What about your sister, Shoshanna?"

Tillman leaned back against the headrest. "She inherited the suicide gene from Mom. Broke up with a guy, drove off a cliff on a motorcycle but didn't finish the job. Traumatic brain injury. She's in a group home. I just hope the part of her brain that remembers our father got destroyed."

Tawny now regretted her earlier harsh judgments of her boss. Moe had provided for his family financially but he'd let them down in every other way. Tillman could have blanked his father from his life. Yet when he learned Moe was at risk of losing his home, Tillman had sent her. On some level, he did care and felt a sense of duty. But he needed her help.

"OK, let me go see if he'll talk to me."

She started to get out of the car but he grasped her shoulder. "I won't let him hurt you. I'll kill him first."

The black promise in his eyes startled her but she managed a wry smile. "Please don't. If the best lawyer in Montana is locked up, who'll defend you?"

His normal scowl returned. "Good point."

She walked up the path to the front door. Tillman followed, staying out of sight behind an arbor vitae hedge bordering the entrance.

She rang the bell and called, "Moe? It's Tawny. Can I come in?"

No answer. She tried the knob. It turned. She cracked the door open.

"Moe? Where are you? Can I talk to you?"

His deep voice echoed in the high-ceilinged room. "Get inside and close the damn door before you let the cats out."

She peered around the edge of the jamb. Moe lay stretched out on the sectional in front of the fireplace, Rambo on his chest. No knife in sight, although it could have been hidden between the cushions. She went inside and pulled the door almost closed but didn't latch it so Tillman could listen and follow her, if necessary. But Moe sounded like his plain old grumpy self now. Thank goodness.

Sugar and two other cats rubbed against her legs. Their greeting had to wait until she found the knife.

Moe stroked the big Siamese. "Place looks nice. You straightened up." His nose twitched. "Smells better, too. But you shouldn't have trashed all my take-out menus. How am I supposed to eat?"

She stepped closer, scanning the living room for the weapon. "I only threw away the ones for restaurants that had gone out of business. The rest are in a drawer." She sidled into the kitchen, not taking her eyes off him, and pulled out the sheaf of menus. "Are you hungry? Want me to order you something?"

On the far end of the granite counter lay what Dwight used to call a "pig sticker," twelve inches long from shank to sharp, shiny point.

She moved to block Moe's view of the knife, fanning the menu selections like playing cards. "What do you feel like? Mexican? Burger? Pizza?"

He scrubbed under Rambo's chin. Noisy purring roared across the room.

She gingerly slid the knife into the pocket of her parka then pulled the front flap tight to cover it.

"Kinda got a hankering for Chinese," he said.

"They're closed today."

"The hell you say. They're open seven days a week."

"Funeral."

"Oh."

The fact that the funeral honored the man Moe had killed apparently escaped his notice. Or he didn't want to acknowledge it.

She took the menus over to him then eased toward the entry. "Uh, I forgot something in the car. I'll be right back."

He sat up, disturbing Rambo, and spread the takeout selections around him on the couch. The Siamese bounded toward Tawny. She scrambled for the front door, more worried about another cat attack than the knife. She raced outside and slammed the door behind her. On the porch, she collided with Tillman.

He steadied her, grasping both arms, concern painting his expression. "You OK?"

"Fine." She pulled the knife out and handed it to him. "I don't know what other weapons he's got in there, but this takes care of one."

Tillman grinned down at her. "Nice save."

Her cheeks heated at the compliment. "He seems calmer. And he's hungry." She turned away. "I better get back inside before he figures out you're still here." She cracked the door, checking for Rambo, but he'd sauntered toward the fireplace, so she slipped in.

"You feel like a big greasy cheeseburger?" Moe asked. "Onion rings? If you order a jumbo drink, you get a free refill next time you take the cup back."

"Sounds great."

"You still got my phone?"

She'd given it to Tillman. "I'll use mine. What's the number?"

After she placed the order, she asked, "Did the cats have breakfast yet? I didn't get here this morning because of the arraignment."

"Yeah, the whole gang met us at the door, hollering and squalling."

"They missed you."

A slight sad smile touched his dour mouth. "I missed them. They're my kids. I've got to take good care of them."

She sank into a chair facing him. "What if something happens to you?" *Like you wind up in prison.*

"I've provided for their futures," Moe said. "Perfect home, plenty of food, unlimited vet care for the rest of their lives. Every last one of them."

"How?"

"Cassandra's taking care of it for me. They'll go to her sanctuary, as close to heaven as a cat can get."

Tawny wondered how much of Moe's dwindling money had gone into Cassandra's venture. "That must be expensive for nine cats."

He shrugged. "They're worth it."

If a man wanted to spend his money on cats, that was his right. Still, Tawny had to wonder. "Have you talked to Cassandra? She's worried about you."

He raked fingers through his thick gray curls. "I suppose by now she knows what happened, along with the rest of the country. Saw myself on the TV news last night in jail. Helluva thing. I look about a hundred and fifty years old." His lanky forearms rested on bony knees, head hanging. "The whole world thinks I killed that retarded guy."

Tawny leaned toward him. "Moe, can you remember *anything* more from that night?"

He shook his head. "Big fat blank. When I was younger, I drank a lot. Blacked out a few times. Couldn't remember a damn thing. I mean, *nothing*. Wiped clean, like it never happened. That's the way I felt that night. I didn't know where I was, how I got there. All I could think of was to call you."

"I'm glad you did." *What am I saying? I'm crazier than he is.*

"You were right," he went on. "I would have frozen to death out there in the middle of nowhere. Although maybe that would've been better. I wouldn't be in this mess now." He sheepishly eyed her and offered a crooked smile. "That doesn't sound very grateful, does it? I do appreciate you saving me. Again." A wink hinted at his old spark. "I owe you more prime rib."

Tawny forced a smile. "Not necessary." She couldn't endure another *thank you* dinner with him.

His head sagged again. "I guess I'm screwed."

"Moe, if anyone can help you, it's Tillman. He's doing his best but you need to cooperate with him." She waited a second, gauging his mood. Depressed but still calm, even after the mention of his hated son. "Will you?"

Head dropped lower, almost between his knees. "Yeah."

Tawny rose and squeezed his shoulder. He looked up, laid

his dry, bony hand over hers, and held tight. The expression in his eyes startled her because Tillman had given her the same strange look the night before.

A look that said he depended on her and had faith in her to help him.

Another layer settled on the heavy yoke of obligation she already felt toward Moe. And Tillman.

She went to the front door and motioned to Tillman, who stepped inside, shivering. "It's OK," she whispered. "He'll cooperate."

He pressed a fist against bluish lips. "Unbelievable," he murmured.

~~~

The uneasy truce between father and son lasted through cheeseburgers and most of the onion rings.

In the laundry room, Tawny was cleaning the litter boxes. A wall muffled their words but she could hear the deep rumblings, so alike in inflection and resonance that she couldn't tell which man was speaking.

Then the conversation detonated.

She rushed around the corner toward the shouting. Father and son stood on opposite sides of the dining table, leaning forward like missiles, poised to launch themselves into a mid-air collision. Onion rings lay scattered as if someone had back-handed the grease-soaked sack.

"I *knew* you were after my money," Moe yelled. "Well, fuck you, it's gone! You're too late!"

"You miserable cocksucker!" Tillman shouted. "You think you can outsmart everyone but you're screwed!"

Rambo streaked across the living room, leapt onto the table, then bounced straight into Tillman's face. His front legs wrapped around the lawyer's neck. Rear claws scrambled against his chest. Fangs gouged his nose and cheek.

Tillman staggered backward, bellowing. He tried to yank the cat off with one hand while the other fist pounded its body. Rambo shrieked but tightened his death grip.

Tawny looked around desperately for a weapon. She grabbed Moe's jumbo plastic soda cup and ripped off the lid. She hurled the drink and crushed ice at Rambo. The wet cold shocked the cat enough to release Tillman and jump free. With a blood-curdling howl, he sprang to an end table, knocked over a lamp with a crash then tore up the stairs.

Moe bounded after him.

Blood and Pepsi dripped down Tillman's astonished face. "Motherfucker!" He slammed a chair to the floor and kicked it across the great room. He stomped in a circle, hands cupped over his bleeding nose.

Tawny hurried to him and reached up to seize his shoulders. "Hold still. Let me look." He squirmed a little but allowed her to study his lacerated face. A fang had ripped clear through his nostril. Blood poured from the ragged wound. More bite punctures rimmed his jaw. Parallel lines of scratches tore deep into both sides of his neck. "Did he get your eyes?"

He shook his head. "Another half second and that monster's neck would have been broken."

"If you hurt that cat, Moe will come after you with a knife again."

"Do I look worried?"

Tawny pulled him by the arm into the bathroom. He sat on the toilet lid while she opened a new bottle of hydrogen peroxide she'd brought after Rambo's first attack. She poured the fizzing liquid over the damage and pressed a washcloth against the river of blood gushing from his nostril. "Hold this on your nose, tight."

Furious dark eyes watched her as she unbuttoned his shredded dress shirt to find more scratches bleeding through the thick black hair on his chest.

"I'm calling Virgie."

The doctor answered her private cell. "Hi, Tawny, what's up?"

"Virgie, the cat that attacked me just tore up Tillman. Are you working at Urgent Care today?"

"Yeah, sweetheart, come right in. I'll let the desk know you're on your way."

CHAPTER 16 – RAMBO 2, HUMANS 0

At the clinic, Tawny sat on a chair in the corner of the exam room while Virgie stitched up Tillman's nose and painted his face and neck wounds with antiseptic. His long legs dangled over the end of the exam table.

"Y'know, if this was a dog bite case," Virgie said, "I'd have to report it and the pooch would be on death row. But I don't think there's a vicious cat ordinance."

"Maybe there should be," Tawny said. Tillman grimaced and she pressed her lips together in empathy. She knew firsthand how excruciating those wounds were, even though they appeared small.

Virgie studied the scratches on his muscular chest. "Mind if I shave you? Makes it easier for your after-care."

Tillman rolled his eyes. "Why not? I've undergone enough other indignities today."

"Don't worry. It grows back." Virgie winked at Tawny. "So, Tillman, Cat the Ripper belongs to your dad?"

"Yeah, dear old Dad who's been charged with homicide." He leaned back on the table as Virgie used a safety razor to mow bare patches around the wounds. "Would you be willing to evaluate him, do a complete workup, including analyzing his prescriptions, as a medical expert?"

"You mean, evaluate his fitness to stand trial?" Virgie asked.

"Not necessarily, although if you find something that indicates diminished capacity, I'll use that."

"Do I have to testify in court?"

"Maybe, although a written report may help me plead him out. I'm hoping this never gets to trial."

Virgie looked over at Tawny. "You work for this guy. Should I?"

Tawny shrugged. "Pay's good but the hours suck. And I don't earn any extra for hazardous duty."

Tillman faced Tawny. "First you fling ice-cold Pepsi on me and now you're angling for a raise?"

She tried to suppress a smile but didn't succeed.

"What do you say, Doc?" Tillman asked.

"I'll probably regret it," Virgie answered, "but what the hell?"

~~~

"What do you think Moe meant about the money being gone?" Tawny spooned chicken salad onto sunflower seed bread. Sandwiches were the best she could do for an impromptu dinner at home.

Tillman sat at the breakfast bar, sipping scotch, his supply replenished by a stop at the liquor store on the way to Tawny's house. "He probably off-shored it. I emailed all the financial records on his computer to my forensic accountant. He can track it further than I did." He watched her cut the sandwiches in half. "I still wish you'd let me take you out for dinner."

She set a plate in front of him. "Have you seen yourself in the mirror? You don't want to go out in public looking like that."

Brown betadine stains seeped from the patchwork of bandages covering his face. His torn nose looked swollen and hot-red under the stitches. Long strips of gauze banded either side of his neck. He'd changed out of the ripped, blood-stained shirt at his hotel. Tawny knew more bandages covered his partly-shaved chest. He shrugged. "OK, but I owe you." He bit into the sandwich then touched his nose as if it throbbed.

"Don't worry. I'll collect." She sat beside him at the bar with her plate, trying to hide the chipped Formica with a napkin. How shabby her old house felt, compared to his opulent lifestyle. Yet he kept returning here, instead of his luxurious hotel suite.

"Hey, this is good," he said. "Did you put cranberries in it?"

"Yep, with chopped celery and almonds."

He smiled, an expression barely familiar to her. Normally he glowered or, if he grinned, there was almost always a sardonic twinge.

They ate in silence for several minutes until Tawny asked, "Do you think you can plead him out?"

"Depends on the medical eval."

"He told me he didn't remember anything from that night," she said. "Compared it to an alcoholic blackout. But, honestly, he didn't seem drunk. He slurred his words but I think that was from hypothermia because, as soon as he warmed up, his speech went back to normal." She sipped orange juice as she reviewed the conversation. "You know, the way he described it, it almost sounded like someone who got slipped a date rape drug."

Tillman snorted. "Nobody has to slip him a drug for sex, except Viagra. Probably pops those like M&Ms. Found plenty in his medicine cabinet."

"Maybe Virgie can come up with an explanation."

He shook his head. "Be damn difficult without a blood sample taken at the time. And we don't have that."

"Now I wish I *had* taken him to the hospital, even though he protested."

"Spilled milk. You takes 'em like you finds 'em."

Tawny tilted her head. "My grandpa used to say that, except he was talking about cards."

"The one with dementia?"

"Yeah. He was a damn good poker player in his day. Later on, he couldn't tell the ace of hearts from this glass of orange juice." She tapped the tumbler with her fingernail, remembering the early signs. "He'd call me up, complaining his phone wasn't working. Dwight and I'd go over to his house and find he was trying to make calls with the TV remote."

"Losing your mind is rough." Tillman finished the last bite of sandwich, chewing slowly, thinking. He knocked back the scotch. "We better go get my car. I need to fly to Billings in the morning. It's my four days with the kids." He cleared the plates and put them in the dishwasher.

Then he turned a slow full circle, scanning her kitchen which appeared tiny because of his height. "Thanks for dinner."

She wondered about his odd expression under the patchy bandages. "Wasn't much."

He gazed down at her. "It was the nicest dinner I've had in a long time. I feel more at home here than I do in my own house."

Realization dawned on her that, despite his wealth and success, this noisy, bombastic lawyer, who boastfully referred to himself as an asshole, was a lonely, unhappy man. Again, a disconcerting connection flickered between them, like she'd experienced when he held her bare foot.

Not sure how to respond, she finally murmured, "Thank you." She moved past him to the mud room. "I'll get my coat."

She felt him watching and wondered if he would approach her. He was her boss. Not smart to cross that line. Yet something had shifted. He'd started to treat her like a confidante. Maybe even a friend. And he sure seemed to need one.

Like his dad did.

He strode to the couch, picked up his suit jacket, and exploded. "Goddammit!"

She hurried to the living room. "What is it?"

"The car keys. They were in my pocket, right here." He

shook his jacket upside down. Only business cards and thumb drives fell out. He unloaded the pockets of his trousers—cell, wallet, the key to Moe's condo, but not the car. Then he dumped the contents of his briefcase on the coffee table. "I *know* they were in my jacket pocket."

"Any chance you left them in the ignition?"

He scowled at her. "I'm a criminal attorney, remember? I *never* leave keys in the ignition."

"What do you want to do?"

"Take me by the rental agency. They'll have a spare set. Goddammit!"

Back to normal. She sighed with relief.

~~~

Tawny made the turn onto Moe's dark street. As the Jeep's headlights swept over his driveway, she and Tillman realized the Escalade was gone.

He blew up again. "That sneaky old prick must have taken the key out of my pocket. Now he's out driving around in a car *I'm* responsible for." He pulled up his cell. "I'm calling the sheriff, reporting it stolen. Let his sorry ass go back to jail. I'm done trying to help him."

Tawny touched his arm. "Wait a second. Let me check inside."

He shot her a furious look. "He doesn't give a shit that he's flouting the judge's orders. His bond will be revoked and I'm out five grand, not to mention wrecking my reputation with the judge. I should have ignored the foreclosure notice, let him get bounced out on the street. I wouldn't even give him a damn shopping cart to push around."

She pressed harder on his arm, feeling the sprung steel of his resistance. "Just give me a minute, OK?"

He flipped her hand off. "Knock yourself out."

Tawny approached the front door. No lights showed through the front window. She rang the bell, waited a few seconds then used the key to enter. "Moe?"

Meows greeted her. She flicked on the entry light as five cats bumped her legs. Tense, she scanned the dimness for Rambo. No sign of the Siamese. Turning on more lights, she checked the living room, kitchen, laundry room, downstairs bath. Entering Moe's house felt like clearing an enemy combatant's territory.

Last, she cracked the door to the office. From inside the darkness, Rambo hissed and spat. She closed the door. Good, he was located and contained.

At the top of the stairs, the bedroom door opened, spilling out a red glow. Moe sprang forth, wearing a black silk bathrobe, not quite tied. "Who the hell's there?"

"It's me, Tawny."

"What the hell are you doing, breaking into my house?"

"You gave me your key, remember?"

A tinkling-crystal voice sounded from the bedroom. "Moshe, darling, what is it?"

He clomped down the stairs, causing the robe to loosen. His Viagra was definitely working. "Give it back, dammit. I don't like being interrupted." He thrust his hand out, palm up. Angry dark eyes snapped.

The jagged edge of the key bit into her clenched palm. "Where's Tillman's Escalade?"

"In the garage, of course. I want my key."

"Not until you give me back the car keys you swiped."

The glare gradually melted into a satisfied grin. "Pretty slick, huh?"

She stared at him. "Moe, driving violates your bond. You'll go back to jail and Tillman's ready to leave you there."

He shrugged. "Cassandra and I went out to dinner. No harm done." A mischievous leer curled his lip. "I'd pay a thousand bucks to see his face when he realized the keys were gone."

"Where are they?"

He folded his arms. "In the ignition. And, if it makes you feel better, *I* didn't drive, Cassandra did." He took one step up the stairs then turned with a jaunty upward nod of his head. "You want to join us? The more the merrier."

Tawny threw his house key on the floor and stalked toward the garage. "Close your damn robe."

~~~

Cassandra twisted on the swing, letting it spin her around in lazy circles, her negligee floating like a swirling see-through cape. Despite the work she'd had done, her body looked much better filtered through filmy lace. However, with the load of Viagra Moshe had on tonight, he'd penetrate chain mail to reach her treasure.

Chemistry was so fabulously versatile. She could crank him up when she was horny, deflate him when she was tired, send him to dreamland he'd never remember visiting, and transform him into a gladiator, ready to impale himself on an enemy sword to protect her.

Except lately, the careful pattern had been disrupted. His stay in jail had allowed certain blood levels to drop precipitously. She needed to reestablish equilibrium. That was proving difficult with the intervention of his lawyer son and that damn Tawny who kept turning up at inopportune times.

Like tonight.

When Cassandra's itch needed scratching.

Their affair should have ended permanently a few nights

before in the freezing car, but Colin had been careless and Moshe didn't cooperate. In a way, she was glad for the reprieve. The old man was an artist in bed and she would miss that.

The $90,000 deferred dividend Moshe was expecting had tempted her to delay a little longer.

But this interlude was over. His son was poking around and she'd heard rumors from neighbors that the consumer affairs agency might start an investigation. As much as she wanted the ninety grand, the risks outweighed the rewards. She'd milked this herd of Montana cows dry. It was time to move on to fresh territory in Florida that Colin had scouted out.

The candlelight under the bathroom door still flickered. "Moshe darling, are you coming out?" He'd been in there ever since he returned to the bedroom after shooing Tawny away. At least ten minutes had passed.

"Are you running a bubble bath for me, darling?"

Still no answer.

Cassandra slid off the swing, wobbling a little on her four-inch platform heels. "Moshe, my handsome stud, you're making me desperate. I might have to start without you."

She pushed the door open but something blocked it. She shoved harder and skinnied through the narrow opening.

Moshe lay on the floor, robe open, his erection shuddering with each snore.

She kicked him with her pointed, feather-trimmed toe. No response. "Goddammit!"

CHAPTER 17 – HE MIGHT HURT YOU

Tawny sat in the clinic waiting room the following morning, pretending to read a magazine but her foot kept twitching. Through her sock, she rubbed the itchy, healing wounds.

Somewhere in the back rooms, Virgie was examining Moe. Tawny longed to be a fly on the wall.

She pondered where privacy ended and legitimate intervention began. At times, Moe seemed completely lucid, at others, hopelessly lost and bewildered. His glee at stealing Tillman's keys put her in mind of a young boy's prank—silly and proud of himself for pulling a fast one on his son, yet no understanding of the possible consequences to his freedom and future.

The sharp edge of the extra key in her pocket scraped her finger. After she'd taken custody of Moe's belongings at the jail, Tillman had instructed her to make several duplicate keys to the condo. She'd objected, wanting to seek Moe's permission first, but now recognized the lawyer's wisdom.

She didn't like being sneaky but she needed to anticipate and outwit Moe's craftiness. From the beginning, this whole assignment had required her to do too many things that made her uncomfortable.

Moe's cell vibrated in her bag. She stepped outside to the parking lot to answer.

"This is Renata Schliefman. Is Mr. Rosenbaum available?"

The fraud investigation lawyer. "Hi, Renata, this is Tawny Lindholm. We met at your talk at Golden Eagle."

"Yes, I remember."

Tawny gave a nervous laugh. "How could you forget?"

A small chuckle in response. "I need to speak with Mr.

Rosenbaum. Is he there?"

"He asked me to hold his phone because he's in an appointment."

"I'm driving over from Helena. Do you know if he'll be free later today?"

"I think so."

"Good. I'll call again when I get there."

Why did Renata want to see Moe? "Is there a message you'd like me to give him?"

A long pause. "Will you be with him this afternoon?"

"Probably. I'm kind of...well, I don't know how to put it. I'm supposed to supervise him on behalf of my boss."

"Babysitting?"

Tawny smiled at the woman's perceptiveness. "That about nails it."

"I'm going to be frank with you, Tawny. Based on complaints I received from a number of people after my talk, my office is opening an investigation into Mr. Rosenbaum's handling of his clients' funds. He may want to have his attorney present when we meet."

Crap. More complications. "Uh, thank you for giving me a heads up. Tillman is on his way to Billings but I'll call him." She disconnected and leaned against the log pillar of the portico in front of the clinic.

Dark clouds hung low over the mountains, the inversion pressing down on the valley like the oppressive problems facing Moe. She hated to think of him cheating his neighbors. Had he done it purposefully? Did he think he was getting away with a prank, like stealing Tillman's keys?

She called Tillman but his phone went directly to voicemail. She left a message about the pending investigation. Too worried and tense to go back inside, she paced the parking lot to keep warm.

Ten minutes later, Virgie and Moe came out of the clinic, laughing. They spotted her and waved.

"Come on," Virgie called. "We're all going to lunch."

Tawny unlocked the Jeep, watching the banter between her best friend and the accused killer-fraudster. Moe pulled the passenger seat forward for Virgie and offered his hand to support her in the awkward climb into the back.

When they were all loaded, Virgie said, "Sweetheart, your next car needs to have four doors. I'm only five-two, but there isn't room enough back here for a toy poodle."

Moe laughed. "None too roomy up here either. Maybe we ought to ride on the roof rack. Probably be more comfortable."

Tawny was used to insults about the old Jeep, and had voiced a few herself but she couldn't bear to part with it because Dwight had loved it. "When I get a raise, I'll buy a different rig."

Moe chuckled. "In that case, Virgie, we better get used to it. If I know my son, she'll have this car for many more years." He swiveled to face the doctor. "Next time, want to sit on my lap?"

Virgie giggled and winked.

He's flirting with my friend and she's flirting back. What the hell?

Tawny hoped Moe's good spirits would last. Every time they'd been in public, he'd acted up. She definitely wouldn't mention Renata Schliefman's pending visit until later. "Where are we going to eat?"

She wanted to send a silent message to Virgie—don't choose your favorite restaurant because you might never be able to go back.

"Let's go to Breezy's," Virgie suggested. "Clam chowder today."

"Sounds fine," Moe agreed.

Homey smells of potatoes, seafood, and salt pork filled the

busy café. It appeared half the county had shown up for the popular special. Servers threaded between packed tables, carrying one-handled pottery ramekins of creamy soup.

Virgie excused herself to go to the restroom. Tawny followed, casting a glance back at Moe, wondering if she dared leave him alone.

At the door, Virgie warned, "Sweetie, it's a one-holer."

Tawny gave her a hard look. "I *need* to talk to you."

Virgie shrugged. "OK, if you don't care, I don't."

Together, they crowded into the little bathroom. Tawny asked, "Do you have lunch with your patients often?"

Virgie made a face. "Of course not. Moe *is* a charmer, though."

"Four wives thought so, too. But he killed a man."

"I know." Virgie's flip tone said it didn't matter as she lifted her skirt and sat.

Tawny turned away to wash her hands.

Virgie asked, "You don't approve of my technique?"

"You're flirting with him."

"Sweetheart, most of my VA patients are older men. I get much better cooperation out of them if they think they're still studs. Since I'm trying to pin down if there's dementia, I figured it might give a more accurate diagnosis to see how he behaves in the regular world rather than simply in a clinical setting."

Now Tawny felt foolish. "I'm sorry, Virg. I should have known you had a good reason." She tugged her braid. "Between him and Tillman, I'm going crazy. And now there's a new wrinkle."

Virgie flushed and washed her hands. "What's that?"

"A fraud investigator from Helena is on her way to question Moe about swindling his neighbors. Tillman had to go back to Billings this morning, so I'm stuck fielding this mess too."

Virgie hugged her. "Sweetie, you're a loyal, devoted friend and there isn't a more conscientious employee than you but Moe is not your father. Tillman's got to shoulder the responsibility."

Tawny melted into her comforting embrace and rested her cheek on Virgie's head. "It's my job. I owe Tillman. He kept me out of prison. I can't just walk away."

"Of course you can't." Virgie patted her back. "But you're letting these guys get to you. You've got to be more detached, keep an emotional distance. Although after three divorces, I'm a great one to be giving that advice, huh?"

A final squeeze and they left the restroom.

Buzzing conversations had given way to shouting in the crowded café.

Across the room, Moe faced off with his bald neighbor, Quentin—the man he'd squabbled with at the fraud meeting. Quentin's wife, Antoinette, tugged on her husband's arm, trying to pull him away. Moe leaned forward while Quentin stretched up, noses almost touching. Their bellowing voices drowned out one another.

Tawny rushed between gawking customers. She caught Antoinette's frightened, jittering glance.

"Moe! Stop it!" Tawny yanked on his right arm, hand already bunched in a ham fist. A heartbeat away from assault.

The wife had pushed her husband sideways, almost out of punching range. "Let's just leave, Quentin!"

Quentin hurled a last insult, "Thief!"

Moe lurched forward, left fist swinging wildly.

Quentin ducked.

The roundhouse sailed over his head and caught Tawny's jaw.

Pain exploded into stars before her eyes. She staggered, throwing her arms in front of her face.

He might hurt you. Emma's warning rushed back, forgotten until this instant.

Fighting to see through black blurs clouding her vision, Tawny balled her hands tight, ready to defend herself.

Horror contorted Moe's face. He retreated a step and stared at his fist, puzzled, as if it belonged to someone else.

"Oh, my God!" he bleated. "I'm sorry! I didn't mean...I would never..." Tears flooded his eyes.

Abruptly, he turned to Quentin. "You lousy jackass! You made me hit my friend!" He lunged again, this time knocking the shorter man into a table that crashed against the wall. Moe bent over him, clutching Quentin's neck, while his fist pummeled his face. "You made me hit my friend!"

Antoinette hammered on Moe's back. "Leave him alone!"

Customers shoved aside chairs and tables in their rush to escape. Dishes crashed. From a long tunnel far away, Tawny heard Virgie calling her name.

Woozy, Tawny pushed forward. "Moe! Stop!"

The pounding continued.

A ramekin fell from an upended table, leaving a wake of spilled chowder as it skidded across the floor. Tawny bent down, grabbed the handle, and swung the bowl hard into the back of Moe's head. The heavy pottery cracked in pieces. Chunks flew in the air.

He wobbled and stumbled sideways. Thankfully, he released Quentin.

Antoinette threw herself between her husband and Moe but the assault was over.

Moe swayed, regaining his bearings, and faced Tawny. Tears dripped off his jutting chin. He feebly offered a hand to her, knuckles raw and bloody. "He made me hit you."

Tawny backed away, nausea rising in her throat.

Sobbing, Antoinette helped Quentin to a chair. Blood

poured from his nose and mouth. Virgie ministered to the injured man, mopping his face with napkins.

Sirens wailed as a police cruiser skidded to a stop in front of the café. Two officers raced inside, hands on their sidearms.

Antoinette thrust a finger toward Moe. "That monster tried to kill my husband!"

The cops approached Moe cautiously but the fight had gone out of him. His head hung while they cuffed him. As they led him past Tawny, he lifted his face briefly. Voice quaking, he whispered, "I'm sorry."

While Moe waited in the back of the cruiser, the officers took statements from Tawny and Virgie, along with other witnesses. The café owner brought Tawny a plastic bag filled with ice, then went to work cleaning up the destruction.

An ambulance arrived for Quentin. On the way out, his wife paused at the chair where Tawny sat, holding ice on her jaw. "Damn small towns," Antoinette muttered. "You're always running into people you don't want to see. As soon as we walked in and saw Moe, I told Quentin we should leave. But he insisted on staying. He says, 'I'm not letting that thief deprive me of my favorite clam chowder.'" She gestured at the broken chairs, upset tables, and shattered dishes. "All this, over soup." She trailed the gurney to the ambulance.

Virgie carefully manipulated Tawny's jaw, up and down, side to side. "I don't think it's broken but I'd feel better if you'd get an X-ray."

Tawny ran her tongue over her molars, checking for looseness. They still felt firm in her gums, although the inside of her mouth puffed like a blood-soaked marshmallow. "I'm lucky he didn't knock my teeth out."

"Come on, sweetheart, let's go get you X-rayed, then I'm taking you home."

Tawny shook her head. "You know what I really need?

Something cold *inside* my mouth." She set down the bag of ice and headed toward the shopping center across the street.

Moments later, they sat side by side on a mall bench, eating Blizzards.

Virgie said, "Guess that settles the question whether Moe's fit to stand trial."

Tawny licked bits of Heath Bar from the long plastic spoon. "I guess." Utterly spent, she wanted to melt to the floor like ice cream and be mopped up by the janitor. Instead she placed another call to Tillman. Still voicemail. She left a message, "Moe's in jail again. Beat the piss out of his neighbor." She disconnected.

Virgie frowned. "You forgot to mention he knocked you silly."

"Oh, I'll tell him. Just not on voicemail."

"Tillman's a pretty hard guy to get a hold of for someone whose father keeps winding up in jail."

"Yeah." Tawny glanced at a *Help Wanted* sign in the Dairy Queen window. "I think I'll quit this damn job and scoop ice cream instead."

"Wouldn't blame you a bit." Virgie took a big bite. "Ooh, brain freeze." She swallowed then added, "Sounds like the Rosenbaum family puts the funk in dysfunctional."

"You got that right. Yesterday, Moe went after Tillman with a knife. According to Tillman, he's thrown tantrums his whole life."

"Definitely anger issues. May be a personality disorder. Or could be drugs. In some ways, he fits a dementia diagnosis but not others. I'd like to see a brain scan on him. I suggested a mental health hold to the cops."

"Will they do a scan while he's in custody?"

"If the court orders it."

"That's Tillman's department." Tawny sighed. "Virgie, I'm

so tired. I've known Moe less than two weeks but I'm ready to throw in the towel. My God, how do people stand it if their husband or wife has dementia?"

Virgie patted her arm. "Not everyone's as extreme as Moe. But, sweetie, I keep reminding you, Moe is not your father. This is just a job. You really can walk away from it and go scoop ice cream."

The sweet chill soothed the inside of Tawny's aching mouth. She wished she could fall into a bathtub full of ice cream. "No, I can't, Virgie. Minimum wage doesn't pay enough that I could ever afford to fix my house."

Virgie licked a drip from the side of her cup. "You're not a quitter, that's for sure. You'll keep your word, even if it kills you."

Tawny closed her eyes. "I keep thinking of my grandpa, old, scared, broke, half out of his mind. But at least he was surrounded by family that loved him. Moe has no one, except Tillman, who hates him, and is about a half breath away from blowing him off for good. After this latest stunt, he just may."

"What about Moe's girlfriend?"

Tawny shrugged. "She's the only one with the magic touch to calm the savage beast. But she strikes me as someone always looking to trade up. I can't imagine her sticking with him through this."

Virgie swirled her spoon in Butterfinger chunks. "Sweetie, has it occurred to you that karma might be at work? Sounds like Moe's abused people for a long time. He's driven everyone away. *That's* why he's alone now. Once the veneer of charm wears off, he's not a very nice man."

Tawny's cell rang, an unfamiliar number. "Hello?"

"This is Renata Schliefman. I'm trying to reach Mr. Rosenbaum but didn't get an answer on his number. I found your card and thought I'd try yours."

Tawny tipped her head backwards, stretching her throat. "Mr. Rosenbaum isn't available now." *And probably not for a long time to come.*

"I take it he's not willing to meet with me."

"No, he can't." *Because he's locked up.* "I'm afraid this is a wasted trip for you."

"Hardly," the lawyer answered. "I'm meeting with his alleged victims. Quite a large group. They've organized a community get-together at the Golden Eagle clubhouse this afternoon for anyone who believes they were defrauded."

Crap. The not-very-nice man's troubles multiplied like cancer cells.

Tillman would undoubtedly want her to attend to find out what evidence they had against Moe.

And, she had to admit, her own curiosity about his suspicious dealings chafed at her. Answers might turn up to the questions she'd raised while combing his records. "Is it appropriate for me to attend the meeting?" she asked. "Or will I be attacked by angry people if I show my face?"

Renata paused for a moment. "I don't really know how they'll react. You're in a difficult position. You're not representing Mr. Rosenbaum, yet you're kind of connected to him."

"Guilty by association."

"Exactly."

"Two weeks ago, I didn't even know he existed. I've never been involved in his business. In fact, I've been trying to figure out what's happening with his finances."

"Well, it appears to be an open public gathering, so come if you want. You can always leave if they start throwing rotten tomatoes."

When Tawny disconnected, Virgie pinned her with a stare. "Don't tell me you're going."

The last bite of Blizzard slid down Tawny's throat. The ache in her jaw would remain whether she stayed home or went to the meeting. She couldn't pass up the opportunity to learn more. "Yeah, I am."

Virgie shook her head. "I should put *you* on a mental health hold."

CHAPTER 18 – CRUEL FRAUD

At the Golden Eagle clubhouse, tables were arranged in long rows with questionnaires and pens at each seat. About seventy-five somber-looking people gathered. Some filled out forms, while others clustered in groups, their conversations tense and worried.

Tawny had arrived late, having stopped at her house to cover her bruised jaw with makeup. Four ibuprofen had eased the pain a little but she kept accidentally biting the swollen inside of her cheek.

At a rear table, she spotted a stack of blank forms and slipped one in her bag to give to Tillman. A few people shot her curious glances but no one seemed overtly hostile. Yet.

In the front of the room, Renata spoke into a table microphone. "Good afternoon, ladies and gentlemen, thank you all for coming. I came to announce that, based on complaints received from many of you, I am opening an investigation into Midas Investments, LLC, and its principal, Moshe Baruch Rosenbaum. May I see a show of hands from anyone who invested funds in Midas, with Mr. Rosenbaum, or with any other entity controlled by him?"

Almost everyone in the room raised their hands.

Renata nodded. The wry humor and vibrant personality she'd displayed at the earlier event were missing. All business now. "I've spoken with a number of you by phone and requested you bring copies of any records pertaining to transactions with Midas and Mr. Rosenbaum. Please fill out the questionnaires on the tables about your investments with as much detail as possible. The more complete your answers, the better job I can do for you investigating this matter. Any questions?"

"Yeah!" a man in a ski parka piped up. "Will we get our

money back?"

Renata's lips creased into a straight line. "I wish I could promise you that. My office will do our best to ensure, if there is fraud or wrongdoing, that the person responsible will be prosecuted. But I must warn you, realistically, recoveries are rare and usually small. Most of the time, the criminal has already spent the money."

Grumbling rippled through the audience. Then people rose one by one to relate their stories while Renata typed notes on a tablet.

A dozen widows had formed an investment club and were doing well until the 2008 crash. Concerned their savings wouldn't last the rest of their lives, they needed a different strategy. Moe had wined and dined them, showing them fantastic returns on investments that more than made up for the beating their stocks had taken. Two women took the plunge. When fat dividend checks began to roll in, the rest turned their savings over to Moe to handle.

Similar tales came from Moe's golfing buddies. As the first few investors made money, more jumped on the wagon that Moe had seemingly hitched to a rising star. Satisfied friends and neighbors referred more clients to Moe. He became the financial savior of the residents of Golden Eagle. They overwhelmingly re-elected him president of the homeowner's association and put him in charge of investing the association funds. For a year, everyone was happy.

Then the dividends stopped.

Moe made excuses—a computer crash, the accounting firm lost records, conversions from foreign currencies required additional time.

A few partial payments temporarily pacified investors, with promises to make up the difference later. They'd trusted their friend and believed his excuses for the next year.

But the dividends never resumed.

Moe stopped giving excuses. Instead, he flew into rages, accusing investors of not having faith in him and insulting his integrity. He became so verbally abusive that people were afraid to confront him and avoided him.

The tipping point came when the HOA accountant sounded the alarm. Treasury funds had disappeared. Residents at last realized most of the community had been defrauded.

As victim after victim revealed stories of loss, Tawny rubbed a hand over her stomach trying to ease the searing pain in her gut. The people in the room weren't greedy Wall Street speculators making windfall profits. They had worked hard, saved, and simply wanted to live out their retirement in peace.

Did Moe intend to defraud people from the start? Or had he been driven to desperation when the recession hit?

Or maybe Tillman's father was simply a con man.

Renata interrupted to ask, "Why didn't you report Mr. Rosenbaum to the authorities before now?"

A stooped man wearing thick glasses answered, "I retired from UM Missoula as an *economics* professor, for God's sake. Embarrassing as hell to wind up being the sucker in a scam. Not something you want to advertise. I thought I was the only one." He waved his hand across the audience. "Now we've learned everyone in this room is a victim."

A woman rose, a flowered scarf covering her apparently-bald head. "Moe was my *friend*. He knew my chemo schedule. He'd always bring his snow blower over and plow my driveway so I could get to my appointments. I couldn't believe he'd cheat me." Her lip trembled. "But he did." She sat down gingerly, as if every movement pained her.

In the rear of the room, a tall man in a ski sweater called out, "Remember what happened to the Kaplans? Alfred killed himself because he was ashamed of filing bankruptcy. Marcia had to beg her jackass son-in-law to let her move in with them. Otherwise, she'd be on the street. All because of this stinking Midas swindle."

Renata frowned and nodded. "Fraudsters and scammers want you to keep silent. The only way to stop these crimes is for people to talk about it, report it, and warn others." She closed the tablet she'd been taking notes on. "Thank you for your courage in coming forward. I'll review your questionnaires and keep you informed about progress. And I *will* contact the FBI."

A cell trilled. A woman answered and listened for several seconds, then waved her phone. "Everyone! Something terrible's happened. Antoinette's calling. Moe Rosenbaum attacked Quentin and almost killed him. Quentin just had a heart attack in the emergency room. If he dies, it's all Rosenbaum's fault."

Ripples of concern swept the room. Now heads began to swivel toward Tawny in her inconspicuous corner. Angry eyes glared.

Her cell vibrated. Tillman. Thank goodness. As she hurried out, she spotted Cassandra on the far side of the room, dashing away even faster than she was. The woman ducked through a rear door to the parking lot.

In the lobby, Tawny kept moving as she answered, "Tillman?"

From a speakerphone on his end, his deep voice reverberated. "The old man called me from jail, blubbering. Said I had to tell you he's sorry, it was an accident, you're his only friend, and he's afraid you'll never talk to him again."

Tawny headed outside toward her Jeep, scuffing on the icy pavement. Across the parking lot, Cassandra's yellow Porsche raced out, tires squealing.

Impatience shrilled Tillman's tone. "You want to fill in

some blanks here?"

"Moe took a swing at his neighbor. The neighbor ducked, I didn't."

Choking. "Are you OK?"

"Yeah, I'm sore and look like a lopsided chipmunk. But, Tillman, he really beat the man badly. I just heard he had a heart attack that his wife is blaming on Moe."

"Motherfucker!"

In the background, she heard noises that probably meant the lawyer was pounding his desk, kicking his chair, and maybe throwing his coffee mug across his office. The parallels between his behavior and Moe's worried her more than the ache in her jaw. She unlocked the Jeep and got in, waiting for the storm on the phone to subside.

It didn't. Finally, she shouted, "Tillman! Take a deep breath. There's more."

"What?"

"It sounds like Moe's scammed about seventy-five of his neighbors. The attorney from the state office of consumer protection is calling in the FBI."

Instant silence. Thinking.

She flipped down the visor and examined her face in the mirror. It had swollen even more and makeup had lost the battle to conceal the bruising.

At last, Tillman said, "Take some time off. He'll be locked up in Pathways for at least forty-eight hours on the mental health hold. He can't hurt you or get in any more trouble. I'll be back in Kalispell for the hearing on Friday. The judge may order him to Warm Springs for further evaluation and treatment."

Warm Springs, the state mental hospital near the prison in Deer Lodge. If convicted, Moe might wind up there, permanently. "Somebody needs to take care of his cats."

"Screw his cats."

Jerk. "It's not *their* fault. I'll feed them."

Heavy sigh. "All right." A pause, then he added, "I forgot to say thank you."

A tiny step of progress. "You're welcome." Tawny had to smile despite the pain in her face.

In the dusky twilight, movement caught the corner of her vision. She turned to find Renata approaching, lugging a stuffed briefcase. Tawny rolled down the driver's window.

The lawyer nodded to her swollen jaw. "You OK?"

"Yeah. My babysitting job got a little rough."

Renata made a face. "That's awful." She patted Tawny's arm in sympathy. "Want to go get a drink?"

Tawny hesitated. Was Renata trying to pump her for information on Moe? She needed to be careful what she said. But she might also learn more. "All right."

Twenty minutes later, they settled into a rear booth at a side-street tavern with peanut shells on the floor and initials carved in the rough wood tables. Renata took advantage of two-for-one happy hour and immediately downed a glass of white wine. "Mmm, I needed that. These meetings are always hard. I hate to hear about people's lives getting turned upside down. But that's the job I signed on for. At least I hope I can make a small difference." She cracked a few peanuts from the bowl on the table and glanced at the wide screen TV over the bar. "Hey, look at that."

Tawny turned to see what had caught Renata's attention. Jerky video played on the screen, apparently from someone's cell.

She recognized Breezy's Café. Moe and Quentin shouting. Tawny and Antoinette trying to separate them. Then the wild swing, Quentin ducking, and Moe's fist connecting with Tawny's jaw.

Immediately, the video replayed, this time in slow motion. The timing of the duck and punch was so perfect, it appeared choreographed.

"Holy shit," Renata murmured.

Another jumpy, crooked clip came on. Moe's fist could be seen crashing down over and over. Tawny's back blocked the camera's view of Quentin's face but she remembered too well the bloody mess. When she thunked the ramekin on Moe's skull, he staggered away. That video also replayed in slo-mo, chunks of broken pottery floating through the air. The ticker read: *Out-of-Control Senior Identified as Father of Prominent MT Attorney.*

Dammit to hell. Tawny shrank back into the booth, hoping no one besides Renata recognized her.

Renata clutched her glass. "A new YouTube star is born." Her tone sounded flippant but concern crinkled her brows. "Here I was whining about *my* hard day." She finished her second glass of wine, held up two splayed fingers to the bartender, then nodded at Tawny's beer. "You sure you don't want a stronger anesthetic than that?"

"I shouldn't even be having this. Ibuprofen's tearing up my stomach."

Renata fluffed her hair to revive the spikes. "Once that video goes viral, Tillman's going to have a tough road defending his dad. By the way, I'm originally from Billings. My family went to temple with the Rosenbaums. I never met the old man but Tillman and Shoshanna were several years ahead of me in school. Their mother went to my bat mitzvah."

"Really? Montana *is* a small town."

"Especially for Jews." Two more glasses of wine arrived. Renata gulped down half of one. "His mother was a lovely woman, elegant, beautifully dressed but terribly shy. So tragic."

Tawny cracked a peanut then thought better of it with her

sore mouth and raw stomach. Mostly she wanted something to occupy her hands because hearing about the Rosenbaum family made her sad and uncomfortable. And she dreaded letting something slip to the woman who would soon be prosecuting Moe.

Renata started on another glass of wine. "I've looked up to Tillman my whole life. He's a brilliant workaholic. That man sets a pace that would kill a triathlete."

"I've noticed." Tawny mentally counted how many days in a row she'd worked. Ten.

"Too bad he doesn't run for governor. He'd be a helluva a lot more effective than most of the clowns at the Capitol." Renata mockingly slapped her hand over her mouth, not completely hiding a mischievous grin. "I should shut up about my bosses."

Tawny smiled. "Not illegal to complain about your job. I do enough of it."

"You have a better reason than I do." She gestured at Tawny's swollen face. "Still, I'm sorry I didn't get a chance to speak with Mr. Rosenbaum before this latest mishap. I'd like to hear his version of events. I've learned there are three sides to every story—the victim's, the perpetrator's, and the truth. I try for the truth, even though sometimes it makes me pretty unpopular in my office."

Tawny sipped beer, watching the woman over the rim of her glass. Was she trying to angle in sideways to get Tawny to reveal incriminating information about Moe? Better change the subject. "How long have you worked for the state?"

"Fifteen years, started there while I was still in law school in Missoula."

"Are you glad you went into consumer protection?"

"Sometimes. We make a dent but mostly it's frustrating. I can prosecute scammers but the victims have still lost their money. Even if we get a conviction, they're disappointed because we can't recover it for them but that's not our function."

Tawny sighed. "There isn't much justice."

"We don't have a justice system. It's only a legal system. Not like the rabbis of olden days who meted out justice." Renata shook her head. "I fell in love with the law because of the rabbinic arguments in the Talmud. Had dreams of someday being on the bench. Now I'm forty and I wonder where all my passion went. That's one reason I admire Tillman. He's never lost that drive to right wrongs."

Tawny gazed up at the TV, now showing a past file clip of Tillman, reciting his favorite tagline: "I'm the asshole who's the opposing counsel's worst nightmare," except the expletive had been bleeped.

Renata gave a low chuckle. "You can't stay under the radar for long when you're around Tillman Rosenbaum. Congratulations on your celebrity status."

Tawny traced initials carved in the tabletop—*SOB*. Seemed appropriate. "That's the last thing I want. Why can't I just live a quiet life? Pay my bills, hike in the mountains, ski a little."

"Downhill or cross-country."

"Cross-country. Flaky meniscus."

"Maybe we could go together sometime."

Tawny studied the woman's face. Earnest, likeable, conscientious. Maybe she *wasn't* trying to pump information about Moe. Too much of Tillman's cynicism was rubbing off. "That'd be fun."

"I could drive over this weekend. Or if you'd like to come to Helena, I know some great groomed tracks."

Sounded tempting since Moe wouldn't be out of custody at least for a couple of days and Tillman had given her time off. "Could we stick around here? I'm pet-sitting."

"Sure." Renata raised her glass. "To this weekend."

Seemed like an odd thing to toast but Tawny clinked glasses with her.

Renata downed the rest and motioned for more.

Tawny's beer was less than half gone and it was pitch dark outside. "I should get going. I've got to feed some cats." She pulled out her wallet.

"Oh, sure." Renata waved off the server delivering more wine. "I need to get on the road too. Long drive back. But this is my treat."

"Thank you. See you this weekend." Tawny slid out of the booth.

Renata rose and clasped Tawny's hand with both of hers in a warm squeeze. And held on. A dreamy look came into her eyes. "You're an amazing woman, Tawny. Even with that lump on your jaw, you're still very beautiful."

Uh-oh. Didn't see that coming. "Thank you, Renata. I enjoyed talking with you but I'm not..."

The lawyer's brown eyes flickered. She finished Tawny's sentence, "Gay?" She let go then backed away. "I should know better than to drink too fast on an empty stomach. I get stupid." Her cheeks flushed.

"It's OK." Tawny felt bad for Renata's embarrassment. "No offense meant, none taken. And I'd still like to go skiing."

The woman fumbled in her briefcase, not looking at Tawny. "Yeah, of course." She pulled out her phone and tapped it. "Oh, I just remembered, I have something going on this weekend. Another time?"

"Sure." Tawny started toward the exit but paused. "Are you OK to drive?"

"Yeah, no worries."

At the door, Tawny looked back once more. Helena was a long two hundred miles away on a winter night. "Be safe."

Still at the booth, Renata lifted her hand in a half-hearted wave.

~~~

Tawny parked in Moe's driveway. The porch light wasn't on and she fumbled in the dark with the duplicate key. Its newness rasped in the lock but the door finally opened. She flipped on the entry light.

The litter box smell made her nose wrinkle. Overdue for another scrubbing with bleach. There'd been too many crises to fit in that job too.

Sugar greeted her as usual with *mreows* and leg rubs. Others lounged on the stairs, bookshelves, or couch. Rambo wasn't in sight. Strangely, they didn't all rush her as they normally did, eager to eat. In the kitchen, she found dishes with fresh traces of food, not left over from this morning. Someone had fed them recently. Couldn't be Moe.

Cassandra? She had a key.

The door to the office opened and Cassandra walked out, Rambo draped over her arm like a fur stole. She spoke into her cell: "You're sure? I don't want this coming back like last time—" When she saw Tawny, she lurched to a stop, blue eyes wide with surprise.

Rambo hissed, fangs threatening. His rear legs scrambled against Cassandra's hip seeking leverage for a leap at Tawny. Cassandra fumbled the phone, which clattered to the floor. With both hands, she pulled the cat free of her pants, tearing the silky fabric, and held the Siamese up in front of her. Both had the exact same jewel-blue eyes.

For an instant, Tawny wondered if Cassandra might throw the cat at her. She tensed, ready to dodge.

Cassandra set Rambo on the floor. He bounded back into

the office. Hand to her breast, she gasped, "You scared me!" She snatched up the dropped cell and spoke into it, "Call you back," then disconnected. "How did you get in?"

Tawny said, "Moe gave me a key. I didn't realize you were here. Your car wasn't out front."

Cassandra waved toward the street. "I walked over to feed the cats." She noticed the swelling on Tawny's jaw. "What happened to you?"

"Accident." Evidently Cassandra had missed the TV news.

"What a shame to spoil your pretty face." Eyelashes fluttered and a sugary tone edged her speech. "You're certainly spending a lot of time with my fella."

"Just doing my job. Don't worry, I don't have designs on him."

"It's not *you* I'm worried about."

Tawny folded her arms. "Didn't I see you at the clubhouse earlier?"

One corner of the pink mouth twitched. "Yes."

"That lawyer plans to call the FBI. Doesn't sound good for Moe."

Cassandra's hand flicked like a bird flitting away. "Moshe will be fine. That investigator won't find anything he did wrong. Most of those people were unsophisticated about their investments. When the crash hit, they needed to blame someone for their own poor judgment. Moshe, being black and Jewish, is the perfect scapegoat for a bunch of white Montanans." A pout pooched her rosy mouth. "I *know* the accusations aren't true because he's done beautifully for me. We've reached our goal for the sanctuary and we'll break ground in March. I'm so excited. It's going to be like no other sanctuary on the planet."

Her version conflicted with the stories from disappointed investors. What was the truth? Tawny needed to keep her talking. "Congratulations. That's quite an accomplishment."

Cassandra gushed, "Let me show you the artist's renderings. I am so proud." She brought up her phone's gallery.

Tawny retrieved her readers and peered over the petite woman's shoulder. Cassandra flicked through drawings of a colonial-style mansion adorned by Greek columns. Doggy wading pools dotted landscaped grounds. Play areas had miniature slides, small-scale merry-go-rounds, and obstacle courses. The separate kitty playground featured climbing trees, high towers to perch on, hiding tunnels, and lounging furniture.

The renderings of the rooms inside the mansion rivaled a five-star hotel, with garden tubs in the bathrooms and in-floor tile trays with drains that Tawny guessed were doggy potties. Luxurious four-poster beds with satin duvets came in varying sizes to fit mini-Chihuahuas to Great Danes. Animal art decorated the walls. Closets displayed designer dog costumes.

A high-end commercial kitchen appeared on the screen. "The head chef will prepare from-scratch meals with fresh, organic ingredients," Cassandra said, flicking to another sketch. "This is the salon. We'll have full-time groomers and a twenty-four-seven concierge."

Cassandra's scheme stank worse than Moe's litter boxes. "Excuse my ignorance," Tawny asked, "but who scoops the poop?"

Her laughter tinkled. "How very practical and earthy you are, dear. The grounds crews will maintain sanitation to the highest standards. Maid service takes care of the interior."

Tawny wondered how employees would feel about shoveling shit for animals that lived in more opulence and ate better than their own children.

Cassandra studied Tawny's expression. "You don't approve. This offends your bourgeois middle-class sensibilities."

Whatever that meant. "I think about hungry children who don't have warm clothes for winter. What the money you're spending on this would do for them."

Again the tinkling laugh. "You don't understand. Pets *are* their children. In fact, in most cases, the pets give infinitely more love, support, and comfort than human offspring. Like darling Moshe, whose children have been a heart-breaking disappointment to him. You wouldn't believe how many people are in similar circumstances. Their pets love them with all their hearts, without conditions, without reservations. You can't put a crass dollar value on such total love. Of course, they want to see their devoted companions rewarded and cared for."

Tawny tried to keep her tone neutral. "I guess I don't understand. So how much would it cost to provide for, say, Moe's nine cats?"

Without a blink, Cassandra answered, "Ninety thousand a year. Ten per cat. Really quite reasonable when you consider the exceptional level of care that's all-inclusive, veterinary, food, grooming, maintenance. Dogs run a little higher, depending on size and breed. Say, fifteen to twenty."

For ten years of care, Moe would spend $900,000. Plus whatever it cost to build the sanctuary. Holy crap. This had to be the sinkhole where his money had disappeared.

Cassandra prattled on, "Endowments are the foundation's life blood but I couldn't have accomplished this without Moshe's brilliant investment strategies. He turned my humble startup into a truly meaningful venture." She shut off the phone gallery, obviously bored with trying to explain sophisticated concepts to someone as lowly and ignorant as Tawny. "Well, the cats are fed, so you can go now."

Tawny suspected Cassandra wanted to push her out of Moe's house to cover up what she had been doing in the office. As weary as Tawny felt, she couldn't leave without learning more. "I still need to clean the litter boxes," she said, moving through the kitchen into the utility room. "Unless *you* were planning to..." She smiled over her shoulder at the bite-a-lemon pinch of Cassandra's pink mouth.

"I'll be going. You're a love to take care of the cats' other needs." Cassandra hustled out.

At the office door, Tawny peeked inside, looking for Rambo. He sprang down from a high shelf, hissed at her again, and escaped into the great room. She stood back, allowing him plenty of space. Thank goodness he didn't force another standoff. Her foot still ached, along with the throb in her jaw.

She found Moe's computer on but in sleep mode. When she moved the mouse, a website flashed up for *This Side of the Rainbow Bridge Foundation*. Cassandra's project was adorned with appealing photos of fluffy cats and sad-eyed dogs to induce donors to open their wallets. Why had the woman been poking around on Moe's computer? Odd. Surely she had her own.

Tawny clicked on a heading titled "Contributions." A spreadsheet filled the screen and went on for several pages, columns totaling more than $4.6 million. It looked like an internal report, something public visitors to the website wouldn't have access to. Cassandra had probably gotten into the page with an administrator password and inadvertently left it open.

Was this file the proof that Moe's money, along with his neighbors' investments, had been sucked into Cassandra's foundation?

Tawny copied the file, emailed it to Tillman, and saved it to a flash drive. His accountant needed to figure out what it meant.

Her cell rang. Emma.

"Mom, you have to come get me."

Emma hadn't been home since she stomped out two mornings before. "Are you all right, honey?"

"Yeah, yeah!" Impatient. "Just come, OK? My car needs a jump."

Not the first time her daughter's junker had left her stranded. "Where are you?"

"Golden Eagle."

"I'm already at Moe's. Give me an address."

Emma described a new section of condos about a mile away.

Tawny left the computer on, figuring she'd come back to search more after she jumped Emma's car.

She locked Moe's house and drove through meandering lanes, up a hill to a newer phase of the development. Since the recession, construction had screeched to a halt, leaving half-built structures covered with snow. The only finished building in that section was a four-plex condo perched by itself at the top of the rise overlooking the golf course and mountains.

One unit had been set up as a model home, with exterior lighting. The rest appeared dark and vacant. The street was empty except for Emma's Hyundai in front of the model.

Tawny parked her Jeep nose to nose with Emma's car. She got out and retrieved jumper cables from the rear.

Headlights illuminated Emma sulking inside her car. The girl needed a spanking.

"Pull the hood latch," Tawny called, since her daughter didn't seem inclined to get out. The hood popped. Tawny brushed thick powdery corrosion off the battery terminals, and connected the jumpers between the dead Hyundai and the Jeep's battery. She got back into the Jeep and revved the engine for a couple of minutes to send charge to the Hyundai. Then she motioned out the window for Emma to start the car.

The engine ground, causing the Jeep lights to dim, but it

finally caught. Tawny unhooked the jumpers and walked to Emma's window.

Reluctantly, her daughter rolled it down.

Tawny wanted to scream, *you ungrateful little shit!* Instead, through gritted teeth, she said, "You're very welcome."

Emma grunted, "Thanks."

Tawny stalked to the back of her Jeep. Fuming, she coiled the cables, put them away, and slammed the hatch. She would never leave her child helpless on a Montana winter night, but, dammit, there were times when it didn't sound like a bad idea. Maybe Emma and Moe should get together in a broken-down car. Kill two brats with one stone.

Emma got out of the Hyundai and approached. Head down but gaze turned up, pleading. "Would you follow me home, Mom? Please?"

Tawny folded her arms. "You stormed out and now you want to come home?"

A nod.

"The teeny-bopper games are over, Emma. If not, you need to find somewhere else to live." The threat pained Tawny's heart but her daughter had to grow up. Someday.

Emma shuffled to her car, head hanging.

Tawny drove behind the Hyundai down the curving hill. The Jeep's headlights shone on the rag still plugging Emma's gas tank. The girl couldn't even take care of her own car.

They were moving past a field of snow bordered by evergreens near the golf course exit when a flash caught Tawny's eye.

More than a flash, a fire. Flames licked up around the edges of Emma's trunk. The gas tank underneath must be on fire. *Oh God!*

Tawny honked frantically and swerved up beside the Hyundai.

Emma was texting with both thumbs, cell propped on the steering wheel, oblivious.

Tawny blasted the horn and shrieked her daughter's name.

Emma's mouth pulled sideways in annoyance until she noticed Tawny's desperate gestures at the trunk. Realization widened her eyes. She slammed on the brakes and jumped out. Tawny flung open the Jeep passenger door. "Get in!" she screamed.

For once, Emma didn't argue. She threw herself into the Jeep. Tawny raced away from the Hyundai before Emma could close the door, and didn't stop until at least a hundred feet separated them from the burning car.

A whooshing tower of flame billowed into the black night. Emma covered her face with her hands and screamed.

Tawny grabbed her close. "Shh, shh, it's OK, you're safe, I've got you."

Emma bawled, clinging desperately to Tawny, hot tears dripping on her neck.

Fingers of flame crept over the body of the Hyundai, bubbling paint. One by one, windows popped from the heat. Jewel-like bits of glass scattered on the ground, reflecting red and orange highlights of the fire. The stench of burning plastic, rubber tires, and gasoline fouled the air.

Tawny ran her hands over her baby's head, neck, shoulders, down her arms and legs, making sure her perfect beautiful daughter was still whole and safe. She damned herself for her horrible thoughts moments before.

Dear God, I didn't mean it. Forgive me.

CHAPTER 19 – WHITE CROSS

Renata Schliefman told herself she wasn't impaired. She lowered the driver's window halfway on her Chrysler, confident the whip of freezing air across her face would quickly erase the effects of four glasses of wine slammed down.

The wine didn't disturb her as much as her embarrassment. What was she thinking?

The day had been arduous, meeting with the Golden Eagle residents, hearing their sad stories, anticipating the mountain of work ahead to build a case against Moe Rosenbaum.

Work didn't bother her. In fact, the challenge exhilarated her, tracing connections, linking evidence piece by piece, like stringing beads on a necklace, to the moment of triumph when she knew she'd cornered a fraudster.

The aftermath brought the letdown. Yes, she'd proved her cases time and time again. Yes, the judge or jury found the defendants guilty. But victims were never made whole. They'd lost their homes and life savings. And they blamed *her* when the thief walked away with a year or two of probation. In fifteen years, she'd never seen fair restitution. Not once.

The case against Moe Rosenbaum was at a dead end before it started. With homicide charges, now to be followed by a criminal assault caught on video, financial fraud ranked way down on the prosecutorial food chain.

In law school, Renata had promised herself to make meaningful differences in citizens' lives. Right the wrongs. Punish the guilty. Restore balance and dispense justice. She should've become a rabbi instead of an attorney.

When the sum total of her life was placed on the scales before HaShem, what value would God give to neat stacks of meticulously-prepared, skillfully-prosecuted cases that failed to make a single victim whole again? Didn't seem like much of a contribution.

Renata appreciated the interest Tawny had shown at the fraud talk. After delivering hundreds of cautionary lectures to audiences all over the state, Renata had reconciled herself to the disappointment that only a handful of people ever really listened to her warnings. Most came after they'd already been scammed and simply wanted to tell their sad stories.

But Renata recognized immediately from the way Tawny leaned forward with rapt attention that she really wanted to learn. She was trying to do a good job for Tillman Rosenbaum, a notoriously demanding lawyer to work for. Renata admired that. Plus, she was a startlingly attractive woman, with her auburn french braid and soft, expressive brown eyes.

And easy to talk to. At the bar, Renata had unpacked the years of frustration she'd been lugging around like a heavy backpack. Tawny really listened, like she cared, unlike most people who dismissed someone else's problems as nothing compared to their own. And God knew, Tawny had plenty of her own troubles with the volatile Rosenbaum clan.

It would have been fun to go skiing and enjoy drinks together. But Renata had blown what might have turned into a really nice friendship.

Forty years old and still dumb enough to get wasted and hit on a straight woman. Pitiful.

Even though Tawny had been gracious about the gaffe, Renata was too mortified now to ever follow through on the ski date. Shit.

In Bigfork, Renata stopped at the market to grab a sandwich then turned on 209 toward the Swan Highway. At least three hours to home. She raised the window, feeling more sober but cold and weary.

Headlights followed her, high beams glaring in her mirror.

She adjusted it.

Maybe she should have taken 93 to Missoula, then I-90 to 12, a more heavily travelled route. But there'd been no snow in the past few days and the two-lane road ahead looked clear and dry.

The lights drew up on her, following too close for winter night driving. Maybe a drunk or goofball kids screwing around. She moved to the right to give the tailgater a chance to pass.

The idiot didn't.

The road now paralleled the Swan River. The Kearney Rapids boat launch was up ahead where she could turn around and backtrack. Yeah, that's what she'd do. Stick to the safer route even if it added almost an hour to the trip.

Idiot stayed on her tail. Must be a damn drunk.

A *thunk* against her bumper made her swerve. Asshole. She accelerated hard to get away.

Damn, where was her cell? In her briefcase, she remembered, in the back seat. She didn't dare take her hands off the wheel to grab for it.

Another bump, harder. Her Chrysler veered over the center line, careening back and forth.

Then he came up on her rear quarter and turned into her, hard, pushing the Chrysler sideways across the lane, close to the drop-off into the river.

She wrestled with the wheel, trying to maintain control. Because of the blinding high beams, she couldn't identify the other vehicle but the impact felt like a heavy rig, a truck or big SUV.

She caught a glimpse of a white cross on the shoulder of the road—the marker of a previous traffic fatality. This son of a bitch was trying to kill her.

The rig backed off for a bare second, then rammed her. The shoulder belt locked with a sharp bite into her neck and chest.

She fought for control but the Chrysler spun one-hundred-eighty degrees. Rear end leading, it hurtled over the embankment on a downward trajectory toward the river, rolling and tumbling.

~~~

The sound of someone crashing down the hillside through brush roused Renata. She didn't know how long she'd been out. "Help!" she croaked. She struggled to call louder, forcing every bit of breath from her scalding lungs. "Help me!"

Miraculously, after tumbling repeatedly, the Chrysler had come to rest upright but the caved-in roof pressed her head sideways, her neck in crooked agony. She couldn't straighten. Hunks of glass from the sunroof gouged her scalp.

Not a single airbag had deployed. A stray wild thought flitted through her mind: *Why the hell did I waste $500 for the rollover option?*

Outside, the crashing noise stopped. Then the car rocked, as if someone was pulling on the door. She couldn't see for the blood in her eyes. She tried to reach the handle but her arm didn't work.

The rear door screeched, metal against metal, as someone yanked on it. An acrid smell of gasoline. A male voice: "Dammit!"

She tried to turn to see her rescuer but her neck screamed. Better stay still for now. Someone was here who would save her from the mashed wreck.

"Help me," she murmured.

The car springs sank as the rescuer climbed in the back seat, huffing hard from exertion. Maybe her door was too damaged to open.

Heavy breathing. Jostling. Rattling of paper. A hard jolt

against her seat that nearly made her pass out from pain. The smell of gas seared her lungs. "Help me, please."

Why didn't he talk to her?

She felt the springs lift as the rescuer got out of the car. Maybe he needed to find a different approach.

Quiet. Then more crashing through brush. He was leaving. To get help. Please.

Blood kept pouring down her face, into her eyes, but she couldn't lift her hand to wipe it away.

Her heartbeat felt like slow weak pats. Hurt too much to breathe. The gas smell faded away. Cold settled over her.

She waited and listened. No sound except for the river trickling through ice.

Surely he'd come back.

Thoughts sluggishly appeared, then lost their way in gray fog. Just before she faded out, she wondered: will they put a Star of David for her beside that cross?

CHAPTER 20 – UP IN SMOKE

Two hours after the volunteer fire department extinguished Emma's Hyundai, mother and daughter curled together at home on the living room couch, covered by the afghan. Emma's head rested on Tawny's shoulder.

"Colin is a complete jerk," Emma said.

Tawny stroked her hair. "What makes you say that?" *Let her tell it her own way, even though you already know he's a jerk.*

"He seemed so cool and funny at first. We were having fun. Then he got all weird."

"Weird, how?"

Emma shifted, pulling away. "I don't want to talk about it."

"OK." *Wait her out.* "Where have you been staying the last couple of nights?"

"With Colin, in that condo where my car was."

"Does he rent it?"

Emma scoffed. "Of course not! He broke in. The builder doesn't even know he's there. Electricity's on 'cause they want to keep it as a model to show to customers."

Great. A burglar and a squatter, as well as a jerk. "If he offered to care-take the place, he might be able to stay there rent-free."

"No reason to. He lives at his mom's. He just wants to get away from her sometimes. Besides, he's always going on trips for the foundation. Why get tied down with a dumb care-taking job?"

Tawny worried what other crimes he'd lured her daughter into. "Is he going on a trip soon?"

Emma shifted again but this time to face Tawny. "Yeah. He promised he'd take me to Venice in Florida, all these awesome mansions built on canals just like the real Venice. Then he says, forget it, I'm too boring and bourgeois. I wouldn't fit in with the crowd he runs with."

That word again. First from Cassandra, now Colin.

"What's *bourgeois*, Mom?"

"We ought to Google it." She pulled out her phone then hesitated. "I don't think it's necessarily a bad thing."

"The way he said it made it sound like I had dog shit on my shoe."

"Do you know how to spell it?"

"I dunno. B-o-o-z-j-w-a?"

Tawny tapped the keyboard. "No, that's not it. I'll ask Virgie or Tillman. They'll know." She squeezed her daughter's hand. "What do you think he meant?"

Emma's gaze dropped. "Might be the opposite of kinky." Her mouth twisted to one side. "He likes weird sex stuff, Mom."

Tawny stiffened. "Did he hurt you?"

Emma shook her head. "Not like that. I mean, he's an awesome crotch cannibal and the first time he gave me nine orgasms. Nine!"

Two hours ago, her daughter would barely speak to her, now she shared a hell of a lot more than Tawny wanted to know. "So what's weird?"

"Just, well, he says he's pansexual. He'll go for anything with anybody. And, like, that's cool. But..."

Tawny forced her muscles to relax so Emma couldn't feel her tension. *Keep her talking.*

Emma's eyes met Tawny's. "He starts talking about how you're really hot and he wants us to do a threesome, you, me, and him."

Tawny could no longer control her flinch nor the disgust that rose in her throat. "What did you say?"

"I told him he made me sick, the idea sucked, and he was a

perv. We started arguing. Then Colin got a call—I think, from his mom—and he took off. I hung around for about an hour, so I could finish telling him off but he never came back. Then my car wouldn't start and I called you."

Tawny realized Emma's earlier snotty attitude probably stemmed from the argument with Colin, rather than the squabble between mother and daughter. A new worry wiggled like a poisonous snake into her mind. "Were you using protection?"

Emma burst into tears and hiccupped for several minutes while Tawny held her. "Mom, I don't know what I was thinking. He said he didn't like it because it took away all the spontaneity, made it seem forced and unnatural. But, jeez, then later he starts talking about all these women he's screwed to get money for the foundation. And men, too. Oh, Mom, I'm scared."

Tawny rocked her, stomach burning with worry. "Shh, shh, honey. We'll get you checked for STDs. Pregnancy too." *Oh, please let my daughter be all right.*

~~~

Colin burst through the connecting door from the garage into Cassandra's condo. The stench of gasoline came with him and wafted across the great room as he moved to the inlaid wood dining table and tossed a blood-spattered briefcase on it. His full lips pouted.

Oh dear, Cassandra thought, he's in another sulk. She approached him, reaching for his dreadlocks. "My adorable bad boy, when Mama needs you, you always come running."

Colin flipped his dreads out of her reach and stalked to the kitchen. He picked up one of the many cans of disinfectant air freshener he insisted on keeping in each room throughout their home. He waved the can in a figure-eight pattern around him but even its perfume couldn't cover up the gas smell.

"I'm done with this hard-core shit," he snarled. "I'll please all the rich old queers and dowagers you want but I'm not getting my hands dirty again."

At the liquor cabinet, Cassandra poured herself a cognac. "Are your balls shrinking, darling?"

"I told you—white collar stuff, finance, hacking, that's cool. Nobody gets bloody. But I almost broke my leg climbing down that cliff. I barely made it back up. That damn woman lawyer, her weak little voice calling 'help.' Blood all over the place. Must have been gallons. I don't need this shit." He moved to the sideboard, snatched the snifter from Cassandra's hand, and drank it down. Rebellion flared in his vivid blue eyes.

She ignored his defiance, refilled the snifter, and carried it to the sofa. Settling into the soft cushions, she sipped and watched him. *He's faltering, too sentimental. He's never been tested this hard before.*

He stalked to where she sat. "Rigging that goddamn gas tank, I'm going to stink for days. I've scrubbed my hands five times already." He grasped Cassandra's jaw with one hand, waving the other under her nose. The stink filled her nostrils. "You like that, huh? My new cologne, eau du ethanol."

His rebellion had just tipped over the edge into unacceptable.

Her hand shot up to pinch his ear, digging her fingernails deep into the fleshy lobe. He grunted, squirmed, and tried to pull free but she twisted harder. Her nails met, puncturing the skin.

His blue eyes widened with panic and pain, probably remembering the time she'd torn a gold hoop clear through his earlobe.

Through clenched teeth, she said, "You are not going to

crack, Colin. Not at this critical time. Do you understand me?"

His tongue flicked over his lips as he lowered his gaze in submission.

Finally, she released him, satisfied to see a little half-moon of blood blossoming on his earlobe.

He scooted away, rubbing the wound.

She crossed to the table where the state investigator's briefcase lay. The dry blood spots easily flaked away under her fingernail. She pulled out a Chromebook and sheaf of complaints from the residents at Golden Eagle. Skimming the pages, she recognized the evidence against Moshe was incontrovertible and damning. Only a few steps of forensic accounting would be needed to establish the connection between Moshe and her.

By retrieving the briefcase, at least Colin had delayed the investigation for a little while. Complaints could be recreated but that took time, time they needed to tie up loose ends.

Cassandra fanned the papers at Colin to soften her earlier rebuke. "Darling, you did well getting these."

He stood at the kitchen sink, steam rising around him, as he scrubbed his hands hard under hot running water. He hazarded a glance over his shoulder at her. Good—not too beaten down this time. Sometimes after punishment, he'd retreat into a fetal ball in his bed for hours, facing the wall.

Cassandra opened the glass door of the fireplace and, page by page, slowly fed the reports into the flames, so they burned completely. As yellow and blue fingers crept along the edges, she drifted back in memory to when she'd learned she was pregnant with Colin.

His father had been her first mark, although she didn't realize it until later. In many ways, the man—what *was* his name?—reminded her of Moshe, once handsome but dissipated, desperately grasping at waning virility, alone and estranged from family because of his temper. They'd met in the retirement home where she worked.

The pregnancy had surprised her, never expecting the seed of a seventy-nine-year-old would still be viable. When she told him the news, he immediately rewrote his will, leaving his entire half-million-dollar estate to her. Three months later, he died of a heart attack, never meeting his unborn son. Along with Colin, Cassandra gave birth to a new business model.

That worked well until the ugliness in New Hampshire forced her to find a different strategy and she'd developed the bogus pet sanctuary. They'd lived comfortably on that model for the past decade, always moving on two steps ahead of authorities.

They'd done well in Montana until Tawny showed up. At first, Cassandra hoped Colin's interest in the woman's skanky daughter might be a useful conduit through which she could keep tabs on Tawny's investigation. But Emma was a self-absorbed ditz who didn't know, or care, what her mother was doing. She simply became a distraction when Colin needed to concentrate.

The car fire should focus Tawny's attention away from Moshe onto her nuisance daughter instead. At least temporarily. That pushy damn woman kept showing up at the most inconvenient times, like tonight when Cassandra had planned to wipe Moshe's hard drive.

During their conversation, Cassandra noticed the flash of realization that crossed Tawny's face when she learned the cost of care for Moshe's cats. Under her phony smiling sweetness, she was smarter than she appeared. Between her, the lawyer-son, and now the FBI, they could piece the plan together.

Moshe's dependence had made the plan work. Cassandra's arsenal of drugs hyped him up when necessary and made him malleable at other times. Between his dementia and drugs, he couldn't follow the financial manipulations she'd orchestrated.

But the old man was no longer worth the risk he posed.

Moshe was the linchpin in any case against Cassandra. Both he and Tawny had to go.

The last page of evidence flaked into black ash in the fireplace.

CHAPTER 21 – ARSON CONFIRMED

The next morning at eight, Tillman called while Tawny was trying to wake up with her third cup of coffee. "How's your face?"

More bruises had blossomed overnight. "Purple."

"Next time you conk my old man on the noggin, use a sledgehammer and make sure you finish the job."

"Are you soliciting me to kill him?"

"Yeah, and I'll gladly defend you for free."

Tawny almost smiled but pain stopped her. "How is he?"

"Well and truly screwed. Aggravated assault charges. That cell video tied the bow on top of his damn case. I called the judge, explained what happened, told her I needed to determine competency to stand trial. She agreed. The psych facility is testing him now."

"How long does that take?"

"Depends. Checking blood and urine. If they find indications of mental illness, he may be placed in a locked unit after the competency hearing. I could buy a Cadillac for what this old man is costing me."

Tawny's heart ached but, in Moe's unpredictable condition, better that he stayed in custody.

Tillman went on: "That stuff you sent last night about the pet sanctuary. My accountant's been at it since five this morning."

She remembered Renata's comment about the lawyer's relentless work ethic. "Is there any point in chasing that wild goose now? Fraud sounds pretty tame compared to the rest of the charges against him."

"If we don't look, we don't know what we'll find."

She sighed. "OK, I'll feed the cats."

He grunted. "About those cats. We have to dispose of them."

"Tillman! You can't. Those are his children. If he ever gets out and they're gone, he'll be devastated."

"Too bad Cassandra's pet sanctuary isn't finished. We could ship them there."

"If it even exists," Tawny answered, "which I seriously doubt. The whole thing smells like a sham."

"Based on what my accountant's found so far, signs point in that direction."

"I'll take care of the cats for now. They're all sweet, except Rambo and he's just being protective of Moe."

"You're a marshmallow, Tawny."

His tone didn't sound as if he meant that as a compliment. "Look, I'll just do it. You don't have to pay me."

A pause, then a grumble. "Keep track of your goddamn hours and mileage, like always."

She smiled at Tillman softening. Then she remembered. "Hey, I might need a little extra time off. My daughter's car burned up last night."

"What?" His sardonic tone switched to real alarm.

"She's all right but the car's totaled. I need to help her find a replacement—"

"How did it happen?"

"She lost her gas cap and has been driving around with a rag hanging out of the tank. I guess that must have caught on fire."

"That's a damn myth," he snapped. "Is there an investigation?"

Why was he upset? "It's an old car. She didn't maintain it. Who knows what happened?"

"Get it checked out, dammit."

"Why?" Tawny didn't like the doubt creeping up her neck.

"Tawny, be careful. I mean it. You've rammed a stick in a hornet's nest."

She pulled on her braid. Tillman's suspicions had an uneasy pattern of coming true. "I will."

"I'm driving over to Kalispell this afternoon. We'll go see how the old man is doing." He disconnected.

So much for a few days off.

Emma stumbled out of her bedroom to the kitchen. "Coffee, Mom, please."

Tawny handed her a mug.

Emma cocked her head sideways and peered at Tawny. "Your face looks worse this morning."

"Gee, thanks."

"Does it still hurt?"

"Aches."

"That old man is bat-shit crazy. Why do you keep working for that prick, Tillman?"

"It's my secret plot to destroy him by making his worker's comp rates go up."

Emma rolled her eyes.

"I've got the morning off. Do you want to look at used cars?"

"No money. My insurance is only liability, no comprehensive." From her slumped posture at the breakfast bar, she looked up at Tawny with a smile that had a hook in it. "Unless you want to lend me the money."

"Are you working?"

"Mo-om."

"The bank would ask you the same thing before they'd make you a car loan."

Emma swirled her coffee. "I'll go back to the Lucky Dragon."

"Seriously?" Tawny leveled a hard stare at her. "Don't you

have a heart? Jim's in love with you and you're screwing around on him."

Emma twisted her hair into a knot and fastened it atop her head. "He'll let me come back. He always does."

Tawny frowned. "Your dad and I didn't raise you to use people. Jim is a really good guy and you're treating him like crap." Another discouraging thought occurred to her. "Get checked out for STDs before you're with Jim again. But I hope he's smart enough to stay away from you."

Emma's eyes flashed defiance. "That's a hurtful thing to say."

"Your behavior is what's hurtful and I'm ashamed of you." Tawny planted both hands on the counter, leaning close to her daughter's face. "Emma, don't you remember last night? Crying and saying how scared you were? Today you're ready to blow it off like nothing happened."

Emma couldn't keep eye contact. "All right, all right."

Tawny suspected she was agreeing simply to stop the scolding.

It was time to pull out the most potent guilt weapon in her mom bag of tricks. Emma had always been *Daddy's girl*. Dwight could get through to her in a way Tawny never could. She gripped her daughter's chin and forced her to look up. "What if your dad was still here? Watching you act like this? What would *he* say to you right now?"

Emma licked her lips and swallowed hard.

Tawny went on: "You could never lose his love but you'd lose his respect and you'd never get that back again."

She watched conflicting emotions play behind hazel eyes. *Please, Dwight, make her listen now.*

"Think about your dad, Emma." Tawny released her daughter's chin and left the kitchen.

~~~

Late that afternoon, Tawny sat in Tillman's Mercedes SUV, enjoying the passenger seat warmer that soothed the chill in her bones as she waited outside the psych unit where Moe was confined. Tillman had wanted her to go inside with him when he talked with the psychiatrist but the claustrophobia of the locked facility felt too scary.

He strode out of the building to the car and folded his long limbs into the driver's seat. "Moe flunked the piss test."

"What kind of drugs?" she asked.

"Like V8 Juice, a little bit of everything." He ticked off the list on his fingers. "Meth, benzodiazepine, cocaine, opioids, PCP, testosterone, steroids. Some of the shit is prescribed, some not." He rotated his head side to side, causing cracks in his neck loud enough for Tawny to hear. "I'm having his hair tested also to see how far back in time it goes."

Tawny wondered about the suspicious pill she'd given Moe at the arraignment. Did it show up on the test? She wanted to ask but Tillman would never tell.

The punctures and scratches still showed red on his face and neck from Rambo's attack.

"I look like I shaved with a hedge trimmer," he muttered and glanced at her. "And you look like you went a couple rounds with Wladimir Klitschko." He rubbed the gashes. "My goddamn pain-in-the-ass old man sure has caused a lot of grief."

She sighed. "Have they checked for dementia?"

"Hard to tell until his system clears out."

Tawny hugged herself. "Poor Moe."

"Poor Moe?" Tillman roared. "He's an idiot! Seventy-five years old and trying to blow his heart out of his chest."

"Maybe he wants to keep up with his girlfriend. She looks

like she's in her fifties, but I think she's had some work done."

"More likely, women try to keep up with him. He's plowed through enough of them."

"What about those drugs you found in his bathroom? Anything illegal there?"

"Being analyzed. We need to go back and completely toss the place, before he gets out."

She faced him. "Do you really think he'll be released?"

He grinned. "I'm good."

She scoffed. "I don't doubt that. But is he safe out on his own?"

"He won't be by himself. You're going to move in with him."

For one horrifying second, she thought he was serious. Then she recognized a mischievous glint in his dark eyes. "You *are* an asshole, Tillman."

"You should've seen the look on your lovely black-and-blue face." He massaged the back of his neck. "Isn't there a gym around here? I'm in knots after driving eight hours."

Tawny pointed. "Next street over. I've got a membership. You can use my guest pass."

He stared at her as if a flower were growing out of her nose.

"What?" she asked, trying to figure out his funny expression.

"I can afford the day fee, Tawny."

"I know."

"Why would you waste your guest pass on me?"

"Why wouldn't I?"

"You don't have to."

"You didn't have to offer me a pay advance, either, to fix my wiring. But you did. And that was nice of you."

His expression grew even more unreadable. What the hell,

she'd never figure out what he was thinking.

Ten minutes later, they met outside the locker rooms. He'd changed into shorts, a tank top, and sneakers. She'd never seen him in less than a dress shirt and trousers, most often a suit. His lean body looked ripped, with dark hair on his arms and legs. Virgie was right—he *was* cute.

"Going to do some lifting," he said.

Tawny flipped him a wave. "I'll be walking."

The oval track ran around the perimeter of the gym, past the basketball court, the Zumba studio, the climbing wall, and weight benches. As she passed with each lap, she watched him doing dead lifts, chest presses, and squats as he added plates to the barbell until it weighed more than three hundred pounds. Sweat dripped from his curly hair and made his bronze skin gleam.

How she used to love watching Dwight work out. And afterward, sliding her hands over the familiar, sensuous ripple of his muscles. What would Tillman's biceps feel like?

Stop that!

She joined a Zumba class to avoid staring at him and the uncomfortable tickle that had started inside her. Once, in the dance studio mirror, she caught a glimpse of him watching *her*. Damn. This wasn't smart. Bosses and employees shouldn't get involved.

After an hour, they met outside the locker rooms again, him fresh from a shower and wearing a crisp dress shirt and slacks he'd retrieved from his suitcase. She felt grungy and sweaty but didn't have her gym bag with a change of clothes.

As they rode in his SUV toward her house, he said, "I ought to take you out dancing."

Uh-oh. Here it comes. "I don't think that's a good idea, Tillman. I work for you."

His dark eyes sparkled. "In your last job, you slept with the boss all the time."

Brat. "My husband and I owned a business. That's a whole different universe than working for you."

"I'm not hitting on you, Tawny."

She had to chuckle. "The hell you say."

He winked and craned his neck, which no longer cracked. Exercise agreed with him, like it did her. "It's just when I heard *Hava Nagila* playing and saw you dancing, it took me back to the farm, being with *Bubbe* and *Zayde*, my grandparents on my mother's side."

"What farm?"

"Outside Great Falls. They grew wheat."

"Really?"

He smirked. "Did you think I was born a lawyer?"

"Just hard to imagine you on a farm, with your Burberry suits and alligator wingtips."

"My grandfather was the founder and president of the Jewish Wheat Farmers Co-op. Also the sole member."

She smiled. "Is that how you got your name? The man who tills?"

He shot her a surprised glance. "Not many people pick up on that. Yeah, *Zayde* named me." He leaned against the headrest and drifted into the past. "Staying with them was the best time of my childhood. *Bubbe* cooking and singing. *Zayde* would come in from the fields and dance her around the kitchen. She was fourteen when the concentration camp at Stutthoff was liberated. She weighed sixty-eight pounds and had watched her parents turned into soap. But now thousands of acres of food surrounded her and she had a man who loved her more than life. She'd tell me, 'Tilly, there is such abundance to be joyful for.'

"Then I'd go back to my parents' house in Billings with the tennis courts, horse paddocks, money coming out my old man's ass, and my mother locked in her bedroom crying." He shook his head.

An invisible hand gripped Tawny's heart. Behind his bluster and rage, Tillman was a disappointed man, longing for family.

Her eyes stung as she remembered Dwight. In spite of their struggles, her family had always been her abundance to be joyful for. She'd lived what Tillman had never known and, sadly, probably never would.

He pulled up in front of her home.

A sudden impulse came over her. "Why don't you come in? I'll cook you dinner."

"I owe you dinner out."

"Last time, *you* looked too bad. This time, *I* look terrible." She opened the SUV's door. "Come on in. My chicken noodle soup would make your grandmother weep."

He got out and, in three long strides, joined her at the sidewalk. "Probably not half as good as *Bubbe's*."

His unexpected eagerness touched her. She grinned up at him. "I accept that challenge."

Emma swung the front door wide, her fair skin even paler than usual. "Mom, the fire marshal called me. They found a bunch of rags in my trunk with some sort of flammable stuff on them and an igniter."

"What the hell?" Tillman blurted. "It *was* arson."

Emma nodded, head down, tears trickling.

Tawny hugged her daughter. "It's OK, honey, it'll be all right."

Tillman stomped into the living room. "What is wrong with you? It is *not* all right. Don't you understand what this means?"

Sobs erupted from Emma. Anger constricted Tawny's throat. "Dammit, Tillman, you're just upsetting her more."

He flung his arms in the air. "Oh yeah, I forgot, I'm on

Planet Pollyanna, where everyone is sweet and helpful and honest as the day is long." He stalked into the kitchen and reached above the refrigerator for the new bottle of scotch.

Tawny pushed her daughter down on the couch and sat beside her, forcing her voice to remain calm. "This is serious, Emma. Someone's trying to hurt you. Do you think Colin could have done it?"

"Who's Colin?" Tillman returned to the living room with a full glass.

Tawny threw him a *shut-up* look. She'd never get Emma to talk if he kept interrupting. "Cassandra's son. Emma and he have been seeing each other and they had a fight." Tawny crooked a finger under her chin and tipped her face up. "Do you think Colin would do that?"

"Maybe. He's a perv."

"Is there anyone else you can think of?"

A long hesitation. Emma looked down and murmured, "Jim?"

Tawny felt as if a balloon in her chest had been punctured and was slapping against her ribs as it deflated.

Please, God, not sweet, loyal Jim. Her daughter had treated him horribly. Was he capable of revenge? As much as Tawny detested the thought, she needed to recognize it was possible. If Jim had learned about Colin, jealousy might have taken control.

"Who the hell is Jim?" Tillman demanded.

She jabbed her hand at him in a *stop* gesture. To Emma, she asked, "Did you mention Colin or Jim to the fire marshal?"

Emma shook her head. "I'm afraid to get them in trouble."

"Have you talked to Jim?"

"Dammit, Tawny," Tillman growled, "don't encourage her to contact someone who might've tried to kill her."

Emma's bawling revved up again. She ran into her room

and slammed the door.

Tawny jumped to her feet and glared at Tillman. "Thank you very much for coming into my home and scaring my daughter."

He slugged down half the glass. "*I* didn't set her car on fire. You keep thinking I'm the bad guy. I'm just the messenger, trying to warn you about evil people out to get you."

She turned away. "Emma's scared. You're just making it worse."

He grasped her arm. "Who is Jim?"

She pulled loose. "Her boyfriend. The one I was hoping would be my son-in-law. He might have been too, until that damn Colin showed up. Jim's mom and uncle own the restaurant where Wilbur worked. You remember Wilbur, don't you? The poor man *your father* ran down."

Tillman's jutting jaw turned to granite.

Tawny instantly regretted her jab. She sank to the couch, head in her hands. "I didn't mean that. It's just I'm so ashamed my daughter treated a really good man like dirt. And now she might have an STD or be pregnant, thanks to this creep, Colin. I was trying not to embarrass her in front of you but you kept butting in on our conversation. And I can't bear to think that Jim maybe committed arson to get back at her."

Tillman lowered himself next to her. "I'm a lawyer." His voice no longer sounded angry but instead weary. "By the time people come to me, their lives are in the toilet and it's half-way through the flush. Nobody needs to be embarrassed. Especially not *you*."

She tried to swallow her mortification, hoping he meant what he said.

He sipped his drink. "Look, Tawny, this scam my old man is mixed up with is unraveling. I'd bet good money that the reason Emma's car was set on fire is probably not jealousy.

She's got to watch out for herself. And you've got to watch out for yourself."

A chill tingled up her back. No, *she* had to watch out for *Emma*.

He placed hands on knees and heaved himself to his feet. "Better get going."

She trailed him to the entry. "I shouldn't have lashed out at you."

He opened the door and looked down at her, again with the strange expression she couldn't, or didn't want to figure out. "I'm used to major-league flogging. Your little remark was like being whipped with dental floss."

Still embarrassed but reassured, she gave him a play shove on the chest.

Quick as a cobra, his cool hand covered hers, pressing it into his shirt. His heartbeat thudded under her palm. "I still intend to find out if your soup is half as good as *Bubbe's*." He let go of her hand. "But not tonight." He moved down the porch steps.

She shut the door and leaned against it for moment, eyes closed, as confusion and fear swirled around her. Then she headed toward Emma's bedroom, wondering how to console her daughter but, more important, how to warn her and make it stick.

CHAPTER 22 – BREAK-IN

At seven the next morning, Tillman picked Tawny up in his Mercedes. Ice fog glowed eerily in the headlights. "We're meeting a locksmith at Moe's place to change the locks. I should've thought of this earlier, with Cassandra having a key. Dammit."

He wore brown slacks and a tan suede jacket, over an apricot-colored sport shirt. Except for workout gear, this was the most casual she'd ever seen him.

"Pull the file out of my briefcase," he said. "See what my investigator finally turned up on the lovely Cassandra."

Tawny put on her readers and pawed through the leather satchel. She opened a folder to a picture of a much younger Cassandra with dark hair instead of platinum, before the neck lift and collagen. It looked like a police booking photo. "What the hell?"

"Cassandra Maza a.k.a. Carmen Matranga. Her grandparents were chemists who founded a successful pharmaceutical company in Italy."

"Moe told me she'd inherited money."

"That was before a tainted batch of their antibiotics killed four children. Shut down the company and wiped out her inheritance. She became a pharmacist. Twenty-one years ago, she was working for a high-end assisted living home in New Hampshire. The residents loved her. She charmed even the most cantankerous ones that no one else on the staff could handle. She became especially close with wealthy ones who didn't have relatives or were estranged from family. See where this is going?"

"She'd drug them and get them to change their wills? Leaving everything to her?"

Tillman nodded. "Without heirs, there was no one to

complain. Until a long-lost relative showed up and demanded an investigation. A detective looked into some deaths involving drug interactions and wrong dosages. She was charged but the prosecution couldn't prove intent, only *accidental* mishandling. She beat it. Never convicted, no jail time, but she lost her pharmacist license."

"Whew." Cassandra's cold blue eyes stared out from the photo. "She's been doing the same thing to Moe. That's why he has all those drugs in his system."

"Maybe." His tone sounded dubious.

How could Tillman miss something so obvious? "What if his crazy behavior isn't dementia, but drugs?" A shiver of excitement ran up her spine. "When he beat up his neighbor, he had drugs in his system. Remember, the night he got lost, I told you he described it like a date rape drug? But once he got warm, he seemed OK, so I figured it was hypothermia. What if he was doped up when he ran over Wilbur?"

Tillman stared at the road ahead. "What if he's been lying to you? Putting on an act? What if the two of them are working together?"

She'd never considered that possibility. She ran the scenario backwards in her mind, reviewing everything Moe had said and done since she'd met him. Yes, he was cranky and difficult, but she'd recognized an underlying tenderness that she doubted he'd ever shown toward his son.

"I'm not convinced," she said. "His behavior is too much like my grandpa's. I don't think he can help what he's doing."

A long moment passed. When Tillman spoke, his tone felt colder than the ice fog. "Congratulations, Moe Rosenbaum. You've fooled yet another gullible woman into believing you."

His insult stung more than it should have. A lot more. Tawny hugged herself.

Why did she ever think she could help Tillman? His

superior attitude shot her down time after time. Just because he'd confided in her a few times didn't mean that friendship and trust were possible between them.

She should keep her mouth shut, do what she was told, and collect a paycheck from the arrogant asshole.

But dammit, her theory fit the facts. Tillman had to see that. Her teeth grated, sending an arrow of pain into her sore jaw. "I think you hate your father so much, you'll believe the worst about him. Even if it isn't true."

He punched the radio on. "Hungry Heart" throbbed inside the Mercedes.

Tawny clamped her hands over her ears and wished she could jump out of the car.

During the half-hour drive to Golden Eagle, the relentless beat of Springsteen hammered on her. Bottled-up frustration made her feel as if she'd swallowed a thistle, a thousand prickles piercing inside. She'd had enough. If the job at Dairy Queen was still open, she'd take it. Maybe ice cream could soothe the holes burned in her stomach from working for Tillman.

When he pulled into Moe's driveway and shut off the engine, the abrupt silence felt like a heavy blanket thrown over her.

Tawny took a deep breath. "Look, you think I'm too dumb and uneducated to work for you, so let's call it quits."

He stared at her with his unreadable courtroom expression then shook his head. "Aw, shut up, Tawny." But the soft tone didn't match his harsh words.

She reached for the door handle, eager to put distance between them and almost didn't hear his low murmur, "Sorry."

"Excuse me?"

"You don't know what I think." His shoulders lifted with exasperation. "You won't follow my instructions without arguing. You take five times longer than anyone else on my staff to read something. Your spelling is so bad, I need a cryptographer to translate." His hard dark gaze met hers. "But you're smart and you're intuitive. You see things I miss. And I don't miss much. That makes you worth more than pearls."

His words flattened her against the seat back, speechless.

He went on: "Your theory about the old man *is* solid. We know he was under the influence when he assaulted the neighbor but, with the damn phone video, diminished capacity will be a hard sell to a jury. And the homicide, without a blood test or other exculpatory evidence from that night, I can't prove it. *That's* what's pissing me off."

He climbed out and came around to open her door. Still stunned, she didn't move.

He rested an arm along the SUV's roof, bending down toward her. "It's been a shitty job and when it's over, if you still want out, I understand." He straightened. "But see this through with me. Please."

She swung her legs out, pressing her hand over the ache in her stomach. "You really meant pearls?"

"Yeah?"

"Not diamonds?"

He snorted and quickly turned away but not before she caught him grinning.

Inside the condo, as she hung up her coat in the entry, something felt off.

Tillman saw her expression. "What?"

"The cats. They always come running for food. Where are they?"

"The hell with the cats." He headed to the office.

Tawny hurried through the great room, calling, "Kitty, kitty, kitty!" Not in the kitchen or utility room. The temperature in the condo felt colder than normal.

Then she noticed the french doors leading out to the golf course. One side gaped open.

"Tillman!"

He came out of the office, rage contorting his face. "Computer's gone."

She pointed at the doors.

"Goddammit!" He yanked his cell out and called 9-1-1. "Yeah, reporting a burglary. One-oh-seven Osprey Lane in the Golden Eagle Golf Club." He answered the dispatcher's questions, then disconnected. "I should've changed the locks before. Do you see anything else missing?"

Tawny scanned the office. No different from the last time she'd seen it, except for a bare spot on the desk where the computer had been, a tangle of wires left behind.

The great room looked undisturbed. No visible gaps showed in the neat stacks of boxes she'd arranged.

Tillman's heavy steps pounded up the stairs to the bedroom. She started to follow then halted. "Be careful, the burglar might still be here."

An angry baritone echoed down the stairwell. "I hope he is!"

Tawny flashed on the memory of him, deadlifting over three hundred pounds. The thief might be better off to jump out a second-story window than to confront the furious lawyer.

Moments later, he thudded down the stairs. "Nothing touched up there, unless he stole some slinky underwear."

"I don't see anything else gone." She pressed her lips together. "Cassandra was working on Moe's computer when I surprised her."

"She must have come back to finish the job." He punched the air. The whoosh whistled across Tawny's face. "Dammit! Why didn't I change the locks?"

The bell chimed. Tillman crossed to the entry and whipped

the door open. "What?" he roared.

A short skinny man in coveralls, toolbox in hand, staggered backward on the porch. He stammered then finally blurted out, "I'm supposed to rekey locks."

Tillman stalked away, cursing, and went back in the office.

Tawny approached the locksmith. "Uh, we just found the place has been broken into. The sheriff is on the way. Can we call you to come back later?"

The locksmith's stare homed in on her bruised jaw, his eyes widening in horror. "Yeah, yeah, sure, no problem." He looked past her shoulder, as if he feared Tillman might return, then sprinted to his truck and raced away.

Crap. The man quite reasonably assumed he'd interrupted a fight and that Tillman must have hit her. Oh well.

She peered out the door that the burglar had left ajar. The sun peeked over the mountains casting weak winter light on the patio. The area had been shoveled, so no footprints showed. A three-foot-tall rock wall enclosed the patio, with a wrought iron gate to the golf course. Beyond the gate, the snow looked tamped down. Maybe the deputy could find the thief's tracks there.

Then she spotted holes in a layer of snow atop the wall.

Cat prints. Moe's cats had escaped through the open door.

The bell chimed again. Tawny checked for Tillman but he remained in the office.

On the porch, Obie stood erect in his brown uniform, body armor bulging under his half-zipped jacket. A ball cap with an embroidered badge covered his shaved head. He zeroed in on her bruises, frowning. "Do you need help?"

She forced a smile. "I'm fine, thanks." Tillman's footfalls sounded heavy behind her, his expression stormy. "Deputy Beaudoin, this is Moe Rosenbaum's son, Tillman."

Obie squinted up at the lawyer then back to Tawny. "Mrs.

Lindholm, would you mind stepping outside with me for a moment?"

"OK." She closed the door, leaving Tillman inside.

Obie immediately asked, "What happened?"

"Someone broke in—"

"No." He pointed at her face. "I mean *this*."

She touched her swollen jaw. Of course he'd want to talk to her alone. Amid the tense atmosphere, with her bruises and Tillman's gouged face, they must look like the poster couple for domestic combat. "No, that's not what the call's about. I'm fine, honestly. It was an accident." She grasped the door handle but Obie moved closer.

"Tawny," he murmured softly, "you still have my cell number? Use it if you need to get out of a problem."

"Thanks for your concern." She didn't say *even though it's misplaced.*

Doubt still shadowed his eyes. He didn't believe her. Let Tillman convince him. She was tired of running interference for the Rosenbaum men.

In the entry, deputy and lawyer faced each other, polite, but testosterone hung heavy in the air. Tillman gave Obie a quick rundown on the burglary, the missing computer, then pointed at the french door. "Intruder must have left this way."

"Let's look in the office first," Obie suggested. He followed Tillman, shooting a glance over his shoulder at Tawny, and closed the door firmly.

She heard the back-and-forth rumble of their voices but couldn't make out the words, although they sounded sharp, verging on anger. After several minutes, though, the sharpness eased. As they came back into the great room, Obie was asking, "Do you have the brand and serial number of the computer?"

Tillman looked at Tawny, hands out, palms up.

Somewhere in the piles of papers, she remembered seeing

an office store service contract dated three years before. "I might be able to find the receipt." Where the hell had she filed it in the thousands of pages she'd combed through? She put on her glasses, squatted before a stack of boxes, and began to dig. Out of the corner of her eye, she spotted Tillman's knee jittering, impatient as ever. "Can't you do something else while I'm searching?"

The men went to check the patio. She watched through the window as they studied the trampled snow beyond the wall then moved around the end of the building toward the street. Moments later, they returned. Obie held a camera, snapping photos of the ground.

Tawny started on a second box but still no receipt. When they re-entered the condo, she shook her head.

Obie said, "That's OK. If you find it, you can call the detectives with the information." He handed Tillman a business card. Once again, he scrutinized her bruises but said nothing more and left.

Tillman sat on the arm of a chair near the boxes she was working on, knee bouncing. Not looking up from the papers, she said, "I won't find it any faster with you watching me."

He shifted position, turning toward the tall windows to the golf course.

She wanted to clamp her hand on that knee to stop its jittering. After several minutes, she couldn't ignore him any longer and looked up.

"He thought *I* hit you," Tillman said. "Imagine that. I had to convince him, nope, not me, it was my damn father. Played the YouTube video on my phone for him. Surprised he hadn't seen it. Everybody else on the planet has."

She touched the swelling. "It was an accident, Tillman. Moe didn't mean it."

The anger seeped out of his tone, replaced by pensiveness.

"The old man told me you're the best friend he's ever had. Of course, you're his *only* friend."

That made her grimace, despite the ache in her jaw.

He went on: "He was the husband from hell but, I have to admit, he never hit my mother. First time in my whole life I heard him cry was when he called, begging me to tell you how sorry he was for hurting you."

Like it or not, she *was* Moe's only friend. And he desperately needed one.

Tawny went back to shuffling the papers in the box. "It'll go faster if you look, too. It's a Staples service contract, folded in thirds, green with red letters."

"Forget it," Tillman said.

"It's in here. I know I saved it because it didn't expire for a few more months."

"Doesn't matter. That computer's not going to wind up in a pawn shop. The hard drive's probably already been yanked out and destroyed."

She sat back on her heels. "So what do you want to do?"

"You takes 'em like you finds 'em. I should have changed the locks the first day I got here. That's what makes me so furious. It's my fault." He pinched his forehead. His torn nostril still looked painfully red. "If you hadn't emailed me the spreadsheet, we'd have nothing. Bupkis. Thank you."

"You're welcome." She picked at crumpled papers to give her nervous fingers something to do. "You want to call the locksmith to come back?"

He rose, moved to her, and extended his hand. "Maybe *you* better do it. I think I made him shit his drawers."

She studied his long fingers, the outreach he was making, felt how hard it must be for him to do. An admission he'd been wrong, compliments, an apology, and a thank you. All in under thirty minutes.

She took his hand and he pulled her to her feet. For an uncertain second, she hesitated, standing close to him, her fingers enfolded in his, inhaling the faint hint of eucalyptus, gazing at the dark hair that peeked through his open collar.

But he let go and took out his cell. He swiped up the number and gave it to her. While she waited for the locksmith to answer, he went outside to the patio.

The man agreed to come back, even though his voice still sounded nervous.

When she returned the cell to Tillman, he didn't look at her. He thrust hands deep in his jacket pockets, dark eyes fixed on the forest far down the fairway where she and Moe had skied. Seemed like months ago.

Chill air nipped at her skin. Mid-twenties, she guessed. Too cold for her light sweater. Yet instead of going inside for her coat, she stayed there, standing beside Tillman. For some unexplainable reason, it seemed like the right thing to do.

Movement in a nearby clump of trees caught her attention. Moe's tuxedo cat crept under the skirt of a blue spruce, sneaking up on unseen prey.

Tillman saw it, too.

"I'll get my coat," Tawny said, "and try to round up the cats. Although that one doesn't look like she'll be in a hurry to be cooped up inside again."

He grunted.

"Moe told me they're all rescues," she added. "Strays used to being outside on their own, hunting for food."

"Why not leave them, then?"

She tilted her head up to him. "Because they're Moe's cats and he asked me to take care of them."

"And a good Girl Scout always keeps her promises."

"Damn straight."

Instead of his normal irritation, his smile surprised her.

~~~

During the hour while the locksmith rekeyed all the doors, Tawny captured three cats.

As she fed them, she listened to Tillman on the phone with a sheriff's detective, recounting the break-in and stolen computer, sharing the findings of his background check on Cassandra, outlining his suspicion that Colin had torched Emma's car, and painstakingly making the connection to a probable case of elder fraud and abuse with drugs administered by Cassandra. He laid out facts in a logical, understandable narrative, and drew conclusions that made any other explanation unlikely.

He was damn good. No wonder he was arrogant.

Suddenly he went quiet, listening intently. He asked a few short questions, then disconnected and came into the kitchen where Tawny washed cat dishes. New strain tightened his narrow face.

"What is it?" she asked.

"Two nights ago, Renata Schliefman went over a cliff in a single-car accident on Highway 209."

Tawny grabbed the counter. "Oh, my God. Is she...?"

"Medically-induced coma in the hospital in Kalispell. She was evidently on her way home to Helena after meeting with the people who'd been scammed."

Tawny's knees wobbled. "I had a drink with her that night."

"Was she drunk?"

Tawny remembered Renata's comment about getting drunk and stupid, her humiliation for coming onto Tawny. "She slugged four glasses of wine in about fifteen minutes." She squeezed her forehead. "I shouldn't have let her drive.

Dammit!"

Tillman folded long arms. "The problem's bigger than that. If you buy that she went off the cliff without help, I *will* fire you."

She pondered for a few seconds. "You think Cassandra...? No, wait, she couldn't have done it because I found her here on the computer." A connection clicked. "Colin! Emma said when they were together, he'd gotten a call and all of a sudden took off. Cassandra must have told him to follow Renata. Oh, God."

She sank against the cupboard until fresh fear jerked her upright. "Emma! What if Colin goes after her?" She called her daughter and told her to stay home and lock the doors. For once, thankfully, Emma didn't argue.

Tawny disconnected, heart fluttering with relief. "She's safe," she said to Tillman. "What about Renata? Is she going to make it?"

His dark brows furrowed. "Detective doesn't know."

"The hospital won't release information, except to family."

Tillman tapped his cell. "We'll get it through the back door." He waited then said, "Chell, Renata Schliefman was in a car accident. Call her mother and find out what's going on." A pause. Annoyance raised his voice. "Because I need to know. Just do it, will you? Call me back." Another pause, another uptick in anger. "No, I can't. That's got to wait. All hell's breaking loose here. You have to take the kids on my next days... I don't know! Listen, this whole goddamn mess is your fault. If you hadn't insisted—" He stared at the phone. "She hung up on me."

As any wife would, if you used that ugly tone, Tawny thought. She'd only met Rochelle Rosenbaum once and felt sorry for the woman, trying to hide pain behind a gracious but cool façade. What did Tillman mean about the mess being her fault? Seemed like an unfair jab at his ex.

Before Tawny could ask, he placed another call and paced the length of the great room. "Detective, Colin Maza may have caused Renata's accident. It happened the same night as the arson fire in Emma Lindholm's car. They might be connected."

After he put away his phone, he said to Tawny, "Come on, I'm taking you home. The detectives are going to pull Cassandra and Colin in for questioning. At this point, we stay out of their way."

Tawny went to the french doors. "I still need to find the rest of the cats."

"Not today, you don't. They'll come around when they get hungry enough. You can capture them then." He strode to the entry.

Discouragement weighed her down as she stared out through the glass. The sky had changed from gray to white, signaling snow. Clouds now obscured the weak morning sun and hung heavy over the mountains like the collection of worries pressing on her shoulders.

The cats lost out in a storm.

Poor Renata, trying to do the right thing.

Moe locked up, detoxing from the drugs in his system.

Emma whose stupidity might haunt her life and destroy any chance of a stable relationship.

And Tillman, eaten up with bitterness toward his father.

No matter how hard she worked, she couldn't seem to help any of them. She rolled her head around, trying to release tension.

Tillman's cool touch on the back of her neck surprised her. She hadn't heard him approach. "You're as knotted up as I am," he said. "Too bad my masseuse is in Billings. We could both use a massage." He took his hand away and she wished he hadn't.

Instead, she longed for him to rub her muscle spasms like Dwight used to do, kneading, easing the pain until she relaxed, and sighed. Then she'd always pull his hands down from her shoulders onto her breasts... *No, this isn't Dwight. It's crazy.*

She pushed the fantasy from her mind but couldn't ignore Tillman's presence close behind her, his exhalations like a feather moving through her hair.

"That deputy wants to ask you out."

She whirled, startled by his statement. "Why would you say that?"

He wore a knowing smirk. "After we settled that I hadn't slugged you, he asked me if you and I were involved."

A flush washed over her like a warm bath. "What did you tell him?"

"That an attorney should know better than to put an employee in a position to allege sexual harassment." A strange little half smile lifted one side of his mouth. "Speaking hypothetically, of course."

"Of course," she said. "Besides, it's felony stupid to get mixed up with the boss." A pulse fluttered in her throat. "Especially a boss with a bad temper."

His head tilted slightly to the side. The hard sharp edge of his expression softened, as it had the night when he'd held her injured foot. But now mischief also lit his eyes.

Inside, her resistance started to melt but she forced herself to be sensible, practical, rational. "If things didn't work, an employee could wind up out of a job. That's a big risk."

The playfulness turned serious. "I wouldn't do that to you, Tawny."

And he meant it. In spite of Tillman's difficult, arrogant, impatient temperament, no matter what happened, she knew he would never leave her out in the cold.

He was waiting. The next step was hers. One step into a trip wire that might explode a landmine. If she moved forward just inches and rose on her tiptoes...

The doorbell chimed.

Tillman jerked his head, cursed, and stalked across the great room to the door. Tawny followed, relieved she'd dodged the landmine but more disappointed by the interruption than she wanted to admit.

Obie stood on the porch, frowning. "You ought to know, I just went by Ms. Maza's condo and the model home where her son was staying. No sign of them. They appear to have taken off in a hurry. Looks like they're on the run."

~~~

A dark blue Toyota sped along Highway 2, Colin at the wheel, Cassandra in the passenger seat. She watched a freight train snake along on the far side of the ravine that cleaved through the mountains between the tracks and the highway.

"OK, stop here," she said.

He veered close to the guardrail and braked. She handed him both of their cells, along with Renata Schliefman's Chromebook and phone that he'd retrieved from the lawyer's briefcase. He got out of the car and, one at a time, flung the devices into the ravine.

Years before at this location a train had derailed, spilling tons of corn that fermented in the summer sun. Bears had come down from the mountains and gotten drunk, putting on a show for drivers. So many watchers clogged the road that accidents skyrocketed, and the highway patrol ticketed anyone who stopped.

Moshe had told her that story, pointing out the spot on their first date three years ago during a drive to Many Glacier Hotel. The aquamarine lake, drinks and dinner at the historic inn, his wit and charm, the diamond pendant she found on the pillow when he took her back to his condo, none of those had impressed her as much as the outlandish tale of drunken bears dancing. It sounded like a vision an old man with dementia might have. She never knew if the story was true or not. She only cared that she'd found the perfect front man for her plan.

It seemed appropriate to now end their interlude in the same place. Cassandra and Colin's identities vanished in the ravine.

Earlier, they'd abandoned her Porsche in the rented garage where the Toyota had been parked in preparation for their escape. Months would pass before the owner of the storage business eventually cut the padlock on the unit for unpaid rent. By then, their trail would be cold.

The Toyota held their new phones and driver's licenses, a laptop, and suitcases. She had already set up a new 501(c)(3) nonprofit corporation to funnel donations through. Colin built a website with a different name, although she reused the same architectural renderings.

That divine architect had done such a beautiful job, envisioning her dreams. She wondered if he'd appreciate how his talent lived on, five years longer than he had.

Colin got back in the car. "Now what?"

"I'm still worried about the FBI questioning Moshe. We've never drawn their attention before."

"They don't have the complaints. You burned them."

"But we don't know what the lawyer already told them. And all that documentation can be recreated. It just takes time."

"We'll be in Florida by then."

She reached over to twirl a rope of his hair. "My bad boy, as much as I love your dreads, these have to go now. Maybe a man-bun next, with the sides shaved." She tugged lightly on his hoop earring.

"Ow! Don't!" He swatted her hand away and rubbed his ear

lobe. The little red half-moon wound from her fingernails still showed.

She opened the visor mirror. Her reflection startled her. It would take time to become accustomed to black hair again. She retouched her cabernet-toned lipstick. "We still need to handle Moshe and that woman. Come on, darling, you're brilliant with creative new ideas. Think of something unique."

"You should've just shot him full of sux, like that architect."

"Too late." That damn Tawny had put her timing off. Moshe's moods had been controllable until she showed up with her questions and snooping. And the famished-wolf looks he gave her. Cassandra didn't care if he lusted after other women but this one was dangerous.

Cassandra had tried to sanitize his condo of evidence, but Moshe was such a disgusting slob, she feared she'd missed places where he'd stashed paper copies of doctored records. At least she'd gotten the hard drive that was the main source. Colin had run it through a wood chipper that the golf course used to make mulch for landscaping the grounds.

He interrupted her musing. "We can't do anything as long as he's locked up. And after half a million people watch him pounding the shit out of Tawny and that other old guy, he's never getting out."

She pulled an eyelash curler from her purse and went to work, crimping her lashes. "His son has a lot of suction. He may well get Moshe out and we have to be ready to act."

Snow fell, increasing as they drove deeper into the mountains. The next half hour passed in silence. White mounds built up on the highway.

At last, Colin said, "We can swat him."

"What?"

"Swatting. I did it in college. If a dude pisses you off, you call nine-one-one from a burner phone and make up some story, like he's bonking a seven-year-old boy in his apartment and he's got automatic weapons. The SWAT team busts down the door and hauls him off to jail."

Cassandra watched excitement ignite in Colin's gorgeous blue eyes. Her lovely boy was so smart.

He continued: "It's really cool. Of course, there isn't any seven-year-old or guns but the guy is still screwed 'cause the cops'll usually find something illegal anyway. Maybe a lawyer can get the dude off but, by then, it's too late. Word's already gotten around about the arrest. He's been expelled, his girlfriend shuns him, his friends all hate him, and his parents are pissed about big legal bills. The call can't be traced to you. You never get your hands dirty. It's sweet."

Cassandra tried to follow. She took for granted Colin could zing through complicated strategy faster than she could. At the same time, she resented his intelligence because it constantly reminded her of the worsening sluggishness of her aging brain. Still, they made a good team—her charm, his brains. "How could that work with Moshe?"

"Take it to the next level. The old dude's been caught on video being violent. He's already charged with murder. We set him up with a weapon and a hostage. Then we call the cops." His tongue trilled like machine gun fire. "The cops do the job for us. Very clean. They'll be so busy dealing with the fallout from shooting a black man in Bumfuck, Montana, we just slip away."

Cassandra smiled, savoring the sensuous way Colin's plan curled like a boa constrictor around Moshe. "Darling, you are too brilliant." She stroked his neck. "I know just the hostage."

CHAPTER 23 – CHOKE HOLD

Friday morning, Tillman worked his magic with the judge. Moe would be released but confined to house arrest with an ankle monitor bracelet until the trial. A no-contact order required him to stay a hundred yards from his neighbor Quentin, who was now home and, thankfully, recovering from his heart attack.

Moe's appearance amazed Tawny when she and Tillman picked him up at the psych unit that afternoon. He was freshly shaved, a new haircut, ironed chinos, and with a spark in his eye that she hadn't seen since the day they'd gone cross-country skiing. She hugged him. "You look great, Moe."

He smiled down at her. "Almost as good as a week at the spa." He tenderly touched the greenish bruise that lingered on her chin. Tears brimmed. "Good thing it was my lousy left hook instead of my killer right cross."

She squeezed his hand. "It was an accident."

In contrast, Tillman was as grumpy as a grizzly with his foot in a trap. Any trace of their connection from the day before had vanished. The stiff collar of his navy dress shirt cut into his neck and his maroon-and-gray striped tie looked tight enough to choke him. When they were loaded in his Mercedes, he turned around to glare at Moe in the back seat. "This is absolutely the last time. If you blow this chance, you'll get a court-appointed attorney and spend the rest of your worthless life in prison. Got it?"

Tawny cringed, holding her breath for Moe's response. Could two men get into a fistfight inside a car? She grasped the door handle, poised to jump out. No way would she let herself be caught in crossfire again.

Surprisingly, Moe winked at her. "Did Tillman ever tell you about the time he was climbing a tree? He was about eight.

Way the hell up. Must have been twenty feet off the ground. The branch broke and down he came. Landed straddling a lower branch like a horse. People heard him hollering all the way to Laurel. After that, I figured he'd never father a child."

Tillman faced forward, jaw jutting, teeth clenched. Tawny covered her mouth and looked out the side window to keep him from seeing her smile. Even though it was cruel for the father to humiliate his son in front of her, it *was* a funny story.

"I'm going back to Billings as soon as I drop you off," Tillman muttered. "*Paying* clients need my attention."

They left Moe at the monitoring office for the ankle bracelet to be fitted, while Tillman drove Tawny home to pick up her Jeep.

"He seems good," she said. "Clearing the drugs from his system helped."

No answer. His mouth looked sour.

"Guess *I* get to break the bad news to him about Cassandra."

Sideways scowl.

His sulk was irritating her. "Tillman, I'm tired of you taking your resentment toward your father out on me."

His head whipped toward Tawny. "You know who made me check up on the old man? Rochelle."

Tillman's ex-wife? Seemed strange.

His knuckles on the wheel paled. "She's the one who first saw the foreclosure notice and started all this shit. You've been blaming me. You ought to blame her. If it had been up to me, he could fall off the face of the earth."

Tawny remembered the odd snippet of his phone conversation with Rochelle. "Why would *she* care?"

Silence.

They arrived at Tawny's house. Figuring he'd never answer, she got out and started up the walk. When she heard the driver's door slam, she turned, surprised that he'd followed her.

He stood on the porch almost vibrating, like a race car revving up for the starting flag. She unlocked the door and motioned him inside but he shook his head. Instead he faced the street with the thousand-yard stare Tawny had seen occasionally in her husband and son, both combat vets. But Tillman had never been in the military.

She waited in the cold, wondering if he'd explain.

His deep baritone rumbled, low, like a beehive, his normal bluster absent. "I never fooled around on Chell. Our problems were legion but not because I couldn't keep it in my pants. I swore I'd never do to my wife what my father did to my mother." A hesitation. "Or to my wife."

She studied his stony expression. "What do you mean?"

Another long pause. Finally, he spoke, "Right before the wedding, I'm taking the bar exam. Chell was flying in from Seattle where she was going to grad school. Old man calls, gives me this line of bull, how proud he is of me, how he understands why my mom banished him from the wedding but at least let him do something to help out, like picking up Chell at the airport. Yeah, yeah, OK, right, just leave me alone so I can concentrate on the exam."

Tawny leaned closer, struggling to make out his quiet words.

"I finish the exam but Chell's MIA. I call, she won't talk to me." He thrust his hands in his pockets. "I figure she's got the jitters, so I let it go. Don't see her until the wedding."

Tawny shivered, not from cold, but in anticipation of the rest of the story.

After a long pause, he spoke again. "Year and a half later, our first daughter's born. Chell goes into heavy-duty post-partum depression. Crying all the time, refuses to nurse the baby. One night, I take her to a party, trying to cheer her up. She gets wasted on mojitos. Drunk on her ass. On the way home, she says she has to tell me something. *In vino veritas.* True confession time."

Tawny knew from the catch in his voice that whatever he was about to confide, he'd never put in words before.

He ran a hand over his face, pulling the skin tight. "Turns out, while I was busting my hump taking the bar, she spent the whole three days before the wedding in the sack...with my old man."

Tawny's throat spasmed. "Oh, Tillman." She longed to touch him but that thousand-yard stare seemed to have taken his body to another dimension as well.

"Real kick in the nuts to a new marriage, huh? I don't blame Chell. She was twenty-two years old, didn't have a chance. The old lech had been through three wives at that point and a hundred mistresses. He knew his way around a woman."

How could Tawny console him for betrayal that deep? "You stayed together, even after she told you. That's amazing."

"Sixteen years." He finally gazed down at Tawny, eyes harder than obsidian. "After all this time, damned if I know why she still cares."

He thudded down the wooden steps to his Mercedes. The SUV took off with a roar.

Shivering, Tawny hugged herself, heart aching.

Despite bitter betrayals by family he should have been able to trust, Tillman still tried to do the right thing.

~~~

Moe squatted on his haunches to pet the three cats that greeted them at his front door. He looked up at Tawny. "Where are the rest? Rambo?"

Time for the moment of truth—the explanation she wished she didn't have to give. "Someone broke in, stole your computer, and left the back door open. The cats got out."

"They got out? Goddamn." He unfolded from the squat and sprinted across the great room. He was out the french door and almost through the gate in the patio wall before Tawny caught up with him.

She grabbed his arm. "Wait, Moe. You can't leave the property. You'll go back to jail."

"But my cats!"

She rubbed his bony back as she'd watched Cassandra do to calm him. "I rounded up those three. I promise I'll look for the rest. Just come back inside. Please."

He resisted for several seconds but finally returned to the condo with her, throwing glances over his shoulder at the fairway. "What about Rambo?"

Nightmares had been haunting her fitful sleep, imagining another encounter with the Siamese. "Maybe we can lure him with food. Or borrow a trap."

He stood vigil at the door while Tawny plugged a charging unit into a nearby outlet and dragged a chair over for Moe to sit in. He needed to stay tethered by a three-foot-long cord while the ankle bracelet recharged for an hour.

She handed him the cell phone associated with the monitor. "You'd better check in so they know you're home." He made the call without protest while she fed the three cats in the kitchen. When she returned to the great room, he was scanning the landscape with binoculars.

He lowered the glasses and faced her. "What the hell has been going on?"

She sat on a window ledge near his chair. The new knowledge that he'd seduced Tillman's fiancé before their wedding sickened her. She'd believed dementia caused most of Moe's bad behavior. But a betrayal from so many years ago couldn't be blamed on that.

Why did the father lash out at his son? She couldn't ask, because that would break Tillman's trust, and she'd never do that. The best course now was to put aside her emotions and do her job.

A deep crevice cut between Moe's bushy gray eyebrows, the intense dark eyes piercing her soul. Again, she glimpsed a preview of Tillman in thirty years and took a deep breath. "A lot's happened. And it's going to upset you. But you need to know."

"Well, tell me already, goddammit." Impatient but not furious.

"First of all, Cassandra appears to have skipped town. The sheriff's been looking for her. Her condo's deserted, her Porsche hasn't been seen. Her son Colin is gone too."

"Why's the sheriff looking for her?" His mind seemed sharper since the drugs had cleared from his system.

"Because we think she's been stealing your money."

"She isn't stealing. I gave it to her."

Tawny pulled the file folder from her bag and showed him the booking photo and arrest report. "She was a pharmacist in New Hampshire. She lost her license for misusing drugs on her patients and stealing from them."

He peered at the photo then flipped through the papers, scanning and frowning.

Tawny waited for him to finish reading. When he looked up, she said, "Tests show you've been ingesting illegal drugs for months." She reached over and ran her hand through his springy gray curls, then sank back on the ledge. "Your hair shows traces of methamphetamine, steroids, cocaine, Viagra, and others. Also the pills in your prescription bottles are not what the labels say."

His eyes narrowed and moved slightly side to side. She'd watched the same expression in Tillman's face. Processing information, sorting, categorizing, discarding or accepting, coming to a conclusion, like a computer.

Two brilliant men, two brilliant brains, one under siege.

She wished Virgie was there to help with explanations. "Your tests show signs of dementia but also serious impairment from drugs." She leaned toward him and searched his gaunt face. "You've been using drugs, Moe."

He blinked several times.

"What kind?" she asked.

He shrugged. "Cocaine. But not that much. We both do it. You wouldn't believe the orgasms you have on coke." His pleading expression really wanted her to understand.

"What about meth?"

He shook his head hard. "Never. That drills holes in your brain, rots your teeth." He bared his teeth in an unexpected grin. "See these pearly whites? Still all my own. I don't want to outlive them."

Tawny grimaced at his pitiful joke. "Did you and Cassandra maybe do some cocktails, combine different drugs?"

"Not a chance. I told you, coke's my one and only vice." A small, sly grin this time. "Well, not quite my *only* vice."

Keep him talking. "Did you ever inject drugs?"

He shrugged. "Sure, testosterone for years. But that's legal." Another grin. "Between vitamin T and vitamin V, I'm a satisfied man."

Glad your sex life is terrific, she thought, because the rest is screwed.

He again raised the binoculars to search for his lost cats. Towering trees cast long shadows on the snow in fading afternoon light.

Change directions, get him back on track. "Tell me about the money orders."

Still staring through the binoculars, he asked, "Know what the shrink said?"

"What?"

"The good news is, I'm not paranoid. The bad news is, they *are* after me."

Tawny stared at him, mystified.

Mischief sparkled in his eyes. "Heard that in the psych ward. Pretty funny, huh?"

Tawny let her head fall back. "Ha-ha, Moe. Good one." Was he purposely deflecting her questions? Or was his attention span really that limited? "Do you have any idea where Cassandra is?"

"Hey, I've been out of touch, remember?" He reached for the cell that the monitoring company had given him and tapped the keypad. "I'll call her."

"You're not supposed to use that unless you have problems with your ankle monitor."

He made a face. "A phone's a phone. Besides, I can't find mine. The jailer must have stolen it. They steal everything from you in jail."

"Use this, OK?" She handed hers over. "I don't want the sheriff showing up here because you broke the rules."

He rolled his eyes and made the call. As it rang, and rang, and rang, his brow crinkled. "Recording says the subscriber no longer has this number."

"I told you, the detective thinks she's skipped town."

"Why would she do that?"

Didn't he remember the explanation Tawny had just given him five minutes before? "Moe, we think she took your money."

"I *told* you, I gave it to her."

"Why?"

"For my cats. To build her sanctuary. Don't you understand?"

She leaned close. "Explain it to me."

"She's going to build the sanctuary and take care of my cats. Not just mine, but a lot of other investors. Doesn't matter if they're dogs, cats, rabbits, pot-bellied pigs, whatever. All pets."

"Were you investing? Or donating?"

"Investing in my cats' future. So they'll be taken care of after I'm gone."

"Did you ever expect to get any money back out of this...investment?"

"Peace of mind. She's taken care of hundreds, maybe thousands, of pets whose owners died."

"If the sanctuary hasn't been built yet, how is she taking care of thousands of pets? What does she do with them in the meantime?" Tawny had a sickening suspicion but needed to learn what Cassandra had told Moe.

"Her son takes them to a foster facility. That's where some of the money goes, for their temporary care until the sanctuary's finished."

"Where is this foster facility?"

He waved his hand vaguely toward the mountains. "Someplace in eastern Montana, I think."

"Have you ever been there?"

"Why would I want to go see dead people's animals?"

Good question.

A parallel occurred to Tawny—she and Dwight had visited several nursing homes before choosing one for her grandpa. "Maybe to check out the kind of care they're getting before you turned your cats over to her."

His face screwed into a don't-be-stupid grimace. "I trust Cassandra. She adores animals. Of course she'll take good care of them."

Right. After Cassandra collected huge payments for perpetual care, Tawny wondered how many pets had been dropped at a pound or left out in the woods to die or be eaten by predators. "Do you know how much money you've given Cassandra?"

Long fingers fluttered. "There are reports somewhere. On the computer."

"Your computer is gone. Someone stole it." She placed her hands on his knees, feeling the knobby joints through his chinos. "Moe, we're pretty sure Cassandra used her key and took your computer to cover her theft. Tillman's accountant has been reconstructing records from files we found before the computer was stolen. It looks like she's taken over a million dollars from you. And from a lot of other people too."

He yanked his knees from under her palms. "What the fuck were you doing in my computer?" He leapt up and paced, jerking the charging cord out of the electrical outlet. The loose wire tangled around his feet but he kept moving back and forth in the great room. Long arms flapped like an angry bat.

Oh no, here it comes. Tawny hurried to the kitchen, putting the counter as a barrier between them. If his rage turned violent, she'd escape through the laundry room, out the back door.

He glared at her across the granite expanse, eyes ferocious. He gripped the edge so tightly, she wondered which would snap first—the granite or his finger bones.

"I trusted you. I told you things I've never told another living soul," he roared. A fist crashed down on the counter, rattling glasses and mugs. "What am I, stupid? Yeah, I'm a stupid putz, all right. And you—you ratted me out to my son, you lousy traitor!"

The guilt that had been eating her suddenly gave way as a

tidal wave of repressed anger surged. "All I've ever done is try to help you with the rotten mess you've made of your life and what do you do but crap on me? You know *why* I'm the only friend you have? Because you're a miserable mean old man who's driven everyone else away."

For a startling second, his face froze, mouth half-open, a pained crease between his bushy brows. Confusion and fear crossed his dark eyes. He looked panicked, as if from one blink to the next, he'd lost track of where he was and who he was.

Then he whirled and stalked away, the charging cord dragging behind like a tail.

Her heart choked. Regret pinched her for lashing out at him. The mean old man had been victimized by a predator who'd taken advantage of his dementia.

And Tawny had taken advantage of his trust, worming her way into his lonely, isolated, unhappy life. She'd made him believe in her then betrayed him. Even if it was for his own good, as Tillman kept reminding her, it was still betrayal. She'd lost her footing, sliding down the road to hell, slick with the black ice of good intentions. Tears burned her eyes.

Moe stood at the high windows, binoculars locked to his face. Still looking for his cats, the only beings he trusted.

Tawny rubbed the back of her hand across her eyes and blew her nose into a paper towel. A hard lump stayed in her chest like a tumor. She crossed the room. "Moe, I'm sorry." A gurgle sounded in her voice.

The binoculars moved, scanning back and forth. "Fuck your apologies. You're always apologizing. Totally useless."

The lump persisted, even when she cleared her throat. "I can't undo what I did. But I was trying to help you."

Silence. He lowered the binoculars, leaned forward, and peered intently at the fairway. "Rambo."

She followed his stare to a small blotch moving low among

trees. The Siamese's cream-colored body blended into the snow but his dark face and ears contrasted against the white. The mahogany-colored tail whipped.

She couldn't make up for breaking Moe's trust but maybe she could earn a little redemption by bringing back his best friend.

In the kitchen, she rushed to open a stinky can of liver, Rambo's favorite. She grabbed a cat carrier from the garage and raced out the rear door.

Deep snow swallowed her feet as she plowed past the adjacent condos, wishing she'd gotten her coat. But if she took that extra time, the elusive cat might disappear.

Rambo must have spotted her because he bounded deeper into a line of blue spruce that ran up a slope toward a row of single family homes. She'd never catch up to him unless he allowed it, and that wasn't going to happen.

With each lumbering, clumsy step in knee-high snow, the carrier banged the side of her leg. Her jeans quickly soaked through, clammy against her skin. Numbness crept into her bare aching fingers, making her fumble the can of liver, nearly dumping it. Her panting breath expelled puffs of steam. This was pointless. No gloves, no coat, twenty degrees, and a cat that didn't want to be caught.

The line of houses fronted on the street that intersected Moe's lane. She clambered up a steep hill and stopped to catch her breath at a rock wall surrounding the patio of a gray house. Shivering, she gasped for air. Wet jeans were already freezing to her skin.

A *For Sale-Bank Foreclosure* sign sat propped inside the window of the vacant dwelling. She remembered seeing a moving van in the driveway a week before. Maybe another victim of Moe's bad investments.

At least no one was there to report her for trespassing if

she cut through the property to get to the road. Be easier to return to Moe's on a plowed street than slog back through the snow-drifted rough of the golf course. She walked under the eaves, teeth chattering and fingers burning from cold.

Rambo had vanished. Stupid idea to run after him. Better to just leave a can of food inside the carrier and set it in Moe's patio. Maybe the lure of an easy meal would tempt the Siamese.

A streak of cream and brown fur zipped past her and disappeared into a slightly open door about ten feet ahead. She approached and peered into a dark double garage.

A growl reverberated. Rambo was cornered.

She slipped inside and closed the door behind her. Dim light shone through a small window on the opposite wall. A dark-colored Toyota was parked inside. The previous occupants must have left the car behind temporarily, planning to return later.

A bowl of dry cat food sat on the concrete floor. Perhaps the owners had been kind-hearted animal lovers, leaving the side door open for ferals to find shelter.

It was too dark to spot the cat. He was likely hiding under the car.

She set the carrier on the floor, wire-mesh door open, placed the can of liver inside, and backed away. "OK, Rambo, we're never going to be buddies but I don't want to hurt you. I just want to bring you home to your dad."

Minutes passed. The icy jeans made her skin burn. Her entire body shivered. Rambo wouldn't come out as long as she stayed. She should shut him in the garage, go back to Moe's, warm up, and figure out how to capture him. She made sure the knob was unlocked, closed the door, and hurried down the sloping street around the corner to Moe's condo.

Once again, he sat in the chair beside the french door, charger plugged in, searching the darkening fairway with binoculars.

"I've got Rambo trapped in a garage."

He stared at her. "No shit?" His anger had faded, maybe replaced by hope of retrieving his best friend. He unplugged and crossed the room as Tawny bundled into her coat and pulled gloves over her icy fingers. "Where?"

"Vacant house around the corner. Somebody left a side door open and he scooted in."

"Let's go!"

"You can't. The ankle monitor."

"The hell with that. I'm the only one he'll come to. We'll go get him and be back before they even realize I'm gone."

"But, Moe, the alarm will go off at the monitoring station. You'll get busted."

A triumphant smirk spread across his face. "Got talking to the guy who hooked me up. He told me there's a ten-minute delay before the alarm shows up on their computer screen. We'll be out and back in less than that. Come on." He elbowed past her through the front door.

She couldn't physically restrain him. Might as well get the cat home and hope the consequences weren't too grave. She followed.

At the curb, he said, "Which way?" She pointed up the hill.

He loped ahead like a father racing to ransom his kidnapped child. At the corner, he checked with her, palms raised in a *where* gesture.

"Second house. The gray one," she called. "There's a door on the right side of the garage."

He rushed to the garage and disappeared inside.

Since Tawny couldn't help with Rambo, she lagged back as she climbed the slight hill. Being so chilled sapped her energy.

From the crest, she surveyed the neighborhood. Because of the curve of the road, the gray house had an oblique but unobstructed view into Moe's condo. The massive staghorn chandeliers glowed bright in his great room.

In the cold, gloomy dusk, the glimpse inside his home appeared warm and inviting. How different reality was, a broken, lonely man understandably shunned by his family, victimized by a con artist, facing foreclosure, assault and homicide trials. And all he cared about were his cats.

Instead of trailing Moe, Tawny went to the front porch on the opposite side of the garage. She hoped to watch the reunion through the window.

The walk and porch hadn't been shoveled and footprints had flattened the grimy snow. After rubbing the glass with the side of her gloved fist, she peered in. Movement, but too dark to see what was going on.

Then a connecting door opened between the garage and house. Soft lantern light filled the dimness. The silhouette of a dark-haired woman appeared in the doorway, her words muffled and unintelligible through the glass. Light caught the side of her smiling face.

Cassandra.

Holy shit.

Tawny grabbed her cell to call 9-1-1.

From behind, a powerful arm looped around her neck in a choke hold.

Her phone dropped to the ground as she grabbed at the vise-like arm. She stomped her foot, aiming for the attacker's instep, but missed. His other arm circled her waist, wrenching her off balance. Her legs flailed wildly, trying to score a kick but nothing landed. She struggled against the strangling pressure on her throat.

Lack of oxygen tunneled her vision. Desperate for air, she tugged at the arm but her fingers fumbled, weak and useless. Her leg muscles softened to mush. All her effort focused on

trying to get a breath.
Just...one...breath.

CHAPTER 24 - SWAT

Voices brought Tawny back to consciousness. She lay on her back, spread-eagled on a mattress. Red light glowed above in her blurry vision. Tight leather cuffs bound her wrists and ankles to four bedposts. She couldn't move. And she was cold. Desperately cold.

Because she was naked. In Moe's bedroom.

Oh, God.

She tried to wriggle out of the fur-lined bindings, bucking and twisting. Her hip bumped something.

Moe lay beside her, knees drawn up in a fetal position, eyes closed, mouth slack. Asleep or unconscious.

Voices murmured again. She turned toward the sound, blinking hard to force her eyes to focus. Through the open door of the bathroom, she saw Cassandra and Colin, huddled over the sink. Cassandra was now a brunette. Colin's dreadlocks were gone, hair cropped close with only a topknot remaining.

She strained, jamming her hip hard against Moe's knee. "Moe? Wake up!" she hissed.

He didn't stir.

Tawny realized while she'd been trying to trap Rambo, she herself had been lured into a trap. Colin had overpowered her and choked her to unconsciousness, while Cassandra handled Moe.

Mother and son had changed their appearances. They must be frantic to cover their tracks and escape.

But why the weird bondage staging?

Maybe they meant to overdose Tawny and Moe, making it look like a kinky sex encounter gone bad.

"Moe!" she whispered, again ramming her hip into his knee. No reaction.

Was he already dead? Had they killed him?

She looked for signs of breathing but in the dim red-hued room, in his huddled position, she couldn't see movement.

Colin's voice: "Hell, no!"

"What's the matter, pussy?" Cassandra taunted. "Too squeamish to get your delicate white hands dirty?"

"Fuck you, do it yourself!"

Cassandra's tone changed to wheedling. "*You* have to. You know I'm not strong enough."

"Forget it! Figure it out. I'm not getting blood all over me."

Blood?

Restraints chafed Tawny's wrists. She tried to scrunch her hands small enough to slip free, but the bindings were too tight. Same with the ankles. No matter how hard she tugged, she couldn't gain any slack.

Cassandra swept into the bedroom and leered down at Tawny. "Well, hel-*low*. Comfy?"

She wore surgical gloves and held a syringe, needle pointed up. She jostled Moe's shoulder. He didn't stir. She plunged the needle through his trousers into his hip. The jab prompted a grunt and a slight spasm.

He was alive. But maybe not for much longer. What was in the syringe?

Colin skulked from the bathroom and sat on the velvet swing, face turned away.

Horrified helplessness paralyzed Tawny. No way to fight back, no way to flee.

Cassandra went to the bathroom and returned a second later, gripping a scalpel in her gloved fist.

Tawny screamed, "Help!"

But no one heard, except Colin. He swayed back and forth on the velvet swing, head bowed. His movements appeared as mindless and mechanical as a metronome.

Cassandra loomed above her. "You ruined it. Damn you."

Tawny's vision fixed on the diagonal blade, barely an inch long, but deadly as a razor. "Nooooo!"

Cassandra raised the scalpel.

"No, Mom!" Colin shouted. He leapt across the room and knocked her wrist sideways.

She twisted toward her son, brandishing the blade in warning. "Back off! This was *your* plan and now you've let me down. If she isn't bloody and dead, the cops might not swat Moshe. We can't leave her alive to tell them about us."

Even though Colin towered over his mother, he shrank back. He returned to the velvet swing, leaned one hip on it and gripped the rope with both hands, hiding his face.

"You are useless!" Cassandra shrilled. Again, she glared down at Tawny.

Tawny bucked and tried to twist out of the way. The blade slashed across her stomach. White-hot agony stole the breath from her screams. Another slice. More searing pain. Blood bloomed from the crisscrossed slashes.

"Colin, help me! Please!" she sobbed. "Don't let her do this!"

But he ran for the bathroom. The sound of retching.

Time halted as Tawny watched her blood roll in lazy red trails from her belly, down her sides and into the furrows of her thighs. The only movement was her heart leaping inside her chest like a frantic grasshopper.

Cassandra's cold blue eyes narrowed as she studied the scalpel, blood dripping from the little blade.

Tawny knew her wounds were painful but not fatal.

Unless Cassandra slashed an artery.

Her mind raced. How to talk her out of the death blow? "Cassandra, you've got the money. Just leave. If you kill us, the cops will hunt you down. You'll never be safe." Her words felt thick, like trying to speak with a cow's giant tongue in her mouth. "You got away with it before in New Hampshire. You won't get that lucky again."

Beside her, Moe stirred and moaned.

Colin emerged from the bathroom, wiping his mouth with the back of his hand. "Mom, she's right. Come *on*. Let's get *out* of here."

Cassandra shot him a nasty glance. "Before putting your brilliant plan into operation? No! Give me her phone." She laid the scalpel on Tawny's bleeding belly, sliding the sharp tip to open the gouge farther.

Tawny flinched. More blood swelled from the gash and ran down to soak into the sheet. The warm wetness quickly turned cold.

Colin's head drooped. He fumbled in his jeans for Tawny's cell, and handed it to his mother.

Cassandra thumbed the phone on. She tapped the screen three times. 9-1-1. Then she shrieked, "Help me, help me! He's got a knife! He stabbed me. He's going to kill me! Help!" She listened for a second, smiling at Tawny, then resumed her hysterical screaming. "Moshe Rosenbaum! He's gone crazy! Golden Eagle. One-oh-seven Osprey Lane. I'm hiding upstairs in his bedroom. Oh God, I hear him coming! Help me!" She let out a long wail, then disconnected, and tossed the phone across the room. In a normal voice, she said, "That should do it."

Colin edged toward the landing and the stairs, whimpering. "Come *on*, Mommy. We've *got* to get out of here."

"No! We have to finish her!" But instead of grabbing the scalpel, Cassandra disappeared into the bathroom. As soon as her back was turned, Colin bolted down the stairs.

Moe stirred beside Tawny. She strained against the straps but couldn't reach him. "Moe! Wake up! Help me!"

His eyes opened, bleary and uncomprehending. Blinking, he slowly sat up on the side of the bed.

"Moe! Unbuckle my hands! Now! Cassandra's going to kill us!"

He stared at her without recognition.

Cassandra returned from the bathroom, another syringe in her gloved hand. She noticed her son had disappeared and screamed, "Colin! Don't you dare leave me!" Then she spotted Moe, awake. She dropped the syringe on the bed between Tawny's splayed legs. Grasping the front of Moe's shirt, she slapped his face hard. Back and forth, back and forth.

He mumbled, "Wha' thell?"

Cassandra clasped his cheeks between her palms and kissed him on the mouth. "Wake up, darling Moshe. It's show time." She grabbed the bloody scalpel from Tawny's belly, tearing the skin another inch.

Tawny choked back a gasp. The death blow would come next. A slice across her throat. She couldn't move, couldn't stop it.

But the final slash didn't come. Instead, Cassandra pressed the scalpel into Moe's palm, wrapping his fingers tightly around the handle.

Fingerprints. She was making sure Moe's prints were on the bloody weapon.

She was staging Tawny's murder so Moe would be blamed.

Cassandra took a step away from him. "Moshe darling, bad men are coming to take your cats away. They're going to kill your cats, your best friends."

Moe grimaced, trying to focus. "Kill my cats?"

Cassandra's syrupy voice continued, "Yes, darling. They're going to kill them. But we won't let that happen, will we, darling? You have to stay here and stop the evil men. You stop them, darling, while I take the cats to a safe place. Do you understand?"

His shoulders went rigid. Fire ignited in his eyes. He leapt to his feet. "They can't kill my cats!"

"That's right, darling. You must protect your cats. Those evil men will come in here and you'll stop them, won't you, darling?"

"Yeah!" he roared. He stomped around the room, gripping the scalpel. "They can't kill my cats!"

Tawny watched in horror as Moe came to vibrant, frightening life, hypnotized by Cassandra's drugs and lies.

Cassandra picked up the syringe, eyes blazing. She grabbed Tawny's naked waist, digging her fingernails deep in the flesh, poised to imbed the fatal needle in her bleeding belly.

Tawny jerked her hips back and forth. The restraints held tight and so did Cassandra's grip. "Moe! Help me!" she screamed. "She's going to kill me! Stop her!"

With her back to Moe, Cassandra didn't see him approach but Tawny did. Confusion painted his expression. When his stare locked with Tawny's, she caught a glimmer of recognition.

"Moe, stop her!" she shouted.

The syringe aimed like a missile at her. Moe's big hand grabbed Cassandra's shoulder and spun her across the room. The syringe flew from her glove and imbedded itself in the carpet.

"Don't hurt my friend!" Moe roared. He slashed the scalpel through the air and planted himself between Cassandra and Tawny.

Rage contorted Cassandra's face.

The scalpel began to jerk, as if Moe's arm had gone into involuntary spasms.

Sirens wailed in the distance. Colin's scream echoed up the stairs, "Mommy! Come *on*!"

Cassandra's head whipped from Moe to Tawny to the pleas from her son. "Fuck you, Moshe! They're going to kill your cats and you can't stop them!" She ran from the bedroom, thumping down the stairs.

The sirens sounded nearer.

Tawny dared to hope. Cassandra hadn't finished her. She was alive. Moe was alive. Help had to be close. The danger was past.

Or was it?

Moe's actions became spastic, lurching as he paced. The whites of his eyes burned red with rage. Spittle sprayed from his mouth as he repeated, "They can't kill my cats!"

Then he hovered above her. Crazed black eyes stared down at her, the bloody blade clutched in his veined hand.

Breath choked in Tawny's throat. "Moe, I'll help you save your cats. Let me loose! Please!"

Pounding on the front door. Muffled shouts.

He stared at her but, unlike seconds before, he no longer showed recognition. His head and arms made jumpy, erratic movements. Eyelids blinked hard and nerves twitched under his skin. The drug Cassandra had injected took over control of his body.

"Moe, please. It's me, Tawny. Unbuckle the restraints. I want to help you!"

Downstairs, a crash sounded, the front door being busted open. "Sheriff's department! Put down your weapons and come out with your hands up!"

"You can't kill my cats!" Moe bellowed, lunging toward the door.

"Moe!" Tawny screamed. "Stop!"

He kept going.

"Don't shoot him!" she shrieked. "Don't shoot him! He's sick! Please! Don't shoot him!"

An explosion rattled the walls. The bed jumped. Picture frames crashed to the floor. The velvet swing flopped up and down. The chandelier swung crazily above her.

Deafened by the concussion, she could only feel reverberations as something thudded down the stairs like a boulder. She bucked against the restraints. "No! No! No! Oh God, Moe!"

~~~

Ten hours ticked by or maybe it was only ten minutes. Tawny couldn't tell. Muffled sounds barely penetrated the ringing in her ears. Finally, Obie burst into the bedroom in bulky body armor, shotgun raking the area, followed by two more deputies. He spotted her on the bed. His mouth moved but she couldn't hear his words.

While other deputies checked the room, closet, and bathroom, Obie set down the shotgun, pressed a pillow hard against her bleeding belly with one hand, and unbuckled the wrist restraints with the other. Sweat beaded on his forehead.

She sat up. "Is Moe dead?"

Through the ringing in her ears, his words sounded muted and hollow. "You're safe. Hug the pillow. It'll slow the bleeding." He wrapped a sheet around her then freed her ankles.

"No, you have to understand!" She struggled to speak. "Moe didn't do this to me. Cassandra Maza cut me. She shot Moe full of drugs that made him go crazy. This wasn't his fault." She lost control of her quivering lips and sobbed. "Is he dead?"

Obie pressed two fingers on the side of her neck, checking her pulse. "Medics are coming. Hang on."

She gripped his hand. "Tell me."

Obie swallowed. "He's not dead but he's hurt bad."

"Did you shoot him?"

He shook his head. "We used a flash bang, that noise that

rocked the house." He pressed his lips together. "Old man took a header down the stairs, like he was trying to fly. May have broken his back. Says he can't move his legs."

"Oh God." She doubled over, gripping the pillow, pain searing her stomach. Then she remembered and straightened. "Cassandra and Colin are getting away. They were hiding out in a vacant house around the corner. It's gray. They may be driving a dark-colored Toyota. And she's got black hair now, not blonde. Her son's with her. He had dreadlocks before, but now his hair is cut close with a man bun."

Obie stared at her, then pressed the radio on his shoulder, and repeated Tawny's description. Squawks sounded, responses garbled by her near-deafness. She rubbed her ears, trying to stop the echo.

Another siren whooped. "That's the ambulance," Obie said. "They'll be right here."

She grabbed his arm again. "They've got to help Moe."

Moments later, two EMTs thumped up the stairs and into the bedroom, jump kits heavy with medical supplies. They spent several minutes checking her vitals and taping thick pads over the slashes. The woman EMT said, "You'll be fine. Cuts are superficial, didn't hit any organs. Tore up some muscle." She offered a reassuring smile. "Trust me, it'll be like recovering from a Caesarian."

Tawny struggled to her feet despite the EMT's protests. She had to see Moe. Her legs felt rubbery but steady enough to hold. Wrapped in a blanket, she slowly descended the stairs, leaning heavily on the woman.

Moe lay on a backboard on the floor of the great room, a hard plastic cervical collar around his neck. Two medics tended to him, one with a blood pressure cuff, the other securing straps to hold him in place. His eyes were closed, brow furrowed, and jaw clenched in pain. Swollen lumps blotched his dark face.

She knelt next to him and stroked his curly gray hair. "Moe?"

Eyelids flickered.

"I'm sorry, Moe."

"Excuse me," one medic said, nudging her.

Tawny straightened, moving away from the broken man, as tears spilled and she hugged the blanket tighter. The woman EMT took her arm again and led her to the door.

A low mumble sounded but Tawny's ears still felt stuffed with cotton. She asked the EMT, "Did he say something?"

The woman rolled her eyes. "He said, 'stop already with the fucking apologies.'"

~~~

Tawny blinked out of nightmares to see Tillman, backlit, framed in the doorway of her darkened hospital room. Still night outside. She rubbed her eyes and sat up, feeling the tug of stitches across her belly, a deep burn in the muscles. "What time is it?"

"Four-thirty." His voice sounded like it came from down in a well.

"Moe?"

"Still in surgery. Four, maybe five displaced vertebrae. Spinal cord damage. May not make it. If he lives, he's paralyzed."

"Dear God."

Tillman moved into the room, closing the door and shutting out the brightness from the hall. A recessed light glowed softly above her bed, casting deep shadows on his solemn face. He still wore the same suit from the previous morning when he'd arranged Moe's release. Now it looked rumpled, tie missing. He shrugged off the coat and tossed it on the visitor chair. Same navy shirt, wilted and creased.

From several cautious feet away, he gazed at her, dark hollows hiding his eyes, mouth pinched.

"You drove all night," she said.

"I'd have been here a lot sooner if you had them call me right away. But no, you wait till I'm practically back to Billings before the hospital reached out to tell me you almost got killed." Underneath the sarcasm, huskiness rasped his deep voice.

She pushed the button to raise the head of the bed, shifted, and winced. "Moe's the one who's bad off. I didn't need to stay overnight. The ER doc and Virgie both said I was fine to leave. But the nurse said some asshole called the administrator at home, woke her up, and threatened if I was released, he'd sue the hospital for so many millions, they couldn't afford to buy a Band-aid."

"A misquote. I said *bedpan*, not Band-aid."

Tawny smiled. "You know, for an asshole, you can be a pretty sweet guy."

"Don't tell anyone."

"It's our secret."

He took a step closer to the bed, almost shyly. "Where does it hurt?"

She gestured across her stomach. "Forty-eight stitches. Sliced abdominal muscles. They gave me pain medicine. I feel pretty loopy." She rotated her hands, studying the bruises that darkened her wrists. Her hips and ankles ached as if they'd been dislocated from straining against the restraints. "Did they catch them?"

"Apparently Cassandra escaped out the french door just before the deputies busted in the front. They slipped out of the complex while the cops were still setting up the perimeter. But your description of them went out over the air right away. Dark-haired mother and son with a man bun driving a dark Toyota. An hour and a half later, tribal police nabbed 'em speeding through Arlee." He pinched his forehead. "Damn, Tawny, you're good."

Not good enough to save Moe.

An irritating memory had run through her drugged, fitful nightmares. "Cassandra said something weird to Colin that the cops were going to *swat* Moe."

"It's known as *swatting*. You call nine-one-one, falsely claiming someone's got a weapon and is threatening great bodily injury. Usually the SWAT team busts in and scares the piss out of some poor schmuck taking a bath. Cassandra and Colin carried it a step further. Get the cops to execute someone for you. Death by proxy. Not a bad plan. Almost worked, except these deputies kept their cool and used non-lethal force.

"If Moe hadn't been hopped up on ketamine, he'd probably have come out OK. But he was in what druggies call the *K-hole*, hallucinations, out of body. Deputies said he tried to fly off the second story landing."

Tawny adjusted the pillows and sank back, weary, sad. "Cassandra had given him a shot and he went crazy. But he saved my life. Cassandra was going to inject me with something and he stopped her."

"Deputies found sux—succinylcholine—in a syringe on the floor." The bass resonance of his voice turned even huskier. "Paralyzes breathing and muscles. You'd have been dead in minutes. That rotten old man finally did one worthwhile thing in his miserable life."

Why did that phrase sound familiar? Then Tawny remembered. Seemed like years ago when Moe had said his son had done one good thing in his life by keeping her out of jail.

Father and son looked alike, talked alike, shared gestures and facial expressions. Yet, so different.

"He did two good things," she said. "He had a pretty amazing son."

Tillman rolled his eyes. But he took another step closer and held out one hand to her, an uncertain offer. "I don't want to hurt you."

She lifted her arms to him, ignoring the burn in her belly. He sank to the bed, cradled her, rocking gently. He kissed her forehead, cheek, eyes. For all the harshness and sarcasm that normally spewed from his mouth, the softness of his lips surprised her. Through his shirt, her hands ran over the muscular contours of his back. He felt strong, solid, and so good.

She scooted sideways and pulled him down to lie beside her, twined his arm around her shoulder, and burrowed her face into his neck. He stroked mussed hair out of her eyes.

"That was the longest drive of my life," he muttered. "Listened to Springsteen's 'I'm on Fire,' over and over again. That line about the edgy, dull knife. That monster was cutting your body and the thought of that cut my soul a helluva lot deeper than a six-inch valley." He shuddered and hugged her tightly. Tears dripped on her forehead, running down the side of her face, mingling with her own.

~~~

Tawny woke at seven-thirty when the door whooshed open as Emma pushed into the room without knocking. When she saw Tillman sleeping beside Tawny, she almost fumbled the folded clothes she'd brought from home. Her chin pulled back in shock.

Tawny held a finger to her lips, slipped out of his embrace, and motioned Emma into the bathroom with her.

"What's he doing here?" An urgent, angry hiss. Her eyes were still red and swollen, as they'd been the night before while she bawled in the ER.

"He drove all night from Billings."

"Jesus, Mom, he's nothing but a big prick, risking your life, and you're sleeping with him?"

Tawny shot her a warning look. "You're hardly in a position to criticize who I sleep with."

A pout.

"Not that I owe you any explanation but all we did was *sleep*."

Emma's head hung. "I'm sorry, Mom."

Tawny's stitches stung as she stepped into fresh panties. "Cassandra and Colin are in custody. They're being questioned."

Emma's shoulders quivered. Tawny imagined she'd flashed on a memory of sex with Colin, a thought now too horrible to accept.

"How did you get here?"

"Jim brought me."

Tawny's heart took a small leap of hope. "Jim? Where is he?"

"Out in the hall, waiting."

"That was nice of him." More than nice. Damn near heroic after Emma had screwed around on him and Moe had killed his friend Wilbur.

Emma shook out folded jeans and offered them to Tawny. "It's another week until I can get tested."

"You're going to use protection from now on, right?"

She flipped hair over her shoulder. "Jim *always* insisted." A stricken look came into her hazel eyes. "But, Mom, he won't have sex with me now, even with a condom."

"Can you blame him?" She rubbed circles between Emma's thin shoulder blades. "Give it time. If he forgives you, he's worth hanging onto." She tried to zip the jeans but pain made her gasp. After tossing aside the hospital gown, she pulled a green hoody over her head, and snugged it down to cover the thick bandage across her belly and the unzipped jeans.

When they came out of the bathroom, Tillman stood beside the bed, smoothing creases down his trouser legs. He glanced at Emma. "Hi."

"Hi."

Two whole words and neither had shouted yet. Maybe there was hope.

"Mom, do you want me to take you home?" Emma sneered over her shoulder. "Or *him*?"

Oh well. Short-lived truce.

Tillman spoke up: "Renata Schliefman's still here. I talked to her mom last night. Do you want to see her?"

Tawny remembered the night she'd had a drink with the dedicated lawyer. If only she'd stopped Renata from driving... She tried to shake off the guilt. "Yes, I would. I also want to thank Jim." She wondered if she dared leave Tillman and her daughter by themselves in the same room for a minute.

Emma looked puzzled but shrugged.

Tawny opened the door to the hall. "Be right back."

In a waiting area, Jim leaned one hip against a couch, watching a TV mounted high on the wall. Local news covered the SWAT operation the previous night at Golden Eagle Golf Resort. The video included lots of flashing lights and wild speculation by the reporter.

She approached cautiously. "Jim?"

He turned at her voice. "Tawny. You OK?"

"Yeah. Thanks for bringing Emma."

"No problem." He looked down, studying his boots. Long

black hair fell forward, partly hiding his face.

"Jim, I'm ashamed how Emma's treated you. She doesn't deserve you. You're a good friend."

A shy smile tugged the corner of his mouth. "Everybody deserves a second chance."

Except, Tawny thought bitterly, this was more like Emma's fourteenth. If she blows this one, I *will* kill her. She brushed Jim's hair. "Thank you."

As Tawny re-entered the hospital room, Emma's protest greeted her: "I don't want to."

Tillman's stern answer: "You don't have a choice. You *will* be questioned. Do you want me there with you or not?"

Emma whined, "I didn't do anything wrong. Why do they have to talk to *me*?"

Tawny stepped between them. To Tillman, she said, "She wants you there." She pushed her daughter toward the door. "Jim's waiting. Thank you for bringing my clothes. I'll see you at home later."

Eye roll, then gone.

Tawny lifted her chin to Tillman. "I don't know what I'm going to do about her. She can't stand being in the same room with you."

He pulled a face. "Hell, most of the time, *I* can't stand being in the same room with me."

She pinched off a giggle and brushed her fingertips along his jutting jaw. "You need a shave."

"And a shower and clean clothes and a six-month vacation." He cocked his head sideways. "You all right?"

She nodded, slipped her hand into his, and experimented with closing her eyes. No nightmare flashbacks for the moment. Maybe they only came in darkness. "Let's go see Renata."

They took the elevator to the neurosurgery wing. Through

the open door, her first glimpse of the injured woman made Tawny's stomach contract, pulling hard on her stitches.

Renata sat in a recliner, surrounded by pillows, neck encased in a cervical collar. Staples crisscrossed incisions in her partly-shaved skull. An oxygen cannula had rubbed raw spots in her nostrils. Soft casts wrapped both arms from shoulders to fingertips.

Beside her sat a short, apple-figured woman Tawny guessed was her mother, spooning ice chips between Renata's swollen lips. The woman rose to stand on tiptoe and kissed Tillman's cheek. "Is this Tawny?"

Tawny extended her hand. "Glad to meet you, Mrs. Schliefman. How is she?"

The mother cocked one eyebrow as they shook hands. "First time she's been up. They're worried about bed sores. Like that's the most serious problem she has."

Tillman patted the woman's shoulder. "Frieda, let me buy you a cup of coffee." They moved down the hall.

Tawny sat in the chair, still warm from the mother's body. "Hi, Renata." She picked up the plastic cup and offered another ice chip. Through puffiness, the lawyer's eyes flickered with recognition. Even her tongue looked bruised as she accepted the ice. An invisible fist gripped Tawny's heart.

"Forced...off...road."

"Tillman told me. The sheriff caught the man we think did it. Colin Maza, the son of Moe Rosenbaum's girlfriend. They also think they found a stolen truck he used." Tawny wondered how much Renata understood. Virgie had told her that a brain bleed could wipe out memory, speech, coordination, cognition. A long rehabilitation stretched ahead for Renata.

"Br-brief...case?"

What did she mean? "I'm sorry, Renata, I don't understand."

"Complaints." The swollen mouth struggled to form words. Frustration flared in her purplish eyes. "Complaints...fraud...took briefcase."

Tawny leaned forward. "Are you talking about the fraud paperwork that people filled out at the Golden Eagle meeting?"

A tiny nod.

"I don't know if they found your briefcase." Helplessness overwhelmed Tawny. This poor woman was still worried about prosecuting her case.

"He...took."

"Colin took your briefcase? From your car?"

"Came down cliff...thought he'd help me...but no..." She tilted her head slightly but winced. "Took briefcase...left me."

Oh God. Tawny gently touched the swollen fingers that peeked out of the cast. Lines of blood showed under Renata's nails. "Are you telling me, after the wreck, Colin stole your briefcase from the car? And left you there?"

Another slight nod. Her eyes closed. The monumental effort of stringing words together had exhausted her.

"You don't have to talk, Renata. I'll tell the detectives. Rest now, OK?"

Feeble squeeze.

Tawny rose and blinked back tears.

A small grunt.

Tawny bent close. "What is it? Do you need something?"

The mouth worked again, twitching, pursing. Eyes pleaded for understanding. "Drunk...stupid...sorry."

She was still worried about the misplaced sexual overture. "Renata, I took that as a compliment."

A tiny smile quivered across cracked lips.

~~~

Tawny met Tillman and Frieda Schliefman coming down the hall. He carried coffee containers in both hands.

"Thank you for letting me visit her." Tawny fought to keep her voice from breaking. She wanted to offer reassurance to the worried mother but feared it would sound hollow.

Frieda gripped Tillman's arm. "I'm taking her home to Billings for rehab. Nice facility. Tilly, you remember my aunt? She went there after her stroke. They do good work with brain injuries."

Tillman kissed her forehead. "You need anything, Frieda, call me or Chell. You've got my private number, right?"

Tawny smiled at the woman's endearment and his tenderness toward her.

They watched her disappear into Renata's room, a few tentative steps on the long road ahead.

As Tillman handed Tawny a coffee cup, her anger boiled up. "After that son of a bitch Colin forced Renata off the road, he came down the cliff and stole her briefcase with all the complaint forms from the people who got scammed. Then the creep left her there to die. We need to tell the detectives."

His face hardened. "Prick." They headed toward the exit. "Practically the same charges as my old man, only in this case, it's *attempted* vehicular homicide. Otherwise, it's a replay— bodily injury, failure to render aid, leaving the scene, failure to report."

Once a lawyer, always a lawyer, she thought.

Under the entrance portico, Tawny noticed a Navigator like Moe's, except this one was silver. A woman was helping her elderly husband into the passenger seat. She closed the door, walked around to the driver's side, and drove away.

Something in the movement triggered a sudden shift in Tawny's thoughts. An unexpected image clicked into place in her mind. "Tillman, what if Moe didn't run down Wilbur? What if *he* wasn't driving that night?"

Tillman's coffee sloshed, dripping on the floor. "What the hell are you talking about?"

Tawny plunged ahead. "Moe said he couldn't remember, like he'd been drugged. What if Cassandra or Colin was driving and they set him up? They'd already stolen his money and wanted to get rid of him."

The theory played behind his eyes for several seconds but ended in a doubtful squint. "You're still looking at that asshole through your Pollyanna glasses."

She felt the truth in her gut, even if Tillman couldn't put aside his hatred long enough to recognize it. "I need to see Moe. Where is he?"

Now his jaw jutted sideways and annoyance oozed from every pore. "Surgeon said he'd be in ICU post-op. And you're not family, so *I* have to get you in there. After that, you're on your own."

She'd hoped they might get through a day without a disagreement but no such luck. Tillman would always assume the worst about his father. And, she had to admit, with good reason. But still...She reversed course toward the ICU. He followed, grumbling.

At the locked entrance, Tillman identified himself on an intercom and they were buzzed into the unit. Nurses monitored from a central station, surrounded by glass-walled patient rooms.

Sweat slicked Tawny's palms. Her last ICU visit had been with Dwight, tubes invading his ravaged body and equipment breathing for him.

"What's wrong?" Tillman peered down at her.

Did she look as pale and nauseated as she felt?

He wrapped his arm around her. "Let's go, you don't need to do this."

She leaned against him, absorbing his strength for a moment. "Yeah, I do." She hurried past the other cubicles, avoiding the sight of patients a whisper away from death. At Moe's room, she pushed open a curtain.

Equipment blipped his heart rate, flashed his blood pressure, oxygen saturation, plus a dozen other readings. With Dwight, she'd known what they all meant but now she couldn't remember, as if forgetting could block out the painful memory.

Moe looked shrunken, almost tiny in the bed, his dark skin now a dull, flat gray. Gone was the imposing, stoop-shouldered giant she'd known.

A steady hiss of oxygen fed into the mask over his nose and mouth. His mouth slacked open, the unforgettable fish-out-of-water face she'd watched in the hours before Dwight died.

And she wondered if she was seeing Tillman thirty years from now...if she would stand beside *him* like this. The idea was startling and made her feel strange. Why had it even occurred to her?

She took Moe's now-fragile, veined hand, avoiding the IV site and the oxygen monitor pinching his index finger. "Moe?"

Although he didn't stir, she knew hearing was the last sense to fail. Maybe—somehow—he could hear her.

"I know you're sick of me apologizing but you have to listen one last time. You trusted me and I betrayed that. But I never wanted to hurt you. I was trying to help you."

"Tawny." Tillman's annoyed baritone rumbled from the doorway.

She waved a hand at him. "Go away. Please."

The curtain dropped and his steps retreated on the tile floor.

She leaned closer. "Moe, I don't believe you killed Wilbur. I think Cassandra and Colin set you up, like they tried to make it look as if you stabbed me. I don't know if I can prove it but I'm going to try."

No movement. Just labored breathing.

"I'll find your cats. They'll be taken care of. For real. Not Cassandra's phony sanctuary. They'll be OK. I promise." She ran fingers through his thick gray curls. "Thank you for saving my life. Now *you're* responsible for *me*." She kissed his forehead, and left.

~~~

Tawny spotted Tillman's mud-spackled Mercedes parked near the hospital entrance, dirty snow plastered in the wheel wells. He'd driven from Kalispell to Billings and back again, almost a thousand miles in one long hard day, with only a couple of hours of sleep.

When she got into the passenger seat, he was operating a tablet in his lap, propped against the steering wheel. He glanced at her. "I called Renata's office and told them about her investigation. Talked to the detective, too." One side of his mouth twitched. "Told him your theory. He wants to talk to you more."

A glimmer of hope ignited in Tawny. Maybe Tillman hadn't dismissed her idea, after all. "When?"

"Soon. If you're up to it."

"Can they wait until this afternoon?"

"Why?"

"Because you need some sleep and I need to round up Moe's cats."

"What the hell?"

"We had Rambo cornered yesterday in the garage of that vacant house when all hell broke loose. You can nap on my couch if you'll let me borrow your car to drive up there."

He stared down his nose. "That house and the old man's

place are crime scenes. You won't be able to get in for several days."

She leaned against the headrest. "Oh."

"Forget the cats already, will you?"

"I promised."

"He's probably going to die." His hand flicked the air, like a magician making a dove vanish. "That cancels your contract."

She looked sideways at him. "Please?"

A long stare but at last he started the engine. "Goddamn Girl Scout."

CHAPTER 25 – A ROLL OF DIMES

While Tillman returned to Billings for a trial, Tawny spent the next four days herding cats. She borrowed traps from the Spay and Neuter Task Force. A volunteer there agreed to foster Moe's cats until permanent homes could be found.

Tawny decided to adopt Sugar herself but that only lasted overnight. The next morning, a neighbor's five-year-old daughter spotted the calico, fell in love, and hauled the cat home with her. Just as well. Tawny's job required too much travel to care for a pet. Still, a purring companion had been nice, even briefly.

Rambo remained at large.

Miraculously, Moe bounced back from death's door and was moved to a regular room. When Tawny entered, he was glowering at a plastic container of pudding. A trapeze hung suspended from a horizontal pole over the bed. A wheelchair sat nearby.

He glanced at her, twirled the spoon, and tossed it on the tray. "Soft diet, hell."

Tawny settled into the visitor's chair. "At least you're not on a feeding tube. I thought you were going to die."

"Is that why I got treated to your heart-rending confession?"

"You heard?"

"ICU's great. You pretend you're out and listen to what people are *really* saying about you."

Tawny felt a blush creep up her neck. "I captured the cats. All except Rambo."

"You'll never catch him."

"I've been leaving food out."

"Probably just attract mountain lions. You're causing a

neighborhood nuisance. The HOA will be down my throat again. Forget it. I'm the only one he'll come to."

He reached up to grasp the trapeze, shifting his position. His legs remained limp and motionless under the thin blanket. Tawny looked out the window to avoid staring at them. "Nice view of Big Mountain," she said.

"Guess *my* skiing days are over."

Crap, why did she mention the ski resort?

"Tillman's ex-wife is setting me up for rehab in Billings. Supposed to be a four-star outfit. Whirlpool, massage, gourmet chef, aromatherapy—whatever *that* is."

"Sounds nice."

Dark eyes skewered her. "I'll finally meet my grandchildren."

She smiled. "I'm glad."

"And all I had to do was paralyze myself." He shrugged. "What the hell, got rid of that nuisance ankle bracelet. This fucking cloud is full of silver linings." He tapped the trapeze, making it swing back and forth. "Now if I could just convince them to replace this metal contraption with a nice velvet swing like in my bedroom."

Tawny chuckled. "That's probably a little too kinky for this hospital."

He grimaced, then punched a button at the end of a cord and inclined his head at a pump on a stand beside the bed. "Morphine. I keep pushing but it only allows me a jolt once an hour."

She noticed a half-full bag of urine hanging low at the side of the bed, a thin plastic tube snaking up under the sheet. Dwight had once told her a catheter was the biggest loss of dignity a man could endure. She tried not to imagine the pain and helplessness Moe was going through.

Several quiet minutes passed. Finally the lines in his

forehead eased. The pump must have allowed the drug to flow into his veins.

Moe sat up a little straighter. "Hey, did Tillman ever tell you about the time he whaled the shit out of me?"

Tawny shook her head, poised for another peek through the cloudy window of Rosenbaum family life.

"He was about twelve, scrawny little piss-ant, hadn't gotten his growth yet. His mom had just tried to commit suicide and he was mad at me about that. I come home from work, walk in the front door and WHAM!" Moe's right fist punched into his palm with a noisy smack. "He tackles me, knocks me right off my feet, and slams me to the floor. Then he starts pummeling. Hell, I was more than a foot taller and outweighed him by a hundred pounds. Busted my jaw, bruised my kidneys. I pissed blood for a month. Kept trying to figure out how this little runt could do so much damage."

The way he rubbed his chin and the expression in his eyes almost seemed like he remembered the incident with fondness.

"Later, I found out he had a roll of dimes clutched in each fist. Old street fighter's trick. Keeps you from breaking your knuckles and turns your hand into a sap. Guys with bigger hands use a roll of quarters. Being little, he figured dimes would fit better. Smart." He nodded slowly, approvingly. "I knew then I'd never have to worry about him."

Moe's perspective was the weirdest father-son bonding Tawny had ever heard. Sick though it was, maybe Moe had a point—early resourceful toughness had made Tillman successful, respected, even feared in the legal community. Still, the lessons seemed too harsh for a child.

She leaned to rest her elbows on her knees but pain burned across her belly. She straightened, trying to ease it. "Would you tell me something, Moe?"

A leer edged his grin. "You know I'll tell you anything."

"Exactly what do you remember from the night when your car broke down?"

One side of his mouth crooked in a rueful grin. "I remember being at Cassandra's, then the next thing I know, I'm freezing my ass off in that field, and the Navigator won't start."

"So you really don't remember driving or hitting Wilbur?"

"Damned if I know. My brain was never the same after my heart attack and it's been getting worse. When I saw the cardiologist a couple months back, he ran me through tests, then wanted to refer me to a gerontologist. A geezer doc, for God's sake. Like I'm some doddering old fart drooling in my oatmeal. Screw doctors, all of them."

Moe's words echoed similar complaints that Tawny had heard from her grandpa—refusing to accept dementia, turning against anyone who questioned or challenged him. She also remembered Virgie talking about how a heart attack sometimes altered personality.

"What about your business, the investments?" she asked. "Did you know you were cheating your neighbors?"

His face lengthened. Dark eyes gauged her.

"I won't tell Tillman if you don't want me to," she said. "I'd just like to know."

His head fell back on the pillow and he studied the ceiling. "I've always been aggressive. Had a real intuitive feel for what investments might take off. Risky? Hell, yes. No balls, no blue chips.

"I thought I could ride out the crash in oh-eight. My neighbors were riding with me. We just had to hang on. I tried different tactics to make up for the losses. Some stuff was a little dicey but if it paid off, we'd all get well.

"Then, not too long after my heart attack, I met Cassandra. I was still recovering, feeling pretty weak, helpless, useless. When your heart fails, man, that's when you know, death isn't

309

an abstract concept way out there in the future, something that happens to the other guy. You can smell its breath in your face."

She waited, watching as his eyes lost focus and turned inward. Silence hung over the room.

Then Moe's expression changed, the sagging jowls and eyelids lifted, infused with new energy. "All my life, I've had beautiful, classy, intelligent women but Cassandra was a goddess. She was like a bottle of Dom Perignon sprinkled with coke. She made you feel her passion for the pet sanctuary, like it was the most vital, exciting project in the universe and you wanted to be part of it with her."

Tawny wondered how many other men had fallen victim to the goddess. Each probably believed he was the one and only. Did their eyes have the same starry look as Moe's?

He reached up to grasp the trapeze, moving it side to side, a nervous gesture. "It became my mission to help her achieve that dream. It was *my* dream, too, because I was building it for *my* cats. They're the only ones that gave a damn about me. Not my children, not my exes, not even my mistresses."

Tawny figured it was pointless to mention the mistresses had triggered the hatred from his family.

He spoke faster, words shooting out in short bursts. "The market got worse. I needed faster, higher returns. Took a few flyers on my own money. Didn't pan out. Had to make margin calls. Started putting friends' money in. Only for a little while, I told myself. I'd pay it back when that horse won the race."

"So you knew, by then, you were gambling. Not investing."

One brow lifted, as much of an admission as Moe allowed. "Damn, I was having such a wild time with Cassandra, the sex, the coke, the adrenaline rush. I'm seventy-five years old. How many more opportunities would come around like that?" For a second, he returned to the present, rubbing his hands up and down his dead legs. "Turns out it *was* my last opportunity."

He gazed through the window at the ski runs but Tawny doubted he saw them.

His voice lowered, energy draining out. "I started losing track. I still ran numbers in my head just fine but then I couldn't figure out where to plug in the totals. Calculations I'd done automatically for years, *poof*, gone. I'd look at a spreadsheet and, all of a sudden, I couldn't recognize a yield factor from my left ear. I got scared but I couldn't tell anybody. I couldn't let them know I didn't have the Midas touch anymore."

His dark gaze penetrated Tawny. "You can't understand how hard that is. All your prestige gone, your whole purpose in life erodes away. Before then, I was important, respected. I stood out—a really successful black man in lily-white Montana. *White* men sought me out for advice. You don't know what that means. Then, suddenly, I'm irrelevant, useless, just a blob of plasma taking up space."

A beseeching look begged for Tawny's understanding. She felt sorry for him but stayed mute.

He pulled himself up again with the trapeze. "Cassandra stepped in to help me. She was damn sharp with finance. She took charge. And I gotta say, I was relieved. But the neighbors started complaining." His tone turned sing-songy. "'Where are my dividends, Moe? I demand a refund, Moe.' Their whining got on my nerves. The hell with 'em. My cats were the only ones that cared."

Because, Tawny thought, they had no other choice.

She rubbed her temples, trying to reconcile Moe's words with his acts. She understood how his health problems made him vulnerable to Cassandra's wiles. But years before then, Moe had betrayed Tillman by seducing his fiancé. What kind of a father did that? She couldn't ask Moe because she would never break Tillman's confidence.

Moe studied her. "You're disappointed."

Disappointment hardly covered her roiling emotions. "Moe, I don't know if you're a villain or a victim."

His chin sank to his chest. "I'm nothing but a broken-down old man."

A broken-down old man leaving a wide trail of misery in his wake. Yet, Tawny reminded herself, he had stopped a vicious woman from killing her.

Finally she rose. "I saved your life. You saved mine. I guess that makes us even."

CHAPTER 26 – FELONY STUPID

A week later, at the breakfast bar in Tawny's kitchen over chicken noodle soup, she pinned Tillman with a look. "Got a call today from my electrician. He received a check for materials and wants to start rewiring my house tomorrow."

Tillman studied a slice of celery on his spoon. "This place is a damn firetrap. Can't have it burning down around a key employee."

Her pride and independence fought with gratitude for his generosity. "I'll pay you back."

"The hell you will. You earned a performance bonus so just shut up about it." He gulped his soup and refused to meet her eyes.

The kindness he tried to hide touched her. She started to reach for his hand but he abruptly jumped up and went to the living room. Seconds later, he returned, swiping his tablet. "Got something to show you."

Tawny put on her readers and peered at the screen where a herky-jerky video played, apparently taken with a cell phone camera. She recognized the inside of the Flathead County jail garage.

Obie and another deputy dragged a thrashing, manacled Cassandra from the rear seat of a sheriff's sedan. A quick zoom showed her bloodshot, smudged raccoon eyes. Acid curses spewed from her mouth. Dark red lipstick smeared her chin. Formerly-perfect hair tangled around her face.

Suddenly the video jolted sideways as shouts reverberated in the enclosed garage.

Cassandra head-butted the deputy, broke free, then tried to kick Obie between the legs. Obie grabbed pepper spray from his holster and shot her square in the face. Her back arched.

She let loose a primal screech. The video abruptly ended.

A haunting chill ran up Tawny's neck. The shriek of the mountain lion that had stalked Moe echoed in her memory. She stared at Tillman. "Wow! Where'd you get *that?*"

His expression was smug. "Confidential source. It's never going to make the ten o'clock news but I thought you'd enjoy it."

Sighing, she leaned her elbow on the counter. "I'm glad we stopped Cassandra and Colin, even though it's too late to help Moe."

Tillman cocked an eyebrow at her. "*You* did that. If it weren't for you, the predators would already be in Florida, bilking a whole new set of victims." He carried his empty bowl to the stove for more soup. His fourth helping.

Her cheeks heated with his compliment. In fact, she was feeling warm all over. When he sat down again, did he scoot his bar stool a little closer to hers?

Yet when he spoke, his tone was crisp and all business. "Settled the charges today against my old man. Closed-door meeting with the county attorney and judge. Moe got probation on the assault charge. He's not much danger to anyone now unless he runs over them with his wheelchair. The judge put it quite eloquently: 'Mr. Rosenbaum has already been sentenced as a prisoner in his own body.' Nice turn of phrase, don't you think?"

Sympathy tinged with disappointment ran through her. Moe had betrayed his friends and his son, yet he'd saved her life. Tawny could never forget that.

Tillman added, "Proceeds from the sale of his condo will go for his neighbor's medical bills. If there's any money left over, the investors he cheated will get it but it won't be much." He dug into his soup with gusto.

She watched him eat for a few seconds, biting back a smile.

"I'm sorry it's not as good as your grandmother's."

The spoon paused mid-air. "If *Bubbe's* was a ten, yours is nine-point-nine." He winked. "But she gets the extra only because she's not alive to defend her title."

Heat continued to rise inside her. This frustrating, irritating man drove her crazy yet underneath his brash exterior beat a good heart she could trust.

Neither of them had mentioned their night together in the hospital, nor the long, wordless, melting hug when he'd arrived at her house earlier this evening. Damn, he'd felt good, solid, strong.

She adjusted the low neckline of her silk blouse. Underneath, she wore a new lacy black bra she'd bought in anticipation of his visit.

"What's your secret?" he asked.

Secret? She fingered the straps. Was the lace showing?

He caught her nervous fidgeting, smirked, then took another bite.

It finally hit her that he meant the soup. "Oh. Simmer the bones from a roast chicken for hours until they get soft. The marrow cooks out of them."

"You sure you're not Jewish? That's how *Bubbe* made her stock too. I could smell it way out in the wheat fields." Memories carried him away for a second, his eyes softening.

Again, she felt the urge to touch him but before she could, he snapped back into lawyer mode. "County attorney said Colin waived his right to counsel and spilled his guts. Wants to make a deal, claiming he knows about several deaths Cassandra caused. He's throwing mommy under the bus. Be interesting to see how that plays out." He leaned back and fixed his dark gaze on her. "By the way, you were right. Moe *didn't* kill Wilbur."

Tawny almost choked on a hunk of carrot. "What?"

"Cassandra had sucked Moe and the Golden Eagle

residents dry and wanted to move on to greener pastures. That night you had dinner with them, she drugged Moe's drinks. Colin drove him out in the country in the Navigator and she followed in her Porsche. They planned to leave him somewhere deserted so he'd freeze to death. But the old man woke up and tried to wrestle the wheel from Colin. Car swerved all over and Wilbur happened to be riding his bike right in their way."

Tawny rested her head in her hand. "Poor Wilbur. The wrong place at the wrong time."

"Yeah," he murmured then straightened. "Anyway, Cassandra gave the old man a nighty-night booster shot. They left him in the Navigator, hidden behind the barn, and took off. Tough old bastard came back to life and called you."

"No wonder Moe didn't remember anything." She visualized the scene around the damaged car. "When we met the tow truck there, I saw other tire tracks but didn't realize what they meant."

"According to Colin, Cassandra was the mastermind and he was the poor, helpless, baby boy being ordered around."

Tawny rubbed her palm over the tender new scar lines across her belly. The stitches had come out that morning. "Might be at least partly true. He did try to stop Cassandra from stabbing me."

Tillman's face turned hard, eyes glinting. "She wanted him to do the stabbing because he's stronger and could do more damage. But he's got a phobia about blood and wimped out."

His teeth dug into his lip and he fell silent for several long seconds. When he spoke again, it was barely above a whisper. "You almost died because of what I sent you into. Maybe you can blow that off, Tawny, but I can't."

The depth of anguish in his dark eyes startled her.

She reached up and touched his cheek, feeling slight stubble under her fingertips. "I'm OK, really."

He moved her hand to his mouth, soft warm lips pressing her palm.

The back door banged open and Emma breezed into the kitchen. "Hi, Mom."

They jerked away from each other. Under his breath, Tillman muttered, "Goddammit!"

Tawny stifled a giggle and turned to Emma. "Hi, honey. Want some soup?"

Emma shot a disgusted glance at Tillman and hurried past. "No, thanks," she called over her shoulder. Seconds later, her bedroom door slammed.

Tillman's sarcasm returned. "I see I'm still her favorite person."

Tawny dropped her voice low. "Her STD tests came back negative. Thank goodness." She sighed. "But she's pregnant."

"Shit. Colin's or that other guy?"

"Colin's, unfortunately. Jim always used protection."

"What's she going to do?"

"I don't know."

"Ought to end it right now."

"Tillman, this is my grandchild you're talking about." Although with him this evening, she'd felt anything but grandmotherly.

"You mean, the offspring of a guy who'll be in prison until it's at least in middle school? The one *you'll* undoubtedly wind up raising?"

That possibility had already occurred to Tawny. "I told Emma if she decided to keep it, she had to be responsible."

Tillman nodded with melodramatic exaggeration. "Oh, yeah, I'm sure that convinced her." Down-the-nose look. "You know damn well you'd never allow anything to happen to that baby. Which translates to another twenty years of parenting for you." He picked up their empty bowls and carried them to the dishwasher.

Emma's timing sucked and, as usual, Tillman was right. Tawny took a Tupperware container from the cupboard and poured leftover soup into it, pondering the unanticipated responsibility of a baby at her age. Still, her heart longed for the warm, soft cuddle of a grandchild. "It's up to Emma. I honestly don't know what she's going to do."

He took the empty stock pot from her, ran hot water in it with a squirt of dish detergent, and unbuttoned his cuffs. "You're loyal to a fault."

"Is that a compliment or an insult?"

He rolled up his sleeves, exposing sinewy forearms. "You figure it out."

Emma breezed through the kitchen, wearing different clothes. "Bye, Mom."

"Bye." Tawny watched through the mud room window as headlights backed away from the garage and disappeared down the alley.

Tillman glanced over his shoulder at her as he scrubbed the pot. "Is the coast clear now?"

Tawny moved behind him, slipped her arms around his waist, and leaned her cheek against his solid back. "Mm-hm."

Still scrubbing, he asked, "Didn't we once have a discussion that it was felony stupid for an employee to get involved with a boss?"

"Yeah, and that an attorney should know better." She moved her hands over the crisp, starched fabric, feeling the firm muscles of his belly and chest.

He rinsed the pot and reached for a dishtowel. "You have forty-eight hours to cease and desist before I file a sexual harassment charge."

She undid a button on his shirt. "Don't you ever forget about the law?"

He dried the pot, still facing the sink. "Last chance to back out, Tawny. This road only goes one way."

Another button undone and she slid her hand inside to stroke the hair growing back on his chest. "I know."

"In the interest of full disclosure, I'm a real asshole."

"You think I haven't figured that out?"

He set the stock pot on the counter. "When's your daughter coming back?"

She rubbed her cheek in circles on his back. "Don't know."

His big hands covered hers, then slowly ran along her arms. "There's my hotel."

"My bedroom's closer and the door has a lock on it."

At last, he turned around and faced her with a crooked smile. "Then I suggest we put it to good use."

THE END

A NOTE FROM DEBBIE

Thank you for reading *STALKING MIDAS*.

I love staying in touch with readers. To contact me for personal appearances, books clubs, teaching, or just to say *Howdy*, visit my website: http://debbieburkewriter.com

If you would like to hear when new books are published, please sign up for my mailing list at: http://www.debbieburkewriter.com/sign-up-for-mailing-list/ I'll never spam you nor sell your information.

What's next for Tawny and Tillman? Check out the sneak preview of *EYES IN THE SKY*...coming soon!

SNEAK PREVIEW OF

EYES IN THE SKY

Frank Grand stood on a wind-swept bluff overlooking the bleak Montana prairie and maneuvered his drone to hover above a rest stop on Interstate 90. He zoomed in on two figures standing in the parking area, the control console focused on his primary target—attorney Tillman Rosenbaum.

At six-seven, Rosenbaum owned any courtroom he entered. Frank had seen him in action, felt the boom of his James Earl Jones voice, and watched as opposing counsel and even some judges shriveled under the fierce obsidian stare.

The slender woman who stood beside him looked about five-ten, with coppery hair in a braid over her shoulder. As Rosenbaum gazed down at her, his long angular face looked like a stick of butter melting in a microwave.

The bigger they are, Frank thought, the harder they fall.

The original plan was to kidnap his children. From the way Rosenbaum looked at this woman, adding her into the equation might drive the stakes even higher.

She touched his arm, an imploring gesture. Rosenbaum's expression hardened. Whatever she wanted, he didn't like the idea.

Frank panned the camera to admire the attorney's Mercedes G-Wagon SUV. Hundred and twenty grand minimum. With his cut of the ransom, Frank might buy one for himself.

The couple got in the Mercedes and merged onto the interstate, eastbound toward Billings.

Frank retrieved the drone, secured it in the hard-sided case, and set it on the passenger seat of his Crown Vic Police Interceptor. He drove down the hill and followed Rosenbaum's SUV.

~~~

Tawny Lindholm studied the dark curly hair, long profile, and jutting chin of Tillman Rosenbaum, her boss and, as of recently, her lover. "I thought we were going to Yellowstone."

Tillman's wrist steered easy on the wheel. "We are."

"You missed the turnoff to Highway Eighty-nine."

"Yeah." The Mercedes continued east on I-90, smooth, steady, its destination predetermined.

A wave of uneasiness crested over Tawny. She shifted in the leather seat, facing him. "Are we going to Billings?" Where he lived on a sprawling estate with his ex-wife in one wing, him in the other, and three teenage children stuck in the middle.

"Do you mind?"

"What are you pulling, Tillman?" Although Tawny adored the brilliant lawyer, she didn't always trust him.

"Tomorrow's Judah's bar mitzvah."

Damn him. He'd manipulated her again. "You lead me to believe we're going on vacation, except now you spring a little detour to shove me down your family's throat."

Tillman faced her, a sheepish grin tugging at one side of his mouth. "Judah likes you. He wants you to come."

"Crap, Tillman, he's only met me once." She recalled the awkward dinner at his home almost a year before when he'd introduced her as his new investigator.

"You made a big impression," he said. "That's three generations of Rosenbaum men you've bewitched."

She hugged herself, again regretting that she'd crossed the line with her boss. "Number one, I don't believe you. Number two, you're an asshole to deceive me. Number three, I am not going to intrude on a sacred family event. Your kids have enough problems without introducing Dad's new girlfriend into the mix."

"I've told them we're together, Tawny. It's not a secret."

"Hearing about someone who lives four hundred and fifty miles away in Kalispell is a whole lot different than coming face to face with the other woman who's the reason their parents won't get back together."

He let out an exasperated huff. "Number one, you were never the other woman. Number two, you already know I'm an asshole. Number three, you're not the reason. They know Chell and I will never reconcile."

"Hope is hard to kill in kids." Tawny stared out the window at the rolling hills, new green growth reawakening from winter. The scent of sagebrush wafted through the air vents. "I don't understand you, Tillman. Why am *I* more concerned about disrupting their lives than *you* are? They're your family."

"You could be my family too . . . someday."

His sideways proposal made her mushy inside but she held strong to her resolve. "No chance of that, at least not until the kids are grown. I'm not making it harder for them than it already is."

"*I* want you there."

"Newsflash, Tillman." She threw back the taunt he'd often used on her, especially when he thought she was being naive. "You're the daddy. That means you have to give up what you want for your kids' sake."

His cell rang through the radio. He punched the Bluetooth. "Judah, my man!"

"Hey, Dad, when are you getting here?" High squeaks alternated with low, gruff tones.

Poor kid, Tawny thought. How well she remembered her own son Neal's embarrassment at age thirteen over his changing voice.

Tillman answered, "Couple more hours."

"Well, hurry up. Mimi and Arielle are fighting World War Three. Mom may kill both of them if you don't get here soon."

"As fast as I can without getting a ticket."

"Hey, Dad, y'know that hot redhead that works for you? Is she coming?"

Tillman slid a sideways glance at Tawny, not bothering to hide his smug smile. "Hang on a sec, got another call coming in." He tapped Judah's call to hold. "Are you going to disappoint him?"

Tawny glared at him. "You're rotten to manipulate me."

"Never pretended to be otherwise." He lifted one shoulder. "Well?"

She stared out the window, irritated, but stuck in a box.

He tapped the speaker. "Yo, Judah. Yeah, that hot redhead's sitting beside me. She can't wait to give you a big, sloppy, congratulatory kiss for becoming a man."

Not in this lifetime, Tawny thought, fuming.

"Da-ad, can she hear what I'm saying? Did you put me on

speaker?" Lots of cracks.

"No worries, son, she's taking a nap." He disconnected.

Tawny didn't know whether to slug Tillman or kiss him for saving the boy from being mortified. How could the man be such a jerk on one hand, yet so sweet on the other?

He settled back in the driver's seat, still steering with his wrist, a little smirk pulling the side of his mouth.

But it was her own fault. She'd broken rule number one: don't sleep with the guy who signs your paycheck.

To Be Continued...

To find out when ***EYES IN THE SKY*** is published, visit: http://www.debbieburkewriter.com/sign-up-for-mailing-list/